has known Grace her whole life. He has visited her dreams every night, and had thousands of "first meetings" with her that Grace doesn't remember. He teaches her about the true origins of the gods La Nuit (Nyx) and Anesidora (Gaia), and their feud. Grace is given a prophecy and tasked with bringing 'forth the Second Age of Heroes.' An attempted meeting with Grace's cousin, Mercy, goes awry, and Bullet is injured. They are rescued by the silent and mysterious Wild, who reluctantly allows them to stay at his nightclub complex, avoiding Grace even though he is her third soul bond. Grace seals her bonds with Bullet and Riot, and hunts down Wild to find out why he's avoiding her, and that is where our story picks up.

GRACE

CHAPTER 1

Oh my... word.

If my life kept going this way, I was going to have to really consider using proper curse words, because 'sugar' just didn't cut this.

I stared at the bank of monitors in front of me in silence, my mysterious third soul bond, Wild, hovering awkwardly in the corner while trying to look like he wasn't actually hovering awkwardly in the corner. He was so controlled, so rigid, that the fact he didn't seem to speak wasn't the reason I had no read on him whatsoever; it was his body language that gave me almost nothing.

Actions spoke louder than words though, and this man—this daimon soul bond of mine—had security footage of *my* apartment, my old workplace, even the streets where I used to go running in the mornings.

Onyx, his business partner, had given me a key to his apartment so I could confront Wild about why he'd been avoiding me. When I'd made the split-second decision to come up here, I hadn't expected this. This was probably the *last* thing I'd expected.

WILD GAME

WILD GAME

STATE OF GRACE 3

COLETTE RHODES

CONTENT WARNING

Please note that this series contains sexual content, violence, and drug references.

"WE ARE ALL IN THE GUTER, BUT SOME OF US ARE LOOKING AT THE STARS."

-*Oscar Wilde*

THE STORY SO FAR

Our angelic agathos, Grace, met bad boy daimon, Riot, outside a club in Milton—a daimon town she'd moved to in a bid to escape her overbearing parents and community. At age 25, Grace had expected to feel a pull towards her four agathos soul bonds by now, but it never came. Instead, she felt pulled to Riot, even though a connection between agathos, worshippers of Anesidora and servants of humanity, and daimons, worshippers of La Nuit and designed to lead humans astray, shouldn't be possible. Grace's parents found out about Riot, and had Grace taken from her job at a shelter and dragged to the basement temple in Auburn for a cleansing ritual to break the connection. Riot was given instructions by the psychic daimon, Bullet, on where to find Grace. With assistance from one of her fathers, Riot rescues her from the agathos attempting to do a cleansing ritual and praying to bond her to recently widowed agathos men. They drive to Bullet's place, where Grace encounters her second soul bond for the first time. While Riot is stuck working for the daimon, Viper, as part of a deal to keep Grace hidden, Grace gets to know Bullet. Bullet, as an Oneiroi,

"Is this... live?" I asked hesitantly. There was nothing particularly interesting happening on the screens—it was early Sunday morning and the streets were mostly deserted. While this whole thing was a little surreal, it was kind of a relief to see that, at least from the outside, my apartment had been left alone for the past couple of weeks. One of my neighbor's cars was parked in its usual spot, the lights flicking on in her apartment while the windows of mine remained dark.

My gaze drifted to one of the other screens as someone stepped out of the front of Hope House, the shelter where I used to work, leaning against the wall and lighting up a cigarette. *The people who stay there are entitled to privacy. This is unethical on about five hundred different levels,* I thought faintly.

Wild nodded once, arms folded across his chest. He was wearing a fitted long-sleeved black top and goddess his biceps bulged when he stood like that. I was trying not to focus on how absurdly handsome he was because it was honestly distracting and I was trying to appear sort of tough while I demanded answers.

Even so, I wasn't immune to those good looks. Wild was at least a head taller than me, and his plain black, borderline militaristic clothes showcased how defined his muscles were. He had rich, dark skin, buzzed black hair, a neat beard that I wanted to run my fingers over, and the most daimonic eyes I'd ever seen. Bullet's were almost entirely amethyst, and Riot's were a mixture of purple and red, but Wild's were almost completely crimson.

Despite his intimidating size and the fact that we were alone in a small, windowless room together, I didn't feel afraid.

It was abundantly clear that he was more afraid of me than I was of him.

"Why?" I eventually choked out, entirely overwhelmed. "Why? Why do any of this? Why not just approach me? Do you know who you are to me? *What* you are to me?"

Another curt nod. *Right, he can't speak. Or doesn't speak.* Goddess, I wished I knew more about him.

He definitely knew more about me.

"Why?" I repeated, leaning into his line of sight so he could see my hands as I signed the word.

His crimson eyes widened a fraction at the gesture, though I wasn't sure if it was in recognition or if he just hadn't expected me to know sign language. I was a little rusty, but many of those who used Hope House's services had been hearing impaired so I'd taken night classes to learn the fundamentals of ASL.

Wild didn't respond, instead opening the top drawer of the filing cabinet behind him and sorting through a few old-fashioned mobile phones, all neatly wrapped in their charging cables, before settling on a chunky, silver one. I watched, slightly bewildered, as he flipped the phone over, adding the number printed on a label attached to the back to his own phone before turning the clunky old one on. Was it a burner phone? Did he have a whole drawer of burner phones? He set it down with the charger on the edge of the desk while the small square screen came to life, the buttons briefly lighting up. The startup sound was jarring in the silence, and I twisted my opal ring on my finger for something to do with my hands.

I should probably take it off. It was a symbol of agathos virtue, and I felt a bit like a fraud wearing it.

The silence drew out, and as far as getting to know my soul bonds, this was by far the most awkward interaction yet. Riot and I hadn't known what the connection between us meant and I thought *that* introduction had been uncomfortable, but at least we'd both been interested in exploring it.

If I'd encountered Wild in the same way and asked him to get in my car with me, I wasn't at all confident he would have agreed. He wasn't kicking me out, but he didn't seem pleased to have me here either. To say it was making me feel insecure was a massive understatement. My entire life up until I'd met Riot a month ago had been a series of moments where my presence was unwanted by almost everyone in the room, and this was bringing up some familiar feelings.

The small room we were in looked like it had been a storage closet, and we'd accessed it by a hidden door in a bookcase that he must have built in front of it. The low sloping ceiling in this cramped space was clearly uncomfortable for Wild with his considerable height, but he moved back into the corner as much as he could anyway, squeezing in the space between the black filing cabinet and L-shaped desk and hunching over to avoid banging his head.

He gave me a pointed look, followed by a similar gesture at the phone.

Right. Pick it up.

The message Wild had sent showed up immediately, and I clumsily stabbed at the arrow buttons, trying to remember how to work one of these phones before I finally got it open.

Unknown Number: *I know who and what you are to me. Keep the phone, message me if you need anything. Goodbye, Grace.*

"What?" I asked, torn between hurt and confusion. "That's it? You don't want to... get to know me? Nothing?"

3

It's not that I thought I was so amazing that anyone would want to get to know me, but we were soul bonds. Chosen for each other by forces beyond our comprehension, our souls linked forever. Wasn't he even a little curious?

You know he's curious. Why else would he do all of this? No one sets up cameras to spy on someone they're not curious about.

Wild didn't acknowledge my question, already trying to inch his not inconsiderable bulk through the small space between me and the desk to get to the secret door.

"You're leaving?" My voice sounded slightly hysterical even to my own ears. He was being so careful not to touch me—did he know that physical contact set off the beginning of the bonding process? He'd set the phone down on the desk, not even risking our fingers touching for a second. He *must* have known.

Wild paused, less than inch of space between us. He was so tall that I had to tip my head back to meet his gaze, and I shivered slightly as his warm breath ghosted over my lips. If I went up on my tiptoes, we'd touch. Just that small movement, that would be all it took, and I'd see if those full lips felt as soft as they looked. One little touch, and the bonding process between us would begin.

Wild's eyes didn't quite meet mine. Instead, he scanned my features like he was memorizing them, from the dark hair I'd smoothed back into a sleek ponytail, to my face with just the barest amount

of makeup still on after wearing it all night. Despite the somewhat modest, agathos-friendly dark green dress I was wearing, I didn't think I'd ever felt more exposed in my life.

Everything in me wanted to give in, to close that small distance between us. There was a tug in my chest dragging me forwards, and fighting against it felt *unnatural*. All agathos were overjoyed to find their soul bonds; there was no need to fight anything. But Wild wasn't an agathos, and nothing about his posture or expression indicated that he wanted any more than this. As unnatural as it was to hold back, it would be even more wrong to take something he wasn't offering.

He exhaled heavily, his eyes shuttering for a moment like he was about to give in—and I had no idea how I'd respond if he did because my ego didn't like the idea of being something he had to *give in* to—but as quickly as the look came, the moment passed. On silent feet, he slipped past me and out into his small apartment, while I stood frozen in place as the front door quietly clicked shut.

My hand clenched so tightly around the phone that the buttons were digging painfully into the pads of my fingers. He'd just left me. In *his* apartment! He must have been really eager to put some space between us if he was running away from his *own* place and he was absolutely running away. I snorted a surprised laugh before clapping a hand over my mouth. There was nothing funny about the situation per se—it was awful he'd been supernaturally connected to someone he had no interest in—but it was all so absurd and unexpected that I had no idea how to respond to it all.

While I was doing my best to unlearn most of my agathos teachings, the ones I had about soul bonds were the hardest to shake. It was meant to be easy. Seamless. We were meant to just *fit*.

They were meant to want me, and I selfishly hated that Wild didn't seem to at all.

It didn't help that I knew he'd kissed Bullet a couple of years ago at the club downstairs. When Bullet had told me that, I'd been strangely comfortable with the idea. I'd never felt like Bullet wanted me less because he'd also found Wild attractive, and Bullet had such a lack of love and comfort in his life that, if anything, the idea of him possibly having more was reassuring. My mind had immediately conjured images of the three of us together, a relationship between us that was separate from what I shared with Riot. A relationship between them that was separate from what they each shared with *me*. It was a naive fantasy of how it could have worked, based on nothing but my own imagination, because as far as I knew, relationships between the men of a bonded agathos weren't ever romantic or sexual in nature. Or if they were, it was one of the many things that the agathos hid and denied.

Maybe I'd had it all wrong. Maybe the connection to me was an annoyance Wild couldn't shake, but it was Bullet who had actually caught his interest. Was that why he left?

What was I going to do if it was Bullet that he really wanted?

Could I stand by and encourage them to pursue a relationship without me?

Would it be better or worse than Wild avoiding all of us forever because he didn't want me?

WILD

CHAPTER 2

Fuck. Fuck. Fuck. Fuck.

Fuck.

I'd always known Grace would track me down and demand answers for why I was avoiding her. I'd even known that when that time came, I'd show her the cameras. Show her that I'd been stalking her like a goddamn lunatic, confident that would be enough to scare any sane person away.

Maybe my sweet little agathos soul bond wasn't quite as sane as she appeared, because while she'd been *confused about the cameras, there'd been a distinct lack of horror and revulsion, and I didn't know what to make of it.*

You should have known, I thought irritably to myself, jogging through the now deserted corridors that led to the back parking lot. *You should have known they wouldn't make a soul bond easy to avoid.*

Who 'they' was—Nyx or the Fates, maybe even Gaia herself—I wasn't sure. I didn't know and it didn't matter because I was going to keep avoiding it, regardless.

I pinched the rough fabric of my sleeves, using it to rub forcefully at the skin on my hands and wrists. An unfortunate habit I'd picked up five years ago, in the time *after*. A weakness that I didn't let anyone else see, because fuck knows I had a big enough weakness that I couldn't hide to give anyone more ammunition against me.

The cold fall air hit me as I shoved open the exit to the employee area used mostly for smoke breaks. The first light was just filtering through the clouds, lighting up the sky and chasing away the remnants of Nyx's night. I shoved the door shut behind me, collapsing back against it and breathing heavily like I'd just gone ten rounds in the ring instead of having a ten-minute conversation with a girl.

Not just a girl, my brain reminded me unhelpfully, the memory of Grace's confused expression floating back to the forefront of my mind. Why hadn't she been angry? Anger would have been easier to deal with. Instead she'd had to go and look hurt when I'd avoided her touch, like I wasn't doing her a massive favor.

Fuck!

I should have gone downstairs. There was a sauna down there that the Keres liked to use for achy muscles after a fight. I found it cleansing—the slime of the curse that had been laid upon me stuck to me like a second skin, and the only time I didn't notice it was when I was sweating or submerged in water.

She'd almost kissed me.

She'd *wanted* to. It had been years and I was rusty, but I remembered what it felt like to have someone look up at me, parted

lips and eyes full of invitation. The last time I'd kissed someone, he'd run from me like he had Kerberos on his tail. And now he was back too. Back in my life after hiding away for almost two years.

Logically, I knew that a curse from the gods couldn't pass from skin-to-skin, but I had visions in my mind that if she'd touch me, the miasma that infected me would infect her too. She'd touch me and she'd know. In reality, Grace could touch me, and nothing would happen to her except that my obsession would grow deeper, impossible to fight off, and that was bad enough. The longer I spent with her, the more likely it was that my curse would become her curse, and I couldn't let that happen.

From the moment Grace had climbed into the back of the van after the shooting and I knew she was returning here with me, the panic that she would throw herself at me and obliterate my self-control had me in a chokehold.

Today had been a close call. Far too close. She'd gotten me alone, in private, looking the way she did, smelling the way she did... Fuck.

My selfish desire to stay close to Grace had almost ruined everything.

Me: *Bring the keys for the Camaro to the back parking lot.*

Unfortunately, the request had to go to Onyx as the only other person with access to my main office, and I'd already annoyed her by sending her Grace's new number and an order to assist her with whatever she needed. At least Onyx had taken a liking to Grace, something I appreciated and slightly resented, since it made it more difficult to stay away from the object of my obsession.

Wait, how had Grace gotten into my apartment in the first place?

Me: *Did you give Grace the spare keys to my apartment?*

Of fucking course Onyx would intervene if she felt like things weren't moving along fast enough. While I'd never told her what Grace was to me, she'd met two of Grace's other soul bonds and knew I'd been following Grace on the cameras, warning every daimon in my employ to leave her the hell alone on pain of death.

Onyx wasn't stupid.

Onyx: *There are so many keys around the place, who knows where they all go?*

Me: *It's your job to know. Bring me the keys for the Camaro.*

Onyx: *Alright, chicken shit, I'm on my way.*

I should fire her, I thought to myself for the millionth time. I wouldn't though. When nearly everyone I encountered tiptoed around me on eggshells, Onyx had been brazenly disrespectful from the moment I met her. She was also fiercely loyal and unusually competent, considering how ruled by our instincts our kind tended to be. And as much as her overstepping frustrated me, Onyx had taken an interest in Grace as a person rather than just as an agathos novelty, and I needed her around to be Grace's point of contact.

I couldn't be what Grace wanted me to be, what she thought we would be, but I wasn't about to throw her to the wolves either. I could help. I could keep her safe.

I moved to the side of the door a second before Onyx slammed it open, glaring at me as she threw the keys and crossed her arms, all hostile confrontation. I'd probably woken her up—she was in baggy sweatpants and slides, unlike her usual skimpy outfit with heeled boots uniform, and it was a little unsettling to see her without a full face of makeup on.

She was a lot less intimidating without all the eyeliner.

"Good girl got you that spooked, huh?" Onyx drawled, somehow looking down her nose at me despite our height difference. "This is idiotic, Wild. I'm sure you have your reasons, but everything about Grace and her little harem of daimons has the hands of the Fates all over it, and you know it. You can't outrun that."

Watch me fucking try.

I inclined my head in acknowledgment before striding across the parking lot to where the cars for employee use were kept. While most of The Underworld network was comprised of the main Asphodel, Elysium and the fight ring complex, I'd purchased a few of the other clubs around Milton, and the daimons who worked there used these vehicles to get between them.

The black Camaro was for my personal use, though I rarely bothered with it because it drew too much attention. Today, I felt like indulging. After I'd stabbed the agathos who'd tried to kidnap Grace and she'd called on Gaia herself to show her disapproval, the agathos who'd been hanging around town had finally left us alone. While I was confident they'd regroup, I could at least enjoy having my town to myself for now.

"Coward!" Onyx yelled before slamming the door behind her, probably pissing off the half-asleep employees who were coming off

their night shifts. I wondered if Grace had gotten used to the daimon nocturnal schedule. She'd looked tired. Gods, all I wanted to do was tuck her up in my bed, sit next to her and truly indulge in my obsession of watching the gift from the goddesses I could never accept.

The vehicle roared loudly to life, undoubtedly pissing off the other half of Asphodel's employees, and I wasn't subtle about throwing it into gear and speeding out of the lot onto Milton's mostly deserted downtown streets.

As tempting as it was to risk a jaunt through agathos territory to get back to one of my properties in Easton, my body physically rejected the idea of going *that* far away from Grace. From Asphodel. From Bullet. Even from that annoying shithead, Riot.

The Fates' wicked webs were already weaving themselves into place, and I was goddamn resentful about it.

I slammed a hand against the steering wheel in frustration, hating that my life was being dictated for me by forces beyond my control *again*, before veering sharply around a corner towards a four-bedroom house I owned in a semi-industrial area near the waterfront. It wasn't particularly luxurious, but it was a comfortable recovery spot for Keres who'd taken a beating and needed somewhere safe and quiet to get back on their feet where Dr. Martinez could visit them.

I'd gotten text requests from the daimons who needed to stay there so I knew only two of the rooms were in use at the moment. *Need to make sure Dr. Martinez was doing regular rounds there,* I reminded myself. Geras daimons made for good human doctors mostly—their priority was to get humans to old age and let them suffer that way—but they needed close management when it came to their daimon patients. Another thing on my endless list, but it gave me purpose.

I would stay at that house, closely work with the daimons there to ensure they were recovering and taking care of themselves, and delegate jobs at Asphodel to Onyx until Grace got fed up and took her loyal lover boys with her back to Bullet's country bolthole. I'd watched her on the cameras enough to know that the impatience had been written all over her face for days. She wanted to go, to pursue whatever it was that had Gaia herself responding to her that day at the community center. Grace was meant for bigger things than the life she was living now. I didn't need the gifts of an

Oneiroi to see that—even the most bloodthirsty Keres at Asphodel had recognized something special in her.

And I would watch from afar, because that was the right thing to do. I'd keep the stench of death as far away from her as I could, because that's what Grace deserved. Eventually, she'd give up on me and leave, and I could continue my life of cursed silence alone. Hopefully, one day she'd understand why it had to be this way.

GRACE

CHAPTER 3

I spent longer in Wild's apartment than I should have. The appropriate amount of time to spend there alone after he'd left was probably zero, but leaving was harder than I thought it would be.

His apartment smelled nice. Like cinnamon and sweat—which *shouldn't* smell delicious, but it absolutely did. It also gave me a tiny insight into who he was as a person, which was more than I was going to get from him directly, apparently. With the pale wood floors and exposed brick walls, the studio apartment had the potential to be beautiful, but it was all very generic and impersonal, with a black leather couch, an oversized bed with plain navy bedding, and fake wood flatpack furniture. How long had he lived here? Bullet had mentioned that Asphodel opened two years ago. I looked at the fitness-related books on the shelves, only occasionally broken up by fancy bottles of liquor. No overly personal touches, no photos, no trinkets...

Wild was layer upon layer of mystery.

Unknown Number: *Hey, good girl, it's Onyx. Bossman gave me your number in case you needed anything from me. I know he's being a dick, but don't worry about it. He'll come around.*

I smiled in spite of myself, quickly saving both her and Wild's numbers. I'd originally been worried—okay, jealous—of the relationship between Wild and Onyx, but the more I'd gotten to know her, the more it seemed almost sibling-like in nature. She seemed almost exasperated with him and his avoidance of me most of the time.

Me: *Are you sure about that?*

With a heavy sigh, I pushed the hidden door to the secret stare-at-Grace room closed, muscles straining at the surprising weight of it. I didn't know who else had access to this place, but I didn't like the idea of anyone else seeing this room. Not just because there were cameras trained on my old apartment and workplace, though that was a big part of it, but also because it felt too personal. I knew nothing about Wild, but I knew that this space was a secret he'd shared only with me, and he wouldn't like that weakness exposed to anyone else.

You are making some bold assumptions there, Grace. You may be soul bonds, but you don't know the first thing about him, and he doesn't want you to know.

I gripped my new phone tightly in my hand, feeling emotionally attached to it already. When the agathos had kidnapped me from work, they'd taken both my regular phone and the burner phone Riot had given me, and I'd been without one ever since. I knew Riot and Bullet had reservations about me having one again, worried that my agathos

15

instincts were going to push me towards confessing my location. Wild probably didn't know or understand their reasoning or he likely wouldn't have entrusted me with one either. I wasn't mad at Riot or Bullet for doing what they thought was right to keep me safe, but this little piece of independence meant something to me.

Passing the small kitchenette, I locked up Wild's apartment and jogged down the spiral staircase to the kitchen and common area, hoping most of the daimons were already asleep. I'd gotten better at handling their sense of humor, but I wasn't ready to face the barrage of jokes that would ensue if they saw me descend from Wild's apartment in the early hours of the morning.

Onyx: *He's been obsessed with you since the moment you arrived in Milton. I don't think he'll be able to stay away for long.*

He might not have a choice, I thought as I shoved the phone into the pocket of my dress. Bullet was healed enough from his gun wound to travel. It was time for us to get back out of Milton. Riot's contact, Viper, had covered our tracks to make it look like we'd gone to Boston, but I doubted the agathos were going to entirely fall for the false trail a second time. Plus my inability to lie was a constant, stifling presence nagging at my brain that lying by omission was no better.

I was sure my parents knew I wasn't in Boston, but at least they no longer had Mercy to use as bait, and hopefully even my mother wouldn't use my baby brothers to lure me back into the agathos fold. Creed was the one who mostly handled their day-to-day care, and he and Chase were more empathetic than my other parents. As intimidating as my mother was, I hoped they'd be willing to go up against her if it meant keeping Leon and Tobin safe from her schemes.

The kitchen was blessedly empty, and I half jogged, half walked past the long counter and giant commercial fridges to get to the corridor where all the bedrooms were.

Since the moment you arrived in Milton. Had Wild really been watching me for that long? Since before I even met Riot? If he'd been watching me for months and been able to avoid reaching out to me, why would he give in now?

Bullet, Riot and I were staying in the largest room at the end of the hall, past all the staff bedrooms. I barely resisted the urge to break into a run as I got closer to them, eager for a little reassurance from the bonded I had to soothe my thoroughly bruised ego.

"You said you were going to get a snack," Riot said the moment I entered the room, somewhat accusingly. While we'd been staying here, he'd taken the time to get his messy black hair trimmed again, and the beard he'd been growing was back to neat stubble. No matter how many times I saw him, whenever those dark purple and crimson eyes landed on me, Riot took my breath away. "You weren't in the kitchen."

"I *was* going to get a snack," I replied quickly, even the implication that I *might* have lied needling those agathos truth-telling instincts. "But no one was around and the stairs up to Wild's apartment were just right there..."

Bullet was lounging on the bed—still in his recovery uniform of sweatpants and no shirt. While I know he didn't like being so dressed down, I quite enjoyed getting an uninterrupted view of his body, inked with tarot cards that had been delivered to him in the visions of the future he received in his sleep from the goddess Nyx, or through the card readings he did that communed directly with the Fates. He pushed his chin-length, messy blonde hair back off his face, watching me with a completely unsurprised look on his face.

What must it be like to go through life already knowing what was going to happen? It never ceased to amaze me that Bullet was so cheerful, in spite of literally everything life had thrown at him.

"Things with Wild didn't go the way you hoped, Amazing Grace?" he asked.

"You didn't *see* that?" Riot countered, looking over his shoulder at Bullet.

"Actually, no, my vision cut out right before the good part started." Bullet grinned, unrepentantly needling Riot whenever possible.

"That's because there was no good part," I told Bullet wryly. Not that I'd actually expected to go in there and jump his bones and seal the bond right away or anything. I'd gone up there purely with the expectation of understanding why he was avoiding me.

Though if I'd gone in there and he'd wanted to seal the bond on sight... I probably wouldn't have said no.

"Was he an asshole?" Riot asked, squaring his shoulders. "I'm better prepared this time, want me to kick his ass?"

Bullet snorted, humming *My Shot* from Hamilton with no subtlety whatsoever. I hadn't known Riot when Wild had beaten him up for selling drugs in his club, but by the way everyone talked about it, it had been a brutal, completely one-sided fight and I absolutely didn't want a repeat of it ever.

"No, no. He wasn't an *asshole*." I grimaced slightly over the word, a lifetime of conditioning reminding me it wasn't ladylike to say, but I was determined not to let my agathos upbringing influence every word choice and decision I ever made. "If anything, *I* was the asshole. I went into his

apartment without asking and demanded answers. Wild was polite, all things considered. He gave me a phone," I added hesitantly, pulling it out of my pocket and holding it up to show them.

"So you can call him whenever you're in trouble and he can swoop in like a stabby knight to rescue you?" Bullet teased, his smile sympathetic.

"We don't need him. We were just caught off-guard that one time because Mercy sold us out. I'll do all the stabbing and protecting from here on out," Riot replied stubbornly, his face still bruised and swollen in places from that last confrontation where the agathos had broken his nose when they'd slammed him down onto the asphalt.

"You are grossly overestimating your fighting prowess," Bullet laughed. "Look in a mirror, my bonded-in-law. You look fucking awful."

Riot shot him a half-hearted glare, knowing that Bullet was right. Riot had taken a beating and Bullet had been shot. But I wasn't going to call on Wild to show up whenever we needed backup. We'd have to find our own way to protect ourselves.

"Talk us through it, Gracie," Riot encouraged. I managed a weak smile, even as I exhaled heavily, my shoulders slumping forwards. I knew they wouldn't judge me, but it was still humiliating to admit that I'd been rejected.

"I don't know what I'd hoped for barging in like that, but it wasn't for Wild to tell me—to text me—that he knew what I was to him and dismiss me regardless. He knew."

Riot frowned. "Sounds like he was being an asshole to me. How did he know? How does he even know about soul bonds?"

19

"I've been wondering that too," Bullet mused, drumming his fingers on his thigh to a tune no one else could hear. "He seemed very well informed on who you were in the dreamscape."

"He's been watching me." I felt my face heat. The idea that he'd been looking out for me was actually quite appealing, rather than inspiring the stalker-like fear it probably should have. "He had cameras on my apartment, outside Hope House, the streets I used to run on... Maybe other places too? I didn't ask."

"But how did he know to watch you in the first place?" Bullet asked. "Most daimons aren't wandering around looking for a soul bond."

"He'd have hardly been the only daimon to be curious about the one and only agathos who decided to move to Milton," Riot pointed out drily.

"Onyx did say he'd been watching me since I moved here," I admitted. "Though I'm not sure if it was curiosity that drew him in or what. Everyone left me alone when I moved here, I really expected more curiosity from the daimons, if anything."

"Maybe they left you alone because of Wild," Bullet countered. "He's got plenty of influence around here, and most daimons don't want to be on his bad side."

Bullet gave Riot a pointed look that he ignored, too busy staring at me, eyebrows disappearing into his messy black hair. "So we're all just cool with the recording Grace thing? No one is weirded out by the stalking except me?"

"Of course not. CCTV footage is, like, so romantic." Bullet swooned dramatically, shooting me a teasing wink. I supposed if anyone knew anything about stalking, it was Bullet. He'd popped into my dreams every night of my life.

"Logically, it's a massive overstep of boundaries and I should be at least a little worried about it," I said slowly, trying to reconcile logic and my unhinged hormonal reaction inside my head. "But I'm not. I don't know why. Maybe because he's my soul bond, even if he doesn't really want to be."

Riot's dumbfounded look morphed into a frown a moment before he pulled me into his arms. I rested my head against his shoulder, relaxing into his embrace. Riot was safety and home and comfort to me. His hugs were like chicken soup for my soul.

"His loss," Riot grumbled. "Well, it would be, though we already know he'll come around eventually. Right, B?"

B! Cute.

"You definitely end up with all four soul bonds eventually, Amazing Grace," Bullet reassured me, a pulse of pleasure going through the bond at Riot's new nickname.

"I mean, we'll see about that," I mumbled back, muffling my words against Riot's body. Bullet had mentioned that his future was uncertain after I found my fourth soul bond, and I'd already told him that I'd rather never find my fourth than risk losing him. He was confident that the Fates didn't work that way, but I was willing to go to battle with them myself if that's what it took.

Maybe Wild was doing me a favor by avoiding me, even if knowing he was mine and yet being out of reach made my chest feel kind of hollow.

"He's buying me out of Viper's deal, regardless," Riot said reassuringly, stroking my back. "Onyx already let me know."

That was good. It was good. Selfishly, I wanted Wild to be responsible for keeping us hidden from the agathos because at least I would be in his life in some capacity and maybe he'd change his mind about getting to know me.

Then again, that was probably a horrible thought because Wild shouldn't be forced to be part of my life just because the Fates had decided we fit together, should he? A few weeks ago, I wouldn't have questioned

that. I'd told Riot that soul bonds were a gift, that mistakes were never made, but I wasn't the same naive person I was then.

Riot had been adamant that you couldn't gift a person, that you couldn't gift a relationship, and he was right. Whatever Wild's reasons for not wanting me were, he was entitled to them.

Even if it hurt.

"Gracie..." Riot sighed, squeezing me close as he felt my internal struggle. He and Bullet both coddled me, I thought to myself with a smile, squeezing him back. And after being alone for so long, even when I'd lived at home with my parents, it was kind of nice to be coddled. But it was a luxury I couldn't really afford to indulge in right now.

"I'm... well not okay, but I'm going to make myself okay. And part of that is deciding where we go next," I said firmly, disentangling myself and snagging Riot's hand to drag him to sit on the bed, squeezing myself between him and Bullet. There were a lot of things that were out of my control right now, but this wasn't. "We can't stay here."

Even if things had gone smoothly with Wild and he'd immediately wanted to bond with me and keep me and live happily ever after, coming back to Milton had been selfish, and staying was dangerous. That didn't mean leaving was particularly tempting though—the daimons here had really welcomed us with open arms, and I was going to miss their company.

Especially Onyx. My female friendships among the agathos in my community had become quite superficial in recent years as they moved ahead with their soul bonds and children and I stayed stuck where I was. Onyx brought something back to my life I hadn't realized I'd been missing.

"Back to the Oneiroi Estate?" Riot suggested, not sounding particularly enthused by the idea. Neither was I, if I was brutally honest with myself. I had a strange itching desire under my skin to do something.

Go somewhere. Get to the bottom of this prophecy that had taken charge of my life without my consent.

Bullet watched me carefully, undoubtedly picking things up through our bond and matching them up with what he knew of the future. Even with the bond in place and a good amount of insight into Bullet's emotional state, the amount he knew, he'd seen, was almost incomprehensible to me.

"Gaia communicated with you," Bullet said carefully, and I winced slightly at the reminder of the small earthquake she'd caused at the community center when I'd asked her to show her approval or not. "Perhaps she'd be willing to say more. Maybe she has answers about what the prophecy means, though there's always a risk she isn't a fan of it."

Riot made a sound of discontent. "And what happens if she's not? Maybe she doesn't want us to liberate the whatever."

"The treasure held in the deep," I murmured automatically. "Where no sweet smelling smoke or prayer can reach."

"And bring forth the Second Age of Heroes," Bullet added. "Don't forget that bit."

"I think it's better to know either way," I said carefully. "We'll plead our case, and hopefully she'll be supportive. Maybe even supportive enough to call off the agathos, to explicitly tell them to stop all the violence against daimons, to stop hunting us."

"Maybe," Riot agreed, not sounding convinced in the slightest. "We better not try contacting her here, unless you're willing to risk flattening Wild's compound."

"Well, I was hoping for a more subtle message than an earthquake, but yes, we do need to go elsewhere." Bullet chuckled. "Somewhere where Gaia's presence can be felt, with a natural spring for Grace to undergo the

traditional cleansing ritual the oracles used to do. Best to start things off on the right foot by showing Gaia respect."

"Do you think it's safe to travel?" I asked a little nervously. Milton was basically boxed in on all sides by agathos settlements. They may think I was in Boston for now, but it still felt like tempting fate for us to drive through the heart of any agathos community.

"Your safety is always my top priority, and I'll always recommend whatever course of action I feel keeps you safe," Bullet replied slowly. The bandage on his arm both backed up his statement and seemed to mock me. Bullet hadn't seemed to struggle at all with picking the path that would result in him getting injured. "While I can't see any issues with us getting there, I'm a little confused about what happens afterwards."

"You're confused?" I asked, reaching between us to link our hands together. It wasn't like Bullet to be confused about, well, anything really.

He pulled his hand away from mine to rub his temple, face scrunched up as though he was in physical pain. There was frustration pouring through the bond from his end, and I was both grateful and concerned that he wasn't making any effort to cover it up when he was usually so conscious about these sorts of things.

"I know we come out of the end of whatever it is okay," Bullet said eventually, squinting slightly. Did he have a headache?

"What the fuck does that mean?" Riot asked, leaning around me to look at Bullet.

"There are some blank patches in my visions coming up." Bullet shrugged, drumming his fingers on his thigh a little slower than his usual frenetic pace since he was using his injured arm. "It's weird and inconvenient. Probably fun surprises from one goddess or another."

"You and I have very different definitions of 'fun,'" Riot groused, pressing in closer to my side like he was worried I was going to disappear.

There was a ripple of tension through the bond that Bullet couldn't quite hide, and I got the sense that despite his casual attitude and his attempts at relaxation, that those "blank patches" were more than just a frustration for him.

"I'm going to try asking the Fates again," Bullet said, already pulling the black pouch that held his tarot cards in it out of his pocket and moving to the small table and chair in the corner of the room. "These are very suboptimal card reading conditions, you know. The lights are fluorescent."

"Snob," Riot snorted, tugging me firmly into his side on the bed. A dangerous position, since I was barely keeping my eyes open as it was and I hated sleeping with makeup on.

We should be sleeping—it was almost impossible to sleep here at night with the pounding bass of the multiple clubs on the property and the sound of voices and drunken laughter seeping through the walls.

"Tired?" Riot asked while Bullet set up his cards, now singing Don't Rain on my Parade under his breath.

"I don't think I'll ever get used to this nocturnal schedule," I admitted, my head lolling against his shoulder. "But I want to, even after we leave here. It's not fair to expect you two to adjust to my schedule."

"Bullet was already on your schedule, and I can sleep whenever," Riot replied, encouraging me under the blankets. Okay, maybe I'd just nap in my makeup, just this once. The idea of getting out of bed now was torture.

There was also a not insignificant chance that if I got into the emotional safe space that was the shower, I'd start crying over Wild, and I didn't want to do that. It would distract Bullet while he was trying to work and stress out Riot, and frankly, it would make me feel like a spoiled brat.

You're not entitled to a relationship, I reminded myself, repeating the words like a mantra to soothe away the sharp edges of my rejection, letting my eyes flutter shut. I vaguely monitored Bullet through the bond, hoping for some rush of excitement or confidence to break up the steady stream of determined focus. Some kind of sign of good news in our future.

Maybe a miraculous change of heart from my parents? An apology from the agathos and a promise to back off and let us live? La Nuit popping up to say 'don't worry about the whole prophecy thing, Grace. You just go on and live your life and be happy?' I'd take any or all of the above.

Riot's thumb rubbed soothing circles into my shoulder, lulling me almost to sleep, when a sudden sharp pain through the bond jolted me awake.

"Bullet!" Riot yelled, both of us scrambling off the bed as Bullet slumped down on the chair, his butt hitting the floor with a thud, blood streaming out of his nose.

I stumbled towards him, quickly pulling his body against mine before he smacked his head on the tile floor. His eyes were closed, body completely limp and heavy against me.

"What's happening?" I whispered to no one in particular. I cupped his cheek, blood quickly pooling in my palm and spilling down my wrist, and quickly moved two fingers down, pressing them against his neck to check his pulse. Strong. Normal. Right? It felt normal. "Bullet! Wake up! Do you think we should put him in the recovery position?"

"I don't know. Maybe?" Riot replied uncertainly, immediately jumping in to help me move Bullet to lie on his side. What was best practice for a bloody nose? Why couldn't I remember a single thing from all the first aid courses I'd taken at work when I actually needed to?

"Fuck. I'm going to run downstairs and find Dr. Martinez," Riot said, standing and running a hand roughly through his hair.

"Okay," I agreed hoarsely. "Okay, that sounds like a good idea. You're going to get Dr. Martinez and I'm going to stay here with Bullet and he's going to wake up soon."

"That's right, Gracie," Riot murmured, already backing towards the door. "He's going to be just fine, you'll see."

But was he? Because that was the thing with Bullet. With his curse, the one I desperately wanted to believe wasn't real. We never really knew if he was going to be just fine.

What if he really did have the Oneiroi curse?

What if the gods had decided to take him from me early?

BULLET

CHAPTER 4

"The Spirit of Dreams," Nyx said, standing over my prone form, her full-body black veil fluttering in the breeze. "You are pushing yourself too hard."

Why was I lying on the ground? When did I enter the dreamscape? I didn't even remember going to sleep.

Feeling more than a little vulnerable under the weight of Nyx's stare, I pushed myself up onto my forearms, surprised at the effort it took, before eventually struggling into an upright position.

The cards. I'd been reading cards. Had I fallen asleep doing a reading? The Fates would not be impressed by that. I'd say I was at risk of losing my special privileges with them, but since I was the last Oneiroi left, I was probably pretty safe in that respect. Silver linings and all that.

"Perhaps I have spoiled you," Nyx sighed, sounding like a long-suffering parent rather than an immortal goddess as she conjured up her usual onyx throne and took a seat. "Between myself and my daughters, we have shown you so much, answered so many of your questions. And how could we not? You're one of our chosen few. My final Oneiroi."

I did not like where this conversation was going on so many levels. I reached out with my senses for that thread that connected Grace and I in the dreamscape, but I couldn't find it. She must still be awake.

Hopefully not panicking about me falling asleep mid-card reading like a total amateur.

"But some things you cannot see," Nyx continued. Right, focus. In the presence of an ancient primordial goddess, now is not the time to slack off. "Some things we cannot show you, not any longer. You know what it is to be an Oneiroi, what the cost is. Do not suffer more than you have to."

It was unusual for Nyx to admit that my gift came with any kind of suffering at all, and that alone shocked me into further silence. While she was always generous to me, she wasn't particularly sympathetic to mortals in general. Our lives were so short to her that what did it matter if we suffered? We weren't around long enough in her eyes for it to really count.

"The players on the board are changing. For centuries, Gaia has been silent. Angry, powerful, but silent. But to your agathos, to the one who accepted the mantle of the prophecy when she prayed to me, Gaia responded. It made other deities pay attention. Daimons and agathos have always been of little interest to other gods and goddesses—barely a step above humans, and pets of either mine or my sister's at that—but no longer, I think."

Ignoring the whole slightly offensive 'pets' concept, holy fuck balls, that was terrifying. Other gods, ones who'd been dormant or uninterested in mortal life for centuries, were suddenly sitting up and paying attention? No wonder my visions were so murky and unsettled recently.

"Return, the Spirit of Dreams. Return to your love. Trust that you will get the answers you need when we can give them to you. Trust your own instincts and those of your new family when I cannot. Return to them, and make the most of the time you have left."

I woke up with a start, the cold floor pressing into my cheek.

"Bullet!" Grace gasped, her soft hands brushing at my cheeks, nose, forehead, checking me over. Or at least that was what it felt like—my head was a big, throbbing mess and I scrunched my eyes shut to avoid the blinding brightness.

"He's awake, that's a good sign," a voice said drily. Dr. Martinez?

"Thank you for that dazzling medical insight," Riot snapped. Aw, was he worried about me again? He really was the best bonded-in-law.

"I'm fine," I croaked, gagging slightly as the taste of blood hit my tongue. "Totally fine. Nothing to see here. I just need to wash my face."

"You collapsed," Grace shot back fiercely. "You are most assuredly not *fine.*"

"How old are you?" Dr. Martinez asked, her voice softening slightly.

"I'm a 29-year-old Oneiroi. You can go, doc. We all know what's wrong with me."

There was a shuffling sound, and I had no doubt Dr. Martinez was following my instructions. All daimons knew there was nothing that could be done for an Oneiroi approaching thirty—they didn't even need medical training for that. Riot knew basically nothing about anything, but he knew what was wrong with me.

"You're leaving?" Grace asked, outraged. I'd never heard her sound so offended in her life. It was so not the time, but the fact that she was getting all protective over me was kind of a turn on. *Saving that snippy tone of voice for the spank bank.*

"Make sure he takes it easy," the doctor replied a moment before the door clicked shut. With an embarrassing amount of effort, I pushed myself into a sitting position, leaning back against the chair I'd been sitting on. Shit, had I passed out and fallen off the chair? That must have been pretty terrifying to witness, no wonder Grace was so anxious.

I could feel Grace and Riot's stares burning into me even though I couldn't quite see them because my eyeballs still weren't being as functional as I would have liked.

Rude of them.

"What happened?" Grace asked, hands still smoothing over my body like she was making sure all the parts were still there. "You were doing a reading and then I felt your pain... Was it a question you asked? Did they not like it?"

They being the Fates, I assumed. My girl was a fast learner, absorbing every lesson I'd given her on the gods and the ways they interacted with mortals.

"I guess I was asking too many questions about things they're not ready to tell me about. There are other gods paying attention after Gaia's big scene, and I can't see their involvement no matter how much I want to. But there's no need to worry," I replied breezily, using the chair to shove myself upright and stumbling towards what I was pretty sure was the direction of the bathroom and knocking my shin hard against the bed frame for my efforts. Fucking *ouch*. "Just a bit of dizziness, I'm going to splash some cold water on my face. I'm probably just suffering the effects of all these microwave meals, you know? I'm a fragile boy, I need fresh fruit and vegetables to sustain me," I rambled, shutting the bathroom door behind me and leaning against it.

"Bullet—" Grace began, her concern pulsing down the bond.

"Just washing my face!" I repeated, my voice too high to be natural as I fell against the sink and turned the faucet on. My lower face and chest were soaked, the blood quickly drying uncomfortably on my skin.

Okay. Okay, not ideal.

31

I'd asked too many questions, fine. There were other gods ready to jump in and make their presence known. Also fine, sort of. Well, I guess that depended whose side they were on. And I hadn't been joking about the microwave meals. As soon as we got back to my place—or wherever we went from here—and I started eating food that didn't come out of a plastic tray, I'd probably feel better.

Sure, nosebleeds weren't an uncommon first symptom of the Oneiroi curse setting in. And sure, Nyx had all but warned me I was speeding up the process of my own demise by pushing myself.

It'd still probably be okay. I had time left.

It was never going to be enough time. That was the simple truth of it. There were a thousand lifetimes I wanted to live with Grace—lazy Sunday afternoons and busy Saturday mornings. School runs, holiday meals, seaside vacations. Trips to Broadway and the West End. Late nights tangled together between the sheets, not knowing where I ended and she began. A million and one scenarios I'd never get to live out, futures that weren't meant for me.

I sucked down a pained breath, forcing myself to stop panicking before the bond showed Grace just how absolutely fucking terrified I was. I splashed my face liberally with water as cold as I could get it, and hummed *Seasons of Love* to myself, exhaling in relief as my blurry vision slowly returned to normal. By the gods, I looked awful—my skin was practically translucent except for the purple shadows under my eyes, and I could have sworn I'd aged five years since this morning. No wonder Grace was hovering outside the bathroom door, the bond alive with fear.

Once I'd scrubbed the last remnants of blood away and dried my face, I pasted my best and brightest smile on my face and let myself out of the bathroom.

"Bullet!" Grace gasped, as though it had been hours since she'd seen me instead of minutes, a blur of black hair as she threw her arms around my middle, hugging me tight whilst simultaneously dragging me towards the bed. "Oh my gosh, you need to rest. Lie down. Riot, get him water! They must have an apple or something in the kitchen. He said he needs fresh fruit—"

Riot made a noise of disbelief, quickly holding his hands up in surrender as Grace gave him a look eerily reminiscent of her terrifying mother.

"I'll go look for an apple or something," he said quickly, edging towards the door. I knew he cared—deep, deep down—but Riot knew as well as I did that what was wrong with me couldn't be cured by vitamins. Grace knew it too, but she wasn't ready to come to terms with that yet and I was happy to indulge her rather than look too hard at the truth. I wasn't ready to come to terms with it yet either.

"Need fruit... May perish..." I sighed dramatically, lying back on the bed and throwing an arm over my face.

"Don't push it, asshole," Riot muttered, somewhat affectionately, pulling the door shut with a *snick* behind him.

"Bullet," Grace said quietly, sitting on the edge of the bed and running a tentative hand down the side of my face. "Be serious for a second and tell me what's going on. *Please.*"

The broken quality of her voice had me pulling my arm away to grab her hand immediately, needing to reassure her despite my every instinct to downplay the situation as nothing to worry about.

"Nyx mentioned there are other deities who are paying attention to us now because Gaia actually responded to you after centuries of silence," I explained, doing my best to smile through it like that wasn't a wholly terrifying concept. "I guess that means I can't push for answers the way I've always done. I'm only Nyx and the Fates' Favorite Boy, not everyone else's."

33

"Then no more pushing for answers," Grace replied decisively, latching on to the one concrete piece of action we could take. "We'll just have to be surprised. See what happens in real time, like everyone else does."

Fuck that.

I mean, I could not push. I wasn't in any hurry to repeat the experience I'd just had. But I had no interest in being like everyone else. I didn't think I was going to stop seeing visions entirely in my dreams anyway—Nyx liked me too much for that—so we'd still have some kind of heads up of what was around the corner for us.

Like everyone else, she says, I scoffed silently. I was the last Oneiroi, I was objectively not like everyone else and I was going to embrace that uniqueness all the way to my deathbed. I didn't have time to feel any other kind of way about it.

No time for bitterness.

"And your health?" Grace asked uncertainly, briefly losing her battle to be in denial about my future.

"It's not a great sign, but I've seen plenty of my life yet to come," I assured her. *Plenty-ish.* 'Plenty' was a subjective term.

Grace linked her fingers through mine, flexing them and rubbing the back of my hand in absent agitation. "Not until after I meet my fourth soul bond, right?"

"Right." As always, I was hit with a healthy dose of guilt and pity square in the chest any time I thought of Dare.

"I meant what I said. I'm never going to meet him," Grace announced, tipping her chin up stubbornly. "I'll just never meet him and then you'll be okay."

"Amazing Grace—"

"I'm not risking someone I know and love for some hypothetical," she clipped, blinking hard to keep the tears at bay. I could feel how much it cost her to say that through the bond. Agathos were raised believing that they should do anything and everything to find their soul bonds, and Grace was already feeling raw from Wild's idiotic rejection.

"I hate to break it to you, but the Fates don't work that way," I replied quietly, adjusting my grip on her hand to keep her fingers still. "Your fourth soul bond isn't some hypothetical, Amazing Grace. I know you don't want to know this, but he'll love you so fiercely you won't know what to do with yourself. He'll make you smile and roll your eyes in exasperation, and he'll complete the missing link in the chain for all of us."

Grace shook her head silently, one lone tear escaping that she rubbed away viciously with the heel of her hand.

"He will," I promised. "And by the goddesses, he is going to need you more than ever soon because the Fates are about to be very unkind to him, and there's nothing any of us can do about it. Nothing *I* can do about it, even though I know what's going to happen, and that fucking hurts. I know you want me safe, Grace, but this has always been bigger than just us. That's our curse to bear."

"That barely scratches the surface of our curses to bear," Grace whispered, disentangling our hands and laying down next to me, cuddling up to my side. I hated that I'd frightened her, but this was also the most snuggly and easily affectionate Grace had ever been with me and I was going to make the most of it. Stupid gun wound, stopping her from properly throwing herself at me. Well, that and the fainting, probably. "I don't want to lose you... I don't want him to suffer either. Please promise me you'll take it easy."

"I promise," I replied solemnly, fighting off the urge to make a joke and lighten the heavy mood.

I wondered if Grace knew that Dare was probably her fourth soul bond? I didn't know for *certain*, in my visions where he appeared with Grace, he still appeared in the garb of The World card, face obscured, but I'd eat my own tarot cards if he wasn't. Dare, Riot and I had all been friends when we were young, and amongst our daimon peers, that friendship had been unusual.

Besides, when I thought of the group of us that Grace had been landed with, Dare seemed like the natural counterpoint to Riot's surly nature, to Wild's stoic intensity, and to my golden-retriever-theater-kid energy. He was relaxed, rolled with the punches, a natural flirt, and personable. If the four of us were together, he'd be the only one who knew how to talk to someone outside of our group like a normal person. He could make—*shudder*—small talk.

Dare really was Grace's missing link.

And while he didn't have my levels of excitement that Grace absolutely found endearing rather than annoying, he could be funny. Hilarious, even. When I was gone, Dare would make her smile.

I tucked Grace's head against my chest, hoping she wasn't paying attention to the bond as I blew out a long breath and schooled my face into a neutral expression. My throat was so tight that it ached, and it didn't matter how much I told myself there was no time for bitterness, I was fucking bitter.

I didn't want to say goodbye to the love of my life. I didn't want to entrust her smiles to someone else and watch her grow old without me from the underworld, waiting to see her again someday, hoping she remembered me. Hoping that after a long lifetime of love and contentment with her other three bonded that she even *wanted* to see me in the afterlife.

I wanted to live. I wanted to love Grace and I wanted her love in return.

I wanted to *live*.

GRACE

CHAPTER 5

I slept restlessly throughout the day, clinging a little too tightly to Bullet considering he was injured and not much of a cuddler when he slept anyway. I couldn't help it—his sudden collapse this morning had terrified me, and I couldn't help but feel like our time together was slipping out of my fingers, as fiercely as I tried to believe that wasn't true.

Bullet and Riot were still sleeping soundly as I carefully climbed out of bed and headed to the attached bathroom, snagging some clean clothes on the way—black leggings that Onyx had procured for me and were the comfiest things ever, and one of Riot's oversized thick navy sweaters, warm enough to travel in.

I was ready to leave.

The phone Wild had given me had been silent since Onyx's messages, and I'd already thrown myself into his way once before. I didn't want to accost him again in his own home. Even before the morning's embarrassing incident in the apartment, I'd been staying here for just over a week now, right under Wild's nose. I'd spent most of that time in the common area at the base of the stairs to his place, and he'd gone out of his way to avoid me. There was only so much rejection a girl could take.

Besides, being here clearly wasn't good for Bullet. He'd been sort of joking about needing fresh vegetables and hating the fluorescent light, but also not joking at the same time. Honestly, Asphodel was overstimulating for *me,* let alone Bullet, who'd lived alone before me, eating an all-organic diet and meditating regularly.

By the time I emerged, Riot was just letting himself back into the room, two coffees in hand.

He kissed my hair as he carefully handed me the cup, and he opened the blinds and took a seat on the low ledge next to the window while I took the seat Bullet had been in yesterday, both of us watching him sleep for a quiet moment. As always, Bullet was motionless, lying flat on his back with his arms rigid at his side. Only the steady rise and fall of his chest and the occasional fluttering of his eyelids gave away that he was even *alive.*

"On a scale of one to ten, how panicked are you after this morning?" Riot asked, sipping his coffee.

"Off the scale panicked," I murmured, rubbing at the relentless ache in my chest that had kept me awake most of the day.

Riot nodded in understanding, turning to stare out the window. It wasn't much of a view—just the slightly dilapidated rooftop of Asphodel, and a few chimneys in the distance from up at this height. *Maybe it was a good thing Wild didn't want me,* I reasoned with myself. At least we wouldn't have to compromise and move into his place.

As spacious as Asphodel was, this wasn't Bullet's scene at all, and Riot hated being around so many people. Or rather, hated so many people being around *me.* His willingness to share my attention only went so far, and I loved that about him.

"I mean, if you were looking for a silver lining," Riot said slowly, watching my reaction carefully, "you and Bullet seemed to really *click* this morning when he was recovering. More than usual."

Guilt snaked through me at that, even though I knew Riot wasn't *trying* to make me feel guilty. Bullet and I hadn't immediately fallen into an easy rhythm with each other, it was something we'd had to work at and we still weren't quite there.

"It was easy with you," I mumbled over the rim of my coffee cup. "It's been kind of hard with Bullet. And then Wild... Well, it's impossible, I guess. He doesn't want me."

Riot hummed thoughtfully, always a smooth lake I could sink into when my emotions felt like a raging ocean. "Wild is a tough nut, but once you crack him, I think that'll be that. You know?"

"No," I replied honestly.

Riot snorted. "I mean, once you break through whatever his barrier is, I think your path ahead will be pretty smooth. He's a warrior, and he'll fight to be at your side every step of the way when he opens himself up to it. He kind of already is, in a creepy, stalkerish sort of way."

I smiled to myself, leaning my head back against the wall and staring up at the ceiling. That was a really nice way of looking at the multiple CCTV cameras Wild had trained on my life.

"And what about Bullet?" I glanced at my still-sleeping soul bond. "Why is it harder with him when we both want this so much?"

I *loved* him. He loved me—I knew those weren't just words, I could feel it through the bond. And yet it still felt like there was something missing. Something that I was missing.

Riot winced, sipping his coffee for a moment before replying. "I've been thinking about this."

39

"Did you come up with any ideas?" I rasped, waiting for his answer with bated breath and dreading it all at once. Riot was smart and observant, despite what he said about himself, and there was a good chance he was seeing the thing I was missing.

"This might sound stupid, I don't really know how Bullet's gifts work and they seem to be changing now anyway," Riot admitted, tapping the side of his coffee cup nervously. "What I do know is that you wake up with a lingering sensation after he visits you in the dreamscape, right?"

"That's right," I said slowly, frowning.

"My theory is that the memories of his visits are there in your subconscious somewhere, you just can't access anything except the most powerful emotion you were left with. If you learned something about him over the years—for example that Bullet had a set expiry date on his life—that might be the kind of thing that might stick in the recesses of your mind without you realizing it. It's the kind of thing that might make you... wary, I guess."

Riot started pouring love and affection through the bond almost instantly as I began to panic. Had I known before I met Bullet in person that he had a short life expectancy? Was that impacting the way I interacted with him? I didn't even want to believe the Oneiroi curse was a real thing, let alone have it impact the way I behaved with him.

"I don't think it's just you," Riot added quickly. "I think your bond is strained on his end too. I try to put myself in his position and think about what I'd be like if I knew I had to leave you behind, and I have no idea how I'd react. Would I push you away? Try to keep some distance to lessen your hurt? Would I make the most of every moment so you'd only remember the best parts of me? Would I try to take on all your burdens as my own so you didn't have to bear them? I don't know, but I can say for sure I have seen Bullet do all of those things at some point or another with you."

A tear I didn't realize had escaped fell with a quiet *plunk* into my coffee as I forced my mind to be still and examine the bonds between us. Despite only being a few days old, they glowed so brightly in my mind, it was like they were made of moonlight. So brightly that it was hard to see small dull patches that dotted the thread, but there was no denying they were there with Bullet though.

They weren't cracks so much as *bumps*. But bumps could be smoothed over, couldn't they? We'd already made progress this morning. We'd had an honest conversation even though it hurt, and I felt closer to Bullet than I had yesterday.

"I know you don't want to believe that Bullet will be affected by the Oneiroi curse—and maybe he won't," Riot said hastily, though not with as much conviction as I'd like. "Nothing about any of us has been normal so far. But *just in case*, don't you want the memories you share with Bullet to be the best ones? Not this weird awkwardness of giving each other everything and nothing at the same time and pretending it's enough?"

"You really are wise," I told Riot, with a weak laugh, feeling a little nauseous at the idea that I may have been holding Bullet and I back inadvertently. But if us moving forward meant me accepting that he was cursed, that he didn't have much time left...

I wasn't sure I *could* accept that. I'd fight for Bullet every single day until I couldn't fight any longer. I wouldn't—couldn't—accept any other option.

From what I understood of Bullet's lessons, our time was finite, a thread of mortality determined by the Fates, and while the paths we could take might change and divert, that length of thread was set. I knew that, I knew that the only certainty in life was death, and yet...

"I'm not wise, but I am a Moros. I've seen a lot of... end of life behavior. I can feel that you're conflicted, Gracie. Just focus on making those good memories, and the rest will come or it won't." Riot shrugged like it was that easy, and maybe it was. Maybe all I had to do was focus on making every day with Bullet the best it could be.

The first step in that plan was getting him out of here. Recovery aside, Bullet had basically holed himself up in the room the entire time we'd been here because the more people he was exposed to, the more visions of the future he'd be bombarded with.

"While we're waiting for Sleeping Beauty over here to wake up, I've got an idea of what we could do," Riot said mildly, a look in his eyes that absolutely promised trouble.

"He needs his sleep, we can't wake him up," I replied, giving him a pointed look.

"What did you think I was suggesting?" Riot laughed quietly to himself. "Get your mind out of the gutter, Gracie. I just want to go for a walk."

I hid behind my coffee cup to hide my blush, even though I knew Riot could feel my embarrassment through the bond. I *had* been thinking he was talking about physical intimacy.

"Where do you want to go? I don't want to be too far from Bullet when he wakes up."

"It's not far. I just want to see the secret camera room Wild uses to stare at you like a fucking pervert."

"We can't go in there," I laughed, careful not to wake Bullet. "It's in Wild's apartment. He's probably there right now. And he's not a *pervert*."

"He's not there. Onyx said he left the property right after you visited him." Riot tapped the back of his phone. "She's such a gossip. It's really convenient for us."

I snorted in spite of myself. Onyx presented herself in such a cool, aloof way that it wasn't immediately obvious that she gossiped like an old woman at a bingo game.

"I can't," I told him with an apologetic smile. "Agathos instincts are saying 'nope.' I guess breaking and entering falls under the lying, cheating and stealing ban. When I went last time, it was because I knew he was going to be there."

"Do those agathos instincts tell you to prevent lying, cheating and stealing?"

I contemplated it, worrying my lower lip with my teeth. "Yes? Sometimes I know you're lying to protect me and it sort of nags at my psyche, but so long as I don't know what the lie is, I don't feel compelled to act, if that makes sense."

Riot hummed thoughtfully, setting his coffee cup aside and standing, pulling something out of his pocket. "And what if you *knew* I stole the keys to Wild's apartment? Would you feel compelled to get them back?"

He dangled them in front of me for a moment, flashing me a grin before darting for the door.

"Riot!" I hissed, quickly setting my own coffee down and racing after him, not even stopping to put my shoes on. Sugar, he could move fast for someone who usually sauntered like he had all the time in the world.

Miraculously, the kitchen was empty, even though I could hear the other daimons who lived here moving around in their rooms. I had no idea what they'd say if they saw me chasing Riot up the spiral staircase that led to Wild's private quarters.

They'd probably laugh, in all honesty. Daimons weren't raised with a crippling fear of authority like agathos were.

Riot was already fumbling with the key by the time I reached the top of the stairs, and I went to grab his arm right as it clicked open. He grinned cockily as he leaned on the door, half falling into Wild's silent apartment, and my breath caught at the look on his face. Riot so rarely smiled—a proper smile with teeth—that I almost forgot for a moment that he was breaking into the apartment of the soul bond who wanted nothing to do with me.

Almost.

"Riot," I grumbled, slipping into the apartment and closing the door behind me, leaning back against it. "We should not be in here. You are in my bad books."

"You don't have bad books, Gracie. You're too nice." He was already poking around the studio apartment with absolutely zero shame, looking in the fridge and cupboards in the kitchen before moving towards the closet. I caught a glimpse of a neat row of black T-shirts before he slid the door closed, moving towards the bookcase.

"You are *so* nosy," I said, torn between outrage and amusement.

"If Wild didn't want you in here, he would have asked for the keys back," Riot replied, like it was the most logical thing in the world.

"He definitely doesn't want *you* in here," I pointed out, laughing quietly.

"Ah, here we go," Riot said triumphantly. Shoot, I thought I'd pulled the heavy bookcase door all the way closed yesterday, but apparently not. Riot hadn't found the handle hidden in the book, but he didn't need to when he was gripping the half-inch edge of the door that was visible and prying it open like it weighed nothing.

He spared a moment to shoot me a victorious grin before walking into Wild's... *office* with a low whistle. With an exasperated sigh, I pushed off the door and followed him. Maybe I could drag him out, if nothing else.

44

"This is quite the setup," Riot said mildly, watching the screens flick between multiple views of my apartment and my old workplace.

What did Wild think of me, seeing me coming and going from work each day in my regulation agathos knee-length skirts and pastel sweaters? The thought of him sitting here in his too-tight black T-shirt, broodily watching as I went through the same mundane routine week after week, hair always perfectly curled and barely-there makeup applied flawlessly, made something stir in me south of my stomach.

Surely that wasn't desire. I wasn't... aroused by that idea. That would be perverse, probably. Inappropriate, for sure.

"What are you thinking about?" Riot asked, his voice way too amused to not know which direction my thoughts had taken.

"Cameras," I replied, cringing at how high my voice was. For the millionth time, I wondered what Anesidora had against the occasional little white lie.

"You want to make a home movie, Gracie?"

"A home movie?"

"The shaky cam, naked kind," Riot replied smugly.

"No!" I swatted his arm lightly before wrapping a hand around his bicep and attempting to drag him out of the room. *I needed to add weights to my workout routine.*

"If it isn't *performing* on camera," Riot mused, easily disentangling my hand from his arm and pulling my back against his chest instead, trapping me in place between him and the desk, "then maybe the idea of Wild *watching* you is what's got you feeling a little hot and bothered there. Does my sweet agathos like the idea of her soul bond sitting in this sad little room, dick in hand, panting after you?"

Oh my.

I *did* kind of like that idea.

Did that make me a terrible person?

Riot didn't give me a chance to analyze it. He ran his hands down my arms, tangling our fingers together before guiding my hands to the desk in front of us and planting them there, dropping a lazy kiss on my shoulder.

"Riot," I warned, face heating. "We shouldn't..."

"I don't think Bullet and I have been doing a good job of showing you the full daimon experience. One of the best things about being a daimon—" Riot's hands slipped around my front "—is doing whatever the fuck you want."

"I'm not a daimon," I breathed, letting Riot's hand slip possessively between my legs anyway, cupping me over my leggings.

Riot hummed, his middle finger working over the seam in a way that should have probably been illegal. "You've got agathos eyes, but the spirit of a daimon. You're something uniquely you, Gracie. One part good girl, one part rebel, all parts having an orgasm in Wild's spy den."

One hand cupped my jaw, encouraging my face towards his as Riot bent down, lips crashing against mine as the fingers that had been stroking over the top of my leggings slipped past the waistband and into my panties.

If whatever deities that controlled my life frowned upon this sort of thing, frankly the punishment would be worth it, I thought idly, parting my lips as Riot's tongue stroked against mine, his middle finger lightly pressing against my entrance. I rocked my hips, groaning at the friction as the heel of his palm rubbed my clit just right.

Riot's hard length pressed against my butt, and he nipped my lip lightly as I pushed back against it, wanting to drive him as crazy as he was driving me.

"Minx," he laughed against my lips, still keeping hold of my jaw. His grip wasn't tight, and I knew he'd release me if I made any attempt at moving away, but I wasn't going to. I liked when Riot got all possessive over me.

"So wet already," Riot mused, a second finger joining the first, pressing deeper until I was biting my lip to muffle my moans. "Hopefully when Wild crawls back here tonight because he can't stay away from you, this tragic little room will still smell like you. Let's see if he can keep his hands off you then."

Maybe I was a terrible, depraved person because Riot's words pushed me over the edge. A leisurely orgasm rolled through me, turning my limbs into noodles, as I imagined Wild in here, reconciling the diligent, by-the-books agathos he'd been watching with the wanton one riding Riot's hand in his office.

"So fucking pretty," Riot murmured, taking his time to pull his fingers free and making a show of licking them clean while I blushed my way through righting the waistband of my leggings. "I could watch you come literally all day. That would probably be my ideal day, honestly."

"You're incorrigible and we are definitely not supposed to be here," I laughed, turning to rest my face against his chest for a moment and catch my breath before resuming my attempts at getting Riot out of here.

"Oh, I know we're not supposed to be here," Riot assured me, patting me on the butt. "I just wanted to help you mark your territory a little. We can go now."

I leaned back to stare at him, my jaw dropping open. "Mark my territory?!"

"Don't let your soul bonds forget who the boss is," Riot replied with a smug smirk. "Come on, Bullet is probably awaiting your return, outraged that he isn't getting immediate attention after his fainting episode this morning. Let's go."

"Close the bookshelf properly," I ordered, dragging Riot out of the small alcove and giving him my sternest look. "And give me back the keys. And I'm going to get you back for this."

"Don't threaten me with a good time, Gracie," Riot snorted, doing as I asked and yanking the bookcase all the way shut with a satisfying click.

I probably wasn't going to show Wild who was boss, but I was going to show him that I was done waiting around for him. I ushered Riot out of the door and tossed the apartment keys onto the counter before pulling the door shut behind me. The loud *snick* seemed to echo behind me, and I briefly closed my eyes, exhaling heavily. Letting it all go. The waiting, the wondering, the second-guessing.

No more, I promised myself. My priority had to be on Bullet and the prophecy, not on gaining the attention of a soul bond who never wanted me.

RIOT

CHAPTER 6

As I expected, Bullet had dramatically complained about how he was a lonely invalid and we'd just abandoned him for *hours* whilst trying to suppress his shit-eating grin until Grace curled up next to him for a cuddle and I'd been relegated to food duty.

I didn't actually mind. Despite all the shit I gave him, I liked Bullet. His sudden turn this morning had scared the crap out of me, and I didn't know how to feel about the fact he was obviously downplaying it. Part of it was him not wanting Grace to worry—which was an impulse I understood—but he was downplaying it for his own benefit too. Neither of them were ready to have a brutally honest conversation about the Oneiroi curse and what it meant for their relationship. For all of us.

As much as I thought they needed to face those hard truths, it wasn't my place to push them into it. It wouldn't help if I did—both Bullet and Grace were great at retreating into themselves and deflecting with pleasantries as an avoidance tactic.

"Riot," Onyx called, her heeled boots clicking ominously over the lino as she crossed the common room, eyes trained on the phone her thumbs were flying over.

"What's up?" I sighed. Was it too much to hope that I'd find some halfway decent microwave meals in the commercial freezer, heat them up, and make my way back to the room without anyone speaking to me? Why were there always people here? Why did they always want to *chat*?

My life was a lot more peaceful when all of these people hated me.

Onyx glanced up from her phone, giving me an appraising look. "How are you so good at pretending not to be a moody asshole around Grace?"

"I'm *not* a moody asshole around her. It's you fuckers that annoy me," I groused, staring through the glass door of the freezer. I had pretty low standards when it came to food—I'd basically survived on tater tots and cocaine when I lived at my dad's place—but even I was getting sick of frozen mac 'n cheese.

"Well if I annoy you, you're definitely not going to be excited to hear who's standing in the parking lot, demanding your presence," Onyx replied drily. "Don't you even check your phone?"

"I left it in the room. Who is it?" I asked, hoping like hell it wasn't my dad. He wasn't allowed on the premises, and it'd be just like him to make a goddamn scene in the parking lot.

"Viper."

"Viper?" I repeated, giving up on food selection and turning to face Onyx. What the fuck was Viper doing here? There was no love lost between him and Wild, and since the deal between us was still in effect, I was basically at his beck and call. He could just demand I go to his place instead.

If I answered my phone.

It must be a really urgent errand for him to risk coming here.

"Right. I'll let Grace and Bullet know, then go see what he wants."

"I'll meet you down there. Don't argue," Onyx added, holding up a hand the moment I opened my mouth. "Wild has decided to go into hiding to avoid the terror that is the dainty, sweet-as-pie Grace, and that means Asphodel and the land it sits on is my responsibility for now. Your snake problem is now my snake problem."

"I thought you said Wild had agreed to make it *his* problem."

"Who do you think I'm messaging?" Onyx gave me a scathing look. Fucking hell, she was scary when she wanted to be. "Get your girl. Meet you downstairs."

She stomped towards the elevator, making some of the most hardened Keres daimons I'd ever seen jump out of her path. No wonder Wild had kept promoting her.

I jogged back to the room, opening the door to find Grace helping Bullet into a shirt. It was the first time I'd seen him completely dressed since the shooting.

"No need to explain," Bullet said breezily, pushing his hair out of his face. "My gift might be on the fritz, but I did see a vision of Viper stopping by while I was sleeping. We're coming with you."

"Of course you are," I deadpanned, grabbing our coats to protect us from the fall chill and handing them out before shrugging on my own.

Grace was pensive as we made our way downstairs, keeping her arm firmly linked through Bullet's good one. There was no way she wasn't replaying the moment where he collapsed on repeat in her mind, and I fully expected Grace to keep a tight grip on Bullet wherever we went for the foreseeable future.

I did my best to repress that version of Riot who cared about those kind of things, not wanting to show any sign of vulnerability in front of Viper. He already knew how much Grace meant to me, and that was far more than I ever wanted him to know.

I swaggered out into the parking lot to meet him, pretending that I had all the might of Wild and his crew behind me even though Wild would probably feed me to the snake if Grace would let him get away with it. Still, I'd done enough bowing and scraping to Viper to last a lifetime.

"You look like shit," I said immediately, blinking in surprise at the state of him. Viper always looked pretty menacing because of the double scars where it seemed like someone had tried to carve out his entire eye, but today the scars were barely even noticeable underneath the swelling and general array of bruises decorating his face. His chin-length brown hair was matted and messy, pushed roughly back off his face, and there was a thin sheen of sweat coating his paler-than-usual skin.

"Fuck you, Riot."

"Hard pass. What do you want?" I asked. Onyx tapped incessantly on her phone nearby, making her presence known in the most obnoxious way possible to Viper. I could feel the mixture of awe and bemusement coming from Grace that was probably due to Onyx's presence. Grace never knew how to feel around Onyx. She liked her, admired her attitude, and was intimidated by her all at once. There was a hint of jealousy there too, despite her best efforts to suppress it. I didn't think she had anything to worry about—as far as I knew, the only thing getting physical attention from Wild was his boxing bag.

"I want out," Viper gritted out eventually, eyes darting around uncomfortably. "Release me from the deal."

"What? Why?" I asked, genuinely baffled. Viper had never asked to be released from a deal before as far as I knew. It was a sign of weakness most daimons didn't like to show.

He gestured at the injuries on his face, upper lip curling in disdain. "It obviously isn't working out well for me."

"If it isn't working well for you, it's because you didn't uphold your end of the bargain," I snapped, squaring my shoulders. I didn't give a fuck that his face already looked like it had lost a fight with a meat grinder, I would absolutely be taking my pound of flesh if he hadn't kept to our terms. Though it appeared Nyx was doing a pretty good job of that for me.

On the plus side, this development meant I didn't have to be his errand boy any longer, nor would I have to enter Wild's service instead. Wild wouldn't need to buy out the deal at all.

"Just let me out of the fucking agreement, Riot," Viper snarled, straightening his spine as though he stood a chance against me in his condition.

"Tell us what you did first," Onyx drawled, still tapping at her phone, not bothering to look up. She was probably relaying this whole conversation to Wild.

Or her new bestie, Dare.

I had no idea why Onyx kept sending selfies of her and Grace to Dare, and she'd basically called me an idiot and rolled her eyes when I asked her. If Onyx had worked out that Dare was likely Grace's fourth soul bond without even being in the same room as them, she was even more perceptive than I thought.

"It's none of your goddamn business, Onyx," Viper replied, cutting her a glare.

"You made it my business when you showed up at Asphodel. Besides, Grace here is my buddy." Onyx finally looked up, giving him a catlike smirk while I ran through the terms of our agreement in my head. "If you've fucked her over, that's something I'm going to have an issue with."

"You asshole, you *told* someone," I sighed as realization set in. He'd been diligent about the other terms of agreement, like covering Grace's tracks and sourcing fake documents for her. "You told someone about our arrangement. What did you say?"

There was a small frisson of fear from Grace that she quickly tried to suppress for mine and Bullet's sakes. If he'd gone and reported everything to the agathos in exchange for a quick buck, Viper wasn't going to walk out of this parking lot alive. Onyx idly pulled her rainbow luminescent butterfly knife out of her pocket, holding it in place behind her phone as she continued to text.

"She's not in any more danger than she was before," Viper scoffed, deflecting. "Break the fucking deal. Nyx is tormenting me."

"Sucks to suck." I shrugged, while Bullet chuckled quietly behind me. Everyone knew that breaking a goddess-sealed deal was a guaranteed recipe for bad luck, and very *public* bad luck at that. A warning from La Nuit to other daimons that someone was unreliable and went back on their word.

"Riot," Grace said quietly from behind me, still hanging back to maintain her grip on Bullet's arm. There was a faintest hint of warning in her voice, like she was reprimanding me for being a dick, which seemed totally unreasonable because Viper was the worst and I had no interest in playing nice with him. Especially if he'd been running his mouth about Grace.

"What is it, Gracie?" I asked, twisting my head back to speak to her without taking my eyes off Viper.

"He looks like he's suffered a lot already..." she hedged.

"The important thing to remember, Amazing Grace," Bullet cut in, still sounding a little worse for wear, "is that Riot may be good to you, but you are very much the exception. We're daimons. We're not good people. We're not compassionate by nature, and Viper broke the deal, so fuck him."

Not only that, but Viper knew too much and he traded in information—going to him for help in the first place had been a calculated risk—and releasing him from all of his obligations would be insanity.

"You are good people," Grace replied stubbornly, and she must have actually believed that since she couldn't lie, which was a slightly alarming thought. We absolutely weren't. Had she forgotten about our little excursion to Wild's secret spy office already? Obviously, I'd played it too safe. Next time, I'd bend her over the desk and have my wicked way with her.

Viper watched with the intensity of a dangerous animal, ready to strike, as Grace guided a limping Bullet forward to stand next to me. He scanned Grace's features like he was looking for something familiar in them, and it was one of the most unsettling things I'd ever seen.

"So, you're the famous Grace."

I did not appreciate Viper's tone, but Grace put a hand on my arm before I could call him out on it.

"And you're the famous Viper. You drove Mercy to Boston," my girl said softly, probably in the voice she used when she worked at the shelter. *Ah, that's why she's being so nice to him.* I could admit that I had no idea why Viper had done that. "Is that who you told?"

Viper looked like he'd rather swallow his tongue than answer, but he probably worked out—correctly—that Grace was his best shot at getting out of this deal. She felt bad for him, it was written all over her face.

"She wasn't exactly going to get in the car otherwise," he grumbled eventually, looking at everything except us and Onyx, who had graduated to absently flipping the butterfly knife around her fingers like it was some kind of fidget weapon.

"Did Dice ask you to drive her?" I asked, still confused as fuck about how this all came to be. Dice and Mercy were soul bonds, though they hadn't actually bonded and probably never would after Mercy sold us all out. We knew that Dice had asked Viper to track her, but I couldn't imagine him wanting Mercy to leave.

I'd never wanted to be away from Grace from the moment I met her. The idea of sending her away, to a whole different state, was insane. But then, she'd never hurt me the way Mercy had hurt Dice. And Wild was living proof that soul bonds *could* stay away from each other, if they wanted to.

Well, sort of. With the assistance of technology and a concerning lack of boundaries.

"No," Viper clipped, cutting a wary glance at Onyx before returning his attention to Grace.

"Then why did you do it?" Grace pressed gently. "That daimon woman, Stellar, who was here the other night already told us that Mercy was going to take a Greyhound to Maine."

"Fucking Stellar and her big mouth," Viper muttered under his breath. "You're really determined to find the good in daimons, Grace the agathos."

His cheek twitched irritably, the movement pulling taut the upper scar that bisected his eyebrow. I frowned to myself, trying to remember the details of the confrontation outside the community center. The whole thing had been chaos and I'd been pinned to the ground for the most of it, but hadn't a stray bullet grazed Mercy's face?

Did that kind of thing scar? Despite my many years of probably deserving it, I'd never actually been shot at.

"Did you feel some kind of..." Grace hesitated, her cheeks flushing. "Connection to her?"

Mercy and Viper as soul bonds? Fucking *gross*.

"She's a kid," Viper scoffed.

"She's eighteen," Grace corrected, looking uncomfortable. "Which is still very young. Younger than you—"

"It's not like that," Viper interrupted sharply. I glanced back at Bullet, wondering if he'd *seen* anything about this, and found him with his head tilted, observing Viper curiously. "Dice asked me to find her, that's it. She was driving around near your old apartment with a bleeding face and no plan. Getting her out of the way before she made a scene and drew more agathos to Milton made my life easier. I was just upholding my end of our agreement." Viper threw another filthy look at me.

"Dice can't be happy with you," I pointed out.

"Dice is a broke teenager, mooching off his sister, and an Ate daimon to boot. Those who don't have anything of value to offer don't get to dictate great terms," Viper replied icily. That made sense. Besides, Dice was young and probably inexperienced with the likes of Viper. I doubted he'd negotiated carefully.

"You made a deal with Mercy," Bullet said suddenly, a look of understanding crossing his face.

"I don't work for free," Viper replied with a cold smile. I didn't know if La Nuit upheld deals made with agathos, but Bullet didn't seem worried so I tentatively hoped Mercy hadn't signed her entire life away. Fuck knows what I would have agreed to if I was eighteen and desperate.

"Can you tell us where she is?" Grace asked. "Did she go to Maine? Where in Maine was she trying to go?"

"I'm sworn to silence, and I'm already dealing with the fallout of one broken deal, so no."

"Thank you," Grace said sincerely before I could argue. "Even if your motivations are selfish, I'm glad that Mercy is out of Milton and that she's hidden if she doesn't want to be found."

It's not like he'd honored *my* secrecy stipulation, but whatever. Maybe this time he'd do a better job of keeping his mouth shut.

"Yeah, I'm basically a hero," Viper deadpanned, crossing his arms over his chest. "Now make your boyfriend release me from this fucking deal."

The second his body language grew more agitated, Wild's Keres daimons seemed to materialize from the shadows, a silent wall of support at our backs.

Well, at Grace's back. These people didn't give a fuck about me.

Onyx pocketed her phone, still twirling the knife around like a lunatic as she moved in closer to where the three of us stood. The rumble of an engine grabbed all of our attention a moment before a black Camaro skidded into the parking lot, the brakes shrieking as it came to a dramatic stop a few feet away from us.

Goddamn, Wild knew how to make an entrance. No wonder he had so many minions. I wondered if he'd give Grace that car if she asked nicely. I'd look good in a Camaro.

He unfolded his massive frame from the vehicle, and Grace sucked in a quiet breath at my side, a bolt of *something* shooting through the bond.

"Wild," Viper clipped, holding his ground but attempting to look somewhat respectful. Anywhere else, he wouldn't have bothered, but this was Wild's turf and Viper wasn't suicidal.

Wild stood with his arms crossed over his chest, angling himself towards Viper. He wasn't standing *with* the three of us, but apparently, he was close enough to catch Viper's attention. His eyes bounced between Wild and the three of us, suspicion followed by disbelief crossing his face before he settled on a more neutral expression.

Grace watched Wild for a moment before looking up at me through thick eyelashes and gently elbowing my ribs. "Can you please release him from the deal? I know better than most how awful it is to be hounded by bad luck."

"Grace..."

"Please?" she asked. I swear to all the goddesses, she batted her eyelashes at me, her lower lip not quite pouting but damn near close to it. Was I going to let myself be swayed by that face?

Absolutely. I didn't stand a chance.

"If you're absolutely sure you don't want a pet snake..." I sighed. Viper practically bared his teeth while Grace raised her eyebrows pointedly at me. "Then okay, fine. I'll just throw away this perfectly good leverage like it's nothing," I muttered.

Wild stepped in front of me before I could say more, positioning himself between us and Viper. Viper pulled his phone out of his pocket, and while I hadn't seen Wild move, I was guessing by the look on Viper's face that the message had come from him.

Grace made a slightly impatient noise, too quiet for anyone except me and Bullet to hear, and I fought back a laugh. Apparently, she wasn't a fan of Wild sweeping in and saving the day? I kind of got that. Grace was only now getting to make decisions truly for herself, and Wild making decisions on our behalf undermined that.

Maybe if he'd deigned to communicate with her first, it wouldn't be an issue. I, personally, was fine with less responsibility.

"You can't seriously expect me to agree to that," Viper groused, eyes flicking nervously between his phone and Wild's stormy expression. "I've always stayed out of your way, you've always stayed out of mine. There's no need for that to change now."

Oh, everything had changed, even if Wild was still mostly in denial about it. Grace fidgeted restlessly next to me, curiosity burning through the bond.

"Wild doesn't negotiate, so I suggest you take the deal," Onyx remarked in a bored voice. "And then get the fuck out of here. We've got a club to open, we can't stand around here all night while you whine."

Viper pursed his lips, glaring at his phone screen again. "Fine. I swear to never speak of the services I provided for Grace the agathos, or Riot, or divulge any of the false information I put out there to distract the agathos, on risk of forfeiture of my Milton properties to Wild Connor. Happy?"

Wild's hand clapped against Viper's, the power of the goddess' magic rippling subtly from where their hands touched and out over the crowd. Grace sucked in a surprised breath, tightening her grip on my arm.

They broke apart, and Viper gave me a hard look. *Right, right. My turn.*

I disentangled myself from Grace and took my time sauntering over to Viper, making the most of these last few seconds where I had something over him.

"I agree to release you from the terms of our deal regarding Grace's safety in exchange for my service," I sighed dramatically, arm outstretched.

Viper snatched my hand painfully, his fury at being in such a vulnerable position written all over his face. "I agree to release you from the terms of our deal regarding Grace's safety," he repeated.

I'd never dissolved a deal before, and the sensation was odd. It had almost a bitter feeling to it, like we'd annoyed Nyx by changing our minds and she was irritated by it. I doubted I'd have come to that conclusion a few weeks ago, but if I'd learned anything from Grace and Bullet's experiences with the divine, it was that they were petulant when they wanted to be.

"Wonderful," Onyx announced, flipping the knife shut and tucking it into her pocket. "Now get the fuck out of here, Viper."

"Gladly," he muttered, already stomping towards his van. "Don't ever come to me for a deal again, Riot. Better yet, don't set foot on my goddamn property. I never want to see your ugly face again."

"Oh no, where else will I find a subpar gym to work out at?" I called after him, enjoying the way he slammed his door a little harder than necessary.

"I'm questioning your judgment a lot right now, Riot," Onyx said, shaking her head as the other Asphodel staff made their way inside. "Viper? Really?"

"All will be revealed in time," Bullet said smoothly, doing his best omnipotent mysterious voice. "I firmly believe there's more to Viper than what we see now."

Unfortunate. That sounded like we weren't rid of him just yet.

"Alright, I'm going to go open up," Onyx announced, staring hard at the still hovering Wild. "You four should go out. Make a night of it. There's an Italian restaurant around the corner that does the best eggplant parmigiana you'll ever eat."

Wild spared her an irritated look before he stalked back to the Camaro, folding himself into the vehicle and slamming the door shut without a look back. Grace let out a shuddering breath as the engine roared to life, and I wrapped an arm around her waist, careful not to jostle Bullet.

"Maybe he doesn't like eggplant parmigiana," Grace laughed weakly. "Besides, we're probably not in any state to dine out."

Bullet looked a little pale, but my face was still pretty bruised from the beating the agathos had given me. I'd draw attention for sure.

"I'll order eggplant parmigiana for all of us," Onyx declared, already tapping away on her phone. "If you can't have your man because he's being a fucking moron, then you can at least have a shit ton of mozzarella as a consolation prize."

GRACE

CHAPTER 7

Onyx made good on her promise of copious mozzarella, sending up one of the daimons with the dinner she'd ordered for us while she managed Asphodel in Wild's absence.

Because he'd just vanished.

Again.

He hadn't even *looked at* me. His resolve to avoid me seemed to be strengthening, if anything. And while, yes, it had only been a *day*, absence had not made his heart grow fonder. *It's fine. It's totally fine,* I told myself as I washed up our dishes in the communal kitchen, the thudding bass from the clubs reverberating through the walls.

That edgy, restless feeling I'd had for days was growing worse after Viper's visit. Wild didn't want me, and the petty part of me didn't want to want him either because my pride was hurt. We'd reached out to him originally to get Riot out of the deal with Viper, and now it was done. Mercy was out there, somewhere, and my guilt over that was driving me crazy.

Why were we still here?

I didn't like to have negative thoughts. I'd been trained not to my entire life, and I struggled not to feel guilty about them when I let those pessimistic ideas take hold in my mind, but I was *filled* with negative thoughts today.

Filled with bitterness and embarrassment that Wild had rejected me.

Filled with rage at the agathos who were taking out their anger on the city of Boston, believing I was there. It was only the fact that the decoy Viper had sent in place looked so unlike me that my instincts were letting me do nothing—Stellar had been so clearly not me that only an idiot would believe she was—but I was still filled with rage at myself for not correcting them anyway. Innocent people would be hurt because of me. *Again.*

I also hated staying awake at night, and it was making me grumpy all the time.

"Ready to go, Amazing Grace?" Bullet asked quietly, joining me in the kitchen. He pulled three to-go cups off the shelf, busying himself making coffee in two and chamomile tea in one with his good arm.

"Now?" I asked, blinking in surprise.

"Why not?" Bullet grinned. "Can you pass me the creamer?"

"You think we should leave today? It's the middle of the night." It was a pretty weak reason even to my own ears, but I wasn't used to just up and going places at midnight. Especially without any prior planning.

"Best time to travel. And you think we should leave today," Bullet corrected, flashing me a grin. "Maybe not in so many words, but you've had enough. You're ready to get out of here. It's only an hour or so to the falls where all Oneiroi are brought for a cleansing ritual when they come of age. Usually, we'd fast for two days first, but we don't have the luxury of that kind of time. I say we take a midnight trip to the falls, dunk you in, then you pay your respects to Gaia and see what side of the coin she lands on with this whole prophecy business."

"Wouldn't that be... sacrilegious?" I asked, taking over the drink preparation because watching Bullet move his injured arm made me nervous. "I'm not an Oneiroi, that cleansing ritual is for you."

"And I'm not an agathos, but we did the ceremony to honor Gaia anyway," Bullet replied with a shrug. "Divinities are big on gestures. Gaia has shown she's willing to speak with you, but I think she'll want to see some kind of *effort* from you, for lack of a better term." He grimaced. "You self selected yourself for the prophecy when you prayed to Nyx, and Gaia's ego might need soothing."

I carefully pressed the lids onto the cups, handing Bullet his and grabbing mine and Riot's. "Do you think I should apologize?"

"No," Bullet replied firmly, staring absently across the room, probably running through visions he'd seen in his mind. "Not for praying to Nyx. Gaia has had a monopoly on the agathos for too long. On mortals for too long. The prophecy says to 'bring forth the Second Age of Heroes.' I don't exactly know what the whole thing means, but that implies future where mortals can seek divine glory. The days of agathos and daimons swearing fealty to one goddess and one alone are over."

Well, no pressure then.

"Can we get out of Milton without bringing attention to ourselves?" I asked warily. It had been my stubborn insistence that we come to Milton in the first place that had put them back on our case.

"Well, my visions are being inconveniently unreliable, but Onyx got us contact lenses, wigs and a vehicle. Ready to see how you look with a bob?"

In the end, we decided not to pack our stuff. We'd need to return the Asphodel vehicle we were borrowing and pick up Bullet's SUV before we returned to his place—it had been parked at the community center during our last confrontation with the agathos, and they'd definitely be looking out for it.

It was a stupid plan, logistically speaking. Even though we all knew it would involve passing through agathos territory multiple times, I didn't want to admit out loud that I was struggling with the idea of leaving Wild behind for good. I was *mad a*bout it too. Why should I struggle when he clearly wasn't? I wanted to have the same nonchalance about him as he had about me—extensive video surveillance system aside—but my brain just wasn't wired that way,

"You good, Gracie?" Riot asked, tossing a day bag into the back while I climbed into the front passenger seat of the borrowed SUV. It felt like so long ago that we'd driven to Milton in Bullet's vehicle to see Mercy, when in reality it had only been a little over a week.

"I'm good," I sighed, the memory of that day with Mercy making my skin itch. Where was she now? Was she safe? Was she missing Dice?

"It could have been worse," Bullet sang, climbing into the seat behind me, already knowing where my thoughts had gone. "Do you want a reminder of all the things that could have gone wrong that day?" he teased.

"Was there an outcome where we never went to Milton at all? Where I hadn't been stupid and naive?" I muttered, face feeling hot. I'd completely disregarded Riot's concerns about that whole day, and he'd been so gracious in not holding it against me.

"Not one that I saw," Bullet replied mildly, scrolling through his phone, undoubtedly looking for a playlist for our little road trip. "There was no scenario where you thought she'd put you at risk. Your trust in Mercy was absolute."

It definitely wasn't now. Now, I only had absolute trust in my bonded.

"Alright, let's get out of here," Riot announced, climbing into the driver's seat and bringing the engine to life. "I can't see Wild, but I can feel him glaring at me from somewhere in the shadows. It's very disconcerting."

"What? He's not here. He drove off, remember?" I pointed out.

"As if distance has ever stopped him from watching you before," Bullet snorted as the dramatic opening notes of *The Phantom of the Opera* came through the speaker, making Riot's eye twitch. "And he's staring at Grace, not you," he added, poking the back of Riot's shoulder. "Do you think he's bugged the car somehow?"

"What?" I asked, whirling around in my seat to look at Bullet. "He wouldn't have, would he?"

"He had cameras set up so he could stare at the *front* of your apartment and your work," Riot pointed out wryly. "As though you just spent your day standing around outside. Ridiculous. Though I guess it's better than installing secret cameras inside your bedroom or something. Boundaries and whatnot."

I scanned the interior of the car as though I'd be able to spot a microphone or hidden camera. "I doubt he's monitoring me now, or he wouldn't have shown me that room. It was probably just a novelty thing, and now he's met me, the novelty has worn off."

"Mm, sure. Keep telling yourself that." Riot shot me a smirk as we pulled out of the parking lot. He and Bullet had both chosen brown wigs and brown contacts, and were layered up enough in their fall clothes to cover most of their tattoos, though Riot had needed to use foundation to cover up the ones on his hands and he kept flexing his fingers like the makeup was bothering him.

Onyx had found me a black chin-length wig and contact lenses that were nearly as dark which were irritating my eyes like crazy. The moment we got free of agathos territory, I'd be taking them out. It *felt* like Anesidora took issue with me covering my agathos opal-colored eyes.

As we made our way through Milton, it was clear how much damage the agathos had managed to do to the properties here. There were boarded up windows everywhere, and a lot of the daimon-owned business looked like they'd been shut down completely. It was painful to see—this town had been theirs, and I'd come here in all my confidence and brought nothing but trouble with me. I couldn't force myself to regret coming to Milton in the first place, my bonded meant too much to me to regret that, but I would live with the guilt of all the damage my presence had caused forever.

"Don't feel bad, Gracie," Riot murmured, eyes moving around constantly as he surveyed the streets for any agathos that might be on the hunt for us. "The agathos made the choices they made, you're not responsible for them."

"The daimons will get their time to shine anyway," Bullet added cheerfully. "Frankly, I think they needed a little kick in the ass to remind them—us—that we're a community. Just because we don't want to be a weird culty one like the agathos doesn't mean we should avoid each other completely, you know?"

"Wild hired a bunch of the people who were worst affected," Riot said, glancing at me out of the corner of his eye. "I heard the Asphodel staff talking about it. The Keres daimons are fired up by all the fighting, they need facilities where they can go to burn off that anger. Those facilities need workers."

"Facilities?" I asked. "Like the basement at the club?"

"That's one option," Riot agreed. "But not all Keres like to fight for an audience. The ones who feel like a slave to their instincts just want somewhere quiet to go work out the rage and then get on with their life."

"I don't think Wild is one of those Keres daimons," I said idly, staring out the window. "I think he *enjoys* the fight. The bloodlust."

I'd seen it in his eyes at the confrontation at the community center. He had been off-balance because I was there and he wanted nothing to do with me, but the violence itself? He'd been all over that.

"I agree," Bullet replied mildly. "You've got a difficult road ahead, Amazing Grace. It would make sense for the Fates to give you a soul bond who didn't mind getting his hands dirty to keep you safe."

"I don't mind doing that," Riot cut in, affronted.

"Yeah, but someone who's actually good at it," Bullet shot back, grinning. Riot narrowed his eyes at Bullet in the rearview mirror before turning the stereo off.

"I take it back! You're the bestest fighter boy there ever was, put my songs back on," Bullet laughed. I felt my lips twitch in spite of myself. It was kind of impossible to be in a bad mood for long with these two around.

All three of us grew quieter as we drove through a sprawling agathos town, but the trip was uneventful. It was the middle of the night, when agathos communities were usually silent, and the violent outbreaks between agathos and daimons had mostly been restricted to cities rather than wealthy suburbs like these ones.

We got through the entire *Phantom of the Opera* soundtrack, much to Riot's distress, before pulling up at a dark, deserted parking spot next to the forest.

"Are you sure this is the right place?" I asked dubiously, quickly taking out my contacts and putting them in a case so I could rub my irritated eyes. "This place seems very... accessible."

"Oh it is," Bullet agreed, also ditching the disguise and accepting the wig Riot handed him, tucking them into a backpack. "It's a popular tourist spot."

"I've personally decided to not question it," Riot said, opening the car door. "I'm trusting that he knows what he's talking about and isn't going to get us killed. I'll drive myself insane otherwise."

"Look at you, learning." Bullet grinned at Riot as he shut his door and walked around the vehicle. "I didn't think you could be taught, but apparently I was wrong."

"Where are we going?" I asked, nudging Bullet with my shoulder to stop him getting too far off-track antagonizing Riot.

"It's close, we're just going to follow the main path," Bullet replied, shouldering the bag with spare clothes and a towel for me and flicking on a flashlight so we could see. It was *freezing* out, and I didn't feel good at all about climbing into a spring in this weather, but to actually have a conversation with Anesidora and find out for sure whether she was friend or foe was worth it. I'd never been the best agathos, but I hoped she'd seen my efforts and remember how I'd encouraged the agathos to better cherish the gift of this earth she'd given us. Maybe she'd understand what the prophecy meant and be willing to help us, if we could just persuade mortals to treat the land with more reverence, the way she'd intended.

"What if a human comes by while I'm mid-prayer?" I asked, frowning to myself as we climbed over a rope barrier and set off on the path into the woods.

"They won't," Bullet assured me solemnly. "Now that we've entered the forest, it'll deter humans until we're done. This is a Gaia-approved spot, and she makes it easy for people to worship her here."

I guess that explained why there was no agathos instinct urging me to stop trespassing, but I supposed if this area was sacred to Anesidora, that would override whatever barriers had been erected by humans.

It was strange there weren't natural wards like this at the temple the agathos used in Auburn, though I already knew that the agathos were wrong in paying their respects that way. Anesidora, *Gaia*, was Mother Nature, the giver of life and earth. Why would she want to be worshipped in a dungeon temple accessible only by agathos blood?

"It definitely feels weird here," Riot muttered, reaching his hand back. I slid my palm into his, giving it a quick squeeze. There were no sounds from birds or insects, even the wind itself seemed muted in here.

"Do what scares you, Amazing Grace," Bullet whispered. His smile was a little strained, and I could feel the nerves he was trying to hide through the bond. "I wish I knew more, that I could see more, but I have a blank spot here."

"It's okay," I assured him, not wanting him to overexert himself and end up collapsing again. "We'll just have to try and see. Most people don't get a heads up about the future whenever they try something new."

"Most people aren't me," Bullet grumbled, sounding genuinely put out about it.

We made our way around well-maintained paths lined with enormous trees, following the sound of running water until we emerged in front of an exquisite waterfall.

"Wow," I breathed, watching the water pour over the terraced rocks into the pool below. The forest floor was blanketed in fallen leaves, the tall trees not quite dense enough at this time of year to stop the moonlight from filtering into the forest, turning everything silver. It felt right that we'd come here now, under the watch of the Goddess of Night. I wanted to bridge the gap between them. I *could*. They didn't need to be at odds, and neither did their followers.

"Does Grace really have to get in there?" Riot asked dubiously, crouching down at the edge of the pool and swiping his fingers through the water. "She'll freeze."

He gave Bullet a withering look, and I felt bad for my psychic soul bond, who looked genuinely upset at the idea of me getting in the cold water.

"I'll be quick, I'm sure it'll be fine," I told Riot, pulling off my coat and shoes, and stripping down to my underwear and an oversized black T-shirt that Bullet had bought for Riot which fell to mid-thigh and would be fast to change out of when wet.

Despite all the things we'd done together and the intimacy we'd shared, I was still struggling not to hunch down and pull the hem of my shirt towards my knees despite no one else being here.

I was in *public* with my *thighs* out.

"Back in the olden days, they did these ceremonies naked," Bullet said, winking.

"I imagine it's a lot warmer in the Mediterranean," I pointed out with a smile, glad he'd lightened the mood. I made my way to the edge of the pool where Riot looked like he was contemplating tackling me rather than letting me climb in, and went up on my tiptoes to kiss his cheek. "I'll be fine. I'll be right out. Hold the towel for me?"

Riot nodded, expression grim, holding my hand as I dipped my toes into the water and sucked in an alarmed breath. Sugar. It was really cold.

Other people do harder things than briefly take a dip in cold water every day, I reminded myself. *We need to know what Anesidora has to say. We need her on our side.*

Chanting those reminders on repeat in my mind, I let go of Riot's hand and put one foot in front of the other, holding my arms out for balance on the slippery smooth rocks. Once I was in waist-deep water, I scrunched my eyes shut, held my breath and dropped down until I was sitting on the bottom of the pool, submerging myself completely in the cleansing waters.

The cold sunk into my bones, and for a brief moment, I was worried that I was too frozen to move. That I'd just drown sitting here because I was too freaking cold to get up again, but fortunately my limbs eventually got the message of what I was trying to achieve and I was able to stand, sucking down a lungful of cold air, my entire body shaking violently.

At first, there was nothing. Nothing was what I expected. My teeth chattered as the cold set into my bones, and I could see Riot struggling to hold himself back at the pool's edge, wanting to dive in and drag me out. I looked to Bullet, whose expression was uncharacteristically serious as he stared down at the water with a frown. We had all put so much faith in this ceremony doing something—*anything*—and none more so than Bullet.

"I'm sorry," I stuttered, my teeth clattering together. "I know how badly you wanted this to work."

The groove between his eyebrows deepened. "I think it kind of did? The air feels... different. Heavier. Do you feel it?"

Honestly, I couldn't feel anything beyond the bone-deep cold, but I attempted to focus on the air around me regardless. No, it was no good. I needed to get out of the spring—Anesidora was the goddess of earth, not water, this wasn't right.

Riot reached for me the moment I made for the bank, hauling me out of the pool and engulfing me in the enormous towel we'd packed in the car for this moment. The moment I wrapped it around myself and stopped moving, I became aware of just how still the air was. Still and thick and heavy with expectation.

"She's listening," Bullet breathed, a few feet away and seemingly unwilling to move closer, to risk disturbing this perfect quiet. "Grace, now might be a good time to pray."

"Anesidora, Sender of Gifts, Great Mother..." I began, taking a step away from Riot and slipping into that traditional agathos prayer opening easily. "I am honored you chose to answer my prayer a few days ago. I'm very thankful that you chose to respond to me, of all your agathos children who vie for your attention."

Shoot, was that bad? Did that sound like I was criticizing her? I pushed on before I second-guessed myself so much that I lost my nerve.

"I don't presume to know the mind of a goddess, but you confirmed what I suspected—that the agathos, or perhaps mortals in general, don't cherish the gift you gave us. The abundant and vibrant earth that you created, the soil that gave us life, the trees, the mountains, the vibrant, beautiful, diverse *life* that populates this planet we call home."

The air grew somehow stiller, as though Gaia was listening carefully, but it didn't feel reassuring. The hairs on the back of my neck stood up, like I was being watched by a predator, one who was waiting for me to trip so they could pounce and make their kill.

By the uneasy looks on Bullet and Riot's faces, they had picked up the same sense of impending doom.

"I used to think I wasn't like the agathos who came before me. That it was *just* me, but that can't be the case because Mercy is different as well. We are different, and we probably won't be the first, nor the last. The Fates imagine a Second Age of Heroes. I don't presume to know what they see, but it sounds like a different future for the agathos, for the daimons, maybe even a future where we're not so divided. But we can't move past that division without your blessing, Anesidora."

I'd been a little unsure on what exactly I wanted from her until that moment, but as I stood in the damp earth, soaked to the skin and freezing, a sense of clarity dawned on me. The agathos were relentless in their pursuit of what they believed Anesidora's will to be. If she made clear that she was in favor of unions between agathos and daimons, that she supported the Fates' vision, the agathos would be forced to concede defeat. No more attacks on daimons, no more banishing agathos that didn't fit the mold, or hunting them down like they were doing to me.

The earth beneath my feet stirred, the soil rising like a small, gentle tornado around me, whipping around my body in an almost testing way. I stayed perfectly still, imagining a wild animal scenting me and not wanting to spook it.

"Prophecy."

My eyes widened, glancing at Bullet and Riot to see if they'd heard that sole word that seemed to drift in on the wind from a feminine, unearthly voice. They both gave me a quick nod in acknowledgment, looking around the trees nervously.

"You smell of prophecy."

I don't think I imagined the hint of accusation in her tone. My heartbeat picked up, a very real sense of terror snaking through me. We were in the heart of one of Gaia's temples and completely at her mercy. *I should have made Riot and Bullet wait in the car in case this all went wrong.*

"There is a prophecy," I agreed carefully, wrapping my arms around my waist as shivers wracked my body.

"Who delivered it?"

Bullet's eyes were wide and fearful, which was the most terrifying sign yet.

"Erebus," I replied. I knew Nyx and Gaia had a fraught history, and against all odds, I hoped that Gaia didn't have the same issues with Nyx's consort.

There was a hiss of disapproval that whistled through the air, immediately killing any naive dreams I may have had of a friendship between Gaia and Erebus. There were only six original primordial gods; did Gaia really hate all of them? What a lonely existence.

"Tell me the prophecy."

Oh sugar, I really, really didn't want to, but there was no way I could deny a direct request from a goddess even though Riot looked like he was considering throwing me over his shoulder and making a break for it.

"Liberate the treasure held in the deep,

Where no sweet smelling smoke or prayer can reach,

Bring forth the Second Age of Heroes."

If the goddess' curiosity had felt like stillness and silence, her anger was anything but. The land rumbled ominously beneath us, and Riot snatched me into his arms right as the ground roiled beneath our feet, a hole opening like the earth was going to swallow us whole.

"Bullet!" I screamed, seeing a flash of his pale blonde hair as he lost his footing, the wave of rolling dirt flowing directly towards him, water sloshing over the rocks of the falls around us, turning the already damp ground to sludge. I dug my nails in, trying to get purchase to crawl onto steady ground—wherever that was—but Anesidora was relentless. Another crash of mud over our heads forced me to give up trying to climb free and I scrunched my eyes shut, using my forearm to shield my face as much as possible and holding my breath. Riot was still crushed against my back, and my chest twinged in panic as he gave a grunt of pain, knocking me slightly before steadying himself.

The noise was overwhelming, the ground consuming us and holding us in place until Anesidora's tantrum was done, and that was all it was.

A cowardly tantrum by a petulant goddess, and I hated her. In that moment, I swore never to pray to her again. Never to fear her again, because no matter how terrifying this was, Anesidora—Gaia—didn't deserve my fear any more than she deserved my devotion.

Riot turned me towards him, pressing my face into his neck and I clung to him as the earth fought and railed against us. A sharp pain on the side of my head was the last thing I remembered, then the entire world went black.

CHAPTER 8

Fuck!

I fought through the earth that was rushing beneath my feet like a river, scrambling to grab hold of branches and roots, whatever I could grasp onto to get me closer to the waterfall.

I didn't know what had happened, whether this was a genuine natural disaster or a vengeful god or goddess playing games, all I knew was that I needed to get to Grace.

Fuck, fuck, fuck.

Why had I hung so far back? I should have just gotten closer, let her see me. I knew they were doing something that made Grace nervous, she'd looked an anxious wreck when she was climbing into the vehicle wearing that ridiculous wig. Why had Onyx given them those without first finding out where they were going? I should have known. I should have been kept in the loop.

Fuck!

This is what I got for trying to keep one foot in the door and one foot out. I should have assigned someone to permanently guard the three of them, to provide consistent backup on the ground, someone they could rely on.

But I couldn't. I'd tried, and I'd never been able to hit send. Because I wanted it to be me, but without Grace knowing. And this was the result, me being too fucking far away and too fucking slow to be there when it counted.

I had no idea how long I fought against the churning earth, my throat aching from countless attempts to yell for Grace, Riot and Bullet despite knowing I couldn't. I'd never felt so helpless. Eventually, the ground stilled enough for me to get purchase, and I scrambled over the displaced rocks and through knee deep mud, looking for any trace of them.

The moonlight seemed to shine brighter suddenly, like the illumination had been turned up a notch so I could see, but there was debris *everywhere*. Where were they? This *had* to be the work of the gods. Earthquakes here were possible but uncommon, and nothing about this looked like a naturally occurring event. Had Grace been *buried alive* by a goddess?

Now that I was focusing on it, the divine magic coating the air was thick and angry. It wasn't like the constant oily presence that I felt—this was much more potent. Much more terrifying. I forced my limbs to keep moving in spite of my fear. I could take on a whole army of mortals single-handed, but an immortal... I felt like I was in that circle of creatures and souls all over again, every inch of me broken and bruised, fighting to stay on my feet.

You're not there. Grace is here. Find Grace.

She had to be alive. I refused to accept any other option.

A pale hand clawed up from the ground, fingers moving weakly. *Bullet*. I didn't hesitate, diving towards him and hauling the dirt back with my hands. *Faster, faster, faster.* They can't *breathe* down there.

79

By the gods, I wanted to be sick.

He was still conscious, his movements weak but frantic as he helped clear the dirt from above his head, eventually a flash of blonde hair—coated with mud—becoming visible. As soon as I could, I snatched his hand and pulled him upwards, glad he still had enough mobility in his legs to use them to push himself out of the hole. I grabbed him under his arms, hauling him out the rest of the way until he was lying half on me and half on the ground.

"Grace, Riot," he spluttered, rolling off me and collapsing face down, coughing up dirt. "They were by the water."

I didn't want to leave him on his own, but I scrambled away, hoping Bullet was alive enough to survive while I looked for Grace and Riot among the worst of the carnage. The ground gave another shudder, the hatred and rage tangible in the air. Whichever divinity caused this, they didn't want me here.

Come on, Grace.

The waterfall had overflowed, flooding the ground around the pool. The earth here was pure mud, I was sinking knee-deep into it with every step. Could they have survived this?

"She's alive," Bullet rasped, rolling onto his back and tapping his chest. "I can feel her, but she's not conscious."

The fear that gripped me was a visceral thing, holding me by the throat and sucking the oxygen from my body. How could I find them if Grace couldn't speak or move? If Riot was conscious, that would help, but I couldn't yell for him because my stupid cursed voice wouldn't goddamn work. Fuck. *Fuck!*

'I will guide you,' a feminine voice whispered in my mind, seemingly blown in on the wind itself.

I looked around in alarm, trying to see who'd spoken, but there was no one in the wreckage of the forest except a barely conscious Bullet.

More gods. Capricious deities playing games with the mortals on their chessboard they'd taken an interest in. What the fuck was Grace involved in?

'*Walk forwards,*' the voice said, a little more insistently this time. '*Let me guide you.*'

The last time a god had spoken to me, I'd been promptly dragged directly to hell, but I didn't have any other ideas. *Hopefully this one is on our side,* I thought bitterly as I moved forwards as calmly and quickly as I could, considering how unstable the ground was beneath me, heading towards the edge of the now almost empty pool.

'*Left,*' the voice commanded.

I was losing my fucking mind. But I went left anyway, inching over mounds of dirt and puddles of mud up to my waist.

'*Move the rock back into the pool.*'

I gulped at the size of the rock—a boulder, really—but moved around it so I could press my back against it and heaved, struggling for purchase on the slippery ground, my feet sinking into the soft earth. For a few minutes, it didn't move at all and I began to panic, wondering if I needed tools, or help, or something, but eventually it budged ever-so-slightly. *Just a little more,* I just needed to get enough traction for gravity to do the work for me.

My muscles burned with exertion as I grit my teeth and gave it everything I had, collapsing into the indent where the boulder had been as it rolled into the empty pool with a slosh.

"Ow, fuck, get off," Riot grumbled, his voice barely above a rasp.

I rolled out of the way in alarm, finding myself half on top of him and Grace, hidden under the branches of a fallen tree the boulder had pinned on top of them. The branch probably saved their lives—that rock would have *killed* them.

I got back to my feet, lifting the trunk of the tree an inch off them and dragging it to the side. They weren't buried in the ground, but they were definitely in a decent-sized trench, one that was too perfect to have just formed naturally. No, they'd gotten lucky. One goddess may have attacked them, but someone had their back at the same time. Maybe the one who'd spoken to me, maybe another. This situation was clearly much bigger than I realized.

Grace's eyes were closed, lips blue, face streaked with dirt and blood, a soaked T-shirt clinging to her skin. Only Riot's arms around her waist and shoulders were keeping her upright, but he didn't look to be in much better shape—blood was trickling steadily from his hairline, coating his face, and despite his surly expression, he was clearly terrified.

"You need to take Grace," Riot gritted out, his arms tightening in direct contradiction to his words. "I think I can climb out, but not holding her. I feel like I've been hit by a truck. Or a tree and a boulder," he added, glaring at the leaves. His eyes moved to mine as he clutched Grace a little closer to him, the blood in his eyelashes making him look more daimonic than I'd ever seen any Keres daimon look. "In any other circumstances, I'd tell you to get fucked because once you touch, the bonding process will start and you've done nothing to earn that right, but I guess we don't have a choice."

I couldn't even blame him for being outraged. I didn't deserve anything from Grace, but I'd always been too selfish to leave her alone.

I nodded once to show him I understood, before reaching down and grabbing Grace under the armpits, half lifting, half dragging her out of the trench. I kept her partially draped over my lap while offering a hand to Riot, who took it a little begrudgingly, wincing as he used it to climb out, and getting unsteadily to his feet. He limped towards Bullet as I stood, scooping Grace into my arms bridal style, her head lolling back immediately. Why was she wearing a goddamn wet T-shirt in the middle of the night in fall? The garment was practically ripped to shreds, and her skin was freezing under my hands.

We had to get out of here.

"C'mon, Bullet," Riot said hoarsely, leaning down to shake his shoulder. "Get up. Time to go."

"'K," Bullet groaned, not protesting when Riot helped him to his feet. The white bandage on his arm from the gunshot wound had turned black with mud, reminding me just how little he could afford another set of injuries.

Why on earth had they come here?

Riot and Bullet leaned on each other, limping and stumbling behind me as I led the way out of the forest with Grace in my arms, my heart beating fast and not just from adrenaline.

Grace. Grace was in my arms.

The ground shook again ominously, feeling an awful lot like a warning.

"Let's fucking go," Riot urged, half dragging Bullet as he attempted to pick up speed. He sounded terrified, and as the trees bent towards us, whipping at our skin with branches that cut like razors, I understood why.

This was *Gaia's* handiwork. The Goddess of Earth was trying to kill them—us—and I was sure it was only the hand of the Fates that stayed the blows that should have been fatal.

Sirens echoed in the distance, and our time to get the hell out of here without attracting human attention was rapidly slipping away.

I tipped my chin at the much larger black SUV I'd driven here, and Riot and Bullet hobbled as quickly as they could to the back seat, climbing in either side then doing their best to take Grace and lay her across them while I dived into the driver's seat, the engine roaring to life a second before I slammed on the accelerator and got us the hell out of the parking lot.

Fortunately, they'd taken one of the Asphodel cars I kept specifically for jobs which had a complicated paper trail leading far away from me and mine, but leaving it behind still wasn't ideal. *There's nothing that can be done,* I reminded myself, my fingers flexing around the steering wheel. It was out of my control, as much as I hated to admit it.

For years, I hadn't let anything be out of my control. But a little had slipped when Bullet had shown up at my club two years ago. And then I'd nearly lost my leash on life completely the first time I'd seen Grace through grainy CCTV footage, only intending to take a quick glance at the plucky agathos who'd thought to move into a daimon-owned town.

One look at her and she'd become the center of my universe. My focus had moved from the club and the Keres daimons around me to Grace. To keeping her safe. To keeping the daimons in Milton away from her so she could live in her apartment peacefully, go for her morning jogs in safety, leave her job at the shelter at any time—day or night—and be free from harm.

But I'd failed today. I'd failed her multiple times. She'd been in an armed robbery in a convenience store that I hadn't known about until after the fact. The agathos had snatched her away from her work via the back of the building where I didn't have cameras, and she'd disappeared from my view for weeks. She'd come back to Milton, only to be put immediately in harm's way again.

You can't keep going like this. She needs more protection.

The road rolled like a wave, cracks spreading out over the asphalt like a rapidly expanding spiderweb, one that we were very much caught in the middle of. If I could speak, I'd be yelling, asking what the hell they'd done. Maybe it was a good thing my voice had been taken from me.

The further we got away from the falls, the more stable the road became. As tempting as it was to make the one-hour drive back to Asphodel where I was confident we could be safe, Grace needed urgent medical attention and we couldn't go to a human hospital without raising questions. There was a Philotes-owned motel not far from here, and I quickly turned onto the street towards it. They'd say nothing for a fee, and I'd contact one of the Geras doctors on my payroll to come out to us.

Grace would be fine, I told myself, fighting off a wave of nausea at how incredibly still she was. She just needed rest. *Clean the wounds. Staunch the blood. Keep her warm.* She didn't seem to be bleeding heavily, but several small injuries added up. What was her blood type? Did Riot or Bullet even know?

"Now what?" Riot sighed, looking at Bullet. "I don't give a fuck what you say, we're never going in one of Gaia's temples again. No prayers, nothing. She's a lunatic."

"Shut up," Bullet groaned, wiping blood off his face with his sleeve. I frowned slightly—was his nose bleeding? Was that fresh? "She might still be listening. Well I guess we know now that Gaia isn't a fan of the prophecy. She's definitely not going to be an ally on that front."

Riot smoothed Grace's matted hair away from her face, staring down at her with a conflicted look, probably wondering the same thing I was. I had no idea what the prophecy was or what instructions they'd been given, but would Grace go through with it, knowing it was against the wishes of the goddess she'd been raised to follow? Could I fulfill a demand if Nyx had made it explicitly clear she didn't want me to?

It took courage to defy the gods. A courage I wasn't sure I possessed, and Grace seemed so meek. Precious. Fragile. In need of protection.

Then again, I didn't really know Grace, did I? She'd come here, to what was apparently one of Gaia's sacred spots. She'd called on the goddess herself, probably after cleansing her body in the falls in the middle of the goddamn night when it was freezing cold.

Maybe I was completely wrong about Grace.

I pulled up outside of the Eros Motel, the neon sign blinking sadly over the parking lot. Riot grimaced but didn't say anything as I parked in front of the office and cut the engine. Options for where I could take three people who looked as awful as they did were limited and we all knew it. I hadn't suffered the injuries they had, but I was still covered in mud and bleeding from the multiple nicks I'd gotten from the clawing trees.

We needed to go somewhere that only cared about their bottom line and didn't ask questions, and this was it.

The dark-haired Philotes daimon at the front desk blinked bright red eyes at me in surprise when I walked in, shoving away the head that was buried between her thighs under the front desk so she could stand, half tugging down a short black dress that had been hiked up over her hips.

What a delightful establishment.

"Hey, aren't you Wild?"

I gave her the same flat look I gave everyone, the one that made people assume I *didn't* speak rather than I *couldn't* speak.

"Right, right stupid question. I guess you want a room. And, uh, maybe a shower. Here." She handed me a key with an enormous plastic tag attached showing the room number. "Just come pay when you're done, I know you're good for it. Besides, I'm a little busy here."

She grabbed a fistful of her lover's hair, the only part of them visible from where they were kneeling behind the desk and dragged them back towards her thighs. I quickly spun away before I saw something I *really* didn't want to see.

Philotes daimons were sex-crazed animals. At least the goddess hadn't made me one of those.

I climbed back into the silent vehicle, moving it to the very end of the L-shaped motel complex. Bullet's head was resting against the back of the seat, his eyes shut and breathing even. The moment we pulled up outside the room and Riot opened his door, Bullet stirred, slumping against the passenger door for a moment like he was struggling to find the energy to open it.

"Unlock the room then come back for Grace," Riot ordered weakly. I wasn't usually in the business of taking commands from anyone, but I'd let him off the hook just this once since the world had quite literally fallen apart underneath him.

While there were plenty of moans and groans coming from the row of rooms, fortunately there was no one outside. I quickly unlocked the door, throwing it open before jogging back to the vehicle for Grace. With Riot's assistance, I was able to pull her into my arms, and she stirred slightly as I brought her into the beige-on-beige motel room, featuring two double beds side by side, an ancient TV on a rickety looking Formica stand, and questionably stained brown carpet.

Why wasn't she waking up? I didn't know how to fix this. I could patch bloody wounds and tape up injured joints and muscles in my sleep, but Grace was so fucking *cold* and her head was swelling and *fuck!* How was I supposed to *fix* this?

Forgive me, I thought silently, setting Grace on the bed and peeling the wet scraps of her T-shirt off her, doing my best to keep my eyes averted.

There was nothing sexual about it, but the agathos I'd grown up around in London were big on modesty, and she'd probably hate the idea of being so exposed in front of me.

Riot limped in with Bullet, kicking the door shut behind him and letting Bullet slump onto the other bed before stomping over with violence in his eyes to remove Grace's bra and underwear himself.

"Fuck's sake, I can't move her under the blankets on my own. You need to help, but don't look," he grumbled, glaring at me.

I nodded, pulling the blankets back, and looking deliberately past Grace as I lifted her up and quickly deposited her on the mattress. Riot was already stripping his filthy, wet clothes off behind me, and wasted no time in climbing under the sheets next to Grace, wrapping his body around her.

There was a slimy feeling crawling up my spine that may have been jealousy, but I refused to acknowledge it. I'd been the one to reject Grace. I'd sent her away.

"This is awkward, but you may have to strip me off too, big guy," Bullet slurred, flopping backwards on the other bed. "I'm not doing too great over here."

Feeling marginally less uncomfortable because at least Bullet was conscious, I pulled him to his feet and ripped the wet clothes off him, planting my hands on his shoulders and guiding him to Grace's other side, helping him into the bed.

It was absolutely not the time, but I hadn't forgotten about the history between me and Bullet either, or failed to notice that Riot did absolutely nothing for me whatsoever.

"These sheets are so fucked," Riot noted, the mud already transferring from their bodies to the linen. Whatever, I'd pay the cleaning fee. I grabbed the blankets off the second bed and the spare ones out of the closet, piling them all on top of the three of them to warm them up.

Satisfied that was as good as it was going to get, I pulled out my phone, shooting off messages to all the Geras doctors within a twenty-mile radius who might be able to respond to an urgent request for assistance. Needing to do something else, I wet washcloths with warm water and handed them to Riot and Bullet, who took a moment to clean their faces and Grace's while I pulled out bottled water from the mini fridge.

Dr. Parker: *I can be there in fifteen. What am I walking into?*

Me: *Hypothermia. Concussion. Scrapes and bruises.*

It was only then that I realized I wasn't experiencing any bloodlust at all. Usually the hint of violence in the air or the scent of blood was enough to tip me into the kind of frenzy that I needed to work out with my fists, but not their blood. Not *Grace's* blood. That just made me anxious.

I fussed like a mother hen, bringing them more warm washcloths and pacing until Dr. Parker pulled up outside, bringing one of his apprentices with him, a young Geras daimon I'd met once before named French.

Dr. Parker stormed in with an enormous black leather bag, barely paying me any regard as he assessed the three of them with brutal efficiency, issuing clipped orders to his assistant and asking Riot and Bullet sharp questions when necessary. Usually, I appreciated his lack of bedside manner—Keres daimons who'd just had the shit kicked out of them in a fight didn't need to be coddled—but it just irked me around Grace. She was hurt, she'd been through so much, couldn't he see that?

"Mild hypothermia," he muttered, fingers carefully exploring Grace's skull. "French, warm up the heat packs. I'm more concerned about the head injury. I don't think there's a fracture, but I can't be sure without a scan."

"Shouldn't she be awake by now?" Bullet asked, vocalizing the question that was running through my head on loop.

"Something about this loss of consciousness feels very... unnatural," Dr. Parker replied slowly. "I don't have a medical explanation for it. It just feels... odd. Not as a doctor, but as a daimon."

Bullet's eyes met mine over the doctor's shoulder, and he cleared his throat before quickly looking away again. "Grace is favored by the gods."

Dr. Parker paused, midway through searching through his bag for supplies. "Then maybe the gods are giving her a moment to heal."

Bullet nodded, looking satisfied by that answer while Riot appeared as frustrated as I felt. There had been so many moments getting out of that forest where it felt like death was on Grace's heels, and only divine intervention had saved her. Maybe this was more of the same.

"You could give me a little more room to work," Dr. Parker said, giving me a pointed look while I hovered close to his back. I crossed my arms over my chest and stared him down, daring him to tell me to move away when *my* soul bond was so clearly injured and in distress. He huffed a sound of irritation before returning to his task, carefully cleaning and bandaging the wound at Grace's hairline.

"Are you going to tell me what happened?" Dr. Parker asked, looking between Riot and Bullet.

"An act of god," Riot deadpanned, slumping back against the pillows, careful to keep his body pressed firmly against Grace's. French had disappeared, returning with an armful of clean, dry linen and making up the other bed to transfer them to.

"Is that so?" Dr. Parker asked, doing a remarkable job of not sounding shocked.

"We pissed off Gaia," Bullet volunteered, adjusting his position on the pillows with a pained groan. "You know how it is. Pray to a goddess, she completely loses her shit and tries to drown you in soil. You got any of those good painkillers, doc? Usually my body is a temple et cetera, et cetera, but the Oneiroi curse has already kicked in and I'm taking it easy on the visions for the foreseeable future. I feel like I should at least be able to enjoy some quality drugs as a consolation prize."

Riot snorted, then immediately winced. "You had the good drugs already for your arm. You know our bodies burn through them faster than human bodies do."

"*More* good drugs," Bullet amended.

"Not on me," Dr. Parker clipped. "French will return with enough pills to keep you comfortable for the next few days. Perhaps some proper food too?" he asked, looking at me. I nodded once in agreement, fishing out some cash from my wallet and handing it to French.

I should go myself. I should go, get food, drop it to them with enough cash to get them back to Bullet's place and then I should drive back to Milton without a second glance. But I couldn't. Dragging myself away from Grace had already felt impossible when I'd left her in my apartment, and that was before I touched her. The connection between us was frail, and I had a horrifying feeling that it was mostly one-sided, but it was still there. I could *feel* Grace, wisps of her pain and discomfort kept brushing against my skin, reaching out to me and holding me in place.

I knew when I pulled Grace out of that hole in the earth that this would change things, but I wasn't prepared for how fierce the need to stay by her side was.

What if she didn't want that? I'd rejected her once, and I didn't even regret it. She'd be better off without me in her life.

Dr. Parker worked in silence for what must have been hours, since the sun was beginning to filter through the blinds. All three of them needed stitches for various injuries, and at one point, French had to get more bandages from the vehicle because he'd exhausted the supply in his bag. I insisted the two of them turn away while Bullet, Riot and I moved Grace to the clean, dry bed, Riot glaring at me the whole time like he'd rather I be standing next to the doctor too with my eyes averted.

"I've done all I can do for now," Dr. Parker announced, standing up and packing his things back into his black leather bag. "As I said, French will return with supplies. Do you have any injuries?" he asked, giving me an appraising look. I shook my head. The scrapes were minor, a reminder that I hadn't been there with them when they'd taken on this ludicrous task. If I'd known they were going to try to communicate with Gaia again, I would have told them how foolish it was to talk to any god willingly. I would have told them that all deities were petulant sociopaths with too much time and power, and not a single deterrent to stop them from playing dangerous games with mortal lives for their own entertainment.

"I'll take my leave then," Dr. Parker said, French waiting dutifully at his side. Geras daimons were so placid, it was unsettling. "Make sure they rest. Don't piss off Gaia again any time soon. I'll return tonight to check on them."

I closed the door behind them, securing the deadlock before turning back to face the trio on the bed. They definitely wouldn't be pissing off Gaia again on my watch. Bullet had already fallen asleep, his head resting against Grace's and mouth slightly parted, snoring lightly.

Not Riot though. Riot was watching me with distrust written all over his face.

"I meant what I said back at the falls," he told me in a low voice, careful not to wake the other two. "The bond between you two is forming now. It'll drive you both mad until you fuck, then it settles into place."

Don't think about fucking Grace, don't think about fucking Grace...

"You'll drive yourselves both insane if you try to run away again now," Riot continued. "And while I couldn't keep Grace safe from a vengeful goddess, I sure as hell can keep her safe from an idiot soul bond with a martyr complex. You followed us. You got her out. You *chose* her. If you run, I'll hunt you like a goddamn animal and drag you back. We clear?"

I raised a disbelieving eyebrow, mildly impressed at the gumption of this asshole when I'd already beaten him to a pulp once before.

"Yeah, yeah, everyone knows you're bigger and stronger than me." Riot rolled his eyes. "Don't underestimate how motivated I am when it comes to Grace. Don't underestimate how motivated *you* are when it comes to Grace. Life as you know it will never be the same again."

GRACE

CHAPTER 9

"Oh good, you're here!"

One moment I'd been standing on a gorgeous beach, wondering how I'd gotten there, the next I was landing on the sand with an oof as Bullet tackled me to the ground, raining kisses all over my face.

"Hi there," I laughed, pushing lightly on his shoulders to roll him off me. "It's nice to see you too."

"Amazing Grace," he said somberly, propping himself up on his side and leaning over me. "Do you remember what happened? Shit, I wondered if you were even going to be here. You're still unconscious back in the real world."

"I am?" I frowned, staring up at the brilliant blue sky above me, hands running through the soft sand. "The falls. The prayer..."

"It didn't go well," Bullet replied gravely, resting his head on my chest with surprising confidence and draping an arm over my waist and a thigh over my legs. I could never remember how our interactions in the dreamscape went, but somehow I found it hard to believe that Bullet was ever this boldly cuddly with me.

Unless things had gone really badly back in the real world, and he'd gotten a huge scare. That would make him cuddly.

"Are you and Riot okay? How did we get out?"

"Ah, lucky for us, Wild is a very dedicated stalker. He wasn't far behind and was able to fish us out of the mud soup Gaia was trying to drown us in. Though I think we probably had a little more assistance than that to be honest. The Fates aren't ready to cut your mortal thread yet, Amazing Grace."

"Great," *I replied weakly, not entirely sure how to respond to the news that the goddess I'd worshipped my entire life had tried to kill me. I was so ridiculously insignificant that the idea of Gaia targeting me was ludicrous.*

To be frank, she probably should have had better things to do.

"This place is beautiful. Do we come here a lot?" *I asked, not wanting to disrupt the peaceful perfection of the moment by thinking too hard about how wrong everything had gone at the falls. Why bother? I was going to forget all of this as soon as I woke up anyway, may as well enjoy it.*

"No, actually," *Bullet replied with a quiet laugh.* "I didn't make this place. I had to track you down and join you here."

"Oh. Does that mean I made it?" *I couldn't imagine myself making a place like this—behind the beach were looming hills covered in lush vegetation as far as the eye could see. I'd never visited a beach like this before.*

"No," *Bullet said slowly.* "You've been brought here by someone. A god or goddess who wanted you to have somewhere safe to rest while your body recovers is my guess."

Well that certainly made the beach less relaxing.

"My guess is Turkey," *Bullet added.* "I've been yanked into visions all over the world so I'm basically a certified travel expert."

I laughed in spite of my discomfort, tangling my fingers in his hair and lightly running my nails over his scalp. So we were on a mystery deity-run dream beach possibly based on one in Turkey and I'd been unconscious for long enough to thoroughly freak Bullet out.

Good. Great. This was all totally fine.

"Shit, I'm being summoned," Bullet groaned, nuzzling his face against my breasts until I shoved him off with a laugh. "I don't want to leave. I'm comfy here."

"I'm pretty sure you don't have a choice," I pointed out, rolling onto my side to kiss his temple.

"Get some rest, Amazing Grace. Sleep it off, then come back to the real world before Riot has a breakdown and Wild panics and runs again. We need you."

Everything hurt.

My eyeballs hurt. My limbs hurt. My head hurt. My freaking *teeth* hurt. Everything hurt.

Light was filtering through my eyelids and I knew I had to open them, to figure out where I was and why I felt *this* bad, but my brain wasn't getting the message to my muscles. I'd never felt so bad in my *life*. No matter how much I'd overextended myself or used my abilities until I dropped, absolutely nothing felt as awful as I felt at that moment.

What happened?

My memory was a fuzzy mess, with sharp edges that stung when I probed too hard at it.

"Gracie?" Riot's voice sounded a million miles away, but as some of my confusion receded, the absolute panic and terror that Riot and Bullet were feeling came through more prominently through the bond.

I forced my eyes open even though they felt like they weighed a thousand pounds, blinking until a peeling beige ceiling came into focus.

"Where are we?" I asked. Was that my voice? My throat felt like it had been put through a shredder, and it didn't sound much better.

"Not far from the falls," Bullet replied, sounding pretty beat up himself. "Wild was a real hero. He showed up, pulled us out of the dirt—literally—got us to this fine daimon-owned establishment, had a Geras doctor come patch us up. We really got the five-star soul bond treatment."

I blinked, struggling to comprehend what he was saying. Wild? Wild came to our rescue?

"Luckily he was stalking you because Gaia really went all out trying to kill us."

"She... what?" I asked, flashes of memory coming to me. The prayer. The falls. The earth itself attacking us. "Surely if she wanted us dead, we'd be dead."

"The length of our mortal threads are determined by the Fates," Bullet mumbled, snuggling into my side, his breath puffing over my naked shoulder. "They alone can cut them. Gaia used to control the threads of the agathos. I bet she's regretting handing them over now."

Because she wanted me dead that badly? Comforting.

"Did I make her that mad?" I whispered, burrowing further down into the blankets. "I didn't mean to."

"Who cares what she thinks, she's a maniac," Riot muttered. "Fuck your goddess."

For once, I made no attempt to chastise him. I didn't care if it was sacrilegious. I had no interest in defending Anesidora's honor any longer.

"Fuck her," I whispered.

Riot and Bullet grew unnaturally still either side of me and Wild appeared out of nowhere, looming over the bed and staring at me with wide eyes.

He was so handsome. Had he really done everything Bullet said? Was he just sitting here listening while Bullet described it?

Bad Grace. He doesn't want you.

But then again, he had dragged us out of earth *Gaia* had attacked us with, which meant he must have followed us there.

"What did you just say?" Bullet asked, sounding much more energetic. "Say it again."

"Aren't you basically a priest? Should you be encouraging that?" Riot asked over my head.

"I'm not Gaia's priest," Bullet shrugged. "I say fuck her."

He tilted my chin up so I could look at his beautiful face, looking worse for wear. There were dark, painful-looking bruises forming everywhere, and a neat row of stitches below his eye that made me want to hunt Gaia down myself and bring her to justice.

"Fuck her," I repeated, with slightly more conviction. "How dare she? How could she do this? Because of the prophecy? I didn't ask for that. I mean, yes, I contacted La Nuit and apparently volunteered myself for it, but I didn't come up with the whole prophecy thing."

Wild sat down on the edge of the bed, handing me a bottle of water that I accepted gratefully while Riot moved his legs closer to mine dramatically, shooting a death glare at my mysterious soul bond. Wild raised an eyebrow at him and I could have sworn he was amused, even though there was nothing in his face that gave it away.

How did I know that?

"You touched me," I breathed, staring at Wild. "The bond..."

The bond between us had started forming because he'd *had* to touch me in order to save me. Not because he wanted to. He actively *hadn't* wanted this. Wild's stare was unflinching as he looked back at me, and I had no idea whether he was happy, sad or indifferent. My insight into his emotions wasn't acute enough to work through feelings that complex.

"Don't feel guilty," Riot said sternly, taking the water bottle off me and unscrewing the cap before handing it back. "He knew what would happen, I told him in advance. I'd have also hunted him down and executed him if he refused to help, so whatever."

Wild rolled his eyes and I blinked at the strangely relaxed movement from the usually calm and controlled daimon.

"Drink," Riot insisted. "You've been out for a full day, Gracie. We've been so fucking worried."

A whole day? I numbly opened my mouth as Riot pressed the water bottle to my lips, going through the motions while panicking slightly that I'd lost an entire day of my life and had no memory of it.

The lights overhead flickered on and off, the mattress faintly shuddering beneath us. Riot cursed as some of the water spilled, quickly snatching the bottle back, but other than that, they looked remarkably unbothered about the freaking *earthquake* that had just occurred.

"It's been happening on and off all day," Bullet volunteered with a grimace. "It could be natural aftershocks. Or it could be an ongoing tantrum by an angry goddess. I'd hoped to get some answers from Nyx while I slept, but she basically told me I was too beat up as it is."

He looked genuinely put out about that too.

"We're not going to leave until you're ready to move, but also... we should go," Riot said, shooting me an apologetic look as he held the water bottle up to my lips again. "I'm not sure it's possible to outrun the goddess of the entire earth, but I'm totally willing to give it a try at this point."

"I feel like I can travel," I replied tentatively, because getting out of here sounded like an excellent idea. "Can I shower first? I feel revolting."

My face felt sort of clean, but below the sheets, I was dirty and not in a good way. This didn't look like the nicest establishment, but I was feeling bad about how thoroughly we'd ruined the bedding.

Bullet let out a strangled snort sound and I glanced at him to find him *asleep*.

"Come on, Gracie," Riot said, shooting Bullet a wry smile. "Bullet's been sleeping a lot on and off, I guess he's still wiped from his collapse back at Asphodel. I'll help you shower. Wild can run across the street to the strip mall and grab us some clothes." He shot Wild a warning look and my jaw dropped for a moment before I slammed my mouth shut at the way Riot was bossing Wild around. Not only was Wild a lot bigger, he'd also beaten up Riot once before and I was not in a rush to see a repeat of that.

Wild didn't react violently though. He just gave Riot an almost indulgent look—in the way a fierce lion might look at a plucky cub—and turned towards the front door. I was so caught up in watching the way he moved, all fluid grace despite his bulky muscles and broad frame, that he was already gone before I had a chance to tack on a polite 'please' to Riot's request.

Riot helped me out of the bed, looking inordinately pleased with himself, and kept one arm around my waist as he guided me to the small bathroom. While he could have done it in a nicer way, I was quietly glad he'd sent Wild away. I was completely naked, and while he'd probably caught a glimpse of that already, the idea of just wandering around without a stitch of clothing on in front of him was more than a little intimidating.

Besides, he didn't *want* me. Didn't want this. Even though he'd followed us and Riot insisted Wild knew what would happen when he touched me, it felt like wandering around naked in front of him would be manipulative somehow. Like I was using my body to try make him interested in me.

I'd already infringed on Wild's liberties more than enough to last a lifetime.

"Don't feel guilty. He knew what he was getting himself into. It's not like you *asked* him to follow us," Riot reasserted, wrinkling his nose at the sorry state of the bathroom. It looked... clean enough. The beige and brown tiles were chipped in places, and I decided not to examine the grout too closely for my own sanity. The entire bathroom was one big, wet room, tiled all over, and Riot cranked the creaky shower on against the wall, removing the handheld hose from the hook. "I'm not sure if you should get the bandage on your head wet, but we can at least rinse the dirt off your body."

I nodded, gripping the porcelain sink to keep myself upright while he fiddled with the temperature.

"How much do you remember?" Riot asked, reaching for me. I grabbed his hand, gripping him tightly as I made my way slowly over to the wall, my legs wobbling like jelly the entire time. I got the feeling the question was more of a subtle attempt to check for a brain injury than genuine curiosity.

"I remember... I remember Gaia said I smelled like prophecy. And when I told her what the prophecy was... she didn't like it."

"She did not," Riot confirmed, mouth pressed into a grim line as he held me up with one hand and used the other to direct the spray of water at my filthy legs.

"And then everything was chaos. And she tried to kill us. I can't remember anything after that."

"A tree fell on us," Riot volunteered, speaking through gritted teeth. "It hit your head and you passed out. But it stopped a giant rock from crushing us, so I guess it could be worse."

I shuddered, tightening my grip on him. If Gaia wanted that boulder to crush us, it should have crushed us. If a falling tree saved us, that could *only* be the interference of another deity. The Fates, perhaps. I doubted Gaia liked that they'd used a tree, which fell under her domain, to protect us.

"How are you feeling about this whole prophecy business now?" Riot asked a little too casually, guiding me to hold the wall so he could scrub the stubborn dried dirt off me with soap.

"I know you want me to say that I don't want to do it. That this has made me realize that I want nothing to do with any of this, but I think it's had the opposite effect if anything," I admitted. "I'm so... angry. She's so powerful, and she has all these people ostensibly doing her bidding even though she doesn't actually bother to bid them to do anything, so they just make up whatever they want and say it's her will because she never contradicts them. And then when other gods are like, 'Hey! This isn't working!' she tries to punish us for it because we were the ones the message was delivered to." I paused, sucking down a long breath. "I'm so angry with her, Riot. It didn't have to be like this."

"No," he agreed quietly, encouraging me to turn. "It didn't. But it doesn't have to be you either, Gracie."

I smiled sadly at the wall. "I think it does now. Because of Gaia. I put myself forward for this prophecy when I prayed to La Nuit, but Gaia is the one that gave my claim weight. She's the one who spoke to me—twice now—and in front of an audience of agathos. She's the one who attacked me. I was nobody before this, not really. Any importance or recognition I have is because she singled me out and responded. She made this *my* problem."

If Gaia had ignored my request in the parking lot, the agathos would have gone on hunting me with the absolute conviction they were doing the right thing. I wasn't sure how they justified it now, but Onyx *had* mentioned in passing that they were driving more eco-friendly vehicles, so maybe they'd opted to take that part of Gaia's message on and ignore anything about violence in her name.

Then again, going by the goose egg on my head, maybe they were right on that front. Maybe Gaia really didn't care about the violence and the bloodshed at all, and that was terrifying.

If she wasn't going to stop the agathos attacking the daimons, then who would?

GRACE

CHAPTER 10

Riot wrapped us both up in towels after we'd finished cleaning up, and I was contemplating just climbing into the fresh sheets Bullet had just finished clumsily putting onto the bed with one arm when Wild reappeared with an enormous bag in one hand which he chucked down on the bed, and a stack of fresh towels in the other. Oh no, between the blood and the dirt, we'd probably ruined *so* many towels and sheets.

Looking almost bashful, Wild went through the bag and pulled out multiple sets of sweatpants with matching sweaters, as well as T-shirts in a bunch of sizes. He handed me a matching set in blush pink that I absolutely *loved*, even if it reminded me of the fact that he'd been watching me from a distance well before I'd even met Riot. This was exactly the kind of thing I would have worn to go for a run in on a chilly morning.

He turned away while I dressed—going commando, which was a very odd feeling. Riot yanked on a black set, looking very nonchalant about it, while Bullet sighed mournfully, mixing and matching slate gray sweats with a black hoodie.

"All these injuries are really ruining my vibe," he said dramatically, gesturing one-armed at his outfit. "I'm a simple man who likes simple things, like pressed slacks, crisp shirts and the odd waistcoat. Is that really too much to ask?"

"Apparently so," Riot said drily, rolling his eyes. "I'm sure we'll be back at your place soon enough and you can return to your indulgent wardrobe."

I climbed into the clean sheets, my body already feeling like an achy mess from the effort of standing and getting dressed. Bullet laid down next to me, wincing slightly as he put weight on his sore arm.

"I don't know," he admitted, frowning. "I went exploring in the dreamscape, but the visions of us—even the ones I've seen before—feel far away somehow. Maybe if I consult the cards, I'll be able to figure out what I'm missing. Something is happening... either because of the gods' games, or you know. Something is happening to me."

There was silence as Riot fairly radiated disapproval at that idea and I attempted to squash down my immediate negative reaction. Bullet had been able to look into the future his entire life, it was reflexive for him, but it was a reflex he had to learn to ignore for his own *health*. I was basically allergic to confrontation, but I was ready to be *very* confrontational about this.

"Bullet, you collapsed during your last card reading. You promised you'd take it easy," I reminded him, as gently as I could manage. While I was getting better at embracing that darkness, that *anger* within me, I didn't want to turn it on my bonded.

Even when they were being idiots.

"I was having an off day," Bullet replied, far too casually. He was carefully avoiding looking at Wild and Riot, who were both standing at the end of the bed with their arms crossed, clearly not buying Bullet's deflection either.

I developed a brand new ache, my jaw hurting from clenching it so hard. I didn't want to fight with him, but I was sort of revving up to do it anyway.

A phone buzzed on the nightstand, and I glanced over, surprised to find it was the one Wild had given me. Where had it even come from? Hadn't I left it in the SUV that we'd left back at the falls?

"Wild had someone go deal with the vehicle," Riot said, answering my silent question. "They dropped our stuff here."

Wow, Wild really didn't leave anything to chance. I couldn't comprehend being that organized.

I reached across the bed, gritting my teeth as every muscle in my body protested, and glanced at the screen.

Wild: *I'll get you some food.*

I looked up, intending to respond to him, but the room door was already quietly clicking shut behind him. "Wow, he moves quietly."

Riot snorted. "Keres often do. They're built like linebackers and move like mice, make it make sense. I'm going to take a shower."

"Oh. Um, okay then." Riot's words had all come out as a jumble and he'd *just* showered with me, though I guessed that was more about getting me clean than him.

Still, he *looked* clean.

"They're giving us alone time," Bullet said sagely, flashing me a grin. "Riot is so subtle about it, I'm not sure how you didn't realize."

Oh. That was unexpectedly sweet, though I didn't know why I was surprised. Riot had encouraged me to make the most of each day with

Bullet, to push past whatever those subconscious concerns were. This was a quiet opportunity among chaos to do it.

While Wild and Riot's interruptions had cooled my ire somewhat, I wasn't going to drop the issue either. "Alone time so we can talk about you seeking out visions? Thinking about doing readings? I know you want answers, I do too, but not at your expense, Bullet. You collapsing like that... it was terrifying."

He hummed in agreement, leaning his head against the top of mine. "I think the only thing more terrifying for an Oneiroi than a nosebleed close to their 30th birthday is being actively hunted by the Goddess of Earth."

I felt my lip wobble and exhaled deeply, trying to stave off the tears that were threatening to fall. I didn't want to cry and make Bullet feel like he had to comfort *me*.

"Amazing Grace, I know you don't want me to push myself, but my time is running out either way. I'd rather spend what I have left doing what I can to make your journey smoother. The curse is part and parcel of being an Oneiroi."

"You're not like other Oneiroi."

"There *are* no other Oneiroi," Bullet sighed. "Maybe because it's a faulty product line, you know? Now defunct. Maybe the gods are ready to release a new model."

"Don't talk like that," I commanded furiously. Despite how weak my muscles felt, how much my head ached, I forced myself upright, clambering onto Bullet's lap and pressing my forehead against his. "You're not faulty. You're not a *product*. You're a person, and if they wanted to do something to keep you healthy, they could. They're divine beings."

"Reow, someone's mad at the gods," Bullet teased, shaking with silent laughter as he wrapped his arms around my waist, half holding me up. *Mad* was an understatement, I was *furious*. I hadn't even begun to get my head around what that meant for the prophecy that had been heaped on me.

"You know, you never told me about your first bullet wound," I said, changing the subject before I went on a blasphemous rant. I brushed my fingers lightly over the faint scar on his chest before moving them up to the golden bullet he still wore on a chain around his neck.

"It's not a very exciting story. My human dad was involved with some fairly unsavory characters. We were sitting on the broken lawn chairs outside our crumbling piece of shit house—it was midday and he was drunk off his ass—and there was a drive-by shooting. Killed my old man and earned me my nickname."

I leaned back so I could properly look at him. "Bullet, that's *awful*. I'm so sorry."

He did his best to shrug with his injured arm. "He wasn't, like, a good dad or anything. Honestly, I probably ended up better off for it. My human aunt took me in. She wasn't overly involved with my life—she had four kids of her own that kept her busy—but I was fed and I had sheets on my bed for the first time in my life. It was nice."

Oh no. The tears were ready to make a dramatic entrance all over again at the thought of young Bullet lying on a bare mattress with an empty stomach.

"It's honestly okay, Amazing Grace," he soothed, comforting *me* when he'd been the one who'd lived through it. "It's not an unusual story among daimons. The kind of humans we pull into our orbit aren't generally upstanding citizens with strong parenting instincts, you know? Most of the time, they're struggling to keep themselves alive. A little demon parasite baby is the last thing most of them need."

"What about your Oneiroi mother?" I asked. "I guess she died... young."

"Yeah, I don't remember her at all. She left the compound long enough to get pregnant, returned to it for the pregnancy and birth before dumping me at my dad's with a birth certificate and nothing else."

"Can I ask what your birth name is or is that a really personal question?"

I'd been wondering about it ever since I met him, but I wasn't sure the etiquette aside from the fact that they all "earned" their nicknames somehow, and seemed to go by them exclusively from that point on.

Bullet snorted, smoothing his hand over my hip before wriggling his fingers underneath my sweater and T-shirt to gently brush my skin. "It's not a personal question, though I've never met a daimon who uses their birth name after they've been nicknamed. My birth name is Tiresias—Oneiroi are more into traditional names that honored the gods and those who came before us, which is how I ended up being named after a famous blind Greek prophet who was turned into a woman for seven years. My dad and aunt always called me 'Ty' though. My aunt still does, on the odd occasion I remember to call her. She lives in Milton."

He leaned up, kissing the tip of my nose. "You don't need to feel bad for me, Amazing Grace. The drive-by was unfortunate, but I got a cool nickname and a swanky piece of jewelry out of it."

I captured his chin, bringing his mouth to mine and pressing a soft kiss to his lips, keeping him in place so I could deepen it. It wasn't about sex, I just wanted him near me. We hadn't had the smoothest journey, and it was still a little bumpy, still a little lopsided from the amount Bullet knew about me and the miniscule amount I knew about him in return. But we were making progress.

And we would *keep* making progress because Bullet wasn't going anywhere. I didn't care which god or goddess I had to fight to make sure of that.

"Mm, this is nice," Bullet hummed, sucking experimentally on my lower lip, and even though it wasn't about sex, there was a little flutter below my belly at the boldness of Bullet's movements. We were both new to this world of intimacy, and it was kind of the blind leading the blind when Riot wasn't in the room giving us directions, but it was fun to learn each other's bodies together.

"Nope," Riot announced. Bullet and I broke apart, and I looked back over my shoulder as Riot threw open the bathroom door and sauntered out in his sweatpants and no shirt, rubbing a towel over his wet hair like he was *trying* to distract me with his flexing muscles. "Rein in your libidos. Neither of you are in any condition for that."

"When did he get so responsible?" Bullet asked, gently cupping my cheek and pulling my attention back to him for more soft kisses.

"When you two hornbags got irresponsible," Riot snorted, dropping the towel around his neck and pulling his buzzing phone out of his pocket, squinting at the cracked screen. "I think Dare is calling me."

Bullet hummed absently, stroking his fingers through my hair and encouraging me to tilt my head to give him better access.

"We're fine, really," I heard Riot say in the background, his voice muffled. "A little beaten up, but you know how it is. Divine earthquakes are a shitshow."

"Don't downplay this, Riot." Dare's voice came through the phone loud and clear despite Bullet's determination to distract me and Riot huddling suspiciously in the corner with the phone. *"You were in an earthquake caused by a goddess you enraged, and I had to hear about it from fucking Onyx."*

"I'll tell her you said that," Riot laughed quietly. "She'll use that scary rainbow knife she carries around to dismember you. We're okay, I swear. We just need a few days to get back on our feet, and then... we'll go somewhere. I'll find a phone charger and let you know, okay?"

"Maybe stop fucking around with goddesses in the meantime," Dare grumbled, the rest of his words getting lost as he and Riot ended the conversation.

I broke the kiss, staring at Bullet, my limbs growing heavier with the effort of keeping myself upright on his lap. "When will I meet Dare?"

"When the time is right," he replied softly, smile a little sad.

I nodded, throat tight, not needing any further explanation. Not wanting any.

Bullet's thumb swiped at the corner of my eye, brushing the tear away before it could fall. "The gods have asked a lot of you, Grace."

"Of both of us," I agreed, arranging my expression into a semblance of calm as Wild let himself back into the room with pizza, giving Bullet and I a strangely guarded look that I didn't understand.

The progress I'd made with Bullet only highlighted how far Wild and I had to go now that we were all but stuck together. And when Riot hung up the phone, sheepishly looking anywhere but at me, just how difficult the journey ahead of all *five* of us would be.

CHAPTER 11

Fuck.

I'd already messaged the motel owner when I'd gone out to buy clothes, asking them to arrange pizzas for us because absolutely anything was available at this place for a fee. But that meant that all I'd done was stand outside the room with the window I'd cracked earlier to air out the earth smell and listened to Grace and Bullet's entire conversation.

I really was a stalker. Apparently, I was getting worse, not better, when it came to boundaries.

I may not be the smartest man, or even the most in tune with the spiritual side of being a daimon, but even I knew about the Oneiroi curse. But *knowing* about it and *hearing* an Oneiroi talk about it were two completely different things.

Bullet was dying. His gift was quite literally killing him, and it didn't sound like Grace was ready to accept that.

Neither was I.

If they had gods giving them prophecies and interfering in their lives, the *least* those gods could do was help Bullet. I didn't trust deities, and I'd rather have nothing to do with them ever again, but if ever there was a good cause...

Grace and Bullet opened the boxes of vegetarian pizzas happily, and I blew out a silent breath that some of the tension between them seemed to be resolved. Keres daimons weren't designed for emotional conflict, we didn't feed off trauma the way Oizys daimons did. As far as I was concerned, all problems should be worked out in the ring. I was already wishing I'd dragged Viper down to the basement of Asphodel and insisted on settling things that way instead of making a deal with him.

A well-placed punch was often more memorable than a goddess-ordained *deal*.

"Thank you for getting us food," Grace said quietly, shooting me a tentative smile as I handed around paper plates. I paused, silently watching her for probably longer than was appropriate as she helped herself to a slice. She was different from the frustrated woman who'd snuck into my apartment, and it wasn't just the injuries. Grace was timid around me now. Because of how I'd acted. Because I'd sent her away and now she was unsure about this burgeoning bond between us.

Well done, Wild. You've made it all a hundred times worse.

"How is it out there?" Riot asked, tipping his chin towards the strip mall across the busy road. I grimaced, pulling out my phone to type my reply.

'A lot of places are closed. People are confused.'

I showed Riot the message, navigating to a local news page while he relayed it to Grace and Bullet, and showing him the news articles. Local officials were calling for calm, saying the aftershocks were easing off, that there was no need to panic, but people were rightly wary. This was a sudden event, unexpected for this area, and even putting it down to an earthquake wasn't sitting right with people—it hadn't felt like a regular earthquake.

I'd only been able to get pizza because there was always at least a few places who didn't give a fuck about their employees' welfare and insisted on staying open. Perhaps with a daimon whispering in their ear, relishing the chaos Gaia had caused.

"We should, um, probably tell you about the prophecy," Grace said nervously, eyes darting between me and her untouched food.

"You eat, I'll talk," Bullet cut in, also looking at her plate. "I am omniscient and all-knowing after all. Or I was," he added, a sullen look crossing his face that I probably shouldn't have found so... adorable. Especially not after what I'd heard.

I sat down on the empty bed with my own food, doing my best not to be jealous of the three of them curled up together because it was entirely my own fault I wasn't there with them. If I'd told Grace I knew she was my soul bond and thrown her down on my bed and kissed her until she was as mute as me, I was almost certain she'd have wholeheartedly accepted me as much as she accepted Riot and Bullet from that moment on.

She was generous, forgiving, and compassionate almost to a fault. I was probably really testing the limits of all three of those traits.

"The gist is," Bullet began, setting his plate down, "the Fates came up with a prophecy—probably centuries ago, who knows how these things work—to usher in a new age. A Second Age of Heroes. An age, judging by our agathos soul bond here and the fact that we're daimons, where our kinds aren't mortal enemies or whatever. I'm sure I don't have to explain to you that our generation of daimons isn't like our parents' one. You've probably been at odds with your own daimon sperm or egg donor most of your life."

Bullet looked at me expectantly, and I nodded once in confirmation. My daimon father was still in London, loudly bragging about what a fearsome warrior I was, despite the fact that I'd *pleaded* with him to stop. I didn't need Thanatos to think I hadn't taken his warning seriously and to come back to teach me another lesson.

"Well, there are others like us out there. You saw Grace's cousin, Mercy, at the community center that day. Dice is her soul bond. We don't know how many others there are—daimons don't communicate and the agathos do horror movie-style exorcisms on their own when they turn up with daimon soul bonds—"

"Bullet," Grace chided with a quiet laugh. "*Katharmos* isn't an exorcism."

"That wasn't katharmos," Bullet shot back, rolling his eyes. "The agathos Basilinnas butcher everything to make it suit their own agenda. Anyway, maybe there were others, maybe they could have been the one landed with a prophecy, but Grace said a prayer to Nyx, who is fond of the prophecy because it pisses off Gaia if nothing else, and basically volunteered herself for the role."

Grace blushed fiercely despite Bullet's almost joyful recounting of the tale.

"Anyway, she met Riot and it all kind of kicked off. I've known Amazing Grace her whole life in the dreamscape which she obviously doesn't remember which is totally fine and not the worst." Grace rested her head on Bullet's shoulder, the love between them obvious.

My fucking chest hurt.

"Anyway, the prophecy is:

Liberate the treasure held in the deep,

Where no sweet smelling smoke or prayer can reach,

Bring forth the Second Age of Heroes."

Bullet finished, picking up his plate and happily digging into his pizza now he'd unloaded all of that information. No big deal. Another day in the life of these three, apparently.

"I know that's a lot to take in," Grace offered. She wasn't looking at me, but Riot's death stare into the side of my head really did the heavy lifting for both of them. "It *is* a lot, and it's a burden that seems to be growing every day. We went to the falls to pray to Gaia, so I could thank her for intervening at the community center and gauge whether she was on our side, whether she'd stop the agathos attacking the daimons. She said she could smell the prophecy on me, and I guess she wasn't the biggest fan of what it entailed."

No, apparently not. I could have told them that. Gaia was at the top of the food chain right now, and no deity would stand aside if some prophecy appeared to challenge that.

"I guess what I'm saying is maybe you were right to run from me." Grace laughed awkwardly. "Laying it all out like this... It seems wrong that I didn't immediately tell you all of this that day in your apartment. If you *had* wanted to pursue the bond with me, I should have been clear about what you were getting yourself into."

I do want to pursue the bond with you! I screamed in my head, the words trapped and burning in my throat. I want to, but I can't. Or rather I'd thought I *couldn't.* I'd avoided Grace because I carried the curse of a god, because I was forever tied to that god and the darkness they brought with them. Because Death haunted my footsteps, and I didn't want Grace to see that. But given what these three had just told me... Well, maybe being cursed wasn't the deal breaker I thought it was.

Being landed with a prophecy big enough to piss off *Gaia* seemed pretty fucking cursed to me.

Maybe we were all destined to be cursed together.

The idea of giving in and accepting the bond between us—showing her the worst parts of myself knowing that she would probably accept them because that was the kind of person she was—was tempting. Did I really want to invite Death into Grace's life, though? Into Bullet's? He was brushing closely with it as it was...

I set my plate aside and patted the mattress to draw Grace's attention. My ASL wasn't as good as it should be—I never used it, preferring people to just assume what they wanted about why I didn't speak—but I wanted to use it with Grace. I wanted to be able to communicate with her while looking at *her* rather than my phone.

'*Thank you,*' I signed slowly, face heating at how much effort it took to remember. '*I do want you.*'

Grace's eyes widened, darting up to my face as if to confirm I'd said what I meant to say. It barely scratched the surface of what I *wanted* to say, but I didn't know where to begin. I also knew it probably wouldn't mean much, not really. I'd left once already and taken any trust Grace might have had in me when I went. That would take time to rebuild, if I ever managed it.

Not to mention, it would take involving myself in her world. A world of immortals and their demands that I'd done everything in my power to avoid.

"Did you, uh, understand that?" Riot asked Grace awkwardly, exhaling in relief when she nodded. "Thank fuck, could have been awkward."

I rolled my eyes, finishing my pizza and clearing up the empty plates. I wasn't sure how I felt about being stuck with *Riot*, but he obviously loved Grace and it made me dislike him slightly less. And Bullet…

Those were complicated emotions I was going to shove into a box and address another day. Or never.

Fed, clothed, and in clean sheets, it didn't take the three of them long to drift back to sleep, even with the earth shifting restlessly below us. They'd taken more of the pills that French had dropped off, and I knew it'd make them drowsy. Had they been anyone else, I might have shaken them awake again—I'd been watching Grace for months and suddenly learned that I had almost *none* of the facts. I wanted to ask more questions, but one look at her long eyelashes resting on her high cheekbones, mouth parted slightly in sleep, and the urge disappeared completely.

Nothing was more important than Grace's recovery. Than all of them recovering. Whatever my obsessive tendencies were, they'd have to wait.

Onyx: *Big shake in Milton. You said this was a goddess' doing?*

I hadn't gone into detail, only telling Onyx that Grace, Riot and Bullet had been injured in a natural disaster caused by a goddess so she knew vaguely what we were dealing with.

Me: *Gaia. Is anyone hurt?*

Onyx: *Well, duh. Earth goddess and all. Not any of our people, but Grace's apartment collapsed. No survivors. It seemed very... targeted to that building.*

Fuck.

I couldn't imagine Grace not feeling some kind of responsibility for those lives lost, not when her heart was so big. Fucking miserable goddesses ruining lives for the fun of it. Killing *humans*. Gaia must be really angry to allow her favored children to be collateral damage.

Me: *Can you hold down the fort? We're not returning to Milton.*

Onyx: *Obviously. Does this mean you finally removed your head from your rectum?*

Me: *I will fire you.*

Onyx: *No you won't, I'm too useful. Do you know where you're going to go?*

I drummed my fingers on the back of my phone, deciding how much to tell her. Onyx was the closest thing I had to a friend, and due to her complete lack of respect for anyone's boundaries, she knew more than anyone else did about me. I'd let that slide to a certain extent because she'd never given me a reason not to trust her, but when it came to Grace's privacy, I was a lot more wary.

Onyx: *I can practically hear you deciding whether or not I'm worthy of bestowing such knowledge from here, oh fearless leader. Fine, don't tell me. Don't do anything dumb with my agathos.*

Not your agathos, I grumbled silently as I rolled my eyes, closer than I'd ever been to saying a prayer to Nyx for strength. *My* agathos.

Onyx: *And you should probably keep Dare updated. He's being very patient, don't make him suffer.*

Dare? The tattoo artist?

I didn't let people touch me, so I had no cause to spend any time with him, but almost all of my staff had been inked by him at some point or another.

Did that mean Dare was Grace's fourth soul bond? Did they both know? Too fucking bad, he'd have to keep being patient. I needed time to figure out my shit with Grace, and I already had two others here to contend with.

Me: *Just keep Asphodel running, I'll be back when I can.*

Part of me still felt like I should go back now. That this was a road that only led to heartbreak, and the longer I was around Grace, the more at risk I put her. This was not a woman who could afford to attract any more attention from the gods.

I'd be prepared. Just in case. I quietly pulled on my jacket and let myself out of the room, crossing to the cash machine across the street so I could withdraw enough to tide the three of them over. Just in case I was man enough to do the right thing and leave Grace alone.

I hit the bag in front of me repeatedly, the rhythmic sensation going some way towards giving me a sense of normalcy after the chaos I'd experienced recently. This was my happy space. This was where I was meant to be. Alone in a dark, sterile gym with nothing but my boxing bag for company. This was my

future. Not beautiful agathos soulmates, not friendships among daimons, or even the temptation of something more. The connection between Grace and I may have started to form, but I was strong enough to break it.

It would hurt, but she had Riot and Bullet to comfort her. She'd forget about me in no time.

My hurt could just go on the list of all the other hurts I had to live with. What was one more?

Bullet walked out of the shadowy corner of the gym and my movements ceased instantly. There was no way this was a figment of my imagination— these dreams were always solitary. No, this was a visit from a very real daimon.

"No Grace?" I asked flatly. Weird. I thought I'd enjoy speaking in the dreamscape, that it would be an opportunity to get out all the words that I kept bottled in, but I'd gotten used to not speaking. The silence was a habit.

Bullet looked strangely uncertain.

"Not that she'd remember any of this anyway," Bullet began with a frustrated look that he quickly wiped off his face. "But I didn't want you to feel pressured to show either me or her what I'm going to ask you to show me."

I'd expected this, mostly. Grace was too polite to ask, to push for answers. Perhaps she assumed I'd been born this way and that was all there was to it.

"You want to see how I lost my voice," I stated.

"No," Bullet replied lightly, tilting his head to the side. He really was so fucking attractive—all angular features and catlike curiosity. "I want to know why you smell of the gods."

"The answers are one and the same." I shrugged, returning my stare to the boxing bag even as my arms stayed frozen at my sides. Was I going to do it? Was I going to share this with him? Something I'd never told anyone?

It was reckless, especially when I would forget this conversation when I woke up. I would be giving Bullet information that I wouldn't remember giving him, and that was antithetical to everything about how I lived my life. Controlled, informed, secretive.

121

It was difficult to say no to Bullet though. Difficult to say no to Grace. Even difficult to say no to Riot, though I felt zero attraction to him. There was still the same sense of them being... my people. Just mine, somehow.

"So it was a punishment," Bullet mused, looking mildly curious at best. These people had no sense of self-preservation. The appropriate response to finding out someone was cursed by the gods was to run very fucking far in the other direction.

Then again, they'd just had an up close and personal encounter with Gaia herself. It would take a lot to rattle them at this point.

"Which god?" Bullet asked.

"Does it matter?"

"Very much so. If Nyx has cursed you, that would make things difficult, though I doubt she has. It's not in her nature, and she favors me, and our Amazing Grace, of course. On the other hand, we know Gaia can be cruel—"

"You think very highly of me to even consider that I might have caught the attention of either Nyx or Gaia," I scoffed. They were at the very top of the food chain, and I wasn't that important.

"Well since most of the others are gone..."

"Not in the underworld," I replied, struggling to keep my voice even. "In the underworld, the gods are as powerful as ever. They reign unchallenged, untouched by Gaia and Nyx and their relentless cold war."

Finally, Bullet had the good sense to look a little disturbed. I knew he was favored by Nyx and the Fates, and he'd probably seen plenty of what they wanted him to see, but there was a whole different group of deities that he hadn't considered.

"Thanatos," I said finally. "That's who cursed me."

Bullet let out a long whistle, shoving his hands into his pockets. "And how'd you get onto the God of Death's radar?"

I paced in front of him, my natural instinct to hide this tale from everyone warring with the strange urge to confess. Perhaps it was because I could speak and be heard, and that was why the whole story came tumbling out as Bullet listened silently. I didn't embellish or leave out my own failures, the hubris that had brought me to that point. I had no doubt that Bullet would relay all of this information to Grace and Riot when we woke up, and she deserved to know what the Fates had landed her with me as her third soul bond. A daimon of violent death, haunted by the personification of death himself.

She deserved to know why I was struggling to stay and why I couldn't leave. Why I'd fought the connection between us no matter what the Fates had in mind. Why I still might, worried about how my curse would affect her in the long run. Affect all of them. Bullet was dying and I was haunted by death.

He didn't look as bothered by that as he should.

"People die in my presence," I reiterated, looking at him seriously. "I started creating spaces for Keres daimons to work out their bloodlust safely because so many I encountered were dying in fights around me. Thanatos would appear to collect their souls, and no one could see him except me. He was always there, watching me."

"And since you started doing that, have you noticed a decrease in the number of dead Keres you encounter?" Bullet asked bluntly.

I blinked at him. "Yes."

"Of course you have," Bullet tutted impatiently. "You obviously think very highly of yourself, but you don't control when someone's time is up. Their threads are determined by the Fates, the same Fates who laid out multiple paths for your future. One of which involved you becoming some kind of guardian angel for angry Keres daimons. I don't know why I'm bothering to explain all

123

of this when you're just going to forget anyway," he added under his breath, massaging his temples.

Despite feeling like I'd just gone through the emotional wringer explaining everything to him, his show of irritation somehow made me feel better. It was so ordinary. Like what I'd just told him wasn't the end of the world.

But would Grace see it the same way?

"You already know I'm going to tell my Amazing Grace all of this, don't you?" Bullet confirmed, echoing my thoughts. Perhaps he could read them when he was dropping into my subconscious. Was he even supposed to be visiting me like this? Was this overextending his gift?

I nodded, reflexively answering silently before remembering I could speak here.

"Why do you call her that?"

Bullet looked at me, eyebrows rising slightly. "You don't think she's amazing?"

"Of course I do," I scoffed. "But I don't believe that's why you call her that. You're too complicated for such a simple explanation."

He glanced at his shoes, cheeks tinging pink. I wondered if he was replaying that kiss between us two years ago at Elysium. As much as I'd thought about it, both recently and when it happened, I wasn't going to bring it up.

Bullet loved Grace. He was committed to Grace. I understood how all consuming that draw to her was because I felt it too. I wouldn't make things awkward by bringing up ancient history.

"Truth for a truth," Bullet challenged, crossing his arms and tilting his chin up. I wouldn't bring up ancient history, but I could still admire how fucking attractive he was. Especially with that stubborn look on his face.

"Sure." I shrugged. I'd already revealed the worst thing about myself.

"What's the harm in telling you? Just more things to forget," he muttered, not quite able to disguise the bitterness in his voice. *"Was Grace that taught my heart to fear, And Grace, my fears relieved."* There was no trace of the sing-song voice he usually used as he recited the lyrics to the old hymn.

"I know that's not what it's referring to," he said wryly. *"But I only fear my curse, my death, because it means leaving Grace behind. And the only reason I don't fear it—some of the time, at least—is because I know eventually she'll return to me at the end of her long life, and hopefully she'll be happy to see me."*

I probably didn't need oxygen to breathe in the dreamscape, but it felt like it had been snatched out of my lungs nonetheless.

"You should tell her what I told you," I said quietly, my voice thick. *"And you should tell her all of that too."*

"I think our girl has enough on her plate without knowing that she's the only thing keeping me this side of sane," Bullet replied tightly. *"Your turn. What will it take to make you stop holding back? What it is you're really afraid of?"*

"That was two questions."

"And you won't remember either of them, give me something here."

I huffed a silent laugh, shaking my head. *"I could quite literally bring Death to your doorstep, Oneiroi. What more explanation do you need? Is that really something you want to risk?"*

"I'm not afraid of dying, Wild. I'm afraid of saying goodbye, I'm afraid of being forgotten, of becoming obsolete to the woman I've loved my whole life. But Death? He can come for me when he's ready. I know to expect him."

My chest ached.

"If I can't be there for Grace when she's old and gray, I'm going to make damn sure her other three soul bonds will be. You're not running away, Wild. I'm not going to let you. Time to wake up."

BULLET

CHAPTER 12

I went from completely asleep to entirely awake, my eyes flying open to stare unseeing at the ceiling. Wild shifted restlessly from the other side of the room, in the armchair he'd dozed off in, and the movement was enough to make Grace stir while Riot continued to cling to her like she was his favorite teddy bear.

I'd known when I decided to pop into Wild's dreams and ask for answers that the ones I got would be hard to hear. The traces of the gods' magic on him weren't subtle, and while I'd predicted *something* like what he'd told me, I was struggling to reconcile the reckless Wild who'd been cursed by the God of Death with the stoic, controlled man he was now.

No wonder he'd earned the nickname 'Wild'.

"Good morning," Grace mumbled, snuggling into my side and pressing a shy kiss to my shoulder. "Is it morning? Are we back to keeping agathos hours? How are you feeling today?"

"It is morning. And I feel better," I assured her. Mostly. "You?"

"Much better. My head still hurts, but I'm ready to travel, I think. If everyone else is." Her eyes darted over to where Wild was leaning forward, elbows braced on his thighs with a frown on his face, rubbing his temples. Left with whatever lingering emotion from our conversation in the dreamscape. Our *two-sided* conversation.

"There's something we need to discuss first, but let's get ready to leave. Do we still have snacks?" I asked, attempting to roll out of bed without letting on how painful the movement actually was. I was pretty sure I'd cracked some ribs in that earthquake.

Riot groaned, burying his face in Grace's hair. "Can't we sleep a little longer?"

"No."

Grace blinked up at me, not used to my authoritative bossman voice. I didn't know if I was pulling it off honestly, but I wanted to get this conversation over and done with. If I couldn't see the future, I was just going to have to make do with the present.

Lame.

Riot grumbled as he rolled out of bed, grabbing the sweatpants and sweater closest to him without considering for even a second if they matched. An absolute animal.

"Stay put, I'll get the snacks," he yawned, running his hand through his hair and ducking into the bathroom. Wild sat silently in his corner, staring up at the ceiling, and Grace looked nervously between us as she shuffled into an upright position and braided her hair over one shoulder, wincing slightly when the movement pulled at the bandage on her head.

"Is everything okay?" she asked. Goddess, sleep-rumpled Grace might be my favorite.

127

"Come here and give me a cuddle," I replied in lieu of a better answer. It had been a rough few days, and while I didn't want to admit it even to myself, I was feeling the pinch of *time* more than ever. Time, time, time.

We all took turns getting up and getting ready while Riot dug through the snacks French had brought us, pulling out various packaged breakfast foods that would play havoc with my body. I supposed it didn't matter anymore—I'd done my best to maximize the amount of time I had, but the clock was running down anyway. What was a little processed sugar at this point?

Grace insisted on us making the bed, and we sat on the edge while Wild hovered in the corner, tapping furiously on his phone.

"I'm not all 'my body is a temple' or whatever like Bullet, but even I'm craving like one vegetable," Riot sighed, unenthusiastically opening a prepackaged snack cake.

"Let's get some on the way... wherever we go," I agreed, looking at my 'breakfast' before setting it down on the nightstand with a grimace. "But I have a story to tell you first."

It wasn't lost on me that we were in a similar position to how we'd been yesterday, except that this time it was Wild's story I was telling the group instead of Grace's. Huh. I was totally the bard of our little bonded family.

I glanced at Wild, who had moved to standing in the corner with his arms crossed, ignoring the cake Riot had chucked on the spare bed. Wild gave me one curt nod, so at least he'd guessed at what we were about to discuss.

I took a deep breath and channeled my inner Homer, ready to tell a story with a not-so-happy ending. "Once upon a time, the Olympian gods interacted with mortals on an almost daily basis. They visited the mortal realm, reproduced with humans, intervened in their lives, they giveth, they taketh away, all that good stuff. How familiar are you with those gods?"

Grace swallowed a mouthful of food, looking between me and Riot like she wasn't sure who I was asking.

"It wasn't something we focused on particularly. The agathos Elders are very moralistic, they disapprove of almost all the Olympians except Hera," she said eventually.

That tracked. Hera definitely embodied agathos puritanical energy.

"The Olympians disappeared after Gaia waged her war against them. They're immortal, so they're not *dead*, but they were sufficiently weakened that she was able to take the top spot." And I had plenty of theories about that, but this moment was about Wild. "Whatever happened to the Olympians, the underworld gods seem to remain unscathed, living and ruling their realm as they always have. Wild knows. He met them."

Boom. Mic drop.

"You *met* the gods of the underworld?" Grace asked, her voice dropping to a whisper as she stared at Wild. "How? When?"

Wild gave me another nod to continue, his expression guarded. There was a wave of longing from Grace through the bond, and I imagined she was craving the connection with Wild that would give her the kind of insight into his feelings that she had into mine and Riot's.

It would be helpful. On the outside, he was about as emotive as the uneaten cake I'd left on the nightstand.

"When Wild was a young, foolish Keres, he rose up quickly through the ranks of the underground fighting scene in London. He was confident, undefeated in the... ring? Cage? I don't know, I don't know shit about fighting. Anyway, he maybe got a little *too* confident one night after a fight, and loudly boasted that not even Death himself could defeat him."

"Death himself didn't like that?" Riot guessed, a slightly disbelieving look on his face. Despite all he'd experienced recently, Riot still wasn't accustomed to the gods and their games.

"He did not. Thanatos, God of Death, decided that if Wild was going to make such grand claims, he needed to back them up. He transported Wild to the palace of King Hades and Queen Persephone in the underworld, a place where mortals can visit—under specific conditions and only by invitation—and challenged him to a fight."

Grace moved like she was going to go to Wild, but he shrunk further back against the wall and she stopped, not quite able to shutter her wave of her rejection before Riot and I picked up on it.

"He lost. Obviously," I clipped, annoyed with Wild all over again for hurting my Amazing Grace's feelings. "Gods and goddesses are rarely content to just leave their victories there. Thanatos cursed him to a life of silence, so Wild could never boast again. This was five years ago. Wild traveled the world since, making his fortune fighting and gaining a reputation for his, you know, silence." Wild's eye twitched. "Then he came to Milton and used his funds to start his Milton mini empire."

Wild cut me a glare again, and I guessed he didn't like his empire being referred to as "mini." I mean, it was impressive enough considering he'd only been there two years, but Milton was tiny and property was cheap. He was hardly some kind of real estate mogul.

"For a long time, Wild saw Keres dying around him. Their bloodlust got the better of them and they fought until they physically couldn't anymore. When that happened, Thanatos would show up to collect the souls, making sure he was visible to Wild, which is obviously not standard procedure."

Wild was looking at me with wide eyes, and I guessed he was surprised he'd shared this part with me.

"That is why Wild goes so hard looking after the Keres daimons in Milton. I guess he carries some misplaced sense of guilt over all those deaths, even though the Fates decided when their time would be up, not Wild."

Damn it, I must have explained it better in the dreamscape. He wasn't looking particularly convinced by my words.

"There must be something that can be done," Grace said softly, giving Wild a longing look. "Some way of reversing it."

Grace and her eternal optimism. It was so tempting to believe it sometimes. To believe she could find a way around my curse. Around Wild's. Fuck, we were an unlucky little crew.

Riot had basically spent his recent years in a cocaine-fueled cocoon of sadness and he was somehow the best off out of all of us.

Wild shook his head, refusing to look at her.

"Is that why you don't want to be my soul bond?"

Riot made a quiet sound of outrage next to her, and I kind of understood the sentiment because the idea of rejecting Grace was insanity to me. I mean, I was *dying*, and I still couldn't stay away from her.

A pained look crossed Wild's face that wrenched at my own heart, and I could feel how much it got to Grace's. At that moment, it was obvious that he wanted to speak more than anything, and he couldn't tell her how he felt.

The ground moved again, this time with a fierce *lurch* rather than a gentle rumble, and Riot and I grabbed Grace at the same time, my heart beating out of my fucking chest. Was this going to be our life now? Was Gaia just going to haunt our steps, trying to circumvent the Fates by killing Grace before she could fulfill the prophecy?

I stiffened as something tugged at my psyche, a sense of wrongness, almost a ripple of *something* through the air.

"Pay attention," Grace whispered, grabbing Riot's hand and reaching for mine. "The voice is saying to pay attention."

What fucking voice?

Grace was hearing voices now?

Wild flattened himself against the wall as the air twisted and contorted in the center of the room, swirling into a fucking *portal*. I pulled Grace off the bed, Riot and I moving in tandem to position her behind us as a figure stepped out of the swirling abyss, dominating the cheap motel room and cutting the three of us off from Wild.

Holy shit.

The enormous feathery, silver iridescent wings were the first thing I noticed because they seemed to span almost the entire length of the room. He appeared as a middle-aged man—with olive skin, shoulder-length wavy black hair and a long, black beard—but I had no doubt he was far older than he looked. Ancient. Immortal.

The god rolled his shoulders impatiently, wings fluttering slightly with the movement. He wasn't dressed in some ancient Grecian garb though. No, this fucking guy was in a blue and silver sequined *suit*, with no shirt underneath. What in the Ziggy Stardust had just portaled into our shitty motel room?

Judging by the terrified look of recognition on Wild's face... Thanatos.

"Ah, if it isn't my least favorite Keres. I was sent on a retrieval trip and it is oh-so-convenient to be able to find you wherever you are. Even easier when you're talking about me—well not *you*, obviously. I applaud myself on my foresight in cursing you."

And I thought Nyx was scary. This guy was terrifying, in a sparkly, unhinged sort of way.

"Isn't this a party?" the god said, his voice mocking as he surveyed the room. "So, three daimons and an agathos walk into a bar... Oh, except it's not a bar. It's the underworld. Come along, mortals. Aunty Gaia is in *quite* the foul mood today."

"Wait—" I objected, digging my heels into the carpet as the portal dragged us forward.

"Oh no, we definitely don't want to wait," Thanatos replied cheerfully.

"What is happening?" Grace gasped, fighting to stay in place, clinging to both Riot and me. There was no point, though. Whatever magic he was wielding couldn't be fought off by brute strength alone. The current dragged us forward, and I crashed into Wild's side as all four of us stumbled through the portal together, briefly blinded by a kind of emptiness that wasn't really empty at all. The veil—the separation between this life and the one after—teemed with vibrance and activity, but none that we could see.

Wild's hand wrapped around my bicep as all four of us fought to hold on to each other through the wind tunnel we were being sucked through. I could faintly make out Thanatos' sparkling wings ahead of us as he swaggered along in his sequins like he was about to march onto a stage rather than... wherever it was we were going.

The underworld. He said we were going to the underworld.

As quickly as it began, the world around us stilled, and I immediately hunched forward, bracing my hands on my knees and trying not to throw up.

"Welcome," a female voice said softly, making me straighten. Grace immediately snatched my hand—the one on my injured arm—but there was no tug of pain. In fact, all of my aches and pains had disappeared. I chanced a glance at Grace out of the corner of my eye, finding her face back to its beautiful flawless state, not a bruise or blemish in sight.

133

Did this mean we were dead? I was going to be pissed if we were all dead. I was the only one on the agenda to die any time soon.

Wild suddenly grabbed the back of my and Grace's shirts and tugged us towards the ground, and I knew right away that he was encouraging us to bow. Not wanting to risk offending anyone, I kneeled the same way I would for Nyx, with Grace following my lead and Riot clumsily hitting the ground with a thud after her.

"Aren't you all sweet?" the voice purred. I chanced a glance up through my eyelashes, finding a terrifyingly majestic goddess staring down at us, wearing a flowing emerald peplos with a thin golden belt that highlighted her generous figure. Her skin was so pale, it looked like she'd never seen the sun, and her waist-length wavy hair was the color of wheat.

She looked like a goddess of harvest and plenty.

Or at least, the daughter of one.

"So polite. Rise. I am Persephone, welcome to my home."

Persephone, Queen of the fucking *Underworld,* led us through the palace to a grand throne room, empty but for one other figure, slumped on an intimidatingly large onyx throne with a bored look on his face.

Hades had the same long, curled dark hair and long black beard that Thanatos had, but none of the jazzy accessories. Instead, he wore a dark chiton with an elaborate blood red himation over top, edged with gold embroidery and secured with an ostentatious bronze fastener at the shoulder.

"Are you sure this isn't an elaborate dreamscape?" Grace whispered to me.

"I am very much not in the driver's seat," I assured her. I was a pretty creative guy, but I didn't have the imagination for *this*. The ceiling above us was at least three stories high, painted with terrifying depictions of what I was pretty sure were the original Moros, sweeping through humanity like a plague of despair. It was a bold choice of decor, but I supposed this room was meant to intimidate and it was doing a great job of it.

I could faintly make out hallways and alcoves behind the enormous Doric columns that lined the palace, though they all appeared to be deserted. Even Thanatos had disappeared, leaving us alone with the two rulers of the underworld.

"This is my husband," Persephone said, gesturing at Hades— *Hades*—lounging on his throne. "He's a little cranky today. Doesn't like having mortals in his realm."

"Sorry," Grace squeaked automatically, leading us as we dropped into a bow again. I chanced a look up, finding Hades looking down at Grace with the faintest trace of amusement.

"Rise," he called, not raising his voice. "My wife wants you here, so here you are."

"Not forever," Persephone said with a light laugh that reminded me of wind chimes or pixies or something. It was too surreal, and I had seen plenty of surreal shit in my time. We climbed to our feet at the bottom of the dais while she took her seat on an elaborate throne of vines and flowers next to her husband's. "Well, you will find your way here permanently at some point—all mortals do—but it is not your time yet."

Grace's hand tightened around mine. That was a good sign, right? At least they weren't all 'hey Bullet, you may as well just stay down here and save Thanatos another trip.' Where had he even gone? I guessed the God of Death was a busy guy.

"I was going to just watch you, to see how your path unfolded, but the ancestral mother is a formidable enemy. You needed to recover."

"Thank you," Grace said nervously, like she wasn't sure if it was appropriate to speak or not. "We're so grateful that you healed us."

Persephone flicked a hand dismissively. "Over the centuries, there have been many attempts to find a new hero among mortals. One to restore things to the way they were before the war destroyed it all. The Fates were coy—as they are wont to be—but I also believe they were finding it difficult to find the right person. The right combination of agathos, daimon, human even. One with a respect for the divine, but a compassion for other mortals, no matter what kind. It was a difficult balance for them to find. To *make*. Until you."

Grace looked about two seconds away from passing out.

"Can you help us with the prophecy? Queen Persephone?" I hastily tacked on the end. For all Nyx's many lessons she had given me over the years, how to address the king and queen of the underworld had never been covered.

She turned those almost golden eyes on me, her expression faintly amused. "You know we cannot give you answers, merely hints. I have no desire to have three furious Fates in my home because I've broken the rules. Oneiroi, you learn more about the divine than most. Whatever you suspect, you are probably correct."

Well, fuck.

Riot shot me an expectant look over Grace's head with a heavy dose of judgment along with it. I hadn't been hiding my theory because I didn't trust them with it, but rather because I'd hoped I was wrong.

I'd hoped whatever it was that Grace had to find would be a 'what' not a 'who'. That made things a lot more complicated.

"Bullet?" Grace encouraged, squeezing my hand. Persephone—*the* Persephone—gave me an encouraging nod. *Cool, cool. Just a normal day.*

"The Olympians. The Olympians are the treasure in the deep."

"They're smarter than I thought they would be," Hades whispered loudly, leaning towards his wife's throne. *Offensive.* "Or that one is, at least."

"Tartarus, to be specific," Persephone confirmed, resting one hand on her husband's arm and using the other to gesture vaguely at the ground below us.

"Can we go there?" I asked dubiously. I knew that was where Nyx resided, but I doubted that was where she brought me in the dreamscape.

"Technically, you cannot go *here*," Hades scoffed.

"What he means to say," Persephone corrected drily, shooting her husband an affectionate look. "You, as mortals, cannot go anywhere you are not specifically welcomed into, whether that is our domain, Tartarus, or the heavenly plane the remaining deities have retired to. Tartarus the *realm* is the domain of Tartarus the *god*. It is an extension of him, and your mortal minds would explode if you saw him in his true form when he wasn't expecting it—the same applies for any god. We are dulling our shine at the moment, as it were."

"How can we liberate them if we can't get to them?" Grace asked, more to herself than anything.

"It is not a matter of stealth or strength, but a matter of brains and faith," Persephone replied, somewhat cryptically. "I do hope you succeed, Grace the agathos. Tartarus is truly in Gaia's thrall—we cannot travel to his realm, or we risk imprisonment too, and it has been many centuries since I've seen my mother."

CHAPTER 13

"I have things to do. Don't fail, Grace the agathos," Hades—fucking *Hades*—said abruptly, standing up and striding off without a second glance.

"He does that," Persephone said, noting our confusion. "Running the underworld is no small task, after all."

This was the weirdest fucking thing that had ever happened to me, and I'd seen some *shit* when I was high. Nothing that quite compared to visiting the goddamn *underworld* and having a full-blown conversation with Hades and Persephone, though.

What was even happening?

Maybe this was some elaborate dreamscape Bullet had cooked up to fuck with me.

"I was intending to collect you regardless—your health was disconcertingly poor—but I had hoped Wild would share his experiences of our realm with you so it would not be quite so alarming," Persephone said, standing with an inhuman kind of fluidity. Aside from the fact that we'd only *just* found out about Wild's excursion to the underworld five minutes before the God of Death showed up to kidnap us, I doubted anything could have prepared us for this anyway.

"Anyway, you probably need a moment to compose yourselves. We are expecting a new resident shortly, someone I'd like you to meet."

All of us froze in place, Grace's dread pouring down the bond.

"It is not time yet, though. Thanatos is busy, he works at his own pace. Orphne, will you show our guests to the balcony? Rest for a while, think of what you will do next. Enjoy this short reprieve where neither Nyx nor Gaia can reach you." Persephone flicked her hand dismissively, and a—what even was she? A nymph?—ushered us out of the throne room. Orphne was what I imagined an underworld goddess to look like—pale with dark sunken eyes, straight black hair that hung like silk to her knees, and black dress that was draped in long layers over her slim frame, trailing along the mosaic floor.

"Stay on the balcony," Orphne ordered in a hollow voice. "If you leave the bounds of the palace, you cannot return to the upperworld."

She held up a flaming torch which only barely illuminated the shadowy marble corridor, though a dim purplish light seemed to glow from the sky above as we stepped onto the semicircular balcony. All four of us headed straight for the railing, where a river below separated the palace from the most vibrant field of flowers I'd ever seen.

"The Elysian Fields," Bullet whispered. "Nyx has shown me visions of this before."

"That's kind of morbid," I noted, frowning at Bullet. "Why was she showing you the underworld?"

He blinked, opening his mouth before closing it again. He'd clearly said more than he intended and I could see the wheels turning in his head as he tried to figure out how to backtrack.

"It's okay, Bullet," Grace said quietly, grabbing his hand and giving it a squeeze. "Just tell us."

"It was meant to be an incentive," Bullet muttered uncomfortably, extracting himself from Grace's grip and carefully removing the now redundant bandage on her head. "Fulfill the prophecy, become a hero, we all end up here together for eternity. The highest plane of the underworld, the place where only a select few spend their immortal days."

Grace stared out over the fields again, eyes pausing on the glinting still lake. There was no sunlight here, but it somehow wasn't pitch black either. Everything about the landscape in front of us was beautiful and appealing, and the idea of spending eternity here wasn't terrible, even if I wasn't in any rush to be thinking about the afterlife.

Bullet didn't have that luxury though. Bullet probably thought about the afterlife a lot.

"You didn't tell me," Grace sighed. "Or you did in my sleep, and I forgot."

"I didn't tell you because I didn't want it to influence you," Bullet countered. "If you decide to fulfill the prophecy, to accept this mantle that's been put upon you, you should do it because you *want* to. Because you believe it's the right course of action. Not because you've been bribed—or worse, because *I've* been bribed and pushed you into it."

Grace pursed her lips but didn't object, and I wondered if Bullet's shortened lifespan and the curse that haunted him were finally getting through to her. No matter how deep in denial Grace was, the signs were all getting a bit too blatant for her to ignore.

140

"So you've been here before?" Grace asked, turning to Wild, opting not to engage in the topic of Bullet's curse.

"Yes."

Wild's voice was so low it took me a moment to realize he'd said the word out loud. Grace's jaw dropped while I contemplated punching him in the face. He could *speak* here, and hadn't said a goddamn word to her.

He was a big guy, but I could probably take him. He needed some fucking sense knocked into him.

"Oh," Grace said quietly. "You spoke."

"I can here."

Awkward as fuck.

"And you fought Thanatos here?" Grace asked, her voice dropping to a whisper. "The god who collected us?"

"Yes," Wild replied tightly, staring out over the fields. "He found us because of me."

"This really seems like a great opportunity for you to have a big ol' conversation with Grace," I observed, crossing my arms over my chest and glaring at him. "Get out all those words you usually have to keep bottled up."

"Riot," Grace chastised, giving me an exasperated look. "Between being given an agathos soul bond in the first place, plus the forced physical contact that kicked off the bonding process, I think Wild has been subjected to enough unwanted *Grace* to last a lifetime."

"It's not unwanted," Wild said quickly, smartly reassuring her before I lost my shit at him for making her feel that way. "It's not a question of *wanting* you, Grace. I'm *cursed*."

"That would be a lot more impressive if the god who cursed you hadn't swung by, picked us up, and dragged us down to the underworld too," I pointed out. "We got all the way fucked up by Gaia a couple of days ago. Grace has some kind of mysterious prophecy about rescuing gods handed down by the Fates. Don't even get me started on Bullet. We're all carrying around baggage the gods gave us—" What the fuck was that noise? "Are you *singing* right now?" I asked Bullet in exasperation.

"*Anything You Can Do,*" Grace answered, shaking her head slightly, giving Bullet an indulgent look before turning her wary attention to Wild. "We have all been impacted by the gods' involvement in our lives, in one way or another. What you've been through, the curse Thanatos put on you... that doesn't scare me. It doesn't put me off. But I'd never take your choice away, Wild."

He looked shocked, though I couldn't imagine why. How could someone watch Grace from a distance for months and *not* come to the conclusion that she was sweet and kind and thoughtful?

"I don't want it to affect you," Wild said slowly, and for a moment I felt a little bad for the guy because it was clear he was out of practice speaking aloud and this was a hell of a conversation to dive in with. "It already is, Thanatos found us because of me. I don't want you to see the God of Death every time someone dies in your presence. I don't want people dying more often around you. Thanatos...He's not always that, er, friendly. I don't want you on his radar."

Shit, that was a rough deal. I didn't want to feel sorry for the guy who'd smashed my face into a pulp a couple of years ago, but I was definitely heading in that direction.

In spite of literally everything that was going on, Grace managed a wry smile as she gestured at our surroundings. "It's a little too late for that. I think at this point, what's one more curse, you know? The only one of us who hasn't been in communication with a deity directly is Riot."

"Don't jinx it," I muttered.

"You're really looking at this all wrong," Bullet pointed out mildly. Wild's attention shifted to him and Bullet's cheeks got all pink like a teenager with his first crush. Fascinating. "We're here because of you, Wild. That's a *good* thing. We got answers about the prophecy, and some magical healing. I'm not complaining."

"Grace had a fucking *head injury*," I added, chest tightening at the thought of just how bad it could have gotten. Grace's fingers lightly drifted over her hairline where the wound had been. "I'm pretty glad for this whole underworld excursion right now."

Wild was an expert at playing his cards close to his chest, but if I had to guess, he looked thoughtful. Or confused. Or angry. Fuck if I knew.

"Agathos are always told that every gift from Anesidora, from *Gaia*, comes with sacrifice," Grace said slowly. "When I use my ability to bestow luck on a human, I pay in bad luck of my own. When I relieve their pain, I take it into myself. Maybe... maybe this connection to the underworld is the *gift* part of the sacrifice you were forced to make. Or maybe it's not, and I'm being too optimistic. But either way, if you want to explore this thing between us, Wild, then let's explore it. And if you don't, that's okay too, you are entitled to make that choice. Just don't make it because you think you're doing me a favor. I *want* you around."

Wild swallowed thickly, and I got the distinct impression that he didn't know how to respond to that, but he didn't move away when Grace stepped into his space, tentatively reaching up to give him a quick, chaste hug. A friendly hug. I knew she was attracted to him, but maybe she didn't want to spook him.

"I want you around. To be around you. To... yeah," he muttered, patting her gently on the back and looking very much on the edge of being spooked.

"He has no game," I mumbled to Bullet. "He's worse than you."

"I have game," Bullet gasped in mock outrage.

"None of you have game," I snorted, not bothering to point out that Grace had resorted to multiple masturbatory showers a day when it had just been her and Bullet staying in the house because they were both too chicken shit to make a move on each other.

Grace took a small step back from Wild, looking back over her shoulder and narrowing her eyes at me before returning her attention to her most mysterious soul bond.

"Did you come to this part of the palace when you were last here?" Grace asked Wild, gently tugging on his arm to guide him back to where I stood, looking out over the field of blossoms.

Olympians. Tartarus.

How could the Fates ask that of Grace? Of any mortal? We weren't qualified for this shit.

"No. The fight—the wrestling match—took place in the throne room. It wasn't empty like today. There were all kinds of creatures and souls surrounding us, cheering him on," Wild rasped.

"You got your ass kicked in front of an audience of dead people and gods?" I asked. "That's rough."

Wild cut me a glare over Grace's head, clearly attempting to remind me with his eyeballs that he could kick *my* ass no problem.

"Play nice," Bullet said, huffing a quiet laugh as he looked out over the field.

"Ah, you're here."

An unfamiliar voice made us jump, and I yanked Grace into my side, wrapping an arm around her protectively as yet another deity showed up like this was just a regular *thing* we did now. Chats with divine beings. No big deal. We should start a podcast.

The goddess in front of us was a lot more intimidating than Persephone and even Orphne. Her dark brown skin was almost completely covered in tattoos—they even trailed in lines of script down her face. Whatever wasn't inked glinted with silver piercings, and her dark hair was done in tight twists, piled messily up on her head and showcasing her tattooed neck.

She wore a Grecian-style red dress thing, and stood with her hands on her hips, surveying each of us silently in turn.

"Sit," she commanded, waving a hand lazily. A wooden bench materialized behind us, scooting into the back of our knees at enough speed to make all of us fall onto it clumsily. She conjured up a slightly grander seat in front of us, folding herself into it elegantly.

It was only a chair, but it was very much a reminder of how powerless we were here. She'd just made furniture out of thin air, for fuck's sake.

"The Spirit of Dreams," she said, staring at Bullet.

"Hecate, goddess of magic, witchcraft, the night, moon, ghosts and necromancy," Bullet responded instantly, like this was a goddamn pop quiz.

Her lips twitched. "Indeed. What to call the rest of you? Only one of you has a grand title, that won't do. You, girl. What have the King and Queen of the Underworld been calling you?"

"Grace the agathos." My girl's eyes were as wide as I'd ever seen them, one hand gripping my thigh, the other resting tentatively on Wild's forearm, with Bullet on my other side. I wondered if she'd even realized she'd reached for Wild—he certainly didn't seem to be complaining about it.

"Grace the agathos," Hecate scoffed. "You see what I'm dealing with? Excellent rulers, of course, but no sense of *poetry*. I suppose I shall have to come up with something."

This was, without a doubt, the weirdest conversation I'd ever had in my life.

Hecate looked at me for a moment, before turning her assessing glare onto Wild. "No titles for you two. A Moros and Keres," she snorted. "As far as daimons go, you could not be any less interesting. Why the Fates chose you two, I have no idea."

Grace frowned, opening her mouth to object because her self-preservation instincts went out the window when her bonded were involved, but both Wild and I grabbed a hand at the same time, giving it a warning squeeze that surprised her back into silence.

"But what to call *you*," Hecate mused, staring at Grace again. "I suppose if you succeed, they'll call you 'the liberator' or something equally as grand."

"Do you want us to succeed?" Grace asked, tilting her head to the side. I did my best to beam *'what the fuck'* into her head with my eyeballs and the bond because were we really going to encourage this? I would argue that we had a net zero of positive experiences with divinities so far, and I'd really prefer to never engage with any of them again.

"No deity should be left unchecked, and Gaia has gone unchecked for far too long," Hecate responded solemnly, nodding her head. "If nothing else, the upperworld is *very* dull now. It was much more fun when there were gods and goddesses who liked to pop in now and then, play with the mortals and keep things interesting."

"Fun for who?" I muttered, vaguely appalled. Now it was Grace's turn to squeeze *my* hand.

"Oh relax, Moros. Mortals are so boring," Hecate mumbled, rolling her eyes. "Things were on a more even playing field for humans then too, you know. Wealthy kings could be cut down to size, poor peasants could rise to greatness, or even just earn Demeter's favor and a generous harvest. Gaia cares not for such trivial things—either the humans worship her and treat her creation with reverence and she is happy—or they do not, and she is angry. Yes, she set her precious agathos loose in the world to do good, but only a little at a time. Eutychia doesn't last long," she added, giving Grace a pointed look.

Hecate sighed, lounging back on her chair. "Then again, there is no guarantee that the Olympians will be just, or that their time in captivity has humbled them. There is no assurance that mortals will come off better, even if it seems as though things couldn't get much worse from the perspective of those mortals who have nothing. There are so few with so much, and so much with so few."

Grace frowned in confusion, and Hecate gave her a feline smile. "Your Spirit of Dreams failed to mention that I am also the Goddess of Crossroads. You, my dear, are at a crossroads."

Well, on that we could agree at least.

"What would you do?" Grace asked quietly. Hecate seemed surprised by the question, her eyebrows hitching ever so slightly.

"What an interesting thought," she mused, adjusting one of the thick silver cuffs on her wrist. "You have asked me the one question that is impossible for an immortal to answer—what would I do if I were mortal? I cannot say. A hundred years is longer than most of you live, and a blink of the eye to me. That sense of urgency that spurs mortals into action, that make them do rash things because they're running out of time, that is something no divine being can truly understand. Just one mortal's life, fleeting as it is, can change the course of history. Fascinating creatures, you are."

Way to not answer the question at all.

"Come," Hecate said, standing suddenly and extending her hand to Grace. "You're wanted back in the throne room, Thanatos has returned."

Grace tentatively pulled her hand out of mine, placing it in Hecate's.

And then she disappeared.

GRACE

CHAPTER 14

I stumbled for a moment, holding out my arms in the empty space in front of me. Somehow, I was back in the empty throne room, *alone*. Where had Hecate gone? How had I got here?

"Don't panic," I muttered under my breath, my limbs shaking violently as I straightened, wrapping my arms around my middle. "Don't panic, Grace."

Except I was panicking because I had no idea where Riot, Bullet and Wild were. Why had they separated us? I wasn't so naive as to think these underworld gods *cared* about me, but I thought they'd been on our side. Separating me from my soul bonds seemed like a not-on-our-side thing to do.

As scary as I found all the deities we'd interacted with so far, being abandoned by them in the underworld was absolutely worse.

"Hello?" I called a little louder into the empty room, my voice echoing around the huge space ominously.

Nothing.

Was this some kind of test? Did they want me to *do* something? I fiddled with the hemline of my sweater nervously, feeling extra ridiculous that I was standing in a grand throne room wearing a blush-colored hoodie, matching sweatpants, and no shoes.

In the absence of any better ideas, I moved into the center of the room, taking a moment to look at the mural on the ceiling above me. It was... horrifying, really. The most beautiful piece of artwork I'd ever seen, undoubtedly created by some gifted immortal being, but horrifying nonetheless.

I recognized Thanatos in the far left corner—a much less glamorous version of him without the sparkly suit—shepherding what appeared to be souls towards a swirling mass in the center that I guessed was meant to be the underworld. There were other deities, and it took me a moment to realize they were *daimons*.

A collection of women with vicious looking wings and faces twisted into snarls, brandishing swords at battling mortals dominated one corner. Keres, perhaps? Were those fearsome women the founders of Wild's line?

The founder of Riot's line was obvious. A grim-looking bearded man whispering in the ears of mortals who reached willingly for the swirling portal of death.

But Thanatos was real, corporeal, we'd seen him with our own eyes. Did that mean the others were still around too? Living out their retirement in the underworld, perhaps?

The doors at the other end of the enormous room swung open with a bang, stopping my musing and making me jump. Sparkly Thanatos appeared in the entryway, giving me a chilling smile that I attempted to politely return because I didn't want him to kill me. I absolutely understood what Wild had meant about him not always being so friendly—there was definitely a scarier side hiding beneath that thin veneer of civility.

Thanatos said nothing, just stared for a moment before standing aside to let someone pass while he hung back. A beautiful woman of Asian descent seemed to glide into the room, giving her waist-length black hair an imperious flick as red and purple eyes came to land on me, one perfectly arched eyebrow rising in an impressive show of judgment for a dead woman. And she was absolutely dead. I didn't know exactly how I could tell, her body still appeared solid, but there a strange dullness to her that was difficult to comprehend. Like her internal light had gone out.

She was tall and elegant, perhaps my mother's age or a little younger, and wearing a simple black peplos that she picked at uncomfortably. Was the black peplos standard issue for souls here? I kind of wished I'd been given one, though I was also exceptionally glad to be... not dead.

"Who are you?" the woman asked, sashaying over to me without a care in the world. Maybe that's what happened when you died? "Ah, an agathos." She grimaced, her hand ghosting over her midsection. "I had hoped to never see one of your kind again."

"Did they... did an agathos... Is that why you're here?" I settled on eventually, dreading the answer.

"Kill me? Oh yes. They broke into my house while I was cooking dinner, stabbed me in the stomach. Barbarians."

Only the fact that I was *starving* prevented me from throwing up. "I'm so sorry. So sorry. That is... That is awful."

"I suppose it could have been worse, at least it was all over quite quickly." She shrugged. "I disliked the idea of growing old and frail, at least I don't have to worry about that anymore."

"I guess not," I agreed faintly. Why was I here? Had Persephone wanted me to see the horror that the agathos wrought first hand?

151

She tilted her head to the side curiously. "You're Grace the agathos, aren't you? From Auburn?"

"That's me," I replied with a weak smile. "Grace the agathos."

"Are you dead?" she asked before I could politely enquire as to what her name was.

"Um, not that I know of."

"Well, thank the gods for that," she sighed. "As far as I know, you're the only tolerable agathos in existence, it would be a pity if you'd died already. I've never seen daimons come together over anything until you and your cause."

"What do they think my cause is?" I asked, genuinely curious.

"The freedom to choose, despite whatever your awful goddess thinks. Perhaps daimons wouldn't be disregarded as third-class citizens—below both humans and agathos—if we had agathos lovers of our own."

"They're my soul bonds, not just my lovers. Relationships gifted by the Fates... I think they like the idea of bringing us all together too."

She gave me an assessing look. "I have a son. He's a good son. Not a very good daimon, but I think I prefer him that way. Perhaps I should have told him that."

"He probably knows," I told her gently, remembering the acrimonious phone call I'd overheard between Riot and his father. She may be an older daimon, but she didn't seem anything like Riot's dad.

"Perhaps," she agreed. "He was a real mother hen of a son. He will worry, and be sad. That distresses me, I find. I hope he discovers an agathos soul bond of his own someday too. He would be good to her."

There was something in her gaze that made me think she was saying more than what she let on, but before I had a chance to figure it out, Thanatos appeared in the doorway, a looming specter of darkness and sequins.

"Time's up. This was a gift to you, Grace the agathos," the God of Death rumbled. "I hope you used it well. Let's go," he added, tipping his chin towards the woman. His voice was gruff but not unkind, and it gave me the faintest sliver of hope.

Taking away Wild's voice had been cruel, but maybe he'd just had an off-day or something. Surely, even immortal beings got carried away in the heat of the moment and did things they regretted. Gaia had shown me that deities were completely capable of irrational overreactions.

"Thanatos," I said quickly, before he could disappear again. "God of Death," I added respectfully, bowing slightly.

He tilted his head to the side in acknowledgment, watching me impassively. My knees trembled, either from nerves or exhaustion or both, but I knew I'd look back on this opportunity with regret for the rest of my life if I didn't at least try.

"It's about Wild. I just... I understand the hubris of what he said, and that you had to punish him for it." And I *did* understand that, even if I didn't like or approve of it. Gods were fickle. "But hasn't he suffered enough? Wild's connection to me means he's got a target on his back and his life is only going to get harder from here even without the curse..."

I swallowed thickly, my bravado faltering under Thanatos' unblinking stare and the curious gaze of the daimon woman.

"The word of gods is adamantine, Grace the agathos. It cannot be broken, dissolved or undone, not even by the one who issued the edict."

My chest felt like it caved in a little under the weight of those words. Wild's curse was *permanent*? What did that mean for him? For Bullet and the Oneiroi curse I tried so hard to ignore? Could *nothing* be done?

Thanatos watched me closely, scrutinizing my reaction. "However, they can be *changed*. Modified. Loopholes found, that sort of thing."

153

"Really?" I breathed, looking at him with wide eyes.

Thanatos nodded, tilting his head back and looking down his nose at me. "Yes. But I will not. I'm sure if you are successful in your task and liberate The Twelve, you will be handsomely rewarded for it," he added dismissively, giving me his back.

I could taste my disappointment. It had been a long shot, but I wanted so much to help Wild. To free him from this curse for both his benefit and my own. I loved hearing him speak, and knowing that it was only temporary was painful.

"I'm glad I got to meet you, Grace the agathos," the woman said softly, turning to follow him. "On a day of terrible surprises, this was a nice one."

"I'm glad I got to meet you too," I replied quietly, watching her leave. I didn't exactly know what this meeting meant or why Persephone had gifted it to me, but I was going to hold it close to my heart and remember it for the rest of my days, that much I was certain of. Every time I was afraid or overwhelmed by the task ahead, I would remember her, murdered in cold blood in her kitchen.

Perhaps that was the point. Perhaps Persephone felt I wasn't motivated enough.

"Grace!"

I whirled around as my three soul bonds ran across the throne room towards me, Riot reaching me first and snatching me off the ground, half hugging me, half patting me down for injuries.

"Are you okay?" Bullet asked, trying and failing to pull me free of Riot's grip before giving up and hugging my back. "What happened?"

Wild stood behind Riot, and I reached over Riot's shoulder before I could second-guess myself, brushing my fingertips over Wild's jaw.

"I met a daimon who was killed by some agathos," I replied thickly, pulling my hand back and squeezing Riot's shoulders before wriggling back down to the ground. "I guess Persephone wanted me to talk to her. To see someone directly affected by the violence. They broke into her house," I choked out, rubbing my sternum the same way she had.

"And we're supposed to take what lesson from that?" Riot asked bitterly. "Because if it's 'work together with the agathos,' I'm not on board."

"Me neither," Wild agreed, cracking his knuckles ominously.

"What do *you* think the lesson was meant to be?" Bullet asked, taking my hands and tugging me towards him.

"I think... I think she was a human face—or a daimon face—to this conflict. A reminder of how they've suffered. How senseless it all is."

"Did you recognize her?" Riot rasped.

"No. She never told me her name." I wished she had, I should have asked. I wanted to be able to put a name to the face when I remembered her.

"What do we do now?" I asked, cringing as my stomach let out a loud rumble. I'd been growing increasingly hungry and thirsty while we'd been here, and it was getting to alarming levels. It seemed like we'd just landed here a couple of hours ago at most, but my body strongly disagreed with that assessment. I was *famished*, and way too dehydrated for just a couple of hours. Time must pass differently here.

I also knew the number one rule of the underworld was don't consume anything.

"Can we leave?" Riot murmured, looking around the now empty hall like he was getting ready to make a break for it.

"You can, actually." Persephone's sudden appearance, seemingly out of a wall, made all of us jump. Apparently, the rules of physics didn't apply

155

in this entire scary realm. "You are healed, you are informed on the prophecy, and Gaia is off your trail for now. Come along, I'll take you to the gate," Persephone continued, sweeping her emerald peplos majestically behind her as she turned and began walking towards one of the walls of columns. "It is time for you to return to the upperworld and fulfill your destiny."

The Queen of the Underworld led us through surprisingly brightly lit marble corridors, along a riverbank of water so black I was too scared to look into it, and then to a rocky tunnel of sorts with a low ceiling, sloping upwards like we could literally just walk back to the world above. It was a little unsettling, to say the least.

"Follow the tunnel, it will bring you to the surface," Persephone instructed. I guessed it was too much to hope that we'd get a fancy portal back out again. "A day has passed while you have been here."

Another day of my life just *poof*, gone.

"Thank you for all of your help," I told her nervously, terrified that my thank you to Persephone would somehow end like my thank you to Gaia had. I would be forever wary of showing my gratitude to goddesses, even knowing that *not* showing my gratitude was probably a higher risk.

"Oh, and before you go," Persephone called, making us all pause at the base of the slope, "I have a gift for you."

Bullet's eyes widened with panic that didn't have anything to do with visions of the future. He'd spent plenty of time emphasizing to me in our lessons how double-edged a gifted sword from a god could be.

But saying no wasn't an option either.

She seemed to glide towards us, stopping right in front of me and producing a dark brown leather pouch—not much bigger than my palm—from somewhere within the folds of her garment.

Not wanting to risk offending her, I accepted it with a smile that only grew more brittle as whatever was in the pouch *rattled*.

"Will I... know the right time to open it?" I asked, feeling a little like Pandora with her amphora of daimons, ready to release havoc on the world.

Persephone scoffed. "No. Frankly, I trust no mortal's judgment—you are barely around long enough to learn basic common sense. Scatter these in the soil when you need to make a big gesture, to *demonstrate* divinity, to force them to pay attention, but only when you are ready to truly come out of hiding and announce yourself to the world. Make sure you have a lot of room around you, and it will infuriate Gaia. You have been warned."

"So I have," I replied faintly, gripping the pouch tightly lest whatever was inside accidentally slipped out. Some kind of seeds? Divine seeds? I wasn't sure I wanted to know. I carefully tucked the leather pouch into the pocket of my sweatpants, hoping I never needed to find out.

"Ah, one more thing," Persephone added, reaching for me and pressing an ice-cold hand to my forehead. I froze in place—whether from fear or magic, I wasn't sure. Probably magic, if the frustrated and alarmed expressions on Wild, Bullet and Riot were any indication. Before I could open my mouth to question it, a splitting pain hit me between my eyes. If my legs hadn't been somehow locked in place, the pain would have taken me to my knees. Something needled its way into my mind, burrowing into my psyche, ravaging, *searching*.

'Ah, there it is,' Persephone's voice whispered, echoing inside my mind. There was a ripping sensation inside my brain, like she'd grabbed a band-aid and *pulled*, tearing off a chunk of flesh with it. There was a brief moment of excruciating pain, and then dark, blissful nothingness.

GRACE

CHAPTER 15

"Grace!" Riot yelled, his heartbeat thundering against my ear. "Wake up, Gracie!"

"She's stirring," Wild's low voice murmured. "Stop shouting at her."

"I'm awake, I'm awake," I assured Riot groggily, blinking at my surroundings. We were still at the base of the slope, all three guys kneeling on the ground around me, hovering with very concerned looks on their faces. "Where's Persephone?"

"Gone," Wild muttered, cutting a glare into the darkness behind him.

"What did she do to you?" Riot asked, helping me to my feet when I pushed upwards. "She wouldn't say. Bullet doesn't know."

Bullet looked distraught about that too, keeping his distance from me and wringing his hands nervously together. He looked so boyish for a moment that it reminded me of the very first time he'd told me he had a crush on me, standing on a beach in the dreamscape when we were teenagers.

I sucked in a breath, freezing in place.

"What is it?" Riot asked urgently.

I opened my mouth to explain before slamming it shut again, so overwhelmed that it felt impossible to speak. Oh goddess, I was definitely crying again. My poor soul bonds probably wondered what they were going to do with me, I was constantly weeping on them.

But I couldn't help myself this time because it was all there in my memories, *all* of it. All the memories Bullet had been carrying alone. Every first meeting, every beautiful dream Bullet had ever created for me, every devastating confession he'd made knowing I wouldn't recall it when I woke up. I remembered everything.

I stumbled out of Riot's embrace and collapsed against Bullet, gripping his sweater tightly as I bawled into his chest, memories running through my mind like a video reel of us playing together as children, or walking under the moonlight as adults while I confided in this stranger each day about my life, knowing deep down that he was my soul bond but unable to line up that knowledge with the fact he was a daimon.

And the futures... So many futures he'd shown me. Beautiful ones, filled with love and laughter and a gnawing kind of *absence,* because Bullet wasn't in them.

"I remember," I managed to get out, sobbing messily into his chest. Bullet's arms wrapped around me tightly, holding me in place. "I remember all of it. Every dream. Every meeting. Everything. Persephone removed whatever was hiding them somehow."

The number of times Bullet had confided in me that he knew his days were numbered, the anger he felt as a kid when he'd first realized what his future had in store for him... By the gods, it hurt. It hurt so much that he'd gone through this all alone. That he'd confessed it to me and I'd just woken up and gone on with my day like it was nothing because he'd always been sure to end things on a positive note. Always thinking of me and accommodating me and *loving* me.

I gasped, struggling to take a proper breath. He'd been suffering for so long and even when we were together, even after I'd fallen in love with him and we'd bonded, I still hadn't truly comprehended the depth of what he'd experienced.

"I'm so sorry," I chanted, my voice strangled. "Bullet, I'm so, so sorry."

"It's okay, Amazing Grace. There was nothing you could have done. Please don't cry." He shook slightly, as though he was trying to contain his own emotions. "I don't like it when you cry. How do I make you stop? Do you want me to sing to you? I'll sing to you."

"We need to go," Wild murmured as I made an ungainly hiccup-like laughing sound against Bullet's chest. "We're not meant to be in this realm. We need food and water."

"Right, you're right," I agreed shakily, forcing myself to take a step back but grabbing Bullet's hand and linking our fingers together. "There'll be time for us to process all of this once we're in the upperworld again."

Riot nodded, though he didn't look confident as he took point, guiding us up the narrow reddish-brown slope, smooth earth beneath our feet.

"Do you think this is going to take us back to Connecticut?" he asked, not sounding very hopeful.

"Definitely not," Wild said quietly, startling me with his proximity to Bullet and I. He was right at our backs, looking around defensively.

"What happened last time you left the underworld?" Riot called back over his shoulder.

"I emerged near Naples, Italy. I didn't take this path though. Mine was rockier than this."

"You just appeared in Italy?" I asked, gripping Bullet's hand a little tighter. "How does that even work? How did you get home?"

"With great difficulty," Wild replied, voice grim. "And that was when I lived in the UK."

Sugar. How were we supposed to cross an ocean without passports? The gods really had no consideration for mortal struggles.

"I'm holding out hope that we'll land in the Appalachians or something," Riot grumbled. "If this is a different path, maybe it's the US-friendly option."

Bullet snorted. "Wow, shit is dire when *Riot* is the most optimistic one in the group."

"Not *that* optimistic," Riot countered. "I'm wondering how many earthquakes we've missed in a day."

I gnawed nervously on my lower lip at that thought. If we emerged somewhere else, was Gaia going to keep torturing the area around the falls where we'd last been? How many innocent people would be hurt or have their lives affected because of me?

"On that note," Wild sighed, still sounding like he was forcing himself to speak even though he found it unnatural. "There was an earthquake in Milton the night before we... arrived here."

The night before we were kidnapped by Thanatos.

"How bad?" I asked, dreading the answer. That dread only grew stronger the longer Wild was quiet.

"Your apartment building was flattened. No survivors," he said eventually, his voice gruff. "The rest of Milton wasn't so badly affected."

161

"She targeted my building," I repeated numbly, thinking of my innocent human neighbors. We hadn't been close, and honestly, I'd gone out of my way to avoid them a lot of the time, needing a break from using my gift. "Surely she knew I wasn't there. That it wasn't me she'd be hurting."

"Yes," Wild said simply, because what else was there to say? More blood on my hands, which were already feeling thick with it after meeting the woman in the underworld who'd been murdered in cold blood in her home.

We struggled up the steep pathway, fighting to catch our breath, and I wept for her, and I wept for the humans who'd died, and the pain Bullet had shared with me over the years that I'd been forced to forget. He held my hand the entire way, his own emotions a turbulent swirl through the bond, jaw set tight.

We'd learned so much on this unexpected excursion to the underworld, and I didn't think any of us were going to emerge from this tunnel the same as we'd come in.

"I asked Thanatos to lift your curse," I told Wild, panting slightly with each word, and glad he was behind me so I couldn't see the disappointment in his face. "He said that's not how the gods' magic works. That whatever they decree, it just is from then on. That it can only be modified, not undone."

"Adamantine Law," Bullet murmured in quiet agreement, a gnawing sense of pity flowing through the bond.

"He refused to modify it. He said... he said that if we freed the Olympians, we'd probably be rewarded for it."

Wild snorted. "Well I suppose we know now that Thanatos is pro-prophecy, if he's using it as motivation."

"Is it?" Riot asked from up ahead. "Motivation for you?"

"I would help Grace fulfill the prophecy if that's what she wants to do regardless of whatever is in it for me," Wild replied immediately, a hint of rumbling warning in his voice that sent a shiver down my spine. "Should we be successful and my curse is somehow lessened, that would be a bonus. But I've lived with it for five years now, I get by just fine."

"Better than fine," I agreed readily, thinking of all the employees Wild managed without speaking a word. I didn't want him to think that I thought less of him because of his curse, or that it would be a deal breaker for me. "I'm disappointed for your sake Thanatos said no, but I think you're amazing as you are, Wild."

He made a slightly strangled sound and amusement flooded the bonds from both Riot and Bullet.

"Thank you," Wild said eventually. He obviously didn't get enough compliments. I was going to do something about that.

"And I'm grateful that you'll help me fulfill the prophecy, but please don't feel like you have to. If we get out of here and you want to go straight back to your life in Milton, I won't hold it against you," I promised. I *would* be quietly devastated, but he didn't need to know that. He didn't need that kind of pressure.

"I'm going to help you," Wild said determinedly. I glanced back over my shoulder, nodding in understanding. It wasn't a promise of anything *more*, and maybe there would never be anything more, but if he wanted to stay and help see the prophecy through, I wasn't going to say no.

We'd deal with the rest as it came.

Light filtered in slowly, a different kind to the flat light that made it possible to see in the underworld even though there seemed to be no particular source. There was a huff of irritation behind me and I glimpsed back, finding Wild massaging his throat.

163

"You can't speak?" I asked quietly. He shook his head, glowering furiously at the ground. Hoping that he wasn't entirely unreceptive to it, I reached back quickly to give his hand a reassuring squeeze, and was surprised when he held on, lightly pulling me out of Bullet's grip.

Bullet looked at him, eyebrows raised for a moment, before moving ahead to fall into step with Riot.

Okay, well hand holding was definite progress. Maybe eventually there would be *more*, and he wouldn't just help us out then go back to the already-established life he'd built for himself.

But if he doesn't want *this to be any more than it is now...*

That was okay. It had to be. He didn't owe me anything, and I hoped that if he decided to walk away, we could still be friends.

"You know, the underworld was nothing like I thought it was going to be," I told him, sort of for the sake of talking. "I imagined it being more tomb-like. Dark. But it wasn't. It was kind of nice even—except for the scary mural on the ceiling. Even the daimon woman who'd just been *murdered* seemed quite relaxed there."

"There's probably a little relief too," Riot said quietly, not turning back. "Daimons are so ruled by their instincts, it's incessant. Maybe it was quite peaceful to die and not feel those constant urges to haunt and torture and ruin anymore."

Bullet nodded silently in agreement and Wild's fingers flexed slightly around mine.

If the gods and the Fates and whoever else wanted me to fulfill this prophecy, I had a few stipulations of my own, I decided. It was cruel that agathos and daimons were second-class mortals, existing to prop up or tear down humans and having our own control of our lives stripped away from us. I was going to fight for *us* too, because somebody finally had to.

There was a narrow rock opening at the top of the tunnel and it took all four of us to pry away the debris blocking it enough for us to fit through. To my surprise, Wild set his hands on my shoulders and guided me firmly back between Riot and Bullet, giving us all a look that clearly said *I'll go first.*

Wild was so broad and bulky, I wasn't entirely confident he would fit, but he turned sideways and squeezed through the narrow gap in the rock, reaching in a hand to help Bullet through when he lined up next.

"Come on," Riot said warily. "Don't let go of my hand, Gracie."

"So far so good," Bullet called through the gap, his voice echoing slightly. "It's more rocks, but now with the bonus of them being slimy and gross. And no pathway. Peachy."

I sucked in a breath as I squeezed through the opening, still gripping Riot's hand while Wild gently took my elbow from the other side to help me through. It *was* slimy in here. That far-off light source that had illuminated the tunnel seemed just as far away in... whatever this was. A cave? There was a quiet drip, drip, dripping sound, and the air was cold. It definitely *felt* like a cave.

"I'll go first," Riot announced, stepping around us. There was some tension between him and Wild, undoubtedly from that fight they'd had years ago, and it surprised me a little that Riot was so willing to leave me with Wild rather than stick by me himself.

Maybe there was a little more trust there than he was letting on.

Or maybe there was posturing happening. It could have been that.

I stayed close to Wild's side as we began climbing over slippery rocks and carefully dodging hanging stalactites. We were still heading up, I was pretty sure, though with only the faint far-off light we were following, it was hard to tell.

"Fuck's sake," Riot muttered from up ahead. "Can everyone swim?"

"I don't think it's very far, if it helps," Bullet added, scrambling up behind Riot and squinting into the distance. Wild and I emerged over the ridge of rocks, finding ourselves facing a still pool, thousands of stalactites hanging above it.

"I'm not the strongest swimmer," I admitted. *Because of my control freak mother and her modesty rules.* "If it's not too far, I'll be fine."

Wild pressed his arm against mine, and I knew without him telling me that he would stick close to me the whole way across.

"Do you reckon there's anything living in there?" Riot asked, kneeling on the edge of the rocks and peering into the dark water.

'*Yes.*'

"Yes," I repeated automatically, drawing everyone's eyes to mine. "Oh no, it's that voice again. I really am losing my mind, aren't I?"

Bullet laughed. "After the day we've had, surely you know by now that nothing is impossible. Even hearing the voice of a god."

"When else did you hear this voice?" Riot asked, sounding much more wary.

"Remember Felix?" I asked. Riot shook his head. "He's one of the bonded of the agathos woman who died—"

"The one the Basilinna wanted you to replace," Riot muttered, a surge of unnecessary jealousy rising through the bond.

"Right. When I called him to warn him what the Basilinna wanted to do, I heard the voice again. And then at the community center when

166

I was praying to Gaia, the voice told me how to do it. And right before Thanatos appeared."

Wild tapped on my arm to get my attention, and I watched carefully in the darkness as he slowly signed to me.

I heard it. He looked briefly frustrated, staring at his hands before mouthing 'waterfall.'

"You heard her speak to you at the falls? After the earthquake?" I confirmed. Wild nodded. Well, at least it wasn't just me hearing things. That was comforting.

"If you hear a deity whispering in your ear, you shouldn't ignore it," Bullet said sagely. Riot gaped at him.

Look amongst the rocks. I could have sworn the voice sounded faintly amused.

"She says we should look amongst the rocks," I relayed, face growing hot.

"Then we look," Bullet shrugged, as though it were that easy.

"Yup, I guess we look," Riot agreed, only somewhat sarcastically. "I guess we're just cool with listening to strange voices, no questions asked, now."

Bullet and Riot split up, clambering over the jagged boulders, while Wild gripped my arm to keep me in place, shaking his head slightly and giving the water a pointed look.

Did he not want me to fall in? That was kind of sweet. In broad daylight, I could probably swim enough to flail my way back to the rocks, but the darkness was absolutely terrifying. I felt like if I fell into *that* water, I'd lose all sense of what was up and what was down.

"Did she tell you how to find us?" I asked Wild quietly. He nodded again, frowning slightly. I had no idea which goddess had deigned to speak to us, but at least it seemed like this one was on our side.

"Got it," Bullet called. "Riot, come give me a hand."

Riot moved across the rocks with just enough speed to terrify me, climbing down into a crevasse with Bullet where I could only just see the tops of their heads. I urged Wild closer, and he maintained a vice-like grip on me as we made our way over the boulders to where they were wrenching an ancient-looking rowboat out from the dry nook it had been sitting in.

Wild gently guided me to sit on a flat boulder and I pressed my lips together to stop myself laughing out loud at his fussing. Like it was nothing at all, Wild leaned over the side of the ditch and hauled the boat free, Bullet and Riot guiding it up until it was sitting on the rocks in front of me.

"Show off," Riot muttered. Wild shot him a cocky smirk that I probably shouldn't have found as attractive as I did, while I kneeled down in front of the boat, pulling my sleeve down over my hand to rub at the dirt on the side of the vessel.

"How old do you think this is?" I asked, scrubbing away at the mud. It was made of wood and while it definitely looked aged, the structure was surprisingly solid.

"Old," Bullet replied with a grimace, dropping down next to me to look at the writing I'd uncovered.

κτῆμα ἐς ἀεί

"*Ktema es aei*," Bullet read, startling Riot and Wild.

"You don't need your dictionary this time?" I teased, bumping him with my shoulder.

"Not for this one," Bullet shot back with a grin. "This one, I remember. It means 'a possession forever', something timeless, like art or literature."

"It is kind of a work of art," I pointed out, rubbing at the dirt to unveil more decorative figures carved into the wood. "Hopefully it's watertight. Ready to get out of here?"

"And find out what country we're in?" Riot added drily. "Very."

Wild and Riot picked up the boat and moved it to the water's edge, and I held my breath as they dropped it the short distance where it landed with a splash. All four of us watched in silence as it rocked for a moment before settling in place.

"Let's get in before it floats away," Bullet announced cheerfully, half climbing, half falling off the boulders into the boat.

"Bullet!" I squeaked. "Give me some warning, would you?"

He grinned back at me, entirely unrepentant. "Come on down, let's go sailing."

"I'll go first, I don't trust him to catch you," Riot said, climbing down the rocks ahead of me while Bullet gripped the ledge to keep the boat in place.

Wild gave me an encouraging nod the moment Riot was settled, and I did my best to channel someone who wasn't afraid of falling to her death in a freezing cold cave as I climbed down slowly, Wild hovering above with one arm outstretched like he'd catch me if I slipped. Riot's hands reached up, settling on my hips and guiding me into the safety of the boat and I exhaled embarrassingly loudly in relief.

Wild didn't hesitate, and I gripped the edge as the boat rocked at the addition of a fourth person. Riot and Wild pulled the oars free and set them up while I stuck as closely as I could to the center of the vessel while trying to look into the dark depths of the water at the same time.

That voice said there were things living in there, and a morbidly curious part of me wanted to know what things were.

169

'Things' could be fish.

'Things' could be strange monstrous and mythological creatures of the gods.

'Things' was a very broad term.

"Do you really want to know?" Bullet asked, arching an eyebrow at me. "If Charybdis is down there, ready to make a whirlpool to suck us down into the depths, I think I'd prefer to be in the dark about it."

"You are terrible at comforting people," Riot observed. "Did you know that?"

"It would be unfair if I was great at everything," Bullet conceded, amethyst eyes sparkling with mischief. Those beautiful eyes that I'd been so intimidated by for so long when I met him in the dreamscape. Every night he'd come to me, and every night I'd been alarmed at the sight of a daimon in my dreams. Fortunately, it seemed I'd never responded with my mother's hysteria which was good, but I hadn't always been warm and welcoming either. I'd been scared—intimidated by what the presence of a daimon in my dreams meant, whether it meant the monster inside me was more than just agathos paranoia and a figment of my imagination.

It didn't take us long to cross the small body of water, and the moment we climbed out of the boat on the other side, it began drifting away to where it came from.

"In spite of all we've seen recently, I still find that weird," Riot remarked as we followed the light towards the mouth of the cave, sinking into knee-deep mud with each step.

"I think I'd be worried if you didn't," I replied, keeping my eyes trained forward instead of watching the creepy unmanned boat navigating the lake. "Reminding ourselves that none of this is normal is probably a wise thing for our sanity."

'Step into the mud where the symbol is. You will pass through.'

The light *did* seem to be filtering through a wall of mud somehow, and it didn't take long to find the spot the goddess described, with a faint symbol on it that I didn't recognize.

"Grace..." Riot warned as I moved further away from them, but it was too late. I leaned ever so slightly on the patch of wall and fell right through with a gasp, landing on my hands and knees on some rocks sharp enough to cut my hands.

"Shoot. *Shit*," I added, standing up and attempting to elbow my way back into the dark cave. The sunlight was almost blinding, and it took me a moment to realize I was hidden in a shallow, rocky cave that was definitely in the upperworld. The air was warm and smelled of the sea, and the sky outside was a brilliant shade of blue. We were out.

Or rather *I* was out.

Before I could spiral into a full-on panic attack at having left my soul bonds in the underworld, Bullet's body crashed through the dirt into mine, knocking me back onto the uneven ground.

"Shit!" he swore, quickly rolling off me and half lifting, half dragging me out of the way. "I don't mean to sound like a dick, but you really shouldn't stand in the doorway."

Riot and Wild came through in quick succession, knocking into each other and exchanging glares.

"See?" Bullet murmured, tugging me out towards the mouth of the cave, half hidden by stacks of rocks that looked like they'd been placed there deliberately. "Imagine if *Wild* had knocked into you. You'd probably be unconscious," he added with a slightly delirious laugh, excited as I was to be out in the fresh air. Sunshine had never felt so good on my skin.

"Oh, we are *so* not in Kansas anymore, Toto," Bullet murmured, nudging Riot with his arm.

"Look at the ocean," I said, walking over the dry rocky ground towards the cliff edge we were standing on in a trance. "Is this Naples?" I asked Wild, turning back to look at him.

He shook his head, hesitating for a moment before signing the letters 'G-R-E-E-C-E.'

"Greece?" I repeated dumbly. "We're in *Greece*?"

'*Maybe*,' Wild signed, looking out over the ocean with a frown, shrugging. I supposed we could be anywhere in the Mediterranean, though I wouldn't have the first clue where. I'd never left North America.

"How the fuck do we get home from Europe?" Riot asked. He pulled out his bronze dragon lighter as he often did when he was nervous, flipping it open and flicking it to light it. He looked down with a frown as it failed to start, thumb dragging the wheel impatiently a few times to no effect. "I just refilled this."

Wild pulled out his phone and hope briefly swelled in my chest that we had a means of communication, but then he sighed heavily, turning to show us the screen. It looked like the inside of the device had *melted*. The phone he'd given me hadn't been in my pocket when Thanatos showed up, but Riot gave up on the light and pulled his cracked device out, huffing a frustrated laugh when his device looked the same.

Bullet was already shuffling his tarot cards—in immaculate condition as always—squinting against the bright sunlight. "Okay, phones are out. We need to find somewhere to stay and regroup. I don't want to be on the edge of a cliff when Gaia notices us again."

"I second that," Riot agreed.

Wild was already moving, walking determinedly inland, and Riot, Bullet and I exchanged a bewildered glance before heading after him. Riot hated making decisions, and Bullet relied heavily on the cards and Nyx to tell him what to do, while I had basically had any leadership skills trained out of me by my mother who'd wanted me to be as invisible as possible.

It looked like our little group had found ourselves a decision maker.

CHAPTER 16

I stood in the aftermath of the massacre in my mother's apartment, looking at the carnage the local daimons were in the process of cleaning up but not *seeing* it. Vaguely, I was aware that my mom's usually spotless stainless-steel kitchen was splattered with red blood. I'd had just enough presence of mind to call Axe when I came home and found my mother's body, knowing that we needed to get the scene cleaned up before the human authorities got involved—or worse, more agathos—but I hadn't moved since.

Not when Axe and a few other local Keres I'd met while I'd been staying in Jersey let themselves into the house under the dark of night, equipped with a heavy white sheet and industrial cleaning supplies. Not when they respectfully laid the sheet over my mother's body, or began cleaning up the evidence around her, or when the stringent smell of bleach filled the room.

Do something, I told myself weakly. *Move. Help them. Anything.*

Daylight would be breaking soon. We needed to be done here before my mom's human neighbors woke up.

My limbs didn't seem to be getting the memo.

Everything felt so barely contained, so fragile. I didn't know if I wanted to cry or go out and stab the first agathos I saw in the gut just to get some goddamn *justice*. The fact that they were still strutting around the streets, self-righteous as fuck, acting like they were the *good* guys in all of this made me feel like a Keres daimon right before a battle. They'd invaded my mother's home, her safe space, and *executed* her.

"Dare," Axe said solemnly, pausing in front of me. "We need to get out of here. We need to move... her. There's a daimon at the local crematorium."

I nodded absently, staring at nothing. Why had I gone out tonight? There were enough daimons here to guard their own businesses and properties, they didn't need me. I should have been at home with her.

"Dare," Axe said sharply. "I'll do my bit to handle the human cops—hopefully those agathos fuckers have done enough damage and their cops stay the hell out of it—but you need to do your bit."

I blinked at him, attempting to clear my head. What was my bit? What was I meant to be doing?

"Get out of here," Axe continued, holding my eye. "Go back to Milton. I'd bet my left nut the agathos targeted this house because there aren't any daimons nearby to deter them. You need to go back to your community, all daimons need to band together right now to keep ourselves fucking *alive*, you hear me?"

"I'll pack my stuff." Was that my voice? It sounded far away.

Axe clapped me on the shoulder. "I'm not kicking you out, kid. This is to keep you safe."

I nodded, walking to the study I'd been crashing in only half aware of where I was going and shoving all of my stuff into a duffel bag. It didn't take long to have my clothes packed up and the foldout bed returned to normal. By the time I'd emerged, the kitchen was spotless. No dead body. No blood. No evidence my mother had even existed in this house.

Bile rose in my throat and I forced myself to shove the burning liquid back down. Axe was right, I needed to get out of here. Not just for my safety, but for my fucking sanity.

"Come on," Axe said quietly, waiting for me outside as I pulled the door shut behind me. "Come with us to do the funeral rites, then get on the road."

"Right," I rasped, heading for my truck. "The funeral rites."

I climbed into my vehicle, following the van that Axe's buddies had brought over without really seeing where I was going. I was vaguely aware of the traditional daimon funeral rites, but I hadn't thought about them in years. Hadn't needed to.

Bullet would know.

Bullet would know about the funeral rites. Bullet would also know my mom was dead. He'd seen this coming—why else would he tell me to stay in Jersey?

I pulled over sharply, glad the roads were mostly empty before dawn, slamming my fist against the steering wheel. He'd known. He'd fucking *known*. And the best he could do was 'stay in Jersey'? That was some goddamn bullshit. He could have told me how to stop it happening if he'd wanted to. He could have *warned* me, and Mom would still be alive.

Throat tight with emotion, I snatched up my phone from the console and stabbed the screen a little harder than necessary.

Straight to voicemail.

I stared down at the phone in disbelief. Bullet *always* answered the phone. He knew we were calling before we even called. It had been like that ever since high school. I hung up and tried it again, getting the same message.

What the actual fuck?

I hung up, pulling up Riot's number instead.

I got a generic voicemail message, and I doubted Riot had ever checked his voicemail in his life. He always had his phone on though. Why weren't either of them answering?

The betrayal ran through me like a crack through my chest. Riot was my best friend in the world and he'd just goddamn *abandoned* me when I needed him most. Had I not been a supportive enough friend to him when he was going through it with Grace?

Or had he guessed that I'd had some more than inappropriate thoughts about his girl? Had Onyx told him?

I didn't have Wild's number, but Onyx seemed to know everything and was always on my ass about Grace anyway so I called her instead.

Fortunately, the phone rang. I'd have probably thrown mine out the window if hers had gone straight to voicemail as well. I was already fighting the urge to yell at her, to take out my rage on the first person who actually bothered to answer me.

"Calling me for more updates on your girl?" Onyx asked in lieu of a greeting, her voice hoarse after probably working at the club all night.

"No," I replied hoarsely, doing my best to shove all thoughts of Grace out of my mind. Grace the agathos. Why did she have to be an agathos? Why was the idea that I couldn't get hold of her either cutting me so deep? "My mom was killed by agathos tonight in Jersey."

There was a pause before Onyx blew out a long breath. *"Shit, Dare. That blows. Where are you? What are you doing?"*

"I'm going to... give her rites. And then come home, I guess."

"Bullet told me..."

"He told you this would happen?" I asked sharply, suddenly contemplating driving to Devil's Den instead of Milton and confronting Bullet in person, if they were even there. Last time I spoke to Riot, they had been in some kind of earthquake near Enders Fall, but Riot had assured me they were fine. He hadn't told me where they were going next though, because no one told me anything. Maybe they didn't trust me.

"No," Onyx replied quickly. *"No, of course not. I don't think Oneiroi can disclose shit like that. He just said you might call someday soon and if they weren't around, to..."*

"To what?"

"Hold on, I'm trying to remember. I'm not a fucking messenger service," Onyx grumbled. Weirdly, her pissy mood was somehow soothing. A slice of normality after a disturbingly abnormal few hours. *"He said something like, 'don't let your anger turn you into someone you can't look at in the mirror.'"*

"I have no idea what that is supposed to mean," I lied around the lump in my throat. It didn't quite stem the rising tide of rage inside me that demanded action, that demanded blood for blood, but it did give me pause.

"Yeah, you do," Onyx sighed. *"I know I'd be out for blood if I was standing in your shoes, but I don't have a pretty little agathos soul bond waiting for me. I don't give a shit if my soul is drowning in red all the way up to my eyeballs, but you might one day."*

I refused to answer that. Onyx was assuming that I was Grace's fourth soul bond, and I didn't have it in me to entertain that hope in that moment. Worse, the guilt at the idea of enacting revenge on *her* people was crushing.

It was easier to believe she wasn't mine. Perhaps more cowardly too.

"You're a Philotes, Dare. You're not meant to be on your own. Come take one of the rooms here. If I could get hold of Wild, I'd run it by him, but he's vanished," she muttered.

"Wild has disappeared? I tried calling Bullet and Riot and it went straight to voicemail." A nauseous feeling churned in my gut.

"Same for Wild, though he's good at disappearing when he's not in the mood to be found," Onyx replied, not sounding particularly worried. *"After the earthquake, they've probably gone to ground to avoid pissing off any more deities while they shake the agathos off their tail."*

Had Bullet known about that too? That they'd disappear? I paused before answering, trying to decide how I felt about him at that moment. There was no doubt in my mind that he'd known what was going to happen to Mom, that this was the reason he was so adamant I stay in Jersey, and yet...

He had to carry that knowledge around with him. He'd spoken to me multiple times and told me to stay put, all because he knew my mom was going to be murdered. How the fuck did he get up every day carrying that kind of darkness with him?

"Let me know if you hear from them," I sighed before cutting the call. I didn't know why they'd vanished, if Riot was annoyed with me, if Grace was even mine to care about, but I wanted Onyx to keep me updated anyway. Even if it was nothing—if I was nothing to them.

Don't let your anger turn you into someone you can't look at in the mirror.

It was seductive though. The agathos treated us like we were monsters, and a not insignificant part of me was tempted to rise to the challenge. To show them just how monstrous daimons could be when we were pushed.

Don't let your anger turn you into someone you can't look at in the mirror.

Fucking Bullet.

I started up the truck and drove out to the crematorium Axe had sent directions to, ready to send my mother off to the underworld with full funeral rites, and reminding myself of everything I had to lose the entire way.

And then I drove home via Auburn, pulling over and giving a posturing group of young agathos dudes an arrogant smile, waiting and knowing they'd throw the first punch.

By the time the sun was high in the sky, I was driving back to Milton with a broken nose, a heart full of rage, and some unconscious agathos assholes on the pavement behind me, and I looked at myself in the mirror just fine.

Why the fuck did I care what Bullet said? He wasn't here.

No one was here.

GRACE

CHAPTER 17

In what was either a stroke of luck or interference from a goddess, we weren't all that far from a small parking lot with a waiting tour van.

The driver was human, but he didn't *act* like a regular human. The moment he saw us, he went all wide-eyed, stuttering in what I was pretty sure was rapid-fire Greek, and ushering us towards the van.

"Is he bowing to us?" Riot asked, bewildered. "He kind of looks like he's bowing."

Wild attempted to hand the man some American dollars he'd been carrying that the underworld hadn't incinerated, but he shook his head vehemently, gesturing at the van and dipping his head again. It *did* look like a bow.

"I'll pay him in good luck," I whispered to Riot.

"The hell you will," Riot shot back. "We don't even know where we are and you want to invite bad luck right now?"

I opted not to answer that because I was probably going to do it anyway. My gift was already rising to the surface, the need to bestow some luck trying to break free. I'd spent so long around daimons recently that I hadn't really encountered any humans, and my gift was restless. It was unagathos to *not* provide assistance to humans.

Surprisingly, it was less pressing than normal, considering how long it had been since I used it. Maybe the driver had a good life and didn't *need* a lot of luck.

"Getting into a strange van is probably not the most sensible decision we've ever made, but the lure of air conditioning is too strong to resist," Bullet sighed, stepping forward to climb into the van. Wild's arm shot out, stopping him from entering, and Wild gave Bullet a pointed look before leaning in and examining the vehicle himself first.

Apparently satisfied, he moved back and gestured for Bullet to enter. I definitely wasn't imagining the faint blush on Bullet's face as he passed Wild. My own face was feeling a little heated too, and not just from being overdressed. The way Wild moved, his commanding confidence, it was all incredibly... sexy.

I followed Bullet into the van, sitting next to him on the long bench at the back, and Riot joined me on my other side while Wild took one of the seats in front of us, twisting sideways so he could watch the door.

We were traipsing dirt all through this poor guy's van with our bare feet. I was *definitely* going to give him a little luck, it was the least I could do.

"Tourist," the human man said, pointing out at the cliff we'd just wandered in from then at the van. Wild nodded once to show he understood, and the guy did his small bow thing again. Strange. Very strange. Humans *were* drawn to daimons, they were naturally alluring, but this felt different.

"Where *are* we?" Riot asked, squinting out the window. "It's all rocks and ocean, what's the tourist appeal?"

"We did just ascend from the underworld through a cave, that's probably a pretty big draw," Bullet said mildly.

"Well yeah, but the humans don't know that."

"Maybe they did," I mused, twisting my hair into a low bun and tucking in the ends in the hopes that it made me look slightly more presentable. "Maybe this is a historical—or a mythological place. Somewhere that was once important."

"The Taenaran gateway, maybe?" Bullet suggested. "It's said to be a gateway to the underworld. I wonder why Persephone wanted us to be somewhere so isolated. We already know there were other options. If we were close to Naples, we would have access to a city."

"Cities have agathos in them. Not that I think I'm important enough for the agathos in *Greece* to be talking about me, but seeing any agathos with three daimons would raise questions."

Hiding among humans would be safer, if I could fight my urge to give everyone having a bad day a big dose of good luck.

"Are you sure I can't have one little conversation with the Fates about why I didn't see any of this, Amazing Grace?" Bullet grumbled, fishing his cards out of his pocket to shuffle them again. The underworld hadn't damaged them at all—if anything the glint of gold on the black cards looked shinier than ever. "I mean, I guess they can't control other gods jumping in and interfering, but still. We don't even have spare clothes."

Nor did we have the *right* clothes. It was so warm, it was basically summer and we were all in heavy sweatpants and sweaters, stained with mud to our knees, and no shoes. I had no idea why the driver had even let us on board, let alone seemed so overly welcoming. Maybe he felt sorry for us.

"This would be a very inconvenient time for you to pass out, B," Riot said absently, staring out the window at the approaching humans.

"Fine," Bullet sighed, tucking the cards away petulantly. Wild's eyes glittered with amusement for a moment as he watched Bullet, before returning his attention to the parking lot.

The human tourists wandered back, chatting amongst themselves as they piled into the vehicle. It was a little unsettling after everything we'd just experienced to see people just... living their lives. They didn't know about the gods in the underworld, or Gaia's rage, or the imprisoned Olympians. There was no prophecy hanging over their heads. What would their lives be like if we successfully liberated the Olympians from their Tartarus prison? What would the *world* be like?

The tourists shot us a few bewildered looks, but as none of them appeared to speak English, we were off the hook for small talk. Or worse, explaining why we were in such a state.

"This is so awkward," Bullet whispered loudly. Wild looked back over his shoulder, raising an eyebrow at Bullet who immediately dropped his eyes to his lap. Bullet was usually pretty unflappable, but it only took one look from Wild to destabilize him. At some point, we'd have a moment of downtime where Bullet and I could actually talk about what that meant. Maybe. Someday.

It was a bumpy ride back to wherever it was we were going, and we only knew when we'd arrived because the driver started loudly speaking to us in Greek, gesturing emphatically at the door.

"I guess this is our stop," Riot groused, climbing out first.

The driver's arm rested along the back of the seat, and I reached out as subtly as I could, pressing a little luck against his forearm with my fingertips as I passed. It wasn't much, but maybe he'd find some money or the ground or something, and it would probably only cost me a bumped knee or a paper cut.

"Gracie," Riot rumbled, pulling me out of the van and into his arms. "What if using your gift alerts Gaia as to where you are?"

"Oh. I didn't think of that," I admitted, blinking up at him. It had just felt so right, so instinctive to help the man...

"You probably don't need to worry," Bullet said, coming to stand next to us. "This place feels *drenched* in the gods' magic, and I'm going to assume it has something to do with Hades and Persephone, since there's an entrance to the underworld nearby."

"You think we're safe here?" I asked. We were standing on the side of a quiet road in front of a pale pink stucco house with a terracotta roof, surrounded by orange trees. It was very picturesque, but I had no idea what we were doing in front of this house, and the driver sped off the second Wild climbed out of the van, shouting something as he went.

"I think we're safe-ish here," Bullet agreed, drumming his fingers impatiently on his thigh. "I'm sure that's *why* we're here at least."

"In that case, should we knock?" I asked, glancing around us at the quiet residential street. "It kind of looked like the driver wanted us to stay here," I added, mimicking the 'stay' motion the guy had made with his hand out the window.

Wild placed a hand on my lower back and I stumbled for a second as he guided me towards the shade of a tree on the side of the road. Wild caught me immediately, wrapping an arm around my waist to hold me up and shooting me an apologetic look. I grabbed his forearm reflexively, staring up at him with moon eyes, but I couldn't help myself. In the afternoon sun, his almost pure red irises glowed like rubies, it was entrancing.

"*Kalispéra!*" a cheerful voice called out from behind us. In half a second, Wild had me standing on my own two feet and positioned his body in front of me, so I had to lean around him to see who was approaching.

A tanned man, flicking messy black hair off his face, was ambling down the street, and it took me a moment to realize that he was a daimon. He was so... happy. If it weren't for the red and purple eyes, I wouldn't have believed it.

"Philotes, for sure," Riot snorted, his posture relaxing instantly. Even Wild relaxed a smidge. I couldn't remember what a Philotes daimon did, but apparently my guys weren't threatened by it.

"I don't suppose you speak English?" Bullet asked him, a little desperately.

"Ah, yes!" the daimon replied, coming to a stop in front of us and wiping the sweat off his brow. From a distance, I'd assumed he was middle-aged, but up close he didn't appear that much older than us. He was just dressed rather conservatively in linen trousers, a half-unbuttoned linen shirt and sandals. "Americans?"

He looked at each one of us, not reacting to my pale agathos eyes at all.

Well, okay then.

"Yes, we're from America," I replied, curious to see how he'd respond to me. "We ended up here a little unexpectedly and were hoping there was somewhere around here we could stay?"

"Of course! You may stay in this house—it is a guest house. Come, come." With no follow up questions about how we'd unexpectedly ended up in his town, the daimon led us on a paved path around to the entrance. There was a shaded porch with a full-sized outdoor table and a smaller seating area that looked out into the orange grove, and now some of the panic of where we were going to sleep was ebbing, I could appreciate how lovely it smelled and how pretty the place was.

He pulled a key out of his pocket and let us in, humming to himself as he went. "Come in, I will need to send for some fresh linen—we haven't had guests in a couple of weeks."

I banged my elbow *hard* on the doorframe, waving away everyone's concerns with a watery smile and doing my best to ignore Riot's exasperated look. As far as payment went for using my gift, a bruise wasn't too taxing.

The guest house was a cozy, old-fashioned place with an open concept kitchen, dining and living area at the front of the house. At the back was a downstairs area with two doors off it, and a narrow staircase that led up to a mezzanine area where I could see a large bed through the balcony railing.

"There's a bedroom and bathroom downstairs," he said, gesturing at the doors. "And another full-sized bed upstairs. I'll have some snacks dropped off with the bedding, you can join me for dinner—my home is on the other side of the orange grove."

"That's very kind, thank you... What was your name, sorry?" I asked. Wild moved in closer, arm pressing against mine. "I'm Grace."

"Ah, welcome to Leonidio, Grace. My name is Vasileios."

Okay. We were in Leonidio. I glanced up at Wild and he nodded curtly, signing '*G-R-E-E-C-E*' again.

Having a firm idea of which country we were in was progress.

"Hi, Vasileios," Bullet replied cheerfully. "I'm Bullet, the brooding giant over there is Wild, and the sulking one is Riot."

"I'm not *sulking*," Riot shot back, rolling his eyes before turning his attention to Vasileios. "How come you're so relaxed about three random daimons and an agathos showing up on your doorstep?"

"You came here for refuge, no?"

"Uh. Sort of. We are wanted by the agathos in Grace's hometown," Riot replied, frowning.

Vasileios shook his head sadly. "They are relentless. Usually, the residents here show up single and perhaps form relationships with each other once they're here, though I suppose not always. Anyway, I won't pry—not until dinner at least. Perhaps some ouzo will loosen your tongues," he teased.

"Are there agathos here?" I asked.

"Oh, yes, though no women. Men who were sent away on the outreach thing." He flicked his hand dismissively, rolling his eyes. "This is a sanctuary of sorts here. Well, other people call it that. They are just misfits—agathos and daimon—who I meet on my travels and invite to my home, sometimes they invite others. The Kakodaimonistai visit here often as they travel around, paying homage to us. Some live here now too—it is a very nice life. I will leave now and get you supplies. Clothes too, yes? You have no luggage. Relax! Enjoy yourself, come join me for dinner later."

Vasileios spun and left, humming cheerily to himself again, leaving us all standing a little shell-shocked in his wake.

"What are the... what he said?" Riot asked, turning to Bullet.

"Uh, the name means 'daimon worshiper,'" Bullet replied, blinking at the front door Vasileios had exited.

"Awesome," Riot said with a grin. Even Wild smirked a little to himself.

I gave Bullet a bewildered look, finding him looking a little less confident than usual too. "Where on earth have we ended up? Who are these people?"

Vasileios sent a diminutive human man named Artyom who spoke no English to the house with an entire wheelbarrow of supplies, including lots of loose-fitting cotton shorts and shirts for the guys, and sundresses for me, and so much fresh fruit I thought Bullet might faint from happiness.

We'd each taken turns showering and dressing for the much warmer temperature—not quite summer weather on reflection, but definitely sundress-and-cardigan appropriate. If we hadn't been dropped here suddenly by a goddess, with another goddess wanting to kill us, it would be a lovely spot for a relaxing vacation.

"Have you been to Greece before?" I asked Wild, grabbing one side of the fitted sheet while he took the other and walked around the side of the bed in the downstairs room. He'd already indicated he'd stay in this smaller bed while the three of us took the one upstairs, and I didn't know exactly how I felt about that.

Disappointed, I decided. I wanted him to *want* to stay with me, though that was a big ask considering where we were in our fledgling relationship.

Wild nodded, tucking in the sheet before spelling out *'A-T-H-E-N-S.'*

"I've always wanted to go Athens. Agathos have to take classes every Saturday morning until we're twenty-one—it's as awful as it sounds—and one of my favorite subjects was the ancient temples. One of my dads, Chance, he said maybe I'd visit them one day with my bonded." I laughed quietly to myself, pulling cases onto the pillows. "Maybe he was right."

I didn't even know why I was telling Wild all of this, or whether he was interested. The connection between us was faint, but I thought I caught the faintest trace of his curiosity as he finished making the bed.

"I miss Chance a lot. And Creed, one of my other dads. They were always nice to me, tried to protect me from the brunt of my mom's corrections, with varying degrees of success. I miss my little brothers too—Leon and Tobin. They're eight and five and don't know me very well, but I still miss them. Or maybe I just miss the idea of them, of the sibling relationship we could have had. They'll grow up thinking I'm this awful person, and they'll *hate* me because they'll be taught to hate me, and that's honestly kind of devastating."

Wild was watching me carefully from the other side of the bed, his face not giving anything away. I shook my head, shooting him a watery smile. "I'm sorry, I don't know why I'm unloading all of this on you. I mean, I do want to talk to you, but I also know I don't really have time to indulge in that kind of self-pity right now. Not when there are a million other things going on we need to deal with. Besides, the sun is setting. We probably need to go join our host for dinner now."

A look of frustration passed over Wild's face, like he wanted to object, but instead he sighed heavily, lightly placing a hand on my arm to stop me from barreling out of the room and pressing a soft kiss to my forehead. I felt the apology in it, the sympathy for how much I was missing my family.

"Thank you," I whispered, grabbing his hand and giving it a quick squeeze before leading him out to join Riot and Bullet in the main living area. They weren't shy about their curious gazes, and I gripped Wild's hand a little tighter in response. One thing we had learned in our agathos classes was that it could be hard for bonded who came along later to find their place within the dynamics of the group, and I didn't want Wild to feel like an outsider even if I wasn't sure if he was going to stay or not yet.

"You're nervous about dinner," Riot said flatly, mouth pressed into a firm line. He had chosen dark gray shorts and a white shirt, all linen, and looked absolutely miserable not to be in his usual all-black uniform. "Maybe we shouldn't go."

"Ugh, it's so annoying not being able to see anything," Bullet groaned dramatically, flopping back onto the couch. He was pulling off a matching pale blue shirt and shorts quite well. "I'm even second-guessing the visions Nyx delivers me when I sleep. There are things now that I realize I thought were happening back home, but it's probably here? Maybe? So many oranges..."

There was a flash of frustration from Riot that he wasn't quite able to smother in time, though he didn't let it show. He knew—we all did—that Bullet couldn't control what he saw—even when he'd had the ability to ask whatever questions he liked, there had never been a guarantee of answers.

"Whenever I try to think about them, my head starts to hurt—"

"Then don't think about them," I said quickly, giving Bullet a reproving look. "We haven't even slept in I-don't-know-how-many days. You're not supposed to be pushing yourself anyway, but especially not today."

"Fine," Bullet groaned in agreement, throwing his arm over his eyes.

"Is *relaxing* such a hard concept?" Riot asked him drily, before returning his attention to me. "Maybe we should just catch up on sleep and go meet all these strangers tomorrow."

"I want to go," I insisted, giving Riot what I hoped was a reassuring smile. "Yes, I'm nervous, but I'm always nervous meeting new people. And these aren't just any ordinary new people. Aren't you curious? Besides, it would be rude not to when Vasileios is letting us stay here."

I glanced up at Wild just in time to see him reach for his pocket before curling his hand into a fist at his side. He'd done it a few times since we'd arrived, and I guessed he was reaching for the phone he usually used to communicate.

It was harder to tell this time around with Riot and Bullet's complete bonds vying for my attention to notice the faint emotional insight I was getting from Wild, but I didn't think I was imagining the hints of irritation I was feeling from him every time he remembered his phone was busted.

Wild looked down at me, my hand still tightly ensconced in his, and even though all he did was tilt his head and narrow his eyes slightly, I got the distinct feeling he was saying 'if you're happy to go, I'm happy to go'. But maybe I was just imagining things.

"Fine. If they're assholes, we're leaving. If they hit on you, we're leaving. If the runaway agathos say shit about you, I'm throwing hands and then we're leaving," Riot muttered, dragging himself unenthusiastically to the front door of the cottage.

"Agreed," Bullet said cheerfully, before breaking out into an honestly impressive rendition of *The Music of the Night* as the four of us meandered through the orange grove under the stars. Wild was a stalwart presence at my side, his grip on my hand a little tense, like he was ready to throw me behind him at the first sign of trouble.

Riot led the way, nonchalant as ever as the trees opened up to reveal a larger version of the house we were staying in with an enormous patio area, the bench seats either side of the long wooden table filled with agathos, daimons *and* humans alike.

Just sitting there. Relaxing. Chatting. Like it was the most normal thing in the world.

It was a little unsettling, but it gave me hope at the same time. Was this what the Fates wanted? The gods like Persephone and Nyx? Because while the idea of resurrecting the old gods that had interfered so freely in mortal lives was terrifying, this was... idyllic. A world where all mortals—regardless of which goddess they'd been brought up to serve, if any—sat around the same table, drinking wine and laughing together, was *everything*. It was a hope to hold on to when everything about what I'd been asked to do felt out of reach.

"Here they are!" Vasileios announced, standing up and ushering us towards the table. People moved down, making room for us in the center, and I sat between Wild and Riot, with Bullet on Riot's other side. "Fresh meat. Welcome, welcome, welcome. Grab a drink, snack, relax."

The driver who'd brought us here waved tentatively and I shot him a beaming smile in return that I could have sworn made him blush. Was he one of those 'daimon worshippers' Vasileios had mentioned? Surely, it was divine intervention that led us to him.

There was an impressive array of meze spread out over the table, a combination of vegetarian and meat dishes, and I was glad the chatter resumed before anyone heard how loud my stomach was grumbling. Without asking, Bullet piled a small mountain of meatballs on a plate and handed it to me with a wink before picking out vegetarian options for himself.

"So, our new American friends, will you introduce yourselves to everyone?" Vasileios asked, sitting on the other side of the table from me. "You don't have to—many of the people sitting at this table chose not to reveal their identities right away. We're all here for our own reasons."

The fact that the agathos men at the table had been silently staring at me from the moment we sat down hadn't escaped my notice. There were five of them I could spot at the table by their eyes, and they all looked to be from different parts of the world. To my surprise, they weren't all sitting together. Some sat next to daimons, some next to humans, and none of them looked particularly uncomfortable to be in mixed company.

They didn't even look uncomfortable about my presence here, just confused.

"Um, well I'm Grace," I said with a lame little wave.

"You're Grace Bellamy," one of the agathos said instantly, making Wild and Riot stiffen either side of me, their biceps pressing firmly against my arms.

"What? *The* Grace Bellamy!" Vasileios laughed, eyes going wide. "We have a celebrity in our presence, I can't believe I didn't realize earlier. This is the one causing all the trouble in America? I should have gotten out the good wine."

Wild sat forward, leaning into my space like he was about to shield me from the table with his body.

"What do you know about Grace?" Riot asked, his voice absolutely lethal, also moving forward in his seat. I huffed slightly impatiently, pushing both of their elbows out of the way so I could see.

"We all keep an eye out on what's happening in our home towns," the agathos man said. Only after hearing Vasileios speak did I register this guy was definitely American. "It's to protect the communities we form here, but also so we know when the outreach trips are happening so we can contact the exiles and offer them a place here if they want it."

"And you've heard of me?" I guessed.

"My family is in New York," he replied with an apologetic grimace. "I'm Foster, by the way. This is my, uh, friend," he added awkwardly, gesturing to the unimpressed daimon woman next to him. "Estrella."

"You're the one they said the daimon stole," she said with a thick accent, Spanish perhaps, staring coolly at me with purple eyes. She was beautiful—all dark hair and long limbs, the kind of interesting natural beauty that would have had modeling scouts chasing after her with business cards.

194

"Riot didn't steal me," I scoffed. I'd been sick of hearing that nonsense when we were Stateside, and it was even more offensive to hear it repeated an ocean away. "Riot is my soul bond. So are Bullet and Wild," I explained, gesturing at each of them in turn. "The agathos in my hometown, the Basilinna, my parents... they all conveniently leave that part out."

"You're actually soul bonds?" Foster repeated, leaning forward and looking at me with wide eyes. "You can feel... you know. For daimons?"

It took me an embarrassingly long moment to realize he was talking about sexual attraction. That none of the agathos sitting at this table could experience physical arousal because they hadn't encountered their soul bonds.

"Yes," I replied, sympathy and embarrassment warring for dominance. "As far as I know, I experience all the things I would experience if my soul bonds were agathos with Riot, Bullet... and Wild."

I glanced at my newest bond out of the corner of my eye, finding him looking down at me with another completely unreadable expression on his face. Did he like the fact I was attracted to him? Not like it? Did he wish I wasn't?

"How'd you do it?" one of the other agathos asked in an Indian accent that briefly reminded me of monthly phone calls with my Indian-born grandmother who now lived in Saskatchewan next door to Mercy's parents. She'd probably disowned me by now too, my mother would have made sure of that. This man was older than us, perhaps in his fifties, with dark skin and wrinkles around his eyes like he smiled a lot, though he definitely wasn't smiling now.

"I didn't do it," I replied carefully. "It was predetermined by fate. By *the* Fates."

"You're sure?" he asked, face falling in disappointment. "My name is Aarav. I am fifty-five years old, and I was exiled from my agathos community decades ago."

"We're sick of living like this," a younger guy said. He sounded like he had a Greek accent, and was the kind of handsome agathos man I'd probably dreamed about having as a soul bond one day when I was younger—all smooth olive skin, thick dark hair that curled slightly at the ends, and a jawline that looked carved from marble. The tattoos on his forearms were surprising though—I didn't know any agathos back home with tattoos. "We're denied our soul bond, then forced into a life of endless celibacy, attempting to recreate romantic relationships with non-agathos while our fucking biology gets in our way."

"It's fucked up, Orion," Vasileios said to him, nodding in agreement. There were disgruntled murmurs and sympathy from the rest of the table, the daimons shooting the agathos pitying looks. "Agathos get a raw deal. We all do in our own ways, I suppose, but I wouldn't trade places with an agathos."

"Maybe with *that* agathos," Orion replied, staring at me. "You seem to have a better deal than the rest of us."

Wild was glaring at him like he was going to eviscerate Orion on the spot with his eyes, and I knew I had to say something.

To say *everything*, because that was what these agathos wanted, wasn't it? The truth. They wanted to know why I had something they didn't.

"I'll tell you my story. I'll tell you everything I can," I promised, my heart breaking for those who'd lived in the miserable loneliness that I'd experienced before I met Riot but for much longer than I had. "But first, I really need to know how we're discussing any of this in front of humans. Sorry," I added with a wince as the human woman next to Vasileios raised one perfectly arched dark eyebrow at me, flicking long dark brown hair back over her shoulder dismissively.

"The Kakodaimonistai aren't regular humans," Vasileios explained. "They are... *initiated*, perhaps. A leftover remnant from the olden days."

He picked up a stoppered ceramic bottle in front of the woman he was sitting next to, shaking it slightly, and she snatched it away from him instantly, giving him a chastising look before returning her attention to us.

"This is *kykeon*," she clipped, holding the bottle close to her chest, long red nails scraping against the ceramic. "So long as we drink it regularly, we can see and know things that we couldn't before. We can see the *truth*."

"That one hundred percent has drugs in it," Riot snorted. Wild's lips twitched as he gave a curt nod in agreement. "What is it? Some kind of hallucinogenic? Mushrooms?"

"It's sacred," the human replied primly, unstoppering it and taking a generous swig.

"This is Alesa, one of my lovers," Vasileios explained. If it bothered her that he listed her as just *one* of his lovers, she didn't let it show. "They drink the kykeon and then they can see us as we are—eyes and all—for days afterwards, and we can speak freely in front of them. It almost certainly has drugs in it."

Bullet's head was tilted to the side, observing each of them carefully. "Drugs, but a little of the Fates' doing too. The trace of the divine on them feels the same as the Fates' magic."

The attention of the whole table moved to him, eyes wide.

"Bullet is an Oneiroi," Riot drawled, piling pita and hummus on his plate. "He says stuff like that. You'll get used to it."

"You will," Bullet agreed, flashing Riot a grin.

"Okay, we explained," Alesa said, staring between us apprehensively. I don't think I missed the awe in her expression as she looked at Bullet, and I tamped down an irrational surge of jealousy. "Now tell us your story."

So I did. From start to finish—from being an agathos who'd never felt quite *right*, to my prayer to La Nuit, to meeting Riot and Bullet, my interactions with both goddesses, the way the agathos treated me, finishing with our journey to the underworld.

No one spoke while I did. They looked as though they were trying not to *breathe* too loud, hanging on to my every word, different individuals responding with their body language to different things. The agathos at the table were clearly uncomfortable when I talked about how the agathos back home had treated me, and terrified when I talked about the goddesses interacting with me directly. The daimons were curious, and the humans were wide-eyed but surprisingly unafraid. *Then again, they weren't regular humans,* I reminded myself.

"So, the gods, with the exception of Gaia, want to return the Olympians to glory," Vasileios said slowly, swilling his wine glass absently in his hand. "They feel that Gaia has too much power, is growing restless and angry with the lack of worship she receives, and needs the others for... balance? Is that right?"

I opened my mouth to reply before closing it and looking to Bullet. I understood the gist of what I was meant to be doing, but the politics of deities was more his arena.

"I'm sure there are many motives, but that's certainly one of them," Bullet confirmed.

"And Nyx wants this?" one of the daimons asked uncertainly. "It sounds like it would benefit humans, which historically has not been her thing."

Bullet shrugged. "Nyx doesn't much care for humans, and I don't see that changing, but she longs for the world as it was where gods and mortals interacted. Maybe even a world that is better for daimons, where we can live in the open. Where this earth belonged to more than *just* humans."

There was a lull of silence, and I was sure they were all considering the ramifications of returning to that kind of world as much as I was.

Wild gave them a moment to think, leisurely helping himself to more pita and hummus before straightening and surveying each of them. He didn't need to say a word to get everyone's attention as he pulled out a notepad and pen—where had he even got those?—and scribbled a message on it. He reached over to show it to me, tilting his head towards Vasileios in a clear request of approval to share it.

It was... sweet. He clearly wasn't someone used to sitting back and waiting for things to happen. Wild *made* things happen.

'You've heard our story, you know what the gods, what the Fates themselves want Grace to do. You've heard how the agathos have treated her so far. Where do you stand?'

I nodded in a sort of bemused acceptance, and he handed the note across the table. It wasn't that I didn't want to know the answer, but I had intended to give them five minutes or so to contemplate their position because it was a *lot* to take in.

Vasileios took a long drink of his wine, scanning his eyes over the note before glancing up at Wild questioningly. Wild gave a curt nod, gesturing to the rest of the table. I hadn't disclosed his curse in my story because it wasn't mine to share, and I was relieved that no one at the table looked inclined to give him a hard time about not speaking.

It probably helped that Wild looked like he could squish any one of them like a bug.

Vasileios read the note aloud before setting his glass down and leaning back, stretching his arm along the back of Alesa's chair. "If Nyx wants this, then that's what we do, surely. I am but a humble servant of hers and whatever the fuck her will is. Is that not what all daimons are?"

"Is that what you feel like?" Bullet asked mildly, reaching for the jug of water in the center of the table. "You never look at older generations of daimons—or agathos—and wonder if you're built differently?"

"We know we're not the same as our parents' generation," Orion replied quietly, shooting an apologetic look at Aarav, who was easily the oldest at the table. He didn't look too upset though. "And maybe if there were other gods around for balance, none of us would be 'humble servants.' Maybe we could have some semblance of control over our own lives. I'd fight for that future."

"As would I," Foster agreed. He shot a longing-look at his impassive daimon "friend," Estrella. Her full lips pressed into a thin line as she caught his glance. "There are a lot of agathos who feel left behind, ones who were never given soul bonds, ones who resent the obligation to make sacrifices for every human in need we stumble upon. Those agathos in Auburn, the ones you grew up with, they're the ones who got the best end of Anesidora's deal. Don't assume that the rest of us will be as willing to uphold the status quo."

A little bubble of hope formed in my chest at the idea of having agathos on my side. I'd resented a lot about my community, but I'd never hated *all* agathos. Leaving them behind, abandoning that part of myself, still hurt.

"Do you think we could have daimon soul bonds? Or human ones? If we prayed hard enough," Aarav tacked on hastily. "Would Nyx give them to us?"

"That is the Fates' domain now," Bullet replied thoughtfully. "Gaia got bored of assigning soul bonds and gave the job to them. Perhaps we can... negotiate, using that as a bargaining chip. They're Team Prophecy, after all. Maybe we can show them that there are agathos who will be Team Prophecy too if they gave them something in return."

I wasn't as convinced in the wisdom of bargaining with the Fates as Bullet was, but I guessed he'd "talked" to them plenty of times over the years through his card readings and knew them better. And I *did* want better for the agathos and daimons, even if I worried that would come at the expense of the comfort and contentment that humans had been enjoying for centuries if we fulfilled the prophecy.

I worried about everything. That my hair hadn't turned gray overnight at some point in the past few weeks was a small miracle.

"Why not?" Vasileios asked, filling up his wine glass before topping up everyone else's within reach. "A world where humans can know about us and all these agathos bastards at my table get to have boners? Where my life has more purpose than just making humans fuck? Sure. I'll fight for that future. But for now, we drink. To new friends and old gods, may neither fuck us over."

"May neither fuck us over," Bullet repeated cheerfully, while I held up my glass to join the toast, my throat thick with emotion. This felt significant. Important. Life changing, even.

We'd been drifting aimlessly, the gods buffeting us from either side with their opinions and will, but now we'd set a course and we weren't sailing alone.

Bring forth the Second Age of Heroes.

CHAPTER 18

Riot was drunk, the irritating little shite. Though I was almost more annoyed with *myself,* for not being as annoyed with *him* as I should have been. He had done most of the talking for our group with our new tentative allies, which I couldn't help but be begrudgingly grateful for since I *couldn't* speak and Bullet used his faintly amused expression to hide the fact that he wasn't used to socializing in large groups.

Grace held her own, but it was clear she wasn't comfortable being the center of attention. *Something that she'd have to get used to,* I thought with a grimace.

"I think we should go," she said with a light laugh as Riot draped an arm over her shoulder, slumping against her. I pushed my chair out so I could move behind them, grabbing the collar of his shirt and yanking him upright before he crushed her. "It's been a really, *really* long day."

"I imagine traveling between realms really takes it out of you," Vasileios laughed, standing at the same time Grace did, Riot somewhat precariously held up between Grace and I. "I'm glad you joined us for dinner though, this has been most interesting."

"Thank you for hosting us, and giving us somewhere to stay. And clothing us," Grace added with a weak laugh. "We're in your debt."

"Not at all," Vasileios shrugged. "This is what we do for any agathos or daimon who comes to our community looking for a place to belong."

His words made something in my chest constrict. I'd invested a huge amount of time and money into creating spaces for Keres daimons where they could let out their anger in healthy ways, where they could fight and be free to be themselves, but also learn not to be so arrogant as to draw the attention of the gods the way I had. Occasionally, I'd hired non-Keres daimons to work at my clubs, if they were useful to me, but other than that I hadn't given them much thought. What did that say about me? It would have never occurred to me to create the kind of sanctuary Vasileios had here.

Grace gave me a curious look from underneath Riot's arm, and I wondered how much she was picking up from me as our connection strengthened.

"I love you, Gracie," Riot slurred, smacking a wet-sounding kiss on her temple as we began to make our way slowly back through the grove, leaving the sound of clinking glasses and laughter behind us. "You're the best thing that ever happened to me."

I snorted. I'd certainly never be able to beat the shit out of Riot ever again, having seen him all soppy and drunk over his missus. And maybe he was growing on me just a little bit.

"Jealous?" Riot teased, elbowing me in the ribs. "You're so fucking jealous, man. You want Grace to love you too, but you had to go and be all difficult about it."

I cut him a glare that I doubted he'd be able to see in the dark, even if his eyes were focusing properly, which was unlikely at best.

"Ignore him," Grace mumbled as I caught a flash of her embarrassment. "You don't have to... I mean, he doesn't know what you want. You don't have to want anything, or tell us anything, or... I'm just going to stop talking now."

As much as it annoyed me to concede Riot had any kind of point, he was right in that I did covet Grace's... affection, at the very least. And I had fucked it up. I had been difficult.

And I didn't know where to go from here.

It wasn't until we'd been to the underworld, until I'd witnessed firsthand what was expected of Grace but also how kind and compassionate she was in the face of the task she'd been given, that I'd realized how much I wanted to stay. How much I cared about staying and cared about Grace wanting me at her side the same way she wanted Riot and Bullet.

I'd given Grace all the worst parts of me, she'd seen the connection Thanatos had to me firsthand, and she still hadn't run. If anything, she seemed worried that I was going to run.

But now we were back in the upperworld, I could no longer speak to tell Grace that, I didn't know enough ASL to communicate the depth of what I wanted to say, and writing it down was an intimidating but probably necessary prospect.

Maybe I should have said all the words out loud when we were walking back through the tunnel, but I'd used the precious speaking time I had to tell her that Gaia flattened her apartment instead. Fucking Gaia.

I'd happily never speak to anyone else again, if I could just speak to Grace, I thought a little desperately. It wasn't quite a prayer, but it was the closest I'd come in years. My attempts at avoiding the divine had failed spectacularly, and I was going to have to get over my aversion to the gods at some point in order to actually help Grace with her task.

"I'll take Riot inside," Bullet volunteered, gently nudging Grace out of the way and dragging Riot's arm over his shoulders instead. "It's a nice night, why don't you two sit out here a little longer?"

Subtle. Bullet caught my eye for a brief moment, a flicker of mischief there that only made him harder to resist. I had no idea how Grace kept her hands off him all day.

Grace gave the back of Bullet's head an exasperated look like she was thinking of how obvious his actions were before turning her attention to me. "Do you want to sit for a moment? It's okay if you don't. I think I will though." She sighed, tipping her head back to look up at the sky through a break in the orange tree canopy overhead. "It's so nice to see the sky again after our little underworld trip. The stars are so much brighter here than they are back home."

If my goddamn *voice* worked, I would point out the Pegasus constellation above us. I'd tell her about how the hero, Bellerophon, tamed Pegasus enough to ride him. Then Bellerophon grew too bold, and attempted to ride Pegasus into the skies to join the Olympians, and fell to his death while Pegasus flew on without him and joined Zeus' stables. I wouldn't tell her because it was a particularly nice story, but because it reflected my fears of bringing long-vanished gods back to power. The stories of the Olympians were all ones of selfish deities who took and took and *took*, and my own experiences with gods hadn't given me any cause to think it would be different this time.

But I couldn't fault the people we'd just had dinner with who were living out here in isolation, outcast from their communities, wanting better for themselves. And I couldn't deny that Gaia having so much power over all mortal life was a terrifying concept. Not after she'd attacked Grace.

205

Not after she'd tried to swallow her into the earth and flattened Grace's apartment out of spite, innocent bystanders be damned. She was dangerously powerful, and maybe we needed to fight danger with danger.

"There's so much going on in your head," Grace laughed quietly, still staring up at the sky. "I wish I knew what you were thinking."

She looked at me suddenly with wide eyes. "Not that I want to *change* you or anything. Don't think that, please. I like you just the way you are."

It was sweet of her to reassure me—and I knew most agathos couldn't lie—but I was fine with feeling a little bit of resentment at the way my life had unfolded and the man it had made me, and I would have absolutely changed things about myself.

I closed the distance between us, tentatively reaching out to run my hands up her arms, resting them on her shoulders, taking a moment to indulge in the simple pleasure of touching her after watching jealously as Riot and Bullet did it with ease. Ever since I'd been cursed, I'd gone off physical touch outside of the ring completely, but I didn't hate it with Grace. She felt like goodness and light under my palms—a goodness that was strong enough to fight off the worst parts of me.

Grace's fingers lightly traced down my forearms, her hands coming to rest over my much larger ones. The faint light through the window of our borrowed house just barely illuminated her bronze skin and wide pale eyes, and it felt like we were entirely alone out here among the stars and the orange trees, alone in Nyx's night and Erebus' darkness.

"There are so many layers to you," Grace whispered. "I hope you'll let me see some of them. I'm being very presumptuous here, hoping you won't leave, hoping that the little touches and long looks mean you actually want to stay after all this is done…"

I want to stay. I took a step closer, hoping she could see my resolve in my expression, feel it through whatever sense of me she was picking up.

"Please stay," Grace breathed, voice catching slightly. "I know we don't know each other very well, and I know I said I wouldn't hold it against you if you left and I *won't*. But I'll miss you every day if you do."

I won't leave, I won't leave, I won't leave, I chanted silently in my head, willing her to understand without me telling her, without me letting her go to pull out my notepad and write it down. Maybe because I was feeling selfish and greedy, and the night felt still and magical around us, but I didn't hesitate to wrap one hand around the back of Grace's head and tug her forwards, pausing with just a hair's breadth of space between our lips as I bowed my head to bridge the height distance. She smelled like the wine she'd drunk at dinner, and I worried that maybe I was taking advantage, but Grace pressed her lips to mine before I could step away.

Gentle. She was so gentle. Tentative. Which made sense because I knew agathos didn't have partners before they met their soul bonds, and she was probably shy as it was, given how new this thing between us was. I tightened my grip in her hair, swiping my tongue over her lower lip, encouraging her to open for me. She brought out the old Wild, the one who moved with confidence, who knew how to give his partners pleasure and never hesitated to do so.

Grace made a pleased mewling sound, melting against me as I gripped her in place, my other hand dropping to her hip to pull her in close as hers came to rest against my chest.

I sucked the sweet taste of lingering wine off her lips, and while I'd intended to keep our first kiss quite chaste, there was nothing chaste about the way Grace was pressing her body against mine, the oh-so-subtle roll of her hips. This was the insanity that Riot had mentioned once—the *need*

207

forcing us together, to cement the bond into something permanent. Grace wasn't ready for that, still hesitant to trust me after I'd walked out on her once before.

We wouldn't be consummating the bond tonight, but I could at least give her pleasure.

Fuck, I hoped I could. It had been years since I'd touched anyone this way.

I slipped my hand down over her hip, moving slowly, giving her time to object. She hummed a quiet noise of pleasure against my mouth, and it was game over. My hand easily spanned the back of her thigh and I dug my fingers in just enough to make her pay attention as I dragged her leg up until she was straddling my thigh, my hand moving to grip her ass.

She had a great ass. I'd been staring at it almost nonstop during our walk back to the upperworld.

There was half a second where Grace paused, her fingers tangling tighter into my shirt like she wasn't sure whether she should do this or not, but then she shifted her hips again and all her hesitation disappeared.

"I don't want you to feel like I'm using you," she whispered, pulling back just enough to look into my eyes.

She wouldn't be worried about that if I could speak. I'd have whispered so much filth in her ear by now, she'd have no doubt of how much pleasing *her* pleased me.

'Come for me,' I mouthed, unwilling to let her go even for a second to sign the words. Judging by the flash of arousal I picked up and the flush on Grace's cheeks, she understood me just fine. Her hands shifted to my shoulders, bracing herself better as she ground her clit on my thigh, dropping her head down. When we were more comfortable together, I'd insist she keep her eyes on me the whole time. Maybe hold her by the jaw and demand she look at me while she took her pleasure. But that wasn't for today, not when she was already pushing herself out of her comfort zone.

"Wild," Grace whispered breathily, rocking steadily against me, her nails digging into my shoulders through my shirt. "You feel so good."

Baby, you have no idea.

I moved my other hand to grip her ass, relishing the way she let out a breathy little moan when I squeezed her cheeks, keeping her firmly in place while she worked her pussy on my thigh like I was her own personal sex toy. My dick was trying to break free of the waistband of my shorts where I'd hastily tucked it into, and I knew that for my own fucking sanity, we couldn't do this again. As much as I loved to see Grace undone like this, I hadn't found pleasure with anything but my own hand for years, and not burying my cock in her now was an exquisite kind of torture.

With a quiet moan that tested my self-control, Grace came undone, gripping me like I was the only thing keeping her tethered to this earth as she rode out her orgasm.

I was never going to wash these shorts. Fuck that. I might frame them.

"That was... wow," Grace mumbled, bashfully removing her leg from mine and crossing her ankles. *Oh so ladylike*, I thought, smirking at her sudden demureness. I captured her wrists before she could take her hands off my shoulders, encouraging her to leave them where they were as I leaned in to capture her mouth again.

Slow. Sweet. Chaste. I repeated the words in my head like a mantra, grateful for the gift Grace had shared with me but not wanting to scare her off by pushing for more now. I'd deliver her safely to her bed with the two bonded she already loved and trusted, then I'd take myself downstairs and fuck my hand until this goddamn ache ceased.

"This really wasn't what I had planned when I asked you to stay out here, but I'm not mad about it," Grace laughed lightly, looking up at me through her lashes. Under the moonlight, her opal eyes looked the palest silver, and it was both beautiful and a little unsettling. "Unless I've made you uncomfortable, then I am mad about it, but only at myself."

I stroked the side of her face, before reluctantly removing my hands to pull out the pen and notepad I'd stored in my pocket before we left the cottage, just in case. I'd never missed my phone so much in my life.

'You worry too much,' I wrote, showing the note to Grace who squinted to read it in the moonlight.

"That's hardly an answer," she replied primly.

I snorted, pulling the notepad back to write more. *'I wasn't uncomfortable. I enjoyed that more than you know, and I want more when we're both ready.'*

Grace tilted her head to the side, chewing her lower lip nervously. "You know that consummating the bond seals it?"

I nodded, scrutinizing her reaction the way she had scrutinized mine.

"Okay. Okay, you know, that's good. And you want to hold off on physical intimacy until we're both ready for the bond? Okay, that sounds like a good idea," Grace agreed, rambling slightly to herself. "Though if you, um, want me to take the edge off now..." She reached uncertainly for me and I caught her hand, pulling it up to kiss her palm before releasing her. "Okay, okay. No returning the favor," she laughed, pressing her palms against her cheeks for a moment.

Way to go, idiot. You've embarrassed her.

'It's been years for me. Since before the curse,' I scrawled clumsily, needing to explain it to her but humiliated as hell about it at the same time.

"Oh. Oh!" Grace said as recognition hit. "So you want to wait until we bond because it's special to you," she surmised with an adorable nod of confirmation to herself like that settled the matter.

I probably should have clarified that being with her would make it special regardless, but the issue was more that if she touched my cock, I'd have her flat on her back in this orange grove before she could blink, and something like a permanent bond deserved a little more thought and care than that.

"But you, um, you do *want* to bond with me? Someday?"

I nodded my head vehemently. *Yes.* If Grace was willing to look past the things I'd told her about, the things she'd seen, then of course I *wanted* her—*wanted* the bond with her. How could she ever think otherwise? I was a right asshole if she'd gotten that impression.

Grace stepped into my space, wrapping her arms around my waist, and I did the same around her shoulders, shoving the pad away and hugging her in close and willing my dick not to prod her in the stomach. The ease at which I could touch her never failed to amaze me after so long hating physical contact from anyone.

With the exception of that one kiss with Bullet. Did Grace know about that? Surely she did. There was no way he'd keep something like that from her.

Did she just not care?

Was it too painful for her to mention?

"We'll make it special," she murmured against my chest. "When we're both ready. Not that I'm *not* ready, but..."

But I'd left, and destroyed her trust in me before it had even had a chance to build.

"I just want you to be absolutely certain," Grace said eventually. "You didn't want this. You didn't ask for it. The Fates forced your hand, and I don't want you to give in to that just because you feel like you have to and spend your life stuck with me against your will. Not just me either—I know you and Bullet have, well, something."

She *did* know. I held my breath, waiting to hear what she'd say next.

I *liked* Bullet. I felt something for him that I couldn't easily explain, and it had been that way from the moment I'd laid eyes on him at my club. But if Grace told us never to touch each other again, I would. Not just because I didn't want to upset her, but I would never risk the love and trust that Bullet and Grace had with each other.

"And I don't mind that. If you two want to pursue something together... I think I'm okay with it, so long as I know about it, I guess?" She winced, like I was going to take issue with her completely reasonable request, and I squeezed her tighter for a moment so she knew I was fine with it. Something in me relaxed at her words, a ball of tension I didn't even know I'd been carrying. "There's also Riot, and I'm pretty sure you don't have *those* kind of feelings for each other."

Not even a little.

"But he's part of my life, an important part. I love him, and I know there's history between you both, and I don't want you to constantly be at odds with each other." Grace sighed, and I got a glimpse of the tension and worry she was feeling as her emotions bled out through the tenuous bond. I guided her to the ground, sitting cross-legged facing each other so I could write more easily even though I wanted to lie down on my back and pull her over my chest so we could stare at the stars.

'Me and Riot are fine. I don't hate him. I won't fight him. I think the reason him breaking the rules at the club years ago bothered me so much was because of the Fates' connection between us through you. I've never gotten that angry before.'

Grace leaned forward, the ends of hair brushing the paper as she read while I wrote. "Oh good," she breathed, some of the tension leaving her posture. "That's good. I've, um, been really worried about that. And your theory is probably right—Bullet thinks that's why he and Riot were friends when they were young even though daimons don't usually have friends. And…"

Her voice trailed off and she swallowed thickly. *And Dare.* I was almost certain that was what she was going to say. I didn't know much about the guy, but I knew Riot hung around him like a bad smell.

Dare was the elephant in the room that Grace didn't want to address. I hoped it wasn't because I'd put her off the idea of meeting her soul bonds completely by acting like a dick.

I contemplated making some clumsy attempt at writing that down, at assuring her he probably wasn't an asshole like me, but Grace swayed slightly in place, distracting me. What an idiot, keeping her out here when she was so clearly exhausted. With our time in the underworld, we were probably approaching two days without sleep.

'You need to sleep. We can talk more tomorrow.'

"You're right, we definitely need sleep," Grace sighed, climbing unsteadily to her feet. "I want to talk more, but I imagine you're as exhausted as I am. I shouldn't have had wine at dinner, that was a rookie mistake."

I placed my hand on her lower back, guiding her towards the house. The sound of Riot's snoring hit before we even got in the door, and Grace's lips twitched into a smile.

"Are you sure you want to sleep downstairs?" she confirmed, pushing open the front door. I didn't, but it felt like the right thing to do. The snoring grew exponentially louder, and she giggled under her breath at my raised eyebrow. "Never mind, I don't blame you."

"Amazing Grace," Bullet sang, not taking any particular care to keep his voice down. "Can you get up here? Riot stripped off before passing out on the bed and you need to come put shorts on him because I am traumatized."

"Oh my gosh," Grace laughed, half jogging up the stairs before pausing to glance back at me. "Goodnight, Wild," she added shyly.

Goodnight, I mouthed. My sweet soul bond.

GRACE

CHAPTER 19

"Nice to meet you, Amazing Grace." Bullet bowed dramatically before straightening, giving me a mischievous grin.

"Nice to meet you too," I laughed, crossing the distance between us and jumping on him, wrapping my legs around his waist. He caught me with an oof—did I still weigh something in the dreamscape? I had assumed I'd be weightless—pulling me tight against him and cuddling me close.

"I remember you," I whispered, toying with his blonde hair. "And I'll remember this when I wake up."

"Feels too good to be true," Bullet mumbled, burying his face against my neck. I clung onto him for a moment before releasing my legs, growing increasingly worried that I, in fact, weighed a lot in the dreamscape and was hurting him.

He captured my lips the moment my feet hit the ground, one hand banding around my waist, the other resting on my butt with surprising confidence as Bullet kissed me like he was still worried I might forget this, like he was trying to imprint himself on my mind.

"Are we... can we do that in the dreamscape?" I asked, running my hands down his arms.

Bullet laughed, patting my butt before stepping back. "As tempting as that is—it would absolutely be the best dream I ever had—I never feel like we're truly alone here, and there are some things I don't want to share with my goddess."

"Me neither," I agreed quickly, the idea of Nyx watching us get it on put an immediate dampener on my desire. "But when we wake up, I'm keeping you all to myself for a little, okay?"

I felt like I was constantly sprinting to catch up with everything that was going on, and I hadn't got to spend the time I wanted with Bullet really enjoying the fact that my memories had been unlocked. I'd already been in love with him, but those feelings had grown with the shared history I now remembered. Like our relationship had suddenly sprouted deep roots overnight.

"Okay?" Bullet laughed. "Um, yes, okay. More than okay. Best thing ever."

"Good. Do you have to go anywhere now?" I looked around, trying to figure out where we were. It looked like we were standing in an enchanted forest, but it wasn't somewhere I'd seen before. I wouldn't be the least bit surprised if Bullet was challenging himself to create new scenery for me now that I remembered all the ones he'd made before.

"So far, I'm not feeling summoned." Bullet shrugged, hugging me close and rocking slightly in place like we were swaying to music only he could hear.

"Do you think bringing me here is a drain on you?" I reached up to toy with his hair. "You're not supposed to be using your gift, remember?"

"This doesn't count," Bullet replied with a cocky grin. "This is as natural as breathing to me, no effort required. And I'm not seeking out visions of the future, I'm just seeing where Nyx takes me. Super casual, low-key, you know how I am. Anyway, where do you want to go tonight? Anyone's head you'd like to pop into?"

"That seems very invasive," I pointed out, even though I was tempted. Tempted to spend time with Wild where I could hear his voice again. Plus, my brain kept reminding me that I had a fourth soul bond out there multiple times a day, and a very good idea of who he was.

Maybe it was selfish, but I didn't want to meet him like this. Not when he wouldn't remember. I'd already met both Wild and Bullet this way, I wanted to see him for the first time in person.

"It's not really that invasive to visit daimons, they're raised to be aware of Oneiroi. You know, like how human children are told that if they don't eat their vegetables, a giant broccoli monster will steal them away in the middle of the night?"

"I'm pretty sure they're not told that."

"Well, it's just like that for daimons," Bullet continued, unperturbed. "Don't ever talk to an Oneiroi, or they'll pop into your head and haunt your dreams. They know what the deal is when they meet me."

"We can just go and visit any daimon you've ever met?"

"Sure. Any daimon and exactly two agathos. You and Mercy."

"We could visit Mercy?" I rasped, grabbing Bullet's arm. "Really?"

"We can, but she doesn't know to expect me," Bullet warned. "I'll leave it to your discretion whether you tell her we're real or let her believe you're just a figment of her overactive imagination."

I already knew I would tell her. Unlike Mercy, I wasn't the kind of agathos who could lie.

"I'm scared it'll make it worse," I admitted. "She's so young and I should just forgive her, but I can't quite let that rage go. I'm worried if I see her, it'll just make me angry all over again."

217

"For what it's worth, I don't think it will," Bullet said gently. "You're a big ol' softie and you know it. Come on, let's go. We can leave whenever you want, she won't remember any of it."

I let Bullet sweep me into his arms, the scenery around us disintegrating into grains of sand and reforming into something else.

We landed in the middle of the Milton community center parking lot, except none of the asphalt was visible under the river of blood up to our ankles we were standing in. Mercy stood, watching everything with wide eyes, silent and helpless as Dice was murdered in front of her. In the few seconds we stood there, me clinging to Bullet in horror, he died at least six different ways, his corpse a gross, ever-changing victim of some new method of torture.

"These are her dreams?" I breathed. If this wasn't the dreamscape, it was a tossup as to whether I'd have thrown up or passed out.

Bullet grimaced, waving a hand and dissipating all the evidence of violence. The streets were clean, Dice's body was gone, all of the attackers disappeared. Mercy gasped—the kind of pained noise someone would make if they were coming up for air after too long underwater—before looking around, terrified eyes settling on us.

"Mercy," I said slowly, holding my hands up and approaching her like I would a wild animal.

"How is this happening?" she muttered, staring at the spot where Dice's body had been. "It stopped. It never stops."

My heart broke for her. "Bullet is an Oneiroi. He can travel through dreams."

"He's a psychic." She shook her head, like she was trying to dislodge an intrusive thought. Or an intrusive older cousin.

"He's a psychic and he travels through dreams. Mercy, look at me."

"You hate me," she said to the ground. "I don't want to look at you. I don't want to see the way you look at me."

"I don't hate you," I replied vehemently, grabbing her upper arms and leaning in until she had no choice but to look at me. "Mercy, I don't hate you. Maybe I did for a little while. I didn't understand... I didn't know the choices you had to make. I still wish you'd just talked to me about it."

"I wish I had too." Mercy threw her arms around my waist, sobbing into my shoulder, and I wasn't sure if she knew that I was real or not, but I pulled her close and cried with her all the same.

"Where are you?" I sniffled. "I can fly you to me. I'll find a way. You can stay with me."

"I can't leave, I don't want to go. I'm safe here. He can't find me."

"Who can't find you?" I asked, guiding Mercy's head back and wiping her tears with my thumbs.

"Dice. I ruined his life, and we never bonded, but he's still looking for me. The need to bond drives him to find me. I just want him to get on with his life," she sobbed. "I want him to be happy. I can't make him happy."

I didn't think Dice would hurt her, but I wasn't going to force her to reconnect with him if she didn't want to. "That's okay. We're in a whole different country. You won't see anyone you know here."

"No, I need to stay with Harbor. Harbor knows what to do."

"Grace," Bullet warned apologetically. "I'm being summoned, time to go."

"I'll come for you," I promised Mercy.

"Harbor," she said more insistently. "I want to stay with Harbor."

Before I could say anything else, we were already gone.

I woke up alone, which was an unsettling feeling. Despite having lived alone for a long time, I'd quickly gotten accustomed to being snuggled up with someone in bed, and it was strange to have the mattress all to myself.

I took some time to shower and get dressed in a pale yellow sundress, finger combing my hair until it looked presentable before heading downstairs and finding a note waiting for me on the fridge.

We're working out in the orchard.

- Riot

All of them? I knew Riot used to work out at a gym and Wild definitely did, but I couldn't see them working out *together.* Maybe they really were growing friendlier. Gods, I hoped they were.

I pottered around the kitchen, making coffee and nibbling on some fruit, my dream visit to Mercy nagging at me. She hadn't wanted to leave wherever she was, which was a good sign, right? She wanted to stay with Harbor. That day the mysterious voice had encouraged me to call Felix, he'd told me about his brother, Harbor, who'd been sent away on an outreach trip and was supposed to be in Russia but sent postcards from Maine. Did that mean there was a community like this one there? I liked to think that Mercy had ended up somewhere this peaceful.

I stirred my coffee before rinsing the spoon in the sink. Then again, that seemed doubtful—this place seemed quite unique with the three mortal kinds intermingling. It was more likely that she'd found a safe community of agathos to take refuge in, which was fine so long as they didn't try to punish her for having a daimon soul bond. Probably more than one daimon soul bond.

Feeling a little lonely and needy, I let myself out of the front door, intending to head into the orchard, but seeing Bullet sitting in the shade made me pause.

"Hey, you. Weren't you supposed to give me some one-on-one time this morning?" I teased, setting my coffee down on the small cafe table on the porch and taking a seat opposite him.

He grinned at me. "It's ten am, Amazing Grace. Patience is not my strong suit."

There was the hint of wistful longing in those last words, and I understood the part he wasn't saying. Patience had never been his strong suit because he couldn't afford for it to be. Because ever since he was a kid, he knew that the sand in his hourglass was falling faster than those around him.

I opened my mouth, trying to come up with something comforting, but Bullet shook his head slightly. He didn't want my meaningless platitudes any more than I wanted to give them.

"This feels more like a vacation than it probably should," I said instead, leaning back in the chair and surveying the sun-dappled orchard. It was beautiful—unlike anywhere I'd ever been. On the rare occasions we'd gone on vacation when I was a kid, it had been to *nice* places that my mother wanted to be seen at, wanted to tell her agathos country club friends about. Nothing as rustic and remote as this.

"I vote that you enjoy it, since it'll probably all get worse from here," he laughed. "Well, maybe not worse. Stressful. But good things are coming too. You and Wild are getting closer."

"We are," I agreed, staring down at my coffee. "We kissed last night."

"Oh, I know. Aside from the fact that *I* could feel you getting all worked up through the bond, *Riot* could also feel it and he was all drunk and mouthy, and basically gave me a play-by-play while he was drunkenly stripping."

"That's embarrassing for all of us," I groaned, giggling a little at the same time as I imagined a drunken Riot narrating his version of events to Bullet while naked.

"Don't be embarrassed, it was hilarious. Well, a little horrific. But also hilarious."

I jumped at a loud *thud* and a grunt, somewhere in the trees just beyond where I could see.

"Don't worry," Bullet assured me. "The sparring is a necessity for Keres daimons—this is definitely better than Wild bottling up his bloodlust and being consumed by it later. And Riot probably enjoys landing a few punches on him—payback for that time Wild beat the shit out of him at Asphodel," he added cheerfully. "Good thing daimons don't get hangovers."

"I'll take your word for it," I replied faintly, hoping both Wild and Riot weren't doing too much damage to each other. "What about you and Wild?"

"What about me and Wild?" Bullet asked, a little too quickly.

"Well, you kissed that one time," I pointed out, trying to hide my smile at the deer-in-headlights look on his face. "And while I am admittedly pretty naive about all of this, the sexual tension between you is obvious even to me. How do you feel about him?"

"I'm with you, we're with you—"

"I know. That doesn't mean you can't explore whatever it was that led to that kiss with each other though." I was surprised at how naturally the words came to me. All I wanted was for them to be happy, and if they made each other happy, I didn't want to get in the way of that.

"Won't that upset you?" Bullet asked, all curiosity and no judgment.

"You'd think so, wouldn't you?" I mused. "But no. If it was anyone else, yes," I added quickly, cutting him a warning look. "I get this sense of fulfillment from Riot that I don't get from you or Wild. Your happiness—yours and his—matters more to me than keeping you each to myself."

Bullet was quiet and thoughtful for a long moment. "I'm not saying no, and I'm not saying you're wrong, but it's a big adjustment in my head. It's always been you."

"I know. I keep having all these memories come up of us over the years." I smiled, taking a long sip of my coffee. "I know you've always been entirely dedicated to me. I don't deserve you, you know."

"Don't say that," Bullet replied sharply.

"It's true—I'm an agathos, one of the truth-telling ones, I couldn't say it otherwise," I teased gently. "You have done so much for me. You were a friend, and an emotional support, and an encouragement. You were so patient, introducing yourself to me every night, never getting mad at me when I asked you the same questions over and over."

"I never felt mad," Bullet said with an easy shrug. "It wasn't your fault you couldn't remember the dreamscape. Sometimes, selfishly, I didn't want you to. When I was having a bad day and I maybe confessed a little more than I meant to."

"I remember those now too. I'm finding it hard to forgive myself for seeing you struggle so many times and doing nothing about it."

"You couldn't have done anything, Amazing Grace. Besides, I didn't tell you those things because I wanted you to fix them, I just wanted... well, someone to talk to, I guess," he said, fiddling with the gold bullet he wore around his neck. "My human aunt and cousins found me creepy and weird, and the daimons I went to school with mostly thought the same, except for Riot and Dare. It was fine, and I was glad I didn't have to move out to the Estate early and be further away from you, but I didn't really have anyone to talk to."

"You'll always have me to talk to," I swore, setting my coffee aside and standing. Deciding to be confident, I moved around the table and sat sideways on Bullet's lap, and he didn't hesitate to wrap his arms around my waist, pulling me in close.

"Ooh, I like snuggly Grace," he teased. "And I always *had* you to talk to. Just because you couldn't remember the background information, don't underestimate how much those conversations meant to me. I looked forward to seeing you every single night, and I wouldn't change any of it."

"So can we go back upstairs then? Because I distinctly *remember* being promised alone time with you," I reminded him, resting my head on his shoulder and brushing my lips over his neck.

"You don't have to ask me to do anything," Bullet laughed. "Give me orders, Amazing Grace. I'll follow you anywhere."

I stood, coffee forgotten, and grabbed his hand, pulling him out of his seat and tugging him behind me back into the house. I knew he wasn't lying—he would be more than happy to take orders from me. He'd *enjoy* it. And I kind of wondered if I'd enjoy giving them? Bullet made me feel powerful, and I could admit that I liked that feeling, maybe a little more than I should.

My grip on Bullet's hand was firm as I led him up the stairs to the bedroom, very conscious of the fact that it was essentially a balcony, with no wall or door dividing it from the rest of the house, and Riot and Wild could walk in at any time. Which made a new wave of butterflies take flight in my stomach at just the thought of them being nearby.

Maybe it was that dark side of me speaking, but the idea of Wild hearing Bullet and I together, giving him the push he needed to embrace the connection between us, watching like he had for so long...

224

"I'd love to know what you're thinking," Bullet laughed, huffing slightly to catch his breath after I'd forced him to jog up the stairs.

"Bad things," I replied, pushing him onto the bed. "Things that good agathos girls don't think."

"Those are my favorite kind of thoughts." Bullet gave me a wicked smile. "I'm at your mercy, Amazing Grace. What are you going to do with me?"

I sunk my teeth into my lower lip, running my eyes down his body, catching on the erection that was already tenting his trousers. What *was* I going to do with him?

"Strip for me," I whispered shakily, bracing myself for him to say no. Or worse, laugh.

Bullet stood slowly, maintaining eye contact as he unbuttoned his shirt, letting it fall open to reveal his inked chest and the golden bullet resting against his skin. He shrugged off the material, dropping the discarded shirt on the floor before pushing down his shorts, kicking them away and opening his arms to display his naked body, as if to say come and get it.

"Lie down," I ordered, stubbornly tilting my chin up. Bullet smirked at me, but the arousal in the bond didn't lie. He found this as sexy as I did.

If only I knew what I was doing, I thought wryly. The idea of taking him in my mouth for the first time was tempting—very tempting—but the idea of being bad at it was mortifying. Especially when I already knew I could make him come with my hands. *Safe. Reliable. Still very sexy.*

I kneeled next to Bullet on the bed, still fully clothed because something about that appealed to me, wrapping one hand around his cock and leaning forward to capture his lips with mine. He tucked his hands under his head, leaving him spread out and pliant beneath me, and a rush of arousal rushed straight to my clit. Bullet groaned against my mouth, sucking my lower lip and scraping it gently with his teeth as I pulled back. The image of him sucking on my clit in this position popped into my head, and the desire in the air between us turned thick.

"Whatever you're thinking, do it," Bullet pleaded. "I want it."

"You don't know what it is!" I huffed a quiet laugh, adjusting my grip so I could twist my hand the way he liked.

"I know I want it," he countered, sounding borderline sullen. "Let me pleasure you, *please*."

Swoop went my belly again at the idea of him craving *my* pleasure, at the idea of me taking it. "Let me know if you change your mind," I told him solemnly, releasing his cock and shuffling up the bed on my knees. I wasn't wearing any panties because there hadn't been any in the supplies we'd been given yesterday. Since we were planning on walking into the village later, that hadn't particularly bothered me, but suddenly, I felt very, *very* bare.

"Oh my gosh, I can't do this," I laughed, sitting back on my heels and clapping my hands over my flushed cheeks. Who did I think I was?

"Hey, Amazing Grace," Bullet said gently, leaning up to tug my wrists back down. "Do me a favor?"

"Anything."

"Sit on my face."

"That is what I was thinking," I admitted, my face growing even hotter as Bullet used his hold on my wrists to pull me over his head, laughing as my sundress covered him completely the moment I straddled him. I quickly pulled it up, before remembering that I had nothing on underneath it, but his face was already there before I could hitch the fabric back down again, brushing soft kisses over my inner thighs.

"I have dreamed about doing this for so long," he murmured, pushing my dress all the way up my thighs and encouraging me closer. Despite my sudden rush of insecurity, I braced myself on the wrought iron headboard behind his head, lowering my body to his eagerly waiting mouth.

The moment his tongue swiped over my slit, I forgot my self-consciousness completely. I already knew I enjoyed this act, but I hadn't been prepared for how powerful being in this position made me feel. Deciding to compartmentalize my shyness and just go for it, I reached between my legs, making a V with my fingers to give Bullet better access, and he rewarded me with a long groan as his tongue swiped determinedly over my core, exploring what I liked.

I already knew where I wanted him though.

"You better tell me if you want to stop," I warned—well, sort of moaned—and with that, I angled my hips so his tongue swiped my clit and rocked against his face with absolutely no shame whatsoever.

It just felt *so* good. I'd question when I became such a wanton woman... later.

Bullet groaned again, and I felt him shifting beneath me, his hips thrusting slightly too as I rolled mine, like he was getting off on pleasuring me so much that *he* was struggling to hold himself back. It was another heady rush of arousal, and I sunk my teeth into my lower lip, throwing my head back and relaxing into the orgasm that was rapidly creeping up on me.

I came with a muffled shriek, my head falling forward as I panted, struggling to catch my breath. Bullet's tongue swiped my overly sensitive clit, and I jolted up on my knees with a squeak.

"Too much, too much, I need a break," I gasped, laughing. "I'm too sensitive!"

"You liked that," Bullet said smugly, licking his lips in possibly the lewdest way possible as he ran his hands up and down my thighs.

"I did. A *lot*. And we're not done yet."

Not when Bullet's arousal was so potent, I was sort of surprised he hadn't come when I had, without me even touching him.

While I was enjoying sitting perched on him like this, having him stare up at me, I was also quietly grateful to still have my dress on as a thin layer of modesty while I was this exposed, so I kept it on while I awkwardly shuffled back down Bullet's body on my knees.

"You are so beautiful," Bullet murmured. "Do you know that? I don't think I tell you enough."

"Don't make me cry during sex," I chastised, fighting a sappy smile as I reached between us, stroking his length before positioning myself over him and slowly sinking down.

"Fuck, Grace," Bullet hissed, grabbing almost desperately at the fabric of my skirt until his hands landed on my hips. "I can't even describe how good you feel. Shit, and I really wanted to last longer this time."

"It's okay, we'll just keep practicing," I promised, draping my body over his so I could kiss him. He tasted like *me*, which I found unexpectedly attractive. Like I'd marked my territory in a cavewoman, primal kind of way.

I heard the door open downstairs, but as I straightened so I could brace my hands on Bullet's abs, sinking even deeper on his cock, I wasn't about to stop for anything. Riot had known exactly what he was walking into—there was no way he'd miss the desire I was feeling through the bond—and I had no doubt he'd have warned Wild. They'd chosen to come inside anyway.

"Please don't tell me you're going to stop now," Bullet panted, bucking beneath me. "I don't think orgasm denial is my kink."

"I'm not stopping," I promised, digging my nails in slightly and rolling my hips, fighting to catch my breath. It wasn't like they'd actually see anything if they came up here anyway—my dress was hiding all the important bits—but I wouldn't have stopped either way. Couldn't stop.

The quiet from downstairs was heavy, and only drove Bullet and I higher. It took minutes for my orgasm to rip through me, and as soon as I tightened around him, he was done, reaching his peak with a low groan that I felt everywhere.

As my senses returned to me, I was vaguely aware that I'd just ridden Bullet like a horse, and instead of embarrassment, all I felt was pleasure. Maybe this dynamic between us would take some time for me to get used to, but there was no doubt in my mind that both of us enjoyed it.

"I call dibs on shower," Riot drawled from downstairs. "Though you're more than welcome to join me, Gracie."

I dissolved into giggles, burying my face into Bullet's chest as he shook with silent laughter beneath me. "Go on," he encouraged, tapping my butt lightly. "Riot's a shower hog, unless you jump in there with him, you're not getting any hot water. Besides, I think you fucked my soul out of my body, I need to lie here for a minute and wait for it to float back in."

"You're ridiculous," I laughed, wincing slightly at the rush of fluid that came free the moment I moved and clamping my thighs together. I heard the shower turn on below us, and the idea of getting cleaned up was tempting enough to make me dart down the stairs, pausing at the bottom when I spotted Wild sitting at the small dining table with a glass of water in hand, watching me with one eyebrow slightly raised, eyes burning with heat. His gaze tracked down my body and I swore he could see the evidence of what Bullet and I had been doing through the fabric of my dress.

I squeezed my thighs a little tighter together, definitely aroused enough that Wild would pick up on it through our burgeoning connection. Maybe it was knowing that he'd watched me for so long already, but the idea of him watching me and Bullet...

I swallowed loudly at that visual.

With a squeak that may have been a greeting, I wasn't entirely sure, I rushed into the bathroom, shutting the door behind me and collapsing against it.

Riot laughed, lazily soaping himself down as he watched me. "If you can't take the heat, don't fuck your bonded on the mezzanine where we can all hear you."

"That is not how that saying goes," I laughed, grabbing a washcloth from the shelf and throwing it at him before pulling off my dress. "In the moment, I felt very sexy and empowered."

"Good," Riot replied, pulling me into the water with him and wrapping his arms around my waist and dropping his head to my shoulder. "Hold on to that feeling, Gracie. That's how all of us want you to feel, always."

GRACE

CHAPTER 20

After a trip to the village for supplies—paid for by Wild's cash stores which he'd converted into euros—we returned to Vasileios' terrace for dinner to find even more daimons and agathos there than yesterday, though the human faces at the table were all familiar. Thirty chairs were now crammed around the long outdoor table, the piles of food higher than they'd been yesterday.

"Friends!" Vasileios called, spreading his arms wide. "We have been filling in our newcomers."

He rattled off the names of four new agathos—Galen, Naom, Emil, and Vincente—and five new daimons—Ovie, Etain, Rue, Fox, and Akouma—in quick succession. They were another interesting mix of people from around the world, all who seemed to have found their way to this little oasis Vasileios had created.

"You all live around here?" Bullet asked as we took the seats reserved for us in the middle of the table again.

"Close enough to here," Vasileios replied with a shrug. "Usually I meet them on my travels, invite them to visit and they stay because I am so wonderful. We are a community, of sorts, but we don't all live together. It is good to have friends nearby."

A few of the people around the table rolled their eyes or shot Vasileios indulgent looks. I wasn't sure he'd consider himself their leader necessarily, but he was obviously at the heart of this mixed community. He'd built it around him.

"It is good," I agreed, blinking in surprise at the sweetness of Vasileios' words considering how adamant most daimons I'd met were that they didn't have friends.

With the further introductions out of the way, Vasileios encouraged everyone to pile their plates high with food while he held court. *There was no way it was a coincidence we ended up here,* I thought to myself, chewing slowly on a small roasted tomato Wild had put on my plate. We knew from his experience that there were multiple exits from the underworld— Persephone had led us to this one on purpose, to these *people* on purpose. Yes, they appeared to be allies for us, but more than anything, they were an example *to* us. Proof that all kinds of mortals could live together, knowing about each other's strengths and weaknesses and existing in harmony regardless.

So far, I hadn't even felt compelled to use my gift again. Perhaps due to the kykeon? Riot, Bullet and Wild seemed to be completely content in the presence of these humans too, not pressured by some urgent need to rain down misery on them.

"How'd you end up here?" Riot asked Foster. They were sitting next to each other, Foster's daimon *friend,* Estrella, on his other side, idly toying with his hair in a way that was definitely more than friendly.

Foster shot us a wry smile as I angled myself towards Riot to listen. "It wasn't a straightforward journey. My assigned outreach trip was in Romania. It wasn't a good experience, to say the least. I've never been great at following directions, which as you know is not a very desirable trait in an agathos. My outreach leader took advantage of any chance to discipline me for my own good."

Estrella pursed her lips in disapproval, and Foster took a moment to collect himself before continuing. "I always thought I'd meet my soul bond. It never occurred to me that I wouldn't, I'd never given any thought to the outreach programs before I was suddenly sent on one, just shipped away overnight so I was out of the way and no longer an embarrassment to my family. I spent a year there, and the contact from home was steadily decreasing. I just woke up and one day and was like, 'what am I doing with my life?', you know? Why was I staying there? The agathos had cast me out, why should I stay in the exile they'd thrown me in and pretend to be happy about it?"

"So you walked away?" Riot asked, sounding impressed.

"I did. I got myself to Bucharest, found a job listing for a call center wanting English speakers. There's a lot of agathos there and I didn't want to attract their attention, so I moved to a part of the city closer to the daimons, hoping they would leave me alone. Most of them did," he said with an indulgent smirk at Estrella, who rolled her eyes.

"I was crashing at my cousin's apartment and I kept seeing this agathos come and go, and I was curious. And he's so pretty," Estrella purred. Foster tipped his head back as she continued to scratch his scalp, and I felt a pang in my chest, wondering if the relationship they wanted was limited by what he was, by the fact that they *weren't* soul bonds. "I kept following him around, asking him why was he here, things like that. Trying to break him. He is so fun to play with."

233

Foster smiled cockily, but he couldn't quite hide the longing in his eyes.

"Anyway, eventually he started talking to me. And then he had visa problems because of the outreach thing." She flicked her hand, making an impatient noise. "So we got married and I took him back to Spain."

"You got married?" I repeated, my eyebrows shooting up.

"In the legal sense of the word," Foster replied, cheeks tinged pink. "We're husband and wife *legally*."

Estrella rolled her eyes. "You don't need to clarify, *guapo*. They all know you can't get it up for me." Poor Foster went as scarlet as the wine in the carafe on the table. "We lived together in Valencia for a few months as married roommates, but the daimons I knew were uncomfortable with Foster being there. Some were violent. We met Vasileios when he was drunkenly fucking our neighbor in the corridor right by our apartment door."

Vasileios laughed, dragging Alesa into his lap whilst winding his hand through the hair of the young human guy next to him. *Mathias*, I recalled vaguely. He was French, tall, blonde and fair, and built like an Olympic swimmer. He also looked at Vasileios like he loved him, though I wasn't sure the feeling was returned.

"Estrella storms out, this raging daimon, yelling at me in Spanish and I don't know what the fuck is happening," Vasileios chuckled. "I think she's going to attack me, then Foster appears in the door, pulling her back before she can take a swing at me and this poor confused human I'm still fucking."

"It's in the top ten most awkward moments of my life," Foster agreed drily, still blushing. "Anyway, Vasileios didn't seem that weirded out to see us together, and just said there was a mixed community where he lived and invited us to visit. The poor woman he had up against the wall was *very* confused."

I laughed in spite of myself. "So then you came here?"

"We visited and never left," Estrella replied, refilling her wine glass. "It's been... two years, maybe? Most of the people at this table—the daimons and the agathos, not the humans—come here alone though. The agathos hear about Vasileios from somewhere and come here seeking refuge. The daimons come because they're curious."

Alesa was straddling Vasileios now, Mathias leaning over, his hand disappearing between the two of them, somewhere around Vasileios' waistband. Vasileios leaned back in his chair, arms behind his head and a cocky grin on his face. "I am very famous. It is my burden to bear."

His eyes flickered for a moment as Mathias' hand reached lower, Alesa making noises that had me staring up at the string of lights overhead in discomfort. "He's a Philotes," Riot whispered in my ear, huffing a quiet laugh. "It's a tough gig, being a walking, talking human aphrodisiac."

"That's what Philotes do? They make the humans around them... aroused?" I whispered back, trying to decide where that fell on the spectrum of Bad Things That Daimons Did.

If I forced myself to look past my agathos upbringing... well it didn't really seem *that* bad.

"Pretty much," Bullet agreed from my other side. "They're very appealing to humans themselves, but their *impulse* is to stir up desire."

There were some sounds coming from the opposite side of the table that I absolutely didn't want to explore, so I focused my attention on Riot who was leaning into my space, shaking with laughter.

I was glad he found this whole thing so hilarious.

"They're not all like this," Riot added. "Dare is a Philotes, and I've never seen him fuck at the dinner table."

Whoosh, the air just seemed to all vanish from my lungs at once. Dare was a sex daimon? Dare had horny humans throwing themselves at him all the time?

Bullet threw a dolmades over my lap at Riot. "Dick. Dare is a broken Philotes—he doesn't just go around fucking for the sake of it."

"Oh yeah, definitely not," Riot said quickly. "Dare really struggles with being a Philotes. He needs to feel emotionally invested in a person first."

Somehow that made me feel *worse*. I didn't even know for sure he was my soul bond, yet the idea of him going out there getting emotionally invested in other people made my heart hurt. I was losing my mind.

"Is he your fourth soul bond?" Foster asked, watching us curiously.

Riot and Bullet grew so still either side of me, I wasn't sure they were breathing. "I haven't met him yet. I guess I'll find out when I do," I replied carefully. "It's tricky right now, with us being kind of in hiding."

"Right, from the agathos in your town, your family, *and* Anesidora." Foster looked thoughtful. "How effectively can someone hide from the Goddess of *Earth*, though?"

"Fuck, Foster," Vasileios groaned. "Right when I was about to come. Can't we talk about this boring stuff later?"

Alesa shuddered in his arms and Vasileios promptly—though not roughly—moved her onto Mathias' lap, where he gently stroked her hair and murmured softly in her ear as she came down from her high.

"If we have to wait for a moment where you're *not* about to come to discuss this, we'll be waiting forever," Estrella said drily, swinging her legs over Foster's thigh and resting her head on his shoulder.

"A good point," Vasileios laughed, adjusting himself under the table with absolutely zero subtlety. "This is your war room, Grace the agathos.

Talk us through your strategy while we drink wine and eat cheese. We may need to stop sometimes to translate—not everyone here speaks English."

"Oh. Um. My strategy?" I looked around the table, alarmed to find everyone looking expectantly at me. Bullet shook with laughter next to me, and I kicked his ankle under the table.

Could I really do this? Could I trust my own decision-making abilities enough to ask others to trust them? I'd done plenty of stupid things in my life. More than that, I'd done plenty of *cowardly* things. It had taken me *years* to have to the courage to talk back to my own mother.

It wasn't enough to be smart. It wasn't even enough to be compassionate, or to be outraged, or to want change. I needed to be *brave*, brave above everything else, and I wasn't sure that I was.

Ugh. Where was that mysterious goddess who liked to pop into my head with advice now? This would be a really great time for some words of wisdom.

Bullet cleared his throat, drawing everyone's attention as he felt me floundering. "Did you know that I've known Grace was mine from when we were kids? I visited her dreams every night, got to know her in the dreamscape, even though she'd forget all of it when she woke up."

"That's so romantic," one of the humans cooed, resting her elbows on the table and leaning forward to listen.

"I mean, sort of. In a Romeo-and-Juliet kind of way," Bullet replied, a flash of misery going through him as he remembered all the years he'd spent alone. I grabbed his hand under the table, squeezing it tight. "She told me once—this was back when she was eighteen or nineteen, after they finished up at some How-To-Be-Agathos event where she was waiting on the street with a bunch of other young agathos—some human kid stumbled into their group, looking real worse for wear, absolutely miserable."

I blinked, rifling through the influx of memories Persephone had granted me. I remembered that day, remembered where he was going with this, but it wasn't until he started speaking that I realized I'd told him about it.

"The kid smelled bad, was real beaten up, was the total antithesis of the fancy Auburn kids in their preppy clothes, milling about before they made their way to their expensive SUVs. And you were standing next to… What kind of agathos was she?" Bullet asked, looking at me with a glimmer of amusement in his eye.

"A Soteria. They can give the gift of safety. Preservation from harm," I listed off, mumbling under my breath.

"Right. And a little preservation from harm would probably be a good thing for a kid who was being beaten up by someone clearly a lot bigger than him. But Little Miss Soteria didn't want to help this kid, because he was disheveled and smelled kind of bad. Because that agathos training that said that some people were more worthy of help than others had thoroughly set in, despite the fact she wasn't even old enough to drink yet. And while Eutychia is kind of the unknown factor as far as gifts go—luck being the fickle beast it is—Grace here didn't hesitate to step in and give this kid as much as she could, while her peers stood around with their noses wrinkled because she was touching a poor person or whatever."

I opened my mouth to object to that characterization of my peers, but I couldn't force the lie out of my throat. That *had* been what they'd done. They'd fought their goddess-given instinct to help and provide because this child hadn't been *cute* enough for them. They'd used my willingness to help as a loophole to do nothing themselves.

"The point I guess I'm making is that Grace didn't tell that useless Soteria to get her shit together and help, she took on the burden of helping the kid herself instead." I gaped at Bullet, trying to decide if he was complimenting me or insulting me. I'd been so sure it was a compliment when he'd started out. "And we're bonded, so right now I can sense how annoyed with me she is, and how much her self-doubt is crippling her. I don't believe the Fates would have even considered Grace for this job if she wasn't cut out for it though, and I just wanted to tell her that in the most embarrassing way possible, in front of all of you."

By the time he was done, most of the daimons were laughing and a few people were translating in different languages to the newcomers. I gave Bullet a withering look, hoping the flush of my cheeks wasn't obvious under the dim lights.

"Thank you for that."

"Oh, any time, Amazing Grace. Just needed to get you out of your own head for a moment," Bullet whispered, giving my thigh a comforting squeeze. Wild caught my eye over Bullet's head, mouthing *'relax.'*

I looked to both Wild and Riot, who were sitting in remarkably similar positions, leaning back on the chairs with their arms crossed, manspreading so Bullet and I were squished together between them. I could feel Riot's confidence, and Wild gave me a curt nod that I took to be his version of encouragement, and I decided I could at least fake bravery. Maybe one day I'd feel it for real.

I did my best to emulate Wild's posture—not the manspreading—but I sat up a little straighter, holding my chin up the way he did. He always looked ready to lead an army into battle.

"Not to pressure you, Grace, but we are not a very motivated group," Vasileios said, while the other daimons at the table made vague sounds of agreement. "You have our support, but you will need to, you know, organize us. Let us help you, and maybe the gods will help us in return."

Foster sat forward in his chair though, as did the other agathos. Maybe they had been forced out of their communities, but if there was one thing agathos knew, it was group projects.

"Well, we can't march into Tartarus' realm and demand he release the Olympians," I said slowly. "We can't go there at all without his express invitation. I think we need to try rattle the cage from the inside, so to speak."

"That certainly sounds like a better alternative to trying to *visit* Tartarus," Foster muttered, rubbing Estrella's thigh.

"*Belief* is what strengthens gods, right? Waning belief is what made them weak enough for Gaia to imprison them in the first place, and even if we free them, it's belief that will make them strong enough to *do* anything," I continued.

"That makes sense," Foster agreed. "So we *believe*? That's it? Like they're fairies and we just need to *believe* hard enough?"

It did sound stupid when he put it that way.

"It's a little more technical than that. We believe, and we make offerings, and so forth," Bullet cut in. "We carry out the old traditions, as best we can. The prophecy tells us that sweet-smelling smoke can't reach them, so that kind of sacrifice would be pointless. It also says prayers can't reach them, but I'm not sure I buy into that. Prayer *requests*, sure. They're not in any state to answer us. But prayers of belief? Of respect?" He shrugged. "Maybe."

"If not the smoke offering, then what?" I asked, frowning. The agathos gave offerings to Anesidora via the soil, but it was only done by the Elders or the Basilinna, it wasn't something I was accustomed to.

"Easy," Vasileios replied with a laugh. "Even I know this one. For tonight, we get drunk on wine, fuck each other, and thank Dionysus for the privilege."

My immediate reaction was to write that suggestion off as a joke, but then again... maybe not? Dionysus *was* the God of Wine & Festivity among other things. And while there were other gods with more sedate traditions and rituals, we were all already here... The wine was here. The participants were willing.

"Are you considering saying 'yes' to the ritual orgy?" Bullet asked, pressing a hand to my forehead as though he was checking for a fever. I swatted his hand away, giving him an exasperated look while trying not to smile.

"It's traditional, right? It was a legitimate form of worship?"

"Oh, for sure. We should probably do libations first, say a prayer, make it official," Bullet agreed enthusiastically, turning his attention to Vasileios. "Got any fancy crockery?"

Conveniently, Vasileios *did* have fancy crockery. He and Bullet set up a small altar-like table at the end of the courtyard, setting a decorative bowl Vasileios apparently had displayed on his wall down in the center.

"It's a *phiale*," Bullet explained, grabbing an amphora of wine and setting it down next to the bowl. "A libation bowl."

Bullet gave me a nervous look, ushering me closer while Vasileios set a basin of water down on the ground and moved back into the crowd.

"Is everything okay?" I asked, picking up on his apprehension. "Are you comfortable doing this? I'm sorry, I just assumed you would do it..."

"Oh, it's fine. I'm the closest thing to a priest here, I guess. I just... Could you pay close attention to the ritual, Amazing Grace? Just in case you ever need to do it on your own."

"I won't need to," I said stubbornly, crossing my arms over my chest. "But I'll pay attention because you asked me to."

Bullet gave me a satisfied nod, crouching down and washing his hands in the bowl of water before drying them on a clean towel he'd asked

Vasileios to get. Alesa approached, handing Bullet a plate of fresh dolmades which he reverently set on the altar.

"Usually, I would lift my hands to the sky for an Olympian," Bullet explained quietly, for my benefit. "But as we know they're in Tartarus, I'm going to keep them lowered towards the ground like I would for an underworld deity."

Bullet kept his fingers pointed towards the ground, arms spread and palms facing up.

"We make this offering to you, Dionysus, and this night in which we celebrate the wine and pleasure you hold dear. We are mere mortals, but on this night, we drink and toast to the return of The Twelve."

He stepped towards the table, picking up the amphora and carefully pouring the wine into the bowl. We all watched in silence as Bullet set the jug down before turning to face us, the respectful priest gone in favor of the mischievous daimon.

"Let's have a party worthy of a god."

A fresh glass of wine appeared in my hand, the daimons and their human followers cheering so loud we would have easily been able to hear them if we were on the other side of the orchard.

Riot grabbed me around the waist, spinning me towards him and landing a hard kiss on my mouth. "Any regrets?"

I carefully held my wine in one hand so it didn't slosh him, resting my other palm on his chest as I looked at the revelry unfolding behind him. Vasileios was already naked, Mathias on his knees at Vasileios' feet, his head bobbing while Alesa gripped his hair, guiding his movements.

"Um," I squeaked. Wow, they were really efficient.

Riot laughed, dropping a hand to grab my ass. "Hey, you wanted them to fuck for Dionysus. They are going to *fuck*. Well, not those guys."

He tipped his chin at the agathos men, who'd made themselves comfortable around the table, eating and pouring themselves wine as though an orgy wasn't breaking out around them. Nine agathos and exactly *one* daimon.

Estrella cleared the table in front of Foster with absolutely no hesitation, climbing up to sit in front of him and draping her legs over his shoulders. With all the comfort and ease of an established couple around horny strangers, he pulled her underwear down her legs and pocketed them, flipping up her dress just enough to bury his head beneath it.

'You're staring,' Wild mouthed, eyes glinting with amusement as he stepped into my line of sight.

"I guess... I guess he can still give her pleasure? That's nice," I mumbled. Riot's hands slipped beneath my dress, careful that the fabric didn't lift up and expose me in front of everyone.

I must be the lamest orgy member ever.

I felt Bullet at my back, briefly kneeling to tug my underwear free with a somewhat delighted laugh. "So, what are we doing?" he teased.

I looked to Wild, still hovering behind Riot. *'I will watch,'* he signed, smirking slightly as he ran his gaze down my body, absolutely undressing me with his eyes. Phew, it was *hot* out here tonight.

"Are you sure this won't be, you know, too much?" I asked with a wince. I didn't mean to sound like I was so irresistible that Wild wouldn't be able to keep his hands off me, but I also didn't want us to accidentally take things too far when we'd agreed that the next time we were together it would be to seal the bond.

Wild shook his head, eyes sparkling as they danced between Bullet and I. Did he want to watch us together? Wow, it was really hot out here.

'I will watch,' he repeated before crossing his arms over his chest in a way that made his biceps *bulge*.

"I'm guessing he's going to watch you, which we already know he has plenty of experience doing," Riot said with a snort. "And Bullet had you all to himself this morning. I'm feeling a little left out, Gracie."

"I got a blanket from Vasileios' couch, he won't mind," Bullet said cheerfully. I tried not to think too hard about the things that blanket might have seen. "Let's move our shy agathos a little further away from all the raging exhibitionists."

I didn't protest at all as they led me further away from the house to the edge of the orange grove, Riot wrapping me in a warm embrace while Wild and Bullet set out an enormous throw blanket for us to... defile? That really seemed like the most accurate word for what we were doing.

"You know you're in charge here, Gracie," Riot murmured in my ear. "If there's anything you don't want to do, we'll stop."

"I know it's an orgy, but I don't really want to get naked." I chewed on my lower lip for a moment. "I don't really want any of you to get naked either."

Riot shook with silent laughter. "You don't have to worry about that. None of those bastards get to see you naked."

"Lucky you're wearing a dress," Bullet said, laying back on the blanket and tucking his hands behind his head. "We could reenact what we got up to earlier. I *felt* how much you liked the idea of Riot and Wild watching."

That was... quite tempting.

"Go on," Riot encouraged, dropping his hands to my hips and encouraging me forward. "What exactly did you do earlier?"

I gave Wild a questioning look as he sat down on the edge of the blanket, double checking he was comfortable. He nodded, gesturing rather magnanimously at Bullet's body as if inviting me to begin the show.

Gods have mercy, these men would be the death of me.

I dropped to my knees next to Bullet's head, calling on the liquid courage from the wine as I lifted myself over him to straddle his face, carefully arranging my dress around us.

Riot let out a low whistle. "You guys are really graduating to the advanced levels now, huh?"

Something like that, I thought briefly before Bullet's hands moved beneath my dress, spreading me wide as his tongue went to work. Shoot, he'd gotten even better at this since this morning. Before I could let out an embarrassingly loud noise of appreciation, Wild leaned in, softly pressing his lips against mine. I didn't hesitate to deepen the kiss, letting him swallow the sounds I was making, his hand gripping my hair just firm enough to ride the edge of pleasure and pain.

While this was most definitely not him *just watching,* I could feel the reassurance he was attempting to convey through both his emotions and his actions. Letting me know that we weren't going to go any further than this, but that this was okay.

Riot laid down on the blanket next to Bullet, watching with a satisfied half smile on his face. It was the kind of cocky expression that usually preceded him spouting some absolute filth, and apparently my body had some kind of Pavlovian response to that look because a tremor of desire ran through me, pushing me further to the peak that Bullet was diligently working me towards.

"When are you going to ride my face, Gracie?" Riot asked lazily, eyes hooded with desire. "I'd love to spend some time with your thighs wrapped around my head and your pretty pussy on my tongue."

"Riot," I hissed, my breathing already growing short as I gripped Wild's shoulders to keep me upright. My stoic, serious Keres daimon shook with silent laughter, his enormous palm cupping my entire hip as he oh-so-generously helped me move.

"What?" Riot laughed, more carefree than I'd heard him maybe ever. "Hurry up and come on him, beautiful. Don't want those quads getting tired before you bounce on my dick."

The way Riot could make me feel both horny and embarrassed at the same time was a true talent. His confidently delivered words combined with the bold *suck* of Bullet's mouth over my clit did me in, and I clawed at Wild, muffing my moan against his bicep as pleasure overwhelmed me.

Wild carefully lifted me off Bullet, cradling me in his lap for a moment as I caught my breath, shooting Riot a half-hearted glare and Bullet licked his lips, closing his eyes like he was the most relaxed he'd ever been.

It didn't escape my notice that Wild was also watching Bullet's mouth, and the image of *him* licking Bullet's lips clean flashed through my head before I had a chance to squash it.

"You should kiss him," I whispered in Wild's ear, loud enough for Bullet to hear.

Bullet grinned lazily up at me, determinedly avoiding Wild's heated gaze. "For Dionysus?"

"For you," I countered, hooking my arm around Wild's neck and dragging him down with me as I leaned over Bullet. Wild was easily three times stronger than me and was absolutely letting me move him, but he came easily, his face close to Bullet's as I pressed my lips to my sweet Oneiroi's jaw. "But only if you both want to," I murmured against his skin.

They both held still and for a moment, I panicked that I'd overstepped. *Too much wine and orgying for you,* I scolded internally. But then they both moved at the same time—both a little tentative, both careful—their lips brushing together in the barest hint of a kiss. It was a little movement but a huge step, and I wasn't surprised when they broke apart rather than going further.

But then Wild leaned forward again, tongue snaking out to swipe the taste of me off Bullet's lips, and I couldn't tell which one of us groaned louder.

"I'm still here you know," Riot snorted, grabbing my arm and half dragging me over Bullet's body.

"Like I could forget about you and your dirty mouth," I told him with a laugh. Bullet and Wild moved apart, sitting up next to each other, though they were close enough for their arms to brush against each other. Closer than usual.

"Glad to hear it, Gracie," Riot replied unapologetically, sitting up and reaching beneath the waistband of his shorts. Even the possibility that anyone else might catch a glimpse of what belonged to *me* had me moving, quickly recentering myself over Riot's lap before that piercing made an appearance.

"Hey there," he murmured with a lazy half smile, banding one arm around my waist, the other still between our bodies. I sucked in a breath as the cold metal of his piercing brushed against my still sensitive clit.

"Hi," I gasped, gripping his shoulders for purchase.

Riot didn't give me a chance to overthink it, positioning himself at my entrance and thrusting up. I didn't quite catch my low moan of appreciation as I let my body relax, sliding further down his cock.

My thighs were already burning, and I was half slumped against Riot's body, letting him set the pace. His teeth grazed my neck before moving up to my earlobe, and I clenched around him in anticipation.

"You have no idea how many of the daimons here wish they were in my place right now. I can see them watching, wondering what it'd be like to have a pretty agathos princess of their own. But you're all mine. Mine, and Bullet's, and Wild's. Aren't you, Gracie?"

I nodded, mumbling something incoherent against his shoulder as he gripped my hips and took over entirely, his muscles bunching and flexing with the effort of keeping us both upright. Wild and Bullet had moved in closer, reassuring me with their presence, their own sexual tension simmering between them so obviously I was surprised I couldn't physically *see* it.

Maybe it was the wine, but having them around me with the cool air on my skin and the stars shining overhead... I'd never felt so alive.

"You going to tell me who this pussy belongs to, Gracie?" Riot rasped in my ear, all dark jealousy as he looked at whatever was happening on the patio over my shoulder.

"My soul bonds," I gasped, my orgasm taking me by surprise. Riot grunted in surprise as I tightened around him, his movements growing choppy as he found his own release.

I wrapped my arms around Riot's shoulders as he did the same around my waist, clinging to him as Wild softly stroked my hair and Bullet murmured gentle encouragement in my ear. Suddenly, I was incredibly overwhelmed. Drained, sensitive, and a little needy, and their reassurance was everything.

"It's okay," Bullet said gently. "You're so beautiful. You did so good. We can snuggle up and eat cheese now if you want."

"Yes, please," I sniffled. "And olives."

"As you wish," Bullet laughed, though it was Wild who stood up and moved back to the food table.

"You good?" Riot asked quietly. "Was I too much?"

"No, never," I assured him, playing with the ends of his hair. "I'm just a little overwhelmed, I don't know why."

"This is still a *ritual*," Bullet said quietly, laying down on his back again next to us. "I mean, yeah it's sex and drinking, but there's an element of sacrifice in it. We're giving some of that pleasure to the divine. It's draining."

Wild returned with an enormous plate of food and I blushed furiously as I climbed off Riot's lap, cleaning myself awkwardly with napkins and hastily yanking my panties back on under my dress.

"No more outdoor sex," I muttered, sitting between Riot's outstretched legs and leaning back against his chest. "Never again. This is too messy, and I need to shower the second we get back to the cottage."

Riot vibrated with laughter behind me as Wild set the plate down on my lap. We had front row seats to a very explicit show, and while I was trying not to look too hard at anyone or anything in particular, there was no denying the daimons were living their absolute best lives. If Dionysus drew extra strength from enthusiasm, then we'd be restoring him to full power in no time with this group.

They were coupled up with each and the humans present while the agathos watched on mildly, and I had to admit, they were impressively calm about the whole thing. I guessed they'd lived here awhile and *seen* some things.

Estrella was straddling Foster's lap, and though I couldn't see very well in the low light and I didn't *want* to be a total pervert and look, it seemed like he was pleasuring her with his hands *while* carrying on a conversation with the other agathos.

"Poor guy," Riot said, reaching around me to grab some food, his attention obviously in the same place as mine. "I'm really glad we're soul bonds."

So was I, but it didn't make me feel any better for the other agathos.

CHAPTER 21

"Welcome," Bullet said magnanimously, bowing dramatically as he pulled back a pale-blue curtain to a fancy tent that was sitting in the middle of a field of flowers for some reason.

"Where am I?" I asked. "What is going on?"

Even in the dreamscape, my dick hurt. It'd been aching since I'd watch Grace ride Bullet's face like it was a mechanical bull, and stolen a sip of her taste from his mouth. That had been three days ago, and my boner hadn't fully gone down yet.

Giving Grace a chaste goodnight kiss before going to bed on my own might have been the most difficult thing I'd ever done. Not to mention the lame wave goodbye I'd given Bullet. A wave. A fucking wave. What a pillock.

"You're going on a date with Grace. Surprise! I can't leave—this is my dreamscape after all—but I'll just be chilling out here while you two get to know each other a little better."

"This wouldn't exactly be how I'd set up a date," I muttered, feeling strangely off-balance as I crossed the small distance between us to the tent. Maybe because of the ease with which Bullet was acting. It was clear that Bullet had done this before, and I wondered how many times I'd had interlopers pop into my dreams without me remembering.

"I took some liberties," Bullet agreed sagely. "I didn't think a sad, empty gym was Grace's idea of romance."

Oh yes. He'd definitely visited my head before.

I spared him a slightly exasperated look as I made my way into the tent, filled with roughly five thousand pastel-colored cushions, and one soul bond, wearing a white sundress and a sheepish smile.

"I wouldn't have minded the empty gym," she said quickly, tugging her knees up so I had room to sit down next to her. "I just wanted to spend time with you. And I know this is a little selfish, since you won't remember any of this—"

"I don't mind," I cut in, surprised at how easily the words came to me when I was so accustomed to silence. "You'll remember. You can ask me... questions. Whatever you want to know."

"That's very kind of you, but I still wish you could ask me questions and remember the answers too." Grace sighed, looking at the curtain of the tent that had fallen shut to where Bullet was waiting on the other side. "I feel like I've learned a lot about your personality over the past few days and none of the basics. Especially with all the rituals we've been working on."

They had been busy working on rituals, I had mostly been watching their backs and pretending I wouldn't have to join in at some point. I wouldn't be able to avoid the divine forever.

"Ask away," I encouraged Grace.

"Oh, okay. What's your birth name?"

My lips twitched at the innocuous question while visions of her throwing her leg over Bullet's face ran through my head. The sweet taste of her cunt on Bullet's lips. We had gone about getting to know each other pretty backwards. "Levi. Levi Connor. I'm thirty years old. I earned the name 'Wild' in my early days in the ring and it stuck."

"I wish I had a cool nickname," Grace said, giving me a relaxed smile I hadn't seen nearly enough of. "Though I'm glad the agathos don't do that—my peers would have come up with something horrific for me. You grew up in London?"

"Yeah, with my Auntie Samira. My story is a pretty typical daimon one—my daimon father impregnated my human mother and left her to it. He's still in London. Got quite attached to me when I was winning fights and making a name for myself. He got very rich off my back."

"And your mother?" Grace asked, undoubtedly expecting another dead human like Riot's mom. A human casualty in the daimons' silent war against humanity.

"Still around, somewhere. She lost custody when I was one. Auntie Samira is actually her aunt. Samira always wanted kids, but wasn't able to have them. Was more than happy to take me in. She died years ago," I added, voice catching in spite of my best efforts.

"I'm sorry," Grace said softly, wriggling a lot closer and moving a pillow out of the way so her leg could press against mine. She still looked hesitant about initiating touch, so I grabbed her hand and linked our fingers together, telling myself I was just taking the decision out of her hands and not that I needed it to ground me.

"I'm not a crusader for justice like you are. The arbitrary unfairness of the gods has never offended me the way it seems to offend Riot, and I don't care much for the grand plans of deities the way Bullet does. Having interacted with a god in person, all I really cared about was never doing it again." I kept my eyes

trained on the fluttering curtain of the tent, absently wondering if Bullet had to consciously conjure up a light breeze for ambience. "I do care about humans like Auntie Samira though. I saw firsthand how difficult it was for her to raise a daimon child without knowing that there was something different about me. She didn't have a lot of money, but she spent it all trying to get me help with what she perceived as regular anger management issues."

If she was still alive, I'd fly straight to London with a bottle of the kykeon the humans here drank and wouldn't leave until she'd finished it all and I'd explained everything to her.

Grace's fingers flexed around mine. "We're all fighting for the same thing in our own ways it seems. Each of us have something we care about. I'm guessing that's not a coincidence."

No, I doubted it was.

"If you tried to avoid interacting with the gods, why did you name your club after the underworld?" Grace mused.

I snorted. "A misguided sort of sacrifice of my own, I think. A dedication to the underworld gods in the hopes I never had to see them again."

"Sorry it didn't work," Grace laughed quietly. "You must be looking forward to getting back there. Running the club again."

I blinked at her for a moment, surprised by her words. "I don't plan on going back to Milton, Grace. Well, unless you want to, but I doubt that will be in the cards for us for a long time. If we succeed with the prophecy, there'll be consequences of that. We won't be returning to our normal lives."

Grace opened her mouth before closing it again, staring blankly at the opening to the tent for a moment. "I mean, I guess I knew that. Logically. Bullet has shown me glimpses of the future and we visit all kinds of places— beaches to mountains and everything in between. I never really thought about how final it would be. That our old lives would be done."

We'd left our old lives behind the moment Thanatos had dragged us to the underworld, but Grace had been running for so long before that, maybe it was hard to see her nomadic life as permanent.

"I'm confident Onyx is doing a great job keeping the club running. And I like traveling," I assured Grace. "In the three years after I lost my voice and before I moved to Milton, I did nothing but travel. You don't need to worry about that future making me happy. I want that future."

"You do? How are you feeling about the whole soul bond thing?" Grace asked tentatively.

"After the other night? Very jealous." Grace scrunched her face up, adorably shy all things considered. "I'm happy to be here, Grace. I'm not good at expressing this stuff. Just know that I'm... happy to be with you. I want to be with you."

Fuck's sake, I was cocking this whole thing up.

"I want to be with you too," Grace replied easily, squeezing my hand. "I'm happy to be with you too."

Maybe I wasn't cocking it up completely. Maybe it was that easy.

"Agathos have four soul bonds, don't they?" I asked, needing to bring it up because it had been driving me slowly crazy. The light breeze abruptly stopped, as though its maker was surprised by the question and listening carefully for the answer. I narrowed my eyes at the curtain, and by the way Grace's lips twitched, I knew she had picked up the change too.

"They do."

"And you know who he is."

"I think I do. Yes," Grace replied carefully, her gaze flicked to the curtain again, a sad smile crossing her face. "I'm not going to meet him."

"Yes, you are," Bullet sang, giving up the pretense that he wasn't eavesdropping.

"No, I'm not," Grace replied stubbornly. "I know that Bullet is safe right now, and nothing else matters apart from that."

"I don't disagree," I said slowly. "But also so much has happened recently that Bullet didn't see. Maybe other things have changed too, maybe that future is less certain than it was."

"You can't argue with that, Amazing Grace!" Bullet called cheerfully.

"I can absolutely argue with that," she shot back with a huffed laugh. She rested her head on my shoulder, looking up at me uncertainly. "Is this okay?"

I snorted, wrapping an arm around her waist and half dragging her onto my lap, remembering exactly how jealous I was when she was on Riot's lap. "You don't need to ask, though it's nice that you do. I didn't like touching people before, I felt like I was too infected. That I'd pass it on to them somehow, but it's never felt like that with you. It feels like your goodness is rubbing off on me," I added wryly.

It felt that way, but I knew that wasn't the case. I was who I was, and Grace was who she was. Maybe we'd learn from each other, but neither of us were making the other anything.

Not wanting to waste our time together, I began to talk. I talked about my childhood in Leyton, playing football in the cold at Drapers Field, making saag paneer at my Auntie's side in the tiny kitchen-dining-living room in our flat—the downstairs floor of a terrace house with a bathroom the size of a closet, two small bedrooms, a combined living space and nothing else. I told her about how my aunt hated my fighting career but was proud of the money I was making. How I'd watched helplessly as she'd been ravaged by cancer, how ashamed I was of the relief I felt when she finally passed, miserable and in pain despite the hospital's best efforts to make her comfortable.

How whatever modesty and humility I'd had died along with Auntie Samira, and that was when I attracted the attention of Thanatos with my hubris.

Throughout it all, Grace listened quietly, her head resting against my chest, hand occasionally squeezing mine to offer comfort or assure me she understood. I was vaguely aware that Bullet was sitting outside, listening to every word, but I found that I didn't mind. Aside from the fact that I felt a connection that differed to what I felt for Grace but wasn't insignificant, I also didn't want her to carry the burden of this knowledge alone when we woke up and I forgot this entire conversation.

Besides, I'd stood outside that motel room what felt like years ago and listened to their conversation. Turnabout was fair play.

"What happened when you came out of the underworld near Naples?" Grace asked, fingers tracing the veins in my forearm in a very tempting way.

"That was an interesting few weeks," I replied, huffing a silent laugh into her hair. "I'd just lost my voice, didn't understand a lick of Italian, and the fabric of my reality had been thoroughly unraveled. I was lucky—or perhaps unlucky—that an Italian Keres spotted me after a couple of weeks of scavenging and living on the streets and threw me into the underground fight scene there. There's one everywhere, if you know where to look, and I'm a big bastard. Daimons take one look at me and know I'm a Keres. Eventually, I worked my way back across Europe for a couple of years, fighting for money."

"And then you moved to Milton?"

"As successful as I was in the ring, as much money as I made from fighting, I would only ever be a small fish in a big pond in London. I wanted somewhere I could build my own empire. I don't know why I chose Milton. Maybe the Fates were pushing me in your direction," I admitted, voicing the thought that had been sticking in my mind recently.

There'd been a fucking blizzard in Milton last winter, and I'd spent plenty of time questioning my sanity in moving there. I could have gone anywhere, why hadn't I gone to a nice, tropical island?

Because of Grace. Because there were forces at work behind the scenes, pushing us in the direction they wanted us to go.

"I think the Fates pushed me to Milton too. I'm glad they did," Grace added. The walls of the tent seemed to waver for a moment, rippling like a puddle that had just been disturbed.

"Damn it, Riot," Bullet laughed. "Sorry, we're out of here. Riot's snoring is waking us all up."

Grace laughed, squeezing me tightly for a moment. "I'll remind you of this when we wake up, okay?"

"Promise?" I asked, the vulnerability in my voice more pronounced than I intended it to be. This moment with Grace, this ability to really connect with her, to tell her about my life before in a way I'd never shared with anyone... It was everything.

Everything. And I was going to forget all about it. How much must it have killed Bullet to go through this every night, knowing Grace wouldn't remember him? He was so much braver, so much stronger, than anyone gave him credit for.

"I promise," Grace said solemnly, pressing a kiss to my lips as the dreamscape around us disintegrated into nothingness.

I stared up at the ceiling, wondering what had woken me. I thought I'd be comfortable sleeping in this room on my own—even when I had come around to staying with Grace permanently, I'd never shared a bed with anyone—but I wasn't really. I still wasn't completely sold on the idea of sleeping on a giant harem bed, or whatever it was that agathos did, but I didn't like being so far away from Grace, and I didn't like being alone.

Should I go upstairs and see her? I always wanted to see her in the morning, but the sensation was more demanding than usual this morning. Waiting around downstairs for her to come down in her tiny shorts, yawning as she piled her hair up on her head and gave me one of those sleepy smiles wasn't going to cut it.

Before I could berate myself any further for my indecision, the door to the downstairs room opened and Grace barreled in, launching herself onto the bed, an *oof* escaping me.

She'd come to see me. She was *hugging* me.

I gathered her up in my arms, rolling her so we were lying on our sides, her head resting on my bicep and my arm draped over her waist. Not that I didn't like her lying all over me, but I didn't want to terrify her with my morning wood either.

"I know you don't remember—shoot, that is frustrating—but we hung out in the dreamscape last night."

We did? Well that explained the lingering need I felt for her this morning.

"You told me all about your childhood in London and making saag paneer with your Auntie Samira, and you played football in the dark, and a Keres in Naples who showed you an underground fight club—"

I pressed my lips to hers, only because she needed to stop talking for a second or she was going to run out of oxygen.

Grace smiled against my lips, and I carefully shifted my hips away from her as she chased me further across the bed. "Sorry," she giggled. "Am I too much? You probably don't want me mauling you first thing in the morning."

I pulled my face back enough that she could see the disbelieving look on my face at that ridiculous statement. I wanted her in every way I could have her all of the time. Confident she could read that from my expression based on the blush on her cheeks and the satisfaction through the bond, I cupped her face and pulled her close again, hoping my morning breath wasn't a deal breaker as I kissed her like I might die if I didn't.

How had I ever thought I could walk away from this? From Grace?

I deepened the kiss, rolling her onto her back and bracing myself over her body, my cock brushing her thigh in my enthusiasm. Grace sighed happily, moving closer, so I guessed she wasn't as afraid of my dick as I assumed she would be. Perhaps it was wrong of me to have assumed that because she was a sweet agathos that intimacy would be a strange concept to her.

Agathos did have multiple lovers after all, and she'd been a willing participant in an orgy a few nights ago.

My hand coasted down Grace's hip as I deepened the kiss, my fingers coasting the side of that delectable ass I'd spent so long staring at from a distance. Grace slid her leg between mine, rolling her hips, her hands running down my chest.

We're supposed to be waiting, I reminded myself. *Waiting until we're ready for the bond.*

Were we ready? Was Grace ready? Because I suddenly realized with perfect clarity that I was absolutely ready. How could I not be?

Maybe we weren't deeply in love with each other yet—though I was confident that would come with time. But bonding, tying our souls together, it was more than love. It was a promise and a commitment, it was a tie to one another when it felt like the entire world was out to tear us apart, to tear *Grace* apart.

I wanted to be by her side forever. I wanted to support her and care for her and protect her. And eventually, I hoped we would love each other as much as she loved her other bonded.

Grace shook her head, sliding her hands down to the waistband of my sleep pants and curling her fingers into the fabric. "I know we're waiting, I know that. Shoot. I'm going to stop now. I just... no, no, I'm going to stop."

Fuck, I hoped that Wild in the dreamscape had been smart enough to tell Grace how much I fucking needed her and wanted her and wasn't worthy of her.

I sat up, which dislodged Grace's hand and made rejection briefly flash over her face which I hated myself for, but I needed her to see my hands.

'I want you,' I signed. *'B-O-N-D. I want you.'*

"You want the bond?" Grace whispered, eyes wide. "You know there's no going back from this. Once we bond, that's it. The connection between us grows stronger and becomes permanent."

It was already permanent as far as I was concerned. There was no going back now. Before I'd even met Grace in person, I'd already set up an elaborate security system to keep tabs on her. That was before I'd met her— what were the chances of me being able to actually leave her alone having met her? Why would I even want to?

'I know,' I signed. *'I want that.'*

"Sometimes I think if I was a better person, I'd let you go," Grace murmured, making my heart drop to my stomach. "You fought this until physical contact forced us together, perhaps the kindest thing to do would be to let you go, but I *can't*."

The last word was uttered with a mixture of fierceness and frustration, the part of Grace that *wanted* rising to the surface despite a lifetime of being trained to suppress it. I laid down again, pulling her close by her hips, gripping her tightly in place and letting her know with my body that I wasn't going to let her go. Maybe I had fought it, maybe I would have held out longer if Gaia hadn't inadvertently pushed us along, but it wouldn't have been *that* much longer.

With Grace and Bullet—even with Riot—I had a family for the first time in a long time.

'Mine,' I mouthed, holding her chin in place to make sure she saw my lips move.

"Yours," she agreed softly, leaning forward to brush her lips softly, tentatively against mine. Such an intriguing mixture of shy and confident was my Grace. Her kisses were soft, exploratory, and I forced myself to be patient and let her lead for now. Once upon a time, I'd be a dominant, confident lover but that was *before*. And those people hadn't mattered to me.

"You're holding back," Grace murmured, gently nipping my lip. "And I think that's really sweet because you're probably worried about how I'll handle... you. Hopefully, I'm not as delicate as you think. You saw me the other night, and you know Riot can be pretty, um, *bold* and I'm comfortable with that. My first time was with Bullet while Riot watched," she laughed, flushing again.

Good thing it hadn't been me there for her first time. I'd have had Grace and Bullet both on their knees if it had been me in the room. Grace's blush deepened, like she could see the filthy thoughts running through my head, or perhaps was picking them up through the faint emotional connection between us.

261

"You can be yourself with me," she encouraged, shyly hitching her thigh over my legs.

I held her in place for a moment, making sure I had her attention as I signed what I hoped was *'Tell me if you want to stop.'*

"Of course," Grace agreed solemnly. "The same goes for you."

That was... unlikely, but I nodded in agreement so she knew I was taking her seriously. And then I flipped her onto her back, bracing myself on my forearm next to her head and raising a questioning eyebrow at her.

Grace's chest heaved underneath, pupils dilated. "I like when you take control. It's nice not to have to think, to get into my own head and worry that I'm doing it wrong or I'm too inexperienced and you won't find me attractive—"

I lowered my weight so she could feel my erection pressing against her leg, cutting her off. If she wanted me to take control, if taking control helped her forget about those insecurities for a little while, I was more than happy to let my beast out to play.

It didn't take long to free Grace from the confines of the shirt and shorts she slept in, exposing the simple, pale cotton panties she was wearing. Who knew I was a cotton panties man now? Grace would look beautiful in lace, but frankly there was something more intimate and meaningful about seeing her *comfortable*.

I leaned forward, holding Grace's jaw in place while I kissed her to test how she'd respond, watching her reactions carefully the entire time to make sure I wasn't pushing her beyond her comfort zone. She made a soft mewling noise that had my cock twitching against her warm thigh through my sleep shorts, and I dragged my hand down her neck to cup her breast.

"Wild," Grace sighed happily, arching her back as I moved down her body to scrape my teeth over her nipple, soothing the sting immediately with my tongue. "That feels really good," she whispered. "Like really, really good."

I appreciated her telling me since I couldn't just *ask* the way I wanted to. The way I would have years ago when sex had been something I'd enjoyed.

I pushed those panties I was getting strangely attached to down her legs before sliding my hand up Grace's silky inner thigh, relishing the simple act of just *touching* her. Grace dropped her knees to the bed, opening herself up for me, and I rewarded her with another bruising kiss, fucking her mouth with my tongue the way I intended to fuck her pussy with it. Someday. I didn't think I had that kind of patience right now.

If I got one taste of her cunt, I'd probably come all over the sheets and humiliate myself.

Instead, I slid my hand up to Grace's pussy, sliding my middle finger into her wetness and dragging it up to her clit, hoping I remembered how to do this. Her hips rocked as I began circling those sensitive nerves slowly, adjusting my pressure until I found what made her moan.

"Wild," Grace said breathily, her nails digging into my skin as she writhed beneath me. "I don't even think I need this foreplay, I want you *now*."

There was the brattiest tinge to her voice that I'd never heard before, and I responded by slowing my fingers, smirking down at her when she gave a little huff of annoyance.

"Are you teasing me?" Grace asked with a mock glare. "Are you a tease, Wild?"

I nipped at her jaw, picking up my pace again until her words became less demanding and more incoherent. Once upon a time, I probably was a tease. I probably would have responded to her demands by pulling her over my lap and spanking that ass that had been consuming my thoughts. Maybe I could discover that part of myself again with Grace.

But regardless of my propensity to tease, I was a big guy everywhere, and I wanted to make sure Grace was completely ready for me. Shit, I should have stolen some of the abundance of lube available at Vasileios' house.

With a quiet moan I would replay on loop for the rest of my life, Grace grabbed my arm as her legs shook, stomach contracting and she found her release.

I couldn't wait any longer. Before she was done shaking, I was already climbing between her thighs, bracing myself over her body and pushing my aching cock into her hot, soaked pussy.

By the gods.

I gritted my teeth, fighting the urge to come *immediately*. How had I stayed away from her so long when she felt like this? This was more than sex. It was *everything*.

Grace shifted slightly beneath me, sucking in a gasp. "You're really... big."

This was not helping in my bid to not immediately come.

"Like *really* big." I gave her a warning look, finding a faintly amused smile on Grace's face. Was she teasing me now? Little minx. "You know I can't lie either."

When I got my hands on my notebook, we were definitely going to outline how she felt about spanking.

Grace rocked her hips beneath me, pretending to zip her lips closed with a mischievous glint in her eye. My sweet, playful soul bond. I leaned forward to nip at her lip, deepening the kiss as I began slowly thrusting into her.

I wanted to be calm and sensual, I did, but my control was slipping away from me fast. Not only did Grace feel amazing, but I could feel the bond forming between us and fuck if it wasn't the sexiest thing I'd ever experienced. I hooked my forearm behind her knee, pressing her leg up and opening her more to me.

"Wild!" Grace gasped, back arching as I hit a spot even deeper within her, grinding my pelvis against her clit with each thrust.

The bond bloomed, the connection forging into something permanent, unbreakable, all encompassing. The urge to have it all, to completely seal what was between us, drove me further. The headboard banged relentlessly against the wall, the sound of Grace's barely muffled moans making it very clear to anyone within hearing distance what we were doing in here and just how much she was enjoying it.

"I can feel you," Grace gasped, hands running over my shoulders and chest like she couldn't get enough of me. "The bond. I can *feel* you."

I doubled my efforts, needing to come before I did something ridiculous like *cry*. I snatched up Grace's hand, sucking her slim middle finger into my mouth, swirling my tongue around her digit until she gasped, then guiding her hand between us.

Grace bit her lower lip nervously, moving with enough deliberation that she'd clearly touched herself before, but enough shyness that I wasn't sure she'd ever done it in front of anyone else. She lost that shyness the moment she began to rub her clit, her knuckles brushing my pelvis.

"I'm so close," Grace whispered. Thank *fuck* for that. The second she began to tighten around me, I was done for. I came harder than I ever had in my life, vaguely worried I was going to drown my new bonded from the inside out.

I lowered the leg I had pinned and half collapsed over Grace, using what was left of my strength to hold my weight off her body. Her cunt clenched around me, and I nearly passed out from pleasure.

"You're mine," Grace whispered, pulling my head down to rest on her chest, her heartbeat thundering underneath my ear. "All mine, Wild Connor. I'm keeping you."

Please keep me.

GRACE

CHAPTER 22

We'd bonded.

Wild and I had bonded.

That wasn't what I'd expected to happen—what I'd *intended* to happen—when I'd rushed in here all high on the happiness of our dreamscape date, but I wasn't disappointed. Not at all. Even if it made me a little bit selfish, or even a *lot* selfish, since he hadn't actually wanted this originally.

"Any regrets?" I asked, my front pressed against Wild's side, head resting on his bicep. He shook his head instantly, but I *felt* his response first. The bond between us ran strong and true, even if it wasn't quite as bright as the ones I had with Riot and Bullet, I was confident we'd get there.

"Do you like pickles?" I asked, focusing on the bond between us.

Confusion. Overwhelming confusion. Probably should have given him a heads up first.

"I thought we could try communicating through the bond," I explained sheepishly. "I just thought... well maybe you could answer me that way. If you wanted to," I added hurriedly. "Just as another option."

To my relief, I felt nothing but amusement coming from Wild. He prodded me in the arm, giving me an encouraging look like he wanted me to try again.

"Do you like pickles?" I asked again, wondering why I hadn't picked a slightly less ridiculous question.

It took a moment while Wild navigated the unfamiliar sensation of sending a particular emotional response through the bond, but eventually there was a clear-cut sense of revulsion. I smiled to myself, pressing my face against his chest. The bond was a powerful, incredible thing to have with each of my bonded, but it was uniquely useful with Wild. It gave us a means of communicating without words even when we couldn't see each other, or didn't have writing utensils handy.

"Do you like grilled cheese?"

A definitely positive emotion, which probably shouldn't have been surprising. Agathos, daimon, or human, who didn't like grilled cheese?

"Can you teach me how to make saag paneer?"

Wild's eyebrows shot up in surprise before he pushed an emotion down the bond that felt a bit like excitement, though a very muted version of it. He wasn't just subtle with his expressions, but even his own feelings were suppressed like he didn't want to let them loose.

"My mom's family is originally from India," I murmured, tracing patterns idly over his ribs. "But my mom..."

There was a sense of encouragement from Wild, and while I knew that he would understand, it was still embarrassing to say out loud.

"Auburn is not the most diverse place, and my mom wanted more than anything for us to fit in," I settled on eventually. "She didn't want to encourage anything that would make us different. She didn't even like when I wore dark colors because they didn't brighten my complexion," I laughed nervously. "It still feels like an act of rebellion every time I wear black."

"You don't have to be angry on my behalf," I assured him, sensing Wild's curiosity and the irritation directed squarely at my mother. "Aside from the fact that she's done drastically worse, I'm angry enough for both of us."

Wild snorted, pulling me closer to his side and smoothing a hand over my head, soothing my ire.

"Welcome to the family, I guess," Riot drawled, walking into the bedroom without knocking, Bullet at his back, grinning slightly maniacally. "Officially."

Wild's lips twitched, a flicker of amusement and pride pulsing down the bond. I laughed even as I pulled the sheet higher up over my chest. It was a little ridiculous—I had no real *reason* to preserve my modesty around any of them, but old habits died hard.

Bullet sat down on my side of the bed, immediately rubbing my ankle through the sheets, while Riot threw himself into the chair in the corner and tipped his head back to look at the ceiling.

I caught a flash of interest from Bullet as Wild sat up in bed, bare muscled chest proudly on display as he helped me back to lean against the headboard. I waggled my eyebrows at Bullet, who narrowed his eyes back at me, scraping his lower lip with his teeth before schooling his expression into something less *interested*.

"What's the plan today?" Riot asked.

"More prayers, sacrifices and libations?" Bullet guessed.

"If everyone's okay with that," I replied, bracing myself for their disappointment. It had been a repetitive few days of different rituals to honor each of the gods, though none as exciting as an orgy. What we really needed was to visit the gods' temples, places that were sacred to them where the rituals would be more potent, but leaving Leonidio meant leaving the safety that the underworld gods provided.

"Cool." Bullet sounded completely nonplussed and Wild shrugged one shoulder in easy agreement, but there was a flash of agitation Riot wasn't quite quick enough to hide.

"What is it?" I asked, shuffling up against the pillows so I could see him better, dragging the sheet up with me.

"I don't mind doing the whole prayer thing again, I just... I want to contact Dare. I feel like Vasileios would give us a phone if we asked for one. It's not like Dare is going to tell Gaia where we are," he added a little irritably under his breath.

"Gaia finding us is a matter of 'when' not 'if.' Telling Dare where we are won't be the deciding factor in that." The caginess in Bullet's voice was impossible to miss—it was so unlike him. This wasn't his regular vague, talking-around-the-future routine. He knew something, and whatever it was he knew *bothered* him.

Riot straightened, glaring at Bullet. "What do you know?"

"I know a lot of things," Bullet replied evasively. Riot sat forward in the chair like he was about to stand and storm over, and Wild immediately stiffened, leaning further into my space towards Bullet, in a clearly protective gesture.

Shoot. Defuse, defuse, defuse.

"Stand down," I ordered, surprising myself with my authoritative tone as I held one hand up towards Riot and gently nudged Wild back with my other. "Let's talk about this. Bullet, what's going on?"

All I'd wanted was a nice moment to enjoy my new bond. But then again... Maybe that's what this was about. Maybe Bullet was acting strangely about the man who was probably my fourth soul bond *because* things were settled with my third.

"Dare's mom died. I don't know how—though I know it was violent. I don't exactly know when—"

"But you did know." Riot's voice was as menacing as it had been when he'd stormed into the agathos temple to rescue me from my family. "That's why you told him to stay in Jersey."

"He needed to be there," Bullet said firmly, eyes flashing with an irritation that I knew was covering his hurt. His *worry*. Bullet may not have been as close to Dare as Riot was, but he'd considered him a friend once too.

"You've always known." Riot shook his head slowly, his voice catching.

"Riot," I said gently, my own emotions a confused a mess. "You know Bullet does what he feels is best for us. For everyone. That he's considering the bigger picture and that puts him in a really difficult position sometimes."

"He told me not to let Dare meet you way back in Milton before your parents even knew about us. On the night of the robbery at the convenience store, he told me to keep Dare away when Dare dropped me off."

There was a pang in my chest as I realized the *depth* of Riot's anger. This wasn't a new issue. He'd been concerned about Dare and frustrated about him being kept in the dark for a long time, and the death of Dare's mom was a tipping point. There was no avoiding this confrontation, it had been too long in the making.

"Things had to happen in a particular order," Bullet gritted out. "I can't—"

"Fuck this and fuck you, Bullet. I'm going to find Vasileios," Riot muttered, pushing out of the chair and storming out of the bedroom.

The bonds I had with both Riot and Bullet felt stretched taut, pulling me in opposite directions. Only Wild's was grounding me in place, suddenly the most stable and easiest to cling to of the three.

Bullet moved like he was going to stand, but I grabbed his wrist, keeping him in place while Wild shook his head at Bullet, a clear instruction not to follow.

"He might just need a minute," I said softly, rubbing my thumb over the four tarot cards Bullet had tattooed on his forearm, the movement pausing over the card of The World. "It'll be okay."

My chest ached. Hadn't Bullet warned me that my fourth soul bond had a lot of trials and heartache ahead of him? I'd done my best to suppress that knowledge, determined not to entertain thoughts of *him*, associating his presence with Bullet's health, but how heartless did that make me?

His *mom* had died.

"This is my guilt to carry, Amazing Grace, not yours," Bullet said flatly, not looking at me. "You and Wild should spend some time together, you just bonded. I'm going to meditate."

Riot was gone the whole morning, and Bullet mostly stayed outside, dragging a lounge chair out into the sun and laying around with his shirt off and not enough sunscreen on. While Riot and Bullet hadn't always gotten along perfectly, it was definitely the most torn I'd ever felt between my bonded.

And I wasn't just pulled in two directions anymore. I had Wild to consider. We worked around each other in the small kitchen, making an enormous Mediterranean-style salad for the four of us to share for lunch despite it only being the two of us. We'd spent a lazy morning in bed, testing out ways of communicating through the bond which I was pretty sure had just been his way of distracting me, but I appreciated it.

Bonding was a very intense process, and Wild and I hadn't entered into it with the same clearly defined feelings as I had with the other two. We were both feeling a little vulnerable, and the only solution for that was spending time together. Finding our rhythm, growing more comfortable.

It would be a lot easier if Bullet and Riot's bonds weren't competing for dominance in my chest, both of them feeling heightened emotions that they weren't quite able to disguise despite their best efforts.

'*You can go,*' Wild signed, tipping his chin at the door and sending a pulse of reassurance down the bond. I made a noise of frustration in response, slamming the knife a little harder than necessary and sending half a baby tomato flying.

"I don't want to go," I replied, a little stubbornly.

Wild began signing before frowning, a clear sense of frustration coming through the bond as he pulled his notebook and pen out.

'*Why do you feel guilty?*'

I chewed nervously on my lower lip, setting the knife down before I took off my finger next. "I don't want to believe the whole Oneiroi curse thing. I understand that it's a real thing and it affected *other* Oneiroi, but I don't want to believe it will affect Bullet because none of us quite fit the mold of our kinds, right?"

Wild looked contemplative, tapping the pen against his jaw in an adorably absent gesture that I wasn't used to seeing from him. He usually moved so deliberately, standing so tall and stiff like his muscles were constantly coiled, ready to attack.

'I think I'm a pretty ordinary Keres—soul bond aside. I enjoy the thrill of the fight. Sometimes, the bloodlust can be distracting, but I don't resent it the way Riot resents his gift.'

"You also manage your gift very carefully, and you built facilities for other Keres to manage their gifts," I pointed out wryly, raising an eyebrow at him. "Is that something that *all* Keres do?"

Wild shrugged, the movement almost bashful. It was hilariously cute considering how enormous he was. Feeling calmer, I picked up the knife again and resumed cutting tomatoes, needing to keep my hands busy while I talked.

"Bullet believes that the curse is very much real and will very much affect him." I swallowed thickly. "Whatever he's seen of his future, it grows less certain after I meet my fourth soul bond."

Wild quietly moved closer, taking the knife from my hand and setting it down before pulling me against his chest, wrapping his enormous arms around my shoulder.

"And while I refuse to believe that Bullet is going to... is going to... I refuse to believe that, I also don't want to risk it by meeting my fourth soul bond. I don't want to risk Bullet, and I've told him that so many times and he always tells me that I can't escape fate."

There was a sense of agreement from Wild, and I supposed he knew better than most what it was to be landed with a difficult path by the Fates.

"Bullet told me that the Fates would be very unkind to my fourth soul bond, that there was nothing either of us could do and it would hurt. It was already hurting Bullet, just *knowing* what was coming. He told me my fourth soul bond would *need* me, and I've done my best to put that knowledge out of my mind because I'm selfish, and I need Bullet to be okay."

Wild's arms tightened around me, one hand moving to stroke my hair, and the fact that *he* was comforting *me* when I was the awful one who'd ignored someone else's suffering for my own peace of mind might have made me feel worse.

"I don't know for sure that Dare is my soul bond, but... well, probably. There's a sense of *something* there when they talk about him, when I see his art on their skin. Plus, both Riot and Bullet get really weird and cagey about him, and they're not as subtle as they think they are."

Wild snorted, pressing a kiss against my forehead before releasing me so he could use his hands.

'Ask.'

"That would be the most obvious solution," I agreed, a sad laugh escaping me. "We've let this fester too long, and now it's come back to bite us."

Wild cocked his head towards the door, a clear challenge in his eyes.

"Fine, fine, fine. I'll go get them. Surely things can't get any worse, right?" I asked, marching outside to where Bullet was lounging. *Famous last words, Grace.*

"You, in," I demanded, pointing at the door.

"Are you trying to tell me off because you know I find it very attractive when you give me orders," Bullet teased, one arm thrown over his eyes and his shorts slung low on his hips as he lounged back in the chair.

"That is super not what I am going for," I sighed in exasperation. "Please go inside so we can have a rational conversation and work this out."

"Mmk, let's see how that goes," Bullet replied cheerfully, as though he hadn't been hiding out here feeling sorry for himself for hours.

I was already making my way through the orange grove before Bullet was in the house, on a mission to find Riot. *It's probably a good thing you're giving Wild and Bullet some alone time. They are suspiciously good at avoiding being in the same room together without me.*

The sound of clinking glasses and laughter greeted me as I approached Vasileios' side of the orchard, and I fought my instinctive urge to pray to Anesidora that Riot wasn't drinking his feelings.

"Grace!" Vasileios called. I immediately averted my eyes, seeing a head move on his lap. Why was there always a head on his lap? "How are you today?"

"Fine," I replied, staring at the sky. *Do I ask how he's doing today? He seems like he's doing just fine.*

Riot emerged from the house, staring down at a phone in his hand. He quickly took in Vasileios' position then me standing there awkwardly, jogging across the patio to drape an arm over my shoulders and turn me back towards the orchard.

"Thanks for the phone!" he called over his shoulder, already guiding me away. "You don't want to show up here unannounced, Gracie. I saw so much dick this morning, I'm traumatized."

"It's not like you *had* to hang out here and watch the orgy," I replied, a little scathing.

"I locked myself in the study, well away from the orgy," Riot assured me. "I only attend orgies when you're there."

We paused in the middle of the grove and I twisted out from under Riot's arm so I could look at him. "I trust you completely, Riot. You know that's not what I'm worried about."

Underneath all the emotions Riot was trying to mask was anger so potent it made my knees shake. I knew it wasn't directed at me, but it didn't make me feel any better that his rage was directed at Bullet.

"I don't know if I can move past this, Grace," Riot sighed, running a hand through his hair, already messier than usual. "Dare is like a brother to me. He's been suffering and alone and Bullet *knew* that."

"I knew my fourth soul bond had suffering in his future, and I suspected it was Dare," I admitted, shame crawling up my throat like bile. "If you're going to be mad at him, you have to be mad at me too."

"Did you know his mom was going to die?" Riot gave me a disbelieving look that said he already knew the answer.

"Well, no. I didn't know that."

"Suffering could have referred to anything, Gracie. Bullet knew a specific traumatic event that was about to take place in Dare's future and just... kept it to himself. And Dare's mom... she was pretty good for a daimon parent. I didn't spend a lot of time with her—Philotes daimons have very active social lives—but she was more engaged than most daimons are with their kids. She found it weird that Dare wasn't out fucking everything with a pulse, but she didn't resent him for it the way my dad resented me for not being a good little Moros, you know?"

"Yeah," I replied quietly, frowning to myself. "I know."

He's a good son. Not a very good daimon, but I think I prefer him that way. Wasn't that what the daimon woman I'd met in the underworld had said?

"Fuck it, I suppose we need to have this out," Riot grumbled, snagging my hand and tugging me back towards the house.

Wild and Bullet were sitting across the small circular table from each other, each picking warily at their bowls of salad when we walked in. I could have sworn the temperature dropped a few degrees when I shut the door behind us, the frostiness between Riot and Bullet unmistakable.

"Okay," I said gently, moving to the center of the room, physically placing myself between them. "Let's talk."

Bullet set his fork down, standing up and crossing his arms defensively over his chest. "Go on, Riot. You look like you've got a lot to say."

"How shocking, that you would have *nothing* to say," Riot shot back. "That's your whole thing, right? Saying absolutely fucking nothing."

"You know that I tell you *everything* I can." Bullet's frustration bled through to his voice. "If sharing what I know is going to make things worse, I don't share it. I'm not going to apologize for that."

"How could it have possibly been *worse* for me to know? For *him* to know? Maybe we could have done something—"

"You couldn't have, that's the whole point! Short of tracking down the Fates and somehow convincing them to lengthen Ruby's mortal thread—a request they'd have never granted, by the way—there was not a goddamn thing either of you could have done."

"So this was the alternative then? Just let it happen?" Riot laughed bitterly. "Why couldn't Dare at least be here, with us? Was it actually about his best interests, or did you just not want Grace to meet him because of *your* future."

"Riot," I warned, blinking back tears.

"Do you think I enjoyed carrying this knowledge around with me, Riot?" Bullet snapped, suddenly looking more tired than I had ever seen him. "Do you think I liked telling Dare to stay put in Jersey, knowing he was going to walk into his mom's house after a night out and find her dead on the kitchen floor in a puddle of blood? Do you think I enjoy seeing a woman who I knew pretty well growing up, whose home I visited and whose food I ate, like that?"

Riot fell silent, and I knew he looked unmoved to Wild and Bullet, but there was a lot more going on beneath the surface than he was letting show.

"I saw a lot of options for Dare's future, and believe me, I steered him onto the best course. If he hadn't been in Jersey, he would have struggled with the guilt his entire life. He'd have always wondered if he'd just stayed a few more weeks, a few more days, if that would have made the difference, and it wouldn't have. It *didn't*. He couldn't have done a goddamn thing to stop the agathos following Ruby home and killing her in the middle of her kitchen for simply existing in a predominantly human area where they felt she didn't belong. There was nothing he could have done. Nothing *I* could have done. The Fates made their choice, her time was up."

Bullet was breathing heavily, and Wild stood silently, moving around to place a supportive hand on Bullet's bare shoulder. Riot watched the movement through narrowed eyes, and I didn't imagine the sense of betrayal that cut through him. The feeling of being ganged up on.

"I met her," I said quietly, drawing their attention to me. "In the underworld. She was the daimon woman I met. She told me..." My voice cracked, and I took a deep breath to steady myself. "She told me that he was a good son, but not a very good daimon, and she liked him that way. She told me that she didn't want him to be sad. And she said.... She said that she hoped he found an agathos soul bond one day too, and that he'd be good to her." I remembered the weighty look she'd given me as she'd said those words. *Ruby*, Bullet had called her. "I think she knew."

"Everyone knows you're meant to be except Dare, it seems. Even his dead mother," Riot clipped, throwing the phone down on the couch. "We

279

have a phone, but I don't have his number memorized. Maybe one of you can figure out a way to get in touch with someone in Milton."

With that, he turned and stormed back out of the house, the pictures on the wall rattling as the door slammed shut. I closed my eyes, trying and failing to keep myself from weeping.

I'm so sorry, Dare. Please be okay.

CHAPTER 23

I narrowly avoided the punch the khaki-clad middle-aged agathos threw at me, ducking under his wide swing and jabbing him in the gut with my elbow. Another one came at me from behind—a younger khaki-clad asshole that was probably his son—and I wheezed at the kidney hit before half stumbling, half spinning to clock him in the face.

At any moment, the ground would probably revolt from underneath me. That was the reality of our life now—a constant stream of natural disasters that were escalating day-by-day. I didn't even have a goddamn apartment or tattoo studio anymore, it had been flattened by Gaia's rage.

"Was it you?" I asked, my breathing sawing in and out painfully. "Did you kill my mom? Sneak into her house and stab her in the gut like a fucking coward?"

"Maybe," the older agathos replied in a raspy voice. "Who knows? I've rid the world of so many daimons recently in Anesidora's name and glory. She is hunting you, shaking your homes into the dirt, and we are finally free to rid humanity of the daimon plague. I don't intend to waste a single second of it."

"Of being off the leash?" I laughed, shoving his son out of the way and tackling Mr. Chatty to the ground. "Such a treat for you. Good little agathos, always doing what you're told, not using a single brain cell of your own."

You're no better, a voice in my head whispered. Maybe it was the tattered remains of my conscience, reminding me that I'd basically been on a rampage since Mom died, not because it was productive or because I thought it was the right thing to do, but just because I goddamn *wanted* to.

Blood for blood.

Everyone I gave a fuck about was gone. Dead, or just out there in the world, not giving a shit about me. What did I have to care about anymore? What was the goddamn *point*?

I never actually killed them, even though I should. Every time I got close, I remembered Bullet's stupid message, haunting me, making me pull my punches. That bastard. He wasn't even here and it was getting to me.

I straddled the guy's chest and rained down punches until he stopped fighting back, then I climbed to my feet, found the next target and did it all over again. I should kill them. Maybe today was the day. It was no secret that they'd been killing daimons, all of them bragged about it and agathos mostly couldn't lie as far as I knew.

But then if I killed them, I'd be no better than them. Whatever I was, whatever these few weeks had shaped me into, all I knew was I didn't want to be like them.

A group of young agathos men rounded the corner, looking like particularly obnoxious prep school gangsters, and I laughed through the pain of my swelling jaw.

Five on one, and they weren't already bleeding and busted. One of them looked like he had brass knuckles.

Too much. I'd taken on too much. Too reckless.

Fuck it.

I had nothing else going for me. If this was the end of the road for me, then I was going to go out fighting against the thing that had taken so much away from me.

I came to slowly, my entire face aching like someone had run over it repeatedly with a ten-ton truck.

"You're a fucking idiot, did you know that? Dice should have left you for dead, that was clearly your goal."

I tried to place the flat, disinterested voice, knowing I'd heard it before but my brain was like soup. A baby—why was there a *baby* here?—made a sudden shrieking squawk-like sound that pierced into the achiest part of my brain and I winced, realizing that I was lying on a couch when I nearly fell off the side of it.

Right. Dice. A baby. An aloof feminine voice. I must be at Rogue's house. How the hell had I got here?

Rogue peered over me, as did the fat, unimpressed looking infant she had propped on her hip.

"Is this hell?" I rasped, attempting to cringe away as some baby drool slowly made its way towards my cheek.

"Ha ha. Next time I'm telling Dice to leave you there," Rogue snapped. "He saw you getting the shit kicked out of you by a bunch of goddamn *teenagers* and for some reason, decided to come to your rescue, which is how you've ended up bleeding out on my couch. He went to

Viper's for help, but Viper said he doesn't deal with associates of Riot and told him to call Onyx instead. You're going to have to pay Dr. Martinez, she's on her way here."

"Great," I mumbled, closing my eyes. "Sounds wonderful."

"No, it does not, and you obviously have a head injury to even say that. What the hell is wrong with you, Dare? What were you trying to prove by taking them all on at once? They'd have killed you, thrown you in the harbor and forgotten about you. You don't gain anything from that."

"Not true," I protested weakly. "I would have gained some glorious peace and quiet."

Rogue made a sound of impatience, but before she could launch into another monotone lecture, there was a knock on the door. "Here," she grumbled. "Hold my offspring while I let the doc in."

A pained *whoosh* escaped my lungs as Rogue dropped her fucking child on what I'm pretty confident was a broken rib. The baby seemed completely unbothered, flopping and wriggling until she was on her stomach and reaching up to prod at my bruised face with a chubby little hand, big red-rimmed purple eyes enquiring as she examined me.

In any other circumstances, I'd probably find it kind of cute, but I was too busy worrying that my lung was about to be punctured to enjoy the baby cuddles.

"Hey, kiddo, what's your name?" I asked, coughing slightly. "You're really heavy, you know. I thought babies were meant to be small and light, but you're really doing a number on my bones here."

"Her name is Quinn," Rogue announced, sweeping back into the small living room with an indifferent Dr. Martinez behind her. Rogue picked Quinn up and the kid made a noise of protest, reaching back for me, her new baby punching bag. "Oh great, do you like him better than me now too? I tore my perineum for you, spawn. The least you can do is like me."

"What's a perineum?" I asked Dr. Martinez.

"Probably the one part of you that isn't injured," she replied drily. "You look like shit. How conscious do you want to be for this patch up?"

There was nothing quite like a daimon doctor. "Knock me out, doc. The less I feel, the better."

"Hold on a minute, I don't want him passed out on my furniture—" Rogue began, but the needle of mystery juice Dr. Martinez stabbed into my veins was already working its glorious magic.

Much to Rogue's disgust, I spent two weeks recovering at her house.

Well she *said* she was disgusted, but I was pretty sure she secretly liked having me here. She had a part-time job as an esthetician and she usually relied heavily on Dice to help look after Quinn, but he'd disappeared on another lead, hunting down *his* agathos girl.

After Rogue had supervised me scrubbing out the bloodstains I'd left on her light gray couch, she'd upgraded me to an actual bed in Dice's room for the meantime. It was a definite improvement over sleeping in my truck, which was what I'd been doing since Gaia flattened my house. Much like many of the other residents in Milton, the ones who hadn't got somewhere outside of the city to go. Rural areas were less affected by Gaia's rage, probably because there were less daimons there.

It was a miracle that Rogue's place was still standing. Maybe Gaia drew a line at squashing infants.

"I'm going out," Rogue called, not five minutes after she'd gotten home from work. "Can you give Quinn dinner?"

"Sure," I replied, limping into the kitchen where Quinn was already sitting in her highchair, the microwave beeping incessantly. Rogue swept past me in a blur of black clothes and blonde hair, snatching her purse off the side table as she went before disappearing out the front door.

Parenting didn't come naturally to daimons. Rogue wasn't doing a bad job, but she wasn't happy either. She went out every chance she got, which was more than usual because I was pretty sure she trusted me more with Quinn than she trusted Dice.

"Alright, Quinbee," I announced, pulling the bowl out of the microwave and stirring the mystery greenish-brown mixture. "The goal for today is to get, like, forty percent of this in your mouth. You think you can manage that?"

She babbled away happily as I checked the food roughly a million times to make sure wouldn't burn her.

"Peas?" I asked, looking at Quinn like she'd answer. "There's definitely peas in there. Maybe some spinach, and I'm going to say... carrots. You're in for a treat," I lied, setting the cool bowl down in front of her.

She reached into it instantly, shoving her entire fist in before pulling it out and examining her filthy hand like she had no idea what had happened to it. Rogue had lost her shit the one time I'd spoonfed Quinn, insisting I was going to spoil her with my indulgent ways, so now I just embraced the chaos and cleaned up afterwards.

"Cool, cool, maybe thirty percent," I told her seriously, hobbling away to grab her sippy cup and pulling out my buzzing phone at the same time. *Onyx.* I blew out a long breath, reluctantly deciding to answer. My old phone had been smashed up in the fight, and I'd only got around to replacing it yesterday.

I'd promptly called both Riot and Bullet, but their numbers had both been disconnected. Only the fact that Quinn was teething and needed extra comfort and attention had kept me from throwing the new device at the wall.

"Hey, Onyx," I sighed, setting the sippy cup on the highchair table where Quinn promptly knocked it off. "What's up?"

"What's up?" she repeatedly darkly. *"What's up?! Where the actual fuck have you been? I've been trying to get hold of you for weeks."*

"I'm in town. My phone broke." I smiled as Quinn licked some mystery goo food off her fingers and laughed in delight.

"Is that a baby? Do you have a baby now?"

"She's obviously not *my* baby."

"Oh good, that would be awkward when you bailed. Wild finally got in touch with me."

"Lucky for you," I muttered. "Let me guess, they're off living the high life somewhere, having a grand old time. Southern California? Florida? Maybe even Hawaii?"

"Greece."

"I— wait, what?"

"Greece, you mopey asshole. They're in Greece," Onyx clipped, sounding remarkably unbothered by the fact that they'd all mysteriously vanished and reappeared on the other side of the world. No big deal, happens every day. *"So you need to get your ass on a plane."*

"I haven't worked in weeks, Onyx. I can't afford a plane ticket to Europe right now," I scoffed, deflecting from my actual reaction which was very much *what the fuck?* I'd talked to Riot right before they dropped off the grid, they'd been caught in one of Gaia's earthquakes and were hiding out in a motel owned by some of the horniest Philotes daimons I'd ever met. How had they gone from that to *Greece?*

Riot didn't even have a passport. I doubted Bullet did either, as far as I knew, he'd never even left Connecticut.

I did. I'd even salvaged it from the remains of my apartment.

Not that it mattered. I wasn't going to use it.

"Don't worry about that, I'm sending you money from the Asphodel coffers," Onyx snorted. *"There are less flights than usual anyway, what with the earth falling apart. Even if you'd been tattooing 24/7 for months, you might not be able to afford it without Wild's money. Just get your ass on a plane, okay? I don't know exactly where in Greece they are—he was vague, as usual—but it can't be that big of a place, right?"*

"I'm not going to Greece, Onyx," I sighed. "I know you've got this idea in your head that I'm in their little group—"

"Because you are," Onyx interrupted sharply. *"Dice told me about you getting your ass handed to you by some agathos teenagers, and I know you've been raging against the world for weeks, and I get that. My mom is a lot less cool than yours, and I'd have still gone on a fucking rampage if some agathos had murdered her. Is your anger really directed at the right people though?"*

"I'm angry at the agathos." I dived for the bowl as Quinn shoved it over the edge of the tray, giving her an unimpressed look as I set it back down in front of her and went to the sink to wash baby food off my hand.

"Including Grace?" Onyx pressed, irritatingly perceptive. *"Grace didn't kill your mom."*

"I know that," I snapped. And I *did* know that, though I couldn't pretend I hadn't felt some anger at her for being an agathos. Why couldn't she be a daimon? Or a human? Why did she have to be the thing I hated so much?

If she was even mine. Was she mine? It made me mad that I didn't know either way.

"And you're not mad at Bullet for not telling you what he saw of your future?" Onyx asked.

"No," I lied.

"Bullshit," she snorted. *"I'd be mad too, and then I'd remember that Oneiroi often have good reasons for not telling us what they've seen. For example, they may have seen a worse outcome that came from you knowing."*

"My mom was stabbed to death in her own kitchen, what could possibly be worse?"

"I don't know, I'm not an Oneiroi. What did Bullet tell you to do?"

"To stay put in Jersey. And that something was going to happen, and I wouldn't forgive myself if I wasn't there." I sounded a little petulant even to my own ears.

Onyx hummed thoughtfully. *"I guess if you weren't in Jersey, and it was going to happen anyway..."* 'It' being the murder of my mom, I guessed. *"Well, maybe it was better that you were there even if you couldn't stop it. Maybe this way... You know you couldn't have stopped it."*

"But I *could* have stopped it if I'd known."

"No one outruns fate, Dare. You know that." The sympathy in her voice was hard to take. Daimons didn't generally sound sympathetic. They usually weren't capable of the emotion.

And I did know that no one outran fate, yet I was struggling to accept it. The idea that my mom's time was just... up. That if it hadn't been an agathos with a knife, it would have been a different agathos and a different weapon, or an accident, or something else was hard to get my head around. Nauseating, even.

"Do you talk to them a lot?" I asked, unable to keep the bitterness out of my voice imagining Riot, Bullet, Grace and even fucking *Wild* off living their best life, drinking ouzo shooters on the beach while I was stuck here, my knuckles permanently bruised and a constant ache in my ribs I couldn't quite shake.

Quinn stared me dead in the eye and dramatically dribbled out a mouthful of food like she was punishing me for forgetting about her.

'Don't worry, Quinbee,' I mouthed. *'You're my new bestie. Riot sucks.'*

"I've only received one message from Wild saying they were in Greece, telling me to keep shit running here and asking that I track you down and get your ass on the next flight to Athens. Which was two weeks ago, by the way, but you goddamn vanished and made things difficult. I've tried to contact him again and let him know but the phone is always off, I'm guessing it's a burner."

Huh. Dr. Martinez and Dice had both done me a solid, not ratting out where I'd been staying to Onyx. I must have looked really pitiful when I showed up here. Either that, or she was just too busy keeping everything running to follow up.

"I tried calling Riot and Bullet last night, but their phones are disconnected," I said, some of the rage I felt like I was constantly carrying around dissipating. The thought of them on the run in a different country using burner phones was quite sobering. I knew the agathos here were after them, had been for weeks. Plus, Gaia had attacked them and was still raging at everyone and everything.

Of course, they had to be careful about their location, it just stung that they were being careful about it with me.

"Bullet has probably dropped into your dreams, you just don't remember."

"I've been taking sleeping pills," I admitted. "Dr. Martinez gave them to me. Bullet told me once that he can't get into someone's head if they've taken sleeping medication, it makes him feel nauseous."

Onyx sighed heavily. *"Come to Asphodel tonight. Grab some food, talk shit with your fellow daimons, stay in the guest room Riot, Bullet and Grace were using. Their stuff is still there. You are a wreck, Dare. Wild told me to get your ass on a plane and I intend to do that, but you're fucked up right now, maybe you should come spend a couple of nights here to get your head on straight. Where are you staying? I'll come get you."*

I contemplated her suggestion, remembering the good old days where I'd occasionally take a night off from working and go out with Riot and get fucked up. It felt like a million years ago, and the idea of being surrounded by daimons who I wasn't close to right now made my skin itch.

Quinn blinked at me, green mush smeared across one eyebrow. "Thanks for the offer, but I'm good here."

"Dare—"

"I'll consider the trip," I interjected, hanging up before she could say anything else and getting a washcloth to clean up Quinn.

My throat felt thick as I worked, attempting to stay cheery for Quinn's sake. Maybe it was because Onyx was the first person to tell me some hard truths about my deep-seated emotional issues in a while, or maybe it was her unwavering confidence that I had a place among Grace's soul bonds even when my own hope had been flagging. Whatever it was, it was enough for me to let go of my bitterness. Maybe even enough to give me hope.

"Alright, Quinbee. Let's look up flights to Athens."

CHAPTER 24

"We need to do more," Grace said, throwing her hands up in exasperation as the TV silently showed footage of a plane from New York that had crashed off the coast of Greece caused by a sudden microburst, like the sky itself was targeting that particular plane. "We're causing this. Our prayers, our offerings, we're enraging Gaia. And she must have figured out where we are now, or at least have a general idea because that one is... close."

Too close. The natural disasters had been increasing in number enough for the doomsday cults to really up their marketing, but this was the first that had been so near to us. The Eastern Seaboard had been ravaged by natural disasters after our departure, moving west across the Americas and then dispersing out across the globe.

An "act of God" the humans said. At first, they'd attributed it to science. "Dynamic stresses" or something, earthquakes triggering other earthquakes, and maybe it was. Those earthquakes had also caused other terrifying events—tsunamis that wiped out daimon-heavy towns, a sudden spate of lake overturns that killed everyone and everything close by via carbon dioxide poisoning, and landslides fucking *everywhere*.

All explained away by frazzled-looking TV personalities. But then came the floods, the droughts, hurricanes, tornadoes, a fucking *fire tornado*. The only thing we were missing at this point was a plague of locusts.

The human explanations had gotten a lot less scientific and a lot more supernatural after that.

People were dying because of Gaia's rage and we weren't doing anything to stop it. If anything, we were making it worse. It wasn't just daimons either—humans were increasingly being caught in the crossfire. Maybe once upon a time, they'd been Gaia's favored children, but she was definitely favoring the agathos now.

"This is awful. What if I try to talk to her again—"

"No," Riot said as I sliced a hand through the air, shaking my head vigorously before Grace could finish that sentence. It wasn't the first time she'd suggested contacting Gaia again, pleading with her to stop the carnage. This clearly wasn't a goddess of mercy though, and I doubted just *asking* her to stop would result in anything other than further injury to Grace and whoever happened to be nearby.

"Fine, but we still need to *do* something," she repeated, frustration pouring down the bond.

On that note, we could agree. We'd spent the past two weeks in a near constant state of ceremony, and the humans here had recruited other Kakodaimonistai scattered around the globe to do the same. Vasileios had reached out to all of the daimons and daimon-friendly agathos he knew to do the same, and I had to admit, it seemed to be working.

Why would Gaia be so enraged if it wasn't? The Olympians were growing stronger under our attention, just not strong enough. Not yet.

'*Temple*,' I signed at Grace, remembering with some dread how potent Gaia's magic had been at the falls when she'd turned on them.

"Right! We need to go to an Olympian temple," Grace agreed, pausing in her pacing to look at us. "The prayers are stronger coming from their dedicated temples, right? That's why we went to the falls to speak to Gaia?"

"Temples or sacred locations," Bullet agreed thoughtfully, lying down on the couch. His face wasn't so pale today, and his eyes were bright and alert. Today was a good day. Yesterday had been... not good. The strain of his ongoing fight with Riot was making things worse.

Grace twisted her ring nervously around her finger. "Maybe we should film it? Send it to the Kakodaimonistai and Vasileios' buddies who have been helping us out. I don't really want to put my face all over it, but the agathos and daimons *here* had already heard of me. Maybe having a person to relate to rather than just an idea or instruction will be more motivating to the people we're asking to help. We need people to actually *believe* in these gods they're praying to, in the power and potential of them, or it's meaningless."

"Wild could send a video to his vast network of Keres daimons," Riot suggested, looking at me like he was daring me to object. I nodded once in agreement, already contemplating the best way to do it. I hadn't been in contact with anyone apart from the message to Onyx sent from a burner phone, reassuring her we were alive and requesting she track down Dare. Grace had been safe here until now, and the idea of reaching out to others, to publishing her location, was... undesirable, to say the least.

I'd turned the phone on occasionally, looking for updates from Onyx, but after the first week of nothing I'd started checking more sporadically. Grace could tell through the bond when I'd heard nothing, and her worry and disappointment radiated out to the other two, ramping up the tension between them.

"It'll encourage other daimons to act. To mobilize," Bullet agreed, glancing at the surly Moros in the corner, still staring determinedly out the window. "I've seen snippets of futures with daimons working together—or more together than they usually do—but I think we're all wary of putting you out there like that, Amazing Grace."

"I don't want to put *myself* out there, but this is my prophecy. My responsibility. I'm the one putting innocent people in harm's way with the prayers and sacrifices, and if I'm going to ask others to help me, to try and stop all of this, then the least I can do is put my name on that." The fierce determination in Grace's voice gave us all pause. She'd never been ambivalent, but her pale eyes were blazing, her hands balled into fists at her side. Grace looked like a queen ready to march into battle.

Suddenly, she deflated, turning back to look at the television. With so many disasters recently, resources were thin on the ground to help people. Footage rolled of crash survivors sitting on the beach, pressing hands and shirts to bleeding wounds, huddling close together for comfort.

It wasn't the first awful footage we'd seen recently and it wouldn't be the last, but something about this was hitting differently. Grace looked and felt *distraught*, and I knew something would have to change.

"So let's talk to Vasileios tonight," Bullet said gently, pushing himself off the couch. "See how quickly we can organize everyone here to travel, figure out how long it takes, then go to the temple ruins at Olympia and make a big fucking scene. Sound like a plan?"

"Yeah," Grace replied, eyes still trained on the screen. "That sounds like a plan. Let's see if we can convince them to come on a road trip."

The footage changed, showing fights that had broken out somewhere in France over food supplies, and I rolled my neck, my bloodlust rising with a vengeance. Between that and the *regular* lust I was constantly trying to keep in check while Grace alternated sleeping in the downstairs bed where

Bullet had holed up with me—awkward and uncomfortable in the extreme, also not ideal for my constant boner—and the upstairs bed she shared with Riot.

They were tearing Grace apart. And each other.

"Come on," Riot said, looking at me and seeing a little *too* much. "You need to work out."

I nodded, standing up to follow Riot out into the orchard. It probably shouldn't have surprised me that he recognized the symptoms of a Keres on edge so well—he'd lived in Milton his whole life, and spent most of it antagonizing the Keres daimons in town who worked as bouncers.

The citrus scent of the orchard was somewhat grounding as we made our way through the rows of trees to a quiet, slightly larger clearing in the center, halfway between the house we were staying in and Vasileios' villa.

We both took a few minutes to warm up and stretch, Riot watching me warily the entire time. I cocked my head to the side, gesturing for him to speak if he had something to say. It was a testament to how much time we'd spent together that he understood what I meant.

"I've mostly come around to the idea of you as Grace's bonded," he began, stretching his arms behind his head. I snorted. As though his opinion on the matter made a difference either way. "But you need to be one hundred percent on top of your bloodlust, you feel me? Grace is adapting to the daimon world so well, but if you hulk out and start smashing shit in a rage, she will be terrified. You feel even a little bit edgy, let me know and we'll spar. Or go make good on all that sexual tension between you and Bullet, if Grace is cool with it," he added under his breath.

I guessed we can't have been that subtle if Riot was picking up on it, but he didn't look disturbed by the idea either. I don't even know why it mattered to me that he wasn't against it—he and Bullet were barely speaking—but I found that it did. As much as I was used to *managing* others, I didn't actually have much experience in taking their thoughts and feelings into consideration until now.

I dropped into a fighting stance, rolling my eyes at him while I raised my fists. However much he'd annoyed me in the past, I appreciated Riot's willingness to *help*, even though the concept of needing help was still foreign and unpleasant to me. A Keres suffering from bloodlust was a dangerous thing—something that I didn't ever want Grace to see.

'B-U-L-L-E-T,' I signed, tilting my head in question.

Both Riot and Bullet had picked up a little ASL from watching Grace and I, and Riot had taken pretty well to the alphabet.

"I don't want to fuck Bullet," he replied, deliberately misinterpreting my question as he dove in to try land the first hit. I elbowed him in the ribs before moving back, giving him a pointed look.

"Cheap fucking shot," he muttered, rubbing the sore spot before getting back in position. "Are you trying to play peacemaker right now?"

I rolled my eyes, taking his awkwardly angled hit in order to land a decent uppercut in the same spot on his ribs. We both pulled our punches and it was never about causing the other pain, but I wanted to make a point as well.

"Ow, fucker."

Riot shoulder barged me to get me out of his space, dancing backwards on the balls of his feet. Considering he didn't have any technical training, he wasn't a bad fighter. For a Moros.

"I'm never going to be okay with Bullet until we find out where Dare is and why he's just dropped off the grid. For all we know, those little agathos shits he was last seen fighting killed him. I don't know, I don't *know* what's happening, all I have is some vague secondhand information you got from Onyx, and that's incredibly aggravating." Riot swallowed thickly, shoving his hair out of his face. "The abstract concept that it's *not his time* yet or whatever else Bullet tries to placate me with isn't actually that helpful. I want to see Dare with my own eyes."

'G-R-A-C-E,' I signed, raising my eyebrows. At the end of the day, Grace was the one who was suffering in Bullet and Riot's rift. She loved them both, and was stuck in the middle, trying to navigate both of their feelings. And she was doing an excellent job—but really, she had enough shit on her plate.

"I know, I know. I don't want to fuck with Grace's head either. I'm not asking her to pick a side, and I'm not expecting her to come out swinging at Bullet or anything." I waited patiently, watching him work through it in his head the way I often did with the Keres daimons in Milton who had gotten carried away in their rage and needed to find a way out of it. Riot sighed heavily, leveling me with a look. "We all know Dare is Grace's fourth soul bond. As much her soul bond as any of us are. So, yeah, a part of me is bitter that *she* isn't mad at Bullet too because Dare deserves all that ferocious love Grace has to give, but I understand that I can't expect her to love him the same yet because she hasn't met him yet. Satisfied?" he asked me warily.

I nodded once, raising my fists and focusing on Riot's movements as he came at me again, his own agitation fueling his movements, making him fight harder than usual.

I'd stood behind Bullet because I could see his pain, I could see how much the knowledge he carried around with him burdened him, especially when it affected someone he knew. But I understood Riot's anger too, because it came from a place of concern. From what I knew of Riot's life back in Milton, his friendship with Dare was really the only thing he'd given up to be here at Grace's side, and it was clearly getting to him.

"Don't hold back," Riot muttered. "I might need this outlet more than you do."

"I'm going to shower at Vasileios," Riot panted as we finished our workout, bracing his hands on his knees. "You can take the shower back at the house. This was good. I just need... a minute."

'*Are you sure?*' I signed, mouthing the words so he could understand. If he didn't want to be alone, Grace would join him in a heartbeat.

"I'm sure. I'm going to wake Vasileios up, suggest the trip to Olympia. Maybe grab some food." I frowned, trying to work out what he wasn't telling me and Riot sighed in exasperation. "We're going to be on the road soon, and then who knows what will happen. Just... have your alone time, the three of you."

Alone time?

Riot disappeared into the grove before I could reply, probably trying to escape the awkwardness of his suggestion. Then again... he wasn't wrong. If Riot hadn't been sleeping above us these past few nights, maybe the strange dance the three of us were doing would be further along than it was.

Or maybe not. Maybe it was all in my head and Grace's fantasies, but never meant to be.

The house was empty when I got back which wasn't overly surprising. The village was within walking distance, and Grace and Bullet often headed down there to stock up on supplies or just whenever they needed some peace and quiet. Being so close to Vasileios and the others that lived around here meant they often dropped by, intrigued as they were by Grace.

It was very inconvenient.

I quickly showered, sensing the moment Grace got back, and walked out into the living area in my shorts, towel around my shoulders as I dried my freshly buzzed head. While I hadn't intended anything by it, I paused in my tracks when I felt the sudden spike of desire from my girl, curled up in an armchair watching me.

Bullet glanced at me out of the corner of his eye, pausing in putting some groceries away. His cheeks tinted pink before he looked away, fumbling the paper bag of mushrooms he was holding, while Grace's curious stare bored a hole into his back.

One part of me thought I should quickly back up and put some more clothes on, the other part of me wondered if Riot had a point. If maybe we should just have this out and see what happened before we were on the road and surrounded by people.

In the end, my curiosity won out.

Whatever emotions Grace was picking up from Bullet had her feeling a strange combination of sympathetic, amused and aroused, and she climbed out of the chair to drag him over to the couch as soon as he started reaching for cleaning supplies.

"Bullet," Grace said softly, sitting so close she was almost on top of him and wrapping her arms around his neck. Her sundress slid up her thighs as she moved, and I thought as many unsexy thoughts as I could before my dick made itself very known in these thin linen shorts. "It's okay," she reassured him. Bullet turned his head, burying it into her shoulder and groaning.

"It's not okay. I'm not meant to feel like this about anyone but you."

"Says who?" Grace asked sharply. "I'm not meant to have daimon soul bonds, and here I am, and all the happier for it. Come on. We can't keep going the way we are with this tension between us."

On that point, I definitely agreed.

BULLET

CHAPTER 25

This moment felt... precarious.

The past few *nights* had felt precarious. With the tension between me and Riot, I'd moved to the downstairs bedroom, sleeping on the furthest edge of the bed while Wild took the other side, and Grace spending every second night between us.

It was exhausting, and all of us were stretched thin by the tension, but there was no getting around it until we found Dare. As much as Riot's stubbornness was pissing me off, he was being careful not to force Grace into the middle of our dispute and I was doing the same. There was no doing that with the tension between me and Wild though. Grace was in the middle, whether she wanted to be or not. I wasn't going to make any decisions that changed the dynamic of our relationship without her input.

"You know I don't mind," Grace reiterated, her cheeks flushing as she maintained determined eye contact with me. She wiggled a little further into my lap, lightly running her nails down my chest. Even with the fabric of my shirt as a barrier, I still sucked in a surprised gasp as she scraped over my nipples.

The little minx was totally giving me a push, letting me *feel* just how okay she was with this idea.

"You really mean that," I told her, frowning slightly to myself. "I mean, I know you can't lie, but I can feel in the bond how much you're okay with it."

Behind Grace, Wild dropped down into an armchair, arms crossed behind his head in a way that accentuated the cut muscles of his chest and arms, his lips twitching into an almost smile.

He absolutely knew what he was doing. It should be illegal for him to walk around shirtless, honestly.

"It really doesn't bother you that this—" I gestured between Wild and myself. "—isn't normal among bonded?"

"We don't know for sure that it isn't," Grace pointed out, leaning in to trail light kisses over my jaw. She had the softest lips. I wanted to suck on them. "Even in Saturday lessons when we were taught about soul bonds, they were very vague on the details of, uh, intimacy."

"Stop distracting me with your feminine wiles," I groaned, tilting my head back to give Grace better access. "Neither of us feel any kind of way towards Riot," I added.

Wild nodded emphatically from the corner and I almost laughed despite the intensity of the moment. Poor Riot. Then again, he was being a dick right now, so whatever.

Grace absently toyed with her opal ring. "Maybe... maybe this is a kind gesture from the Fates. The two of you have been so alone, both bearing the weight of the gods' will in different ways, and maybe they thought that you needed some extra lo—, er, *affection* in your lives."

Wild and I glanced at each other before both looking away quickly, and I wouldn't be surprised if he was feeling as weirdly shy as I was.

'Love' was what Grace had almost said. We weren't there yet, and I wasn't sure we ever would be. Love required vulnerability. Both Wild and I were pretty great at reserving our vulnerable sides for Grace alone.

"That's a nice theory," I murmured, running a hand over her hip. "That some extra affection would be a little recompense for our lonely Grace-free lives."

"Not just Grace-free," she chided. "Just the time... before. I was lonely too."

"You'll never be lonely again, Amazing Grace." I gripped her leg, pulling Grace over my body until she was straddling me, my boner pressing rudely against her inner thigh, despite my conflicted thoughts.

I hated that Grace had been lonely, that I'd been forced to wait until she made her way into this world of prophecies and divine pressure on her own. I hated that I'd been right there, just out of her reach. Grace should have never been lonely a day in her life.

Wild shouldn't have been either. He'd kissed me and I'd left him, avoiding him ever since.

"Neither will you." Grace leaned down, brushing a kiss over my lips. "Do you want to do this? All of us? It can be... whatever we want it to be. It can go as far as we want it to go."

"Look at you, breaking all the rules, ignoring social norms," I teased, sliding the hem of her dress up just a little.

"Auburn Grace in my pastel-colored swing skirts and high-necked blouses wouldn't recognize this hussy," Grace laughed. Wild almost smiled, watching our girl in a rare moment of pure, unadulterated happiness. They were fewer and farther between these days. "So?" she pressed.

"You can *feel* what we want to do," I pointed out, slipping my hands underneath her dress and rubbing circles over her smooth thighs with my thumbs.

"I can, but I'm not letting you off that easily. I need us to be on the same page. I need you to *tell* me," she replied primly, sticking to her guns.

She twisted to look back at Wild, who nodded once, crimson eyes set firmly on me. *Be cool, Bullet. You've totally got this.* Grace tutted, giving him a pointed look, and he shot her a devastating smirk as he signed something.

"He said he wants this," Grace whispered breathily, her arousal ratcheting up in time with my own.

It was up to me. They'd both laid their cards out on the table, and now it was my turn. I had absolutely no doubt that if I said no, neither of them would hold it against me.

"Bullet?" Grace asked softly, turning back to face me.

"You know I love you right, Amazing Grace?"

"There's no doubt in my mind," she promised. That was all I needed. Loving Grace had gotten me through every difficult moment of my life, every hard choice I'd ever had to make, and that was before she even knew I existed.

"Then yes," I told her, desire and shyness battling for dominance. Had I imagined this thing between the three of us turning into something a million times? Yes. Had those thoughts got a hundred times more explicit post-orgy? Also yes. But I also had no idea what I was doing.

Wild probably knew exactly what to do, but he was taking his cues from me and Grace, clearly holding himself back to make sure we were both comfortable.

Which left Grace to take the lead.

She knew it too, a sense of steely resolve coming over her that Wild and I both sensed through the bond, making that delicious smirk appear around his mouth again.

Be cool, Bullet! You are going to humiliate yourself.

"Bedroom," Grace ordered, probably not wanting Riot to walk in on something that might traumatize him. She climbed off my lap, grabbing my hand with surprising assertiveness and pulling me towards the downstairs room. She didn't *need* to pull me, I was following with a borderline embarrassing level of enthusiasm.

I couldn't help it, I loved when Grace got all bossy with me. The moment we were in the bedroom, she pushed me to sit on the edge of the bed, standing confidently between my thighs, and I almost came then and there.

"On the bed, by the headboard," she ordered Wild, pointing at the pillows with slightly less confidence. Wild did *not* seem like he'd jizz his pants from being bossed around, and he was clearly indulging Grace as he oh so slowly prowled to the top of the bed, all cat-like grace despite his bulk. I swallowed thickly as the mattress dipped behind me, keeping my eyes trained forward as I imagined him lounging against the headboard, crossing his arms behind his head again and displaying all that rippling muscle.

Judging by Grace's sudden spike of arousal, that was exactly what he was doing. Whatever it was, it boosted her confidence, and she shot me a mischievous smile as her hands rose to slowly untie the halter neck strap that was holding her floaty sundress in place. She caught the material before it slipped over her breasts, my eyes obsessively following the movement.

"Hi," she whispered, her dress slipping slightly as my hands came to rest on her hips.

"Hi," I whispered back, tugging her down to my lap, needing to close the distance between us. She caught herself with one hand braced on my shoulder, her dress exposing one nipple. "You're a dream, you know that?"

"I've seen your dreams," she teased, a reminder that never failed to give me the warm and fuzzies. "I think we can do better. Lie down."

"Yes, mistress."

"We're not there yet," Grace laughed, swatting my chest as I laid down. She moved up my body to reach my mouth, draping herself over me and attempting to undo the buttons on my shirt between our bodies.

"You know we can stop whenever you want too," I mumbled against her lips, pushing the fabric of her dress down until it pooled at her waist. "I can feel how much you're thinking about our comfort, rather than your own."

"Oh, I'm very comfortable," Grace assured me, somewhat aggressively tackling my buttons. "There is something I wanted to try. Something I've been wanting to do but kind of wanted some extra, um, *guidance* on..."

I was about to ask what, but Grace finally got the last button undone, and her hand came to rest right above the waistband of my shorts, that mischievous glint back in her eye. Nothing made me happier than seeing Grace come into her own. The way she was learning to ask for the things she wanted, and not to feel ashamed of the desires she had.

"Whatever you want, Amazing Grace."

She crawled down my body, running her hand over my stomach and tugging off my shorts. I barely had a moment to give my dick a calm down pep talk before Grace was wrapping her fingers around my cock, adjusting her grip and monitoring my reactions until she was right where I wanted her. We'd done this before, so if there was something different she wanted to try...

I sucked in a loud breath, fisting the blankets either side of me as Grace lowered her head, swiping up a bead of precum with her tongue. Oh *fuck*, that felt good. While Grace and I hadn't done this before, I'd sort of assumed she had with Riot or Wild, but judging by the experimental way she was licking my cock like it was a particularly fascinating lollipop, maybe not?

Honestly, all she had to do was breathe near my dick and my stomach muscles were contracting, ready to end the party before it even began.

Grace smiled, looking pleased with herself before shooting a slightly pleading look through her eyelashes at Wild, clearly asking him for help. I didn't know exactly what that would look like, but I decided I'd be open minded. We had so much heavy shit going on in our lives, why not indulge our carnal desires for a little while?

Wild's hand brushed over my hair as he moved down the bed, letting me know he was moving closer, and I shuddered in anticipation. I couldn't communicate with him the way Grace could, which meant everything about the attraction between us had an added air of mystery. It just *felt* right.

That didn't mean it wasn't scary.

It didn't stop my heart from trying to beat out of my chest as Wild leaned over me, his lips brushing over mine in the same whisper of a kiss we'd shared the night of the the ritual for Dionysus. Slowly, purposefully, Wild repeated the gesture. Teasing me, inviting me to take more. I leaned up, chasing him and I could have sworn I felt the corners of his mouth tilt up as he rewarded me with another soft almost-kiss.

I had a feeling that if we were further down this road, Wild would have me more than just chasing. He'd probably have me *begging*, but today he was easing me in.

There was a surge of desire from Grace as Wild repeated the gesture, and I huffed a faint sound of irritation at being left unsatisfied. Apparently, that was the encouragement he'd been waiting for as he pressed his lips hard against mine, forcing my head back onto the mattress as he *finally* kissed me properly.

Again. Just like two years ago at the club, yet so, *so* much more.

Wild's enormous hand cupped my jaw, keeping me in place as his tongue swept my lower lip, demanding entry with that calm, unwavering confidence I found impossible to resist. I went pliant for him, vaguely aware that my hips were shifting, thrusting into the hand Grace had kept tightly wrapped around my dick. I tried to check the bond, to make sure Grace was still comfortable, but the desire she was feeling was so acute that I had to pull back or I really would end this show before it even began.

I guessed she was fine then.

Slowly, Wild pulled back, tugging my lower lip with his teeth for a moment, just enough to sting but in the best kind of way. He hovered above me for a moment, giving me a look so full of filthy promise that no words were necessary. I fucking *panted*, struggling to catch my breath as he ran a hand down my chest, all cool and confident, before shifting down the bed and settling next to my leg.

I expected to feel shy being naked in front of him, but Wild looked at me like I was hot as fuck, and that helped a lot. When he ran his hand up the back of Grace's neck to the back of her ponytail, all controlled dominance, that helped even more.

"Yes please," she said to whatever sense of a question he'd asked through the bond, arching back into his touch like a cat. "Show me what to do."

"I am not going to last long, you know that, right?" I confirmed, lifting my head off the mattress.

"Try," Grace replied, blowing me a kiss.

"Temptress," I groaned, flopping my head back down.

Before Grace could tease me any more, Wild gently used his hold on her hair to guide her gaze towards him, Grace's hand still rhythmically pumping my shaft. I watched, semi-pained by the effort of not coming, as

Wild gripped her chin and gently tugged Grace's mouth open, giving her one of those sinful looks as he pressed his thumb in her mouth and used his fingers to push her jaw up.

Holy fuck. I was jealous of Grace's mouth and Wild's thumb all at once.

She maintained eye contact with him, a questioning look on her face as she experimentally hollowed her cheeks, sucking his digit further into his mouth and swirling her tongue slowly around it.

"Nope, no, definitely not going to last," I breathed. Oh, how I loved when Grace completely dropped those agathos hangups and just embraced what she felt. "Are you trying to kill me?"

Wild pulled his thumb free, guiding Grace's head back down to my lap, eyes sparkling with amusement. Wild wrapped his hand around hers, guiding her movements as Grace took the head of my cock into her mouth, swirling her tongue teasingly again.

"Fuck," I hissed. "Fuck, fuck, fuck. That feels so good, you have no idea."

She probably had some idea—the pleasure was almost an avalanche of sensation through the bond, and Grace was practically grinding on my leg for some friction.

Wild maintained his grip on Grace's hair and hand, guiding her movements, and it was perfect because if he'd switched places with her, I probably would have freaked out just a little. I wanted this, I wanted him, but the idea of intimacy with anyone other than Grace was still a little overwhelming after a lifetime of thinking otherwise.

My teeth were digging so hard into my lower lip, I was surprised I hadn't broken skin. I watched as Wild released Grace's hand and gently stroked her throat as if to say '*relax*,' and exhaled heavily as she followed his silent instructions, taking me even deeper.

Nope. There was no way I could hold out after that.

"I'm going to come," I groaned, twisting the sheets into knots either side of me. "Grace, stop."

Frowning a little, Grace pulled back right as I came with an almost pained sigh all over my still twitching stomach, my entire body going limp immediately afterwards. While I didn't think I enjoyed making myself wait necessarily, the eventual pleasure had been even more all-consuming than usual.

Maybe there was something to be said for this whole orgasm denial thing after all.

"Can I not stop next time?" Grace asked, blinking at me innocently.

"You're a cruel mistress," I panted. "No teasing right now. My dick is like, overstimulated or something."

Grace snorted, but Wild was clearly in a less playful mood. Oh so slowly, he swiped his finger through the cum on my stomach and held his finger up to Grace's mouth. She didn't hesitate for one second to part her lips, licking the salty liquid from Wild's skin. He maintained eye contact with me as he sucked the remainder off his own finger, and my lower belly clenched with desire so potent I sucked in a breath.

"Oh, I am for sure going to come again," I muttered, looking between us. "Just give me, like, five minutes."

Wild shook with silent laughter, already moving, and I laid back and relaxed, knowing he was about to give Grace some much needed attention.

She blushed furiously as he climbed off the mattress, kneeling at the end of the bed and grabbing her hips, tugging her backwards and encouraging her onto all fours. Her eyes went wide at the *exposed* position, and I grinned at her as I practically watched her fight down the urge to clamp her legs together in real time. Wild didn't give her a chance, pulling Grace's scrunched-up dress and panties off before his hands smoothed reverently up and down the back of her thighs. I pushed my desire for Grace through the bond, confident that Wild was doing the same, encouraging her to relax, to know that she never needed to hide from us. Grace rewarded me with a beaming smile that turned into a breathy moan as Wild's face moved between her thighs.

Maybe Wild had been content to sit back and let Grace call the shots in the beginning, but he was definitely leading this dance now.

I shuffled further down the bed, forcing my weak limbs to move so I could get a better view as Wild tilted his head to the side and french kissed Grace's pussy with absolutely zero hesitation. Grace made a noise somewhere between a choke and sob, and I angled myself further towards him so I could study his technique.

I knew when I was watching a master at work.

"That good, huh?" I asked Grace with a lazy grin. "I'm going to take notes."

Wild pulled back for half a second to meet my gaze, all lazy arrogance like he was *inviting* me to watch and learn.

My dick stirred against my better judgment. I was going to need to nap for a solid ten hours after this.

WILD

CHAPTER 26

Grace's pussy was so slick, the feel and scent of her practically calling out to me. I knew she was shy about being in this position, so I continued to run my hands over her body, letting her know with my actions how attractive I found her as I *devoured* her cunt. There was going to be no room in Grace's head for anything but pleasure if I had my way. Not after that glorious little performance with Bullet. My dick was hard enough to hammer nails, and I needed her to be good and wet so I could bury myself in her before I lost my fucking mind.

Grace fell forward onto her forearms with a breathy moan, braced over Bullet's body. The moment my tongue found her clit, any traces of shyness vanished completely. Her body rocked back against my face, grinding experimentally to get me where she wanted me, and I reveled in her growing confidence with her own sexuality. Beneath that good girl agathos exterior was my horny, greedy soul bond and I intended to give her everything she ever wanted before she even had to ask for it.

I could feel Grace getting closer, but I didn't want her to come on my tongue this time. Not when we were introducing Bullet to the idea of a sexual relationship between the three of us.

Would it be too much for Grace to come on his tongue while I was fucking her from behind?

Maybe. This time, at least.

Still, this time he could appreciate the view.

I stood, wrapping an arm around Grace's waist and easily lifting her body further up Bullet's until her pussy was positioned over his renewed erection. She gasped—a quiet, needy sound—as I lined my cock up behind her, slowly pushing into her soaked pussy with no resistance. I'd never get sick of how this felt—like we were made for one another—but not just each other. Not when most of the purple of Bullet's eyes had been eaten up by his dilated pupils, his abs contracting, cock twitching beneath Grace as though it was trying to get closer to us.

"Wild," Grace moaned as I pulled her upright, her back flush to my chest. I wrapped one arm around her middle, hand kneading her breast as I rocked into her slowly, stoking Grace's arousal while putting on a goddamn show for the Oneiroi lying beneath us, breath loudly sawing in and out of his lungs.

I'd never wished more that I could *speak*. That I could whisper filth in Grace's ear until her pussy was clenching around me and her face was flushed scarlet, but I couldn't. I'd just have to show her with my body.

My eyes met Bullet's over Grace's shoulder as I slid one hand down her front, applying enough pressure to make her movements still, her body growing pliant beneath my ministration. She exhaled in relief as I circled her clit with my middle finger, her pussy clenching hard around my cock. My own eyes briefly rolled back into my head at the sensation.

313

"Don't stop," Grace breathed, her slim fingers wrapping around my wrist, keeping my hand in place. "I'm so close."

I won't stop, I promised her silently, hoping she could feel my determination if nothing else. I made sure to keep doing *exactly* what I was doing because I wasn't about to argue with my girl when she told what was going to get her over the edge. Within seconds, Grace was tightening around me, nails digging into my wrist as she curled forward as much as she could in my embrace, arousal flooding the bond between us.

"That's the prettiest thing I've ever seen," Bullet murmured, entirely transfixed as Grace rode out her release, dark hair escaping her ponytail and falling forwards over her face. *This* was the divine. I didn't give a fuck about interfering gods and goddesses—Grace in the throes of passion was the sacred eternal made flesh.

She let me lower her body with no protest as I draped her over Bullet, careful to keep us connected because the idea of pulling out of her hot, wet pussy was impossible. My own restraint flagging, I gave Grace just enough time to prop herself up on her forearms either side of Bullet before I curled over her body and fucked her like I goddamn *meant* it.

Bullet's hands tangled in Grace's hair, holding her gently in place—each thrust grinding her clit against his cock. I tipped my head back, closing my eyes at the fucking *bliss* that was having them both beneath me. *Mine.* Mine to cherish. Mine to protect. All fucking mine.

"It's too good," Grace whined, voice muffled against Bullet's chest.

"Please come," Bullet begged, face half hidden by Grace's hair. "Because I'm for sure ready to go again and I'm gonna need you to join me."

Was he worried Grace would find his lack of control off-putting? That I would? *Cute.* I was pretty sure both Grace and I would like nothing more than to see how many orgasms we could wring out of our needy Oneiroi.

"Wild, Wild," Grace chanted breathily. I could feel that she wanted me to get there with her, even if she was struggling to find the ability to speak. That meant I was doing something right.

Not wanting to disappoint her, I picked up my pace, feeling my spine tingle with my impending release. Grace must have picked it up through the bond because that seemed to be the permission she needed to let herself ago, writhing against Bullet as he bit down hard on his lower lip, stilling completely beneath her.

I came so hard, my vision wavered for a moment, the pleasure almost cripplingly good. I was only just holding my weight off Grace's back—my mind running through a series of filthy scenarios that all required Grace sandwiched between Bullet and I—and I forced myself to think calm relaxing thoughts as those visions tried to morph into the possibilities with *Bullet* pinned in the middle.

We were all sticky, messy and sated, and had probably pushed each other's comfort levels enough for one day without me getting overexcited all over again.

Reluctantly, I pulled back, biting my lip at the sight of my cum on Grace's inner thighs. I dropped a light kiss between her shoulder blades before darting into the bathroom next door to clean up, returning with two damp washcloths and handing one to Grace who accepted it gratefully before handing one to a startled-looking Bullet.

"Thanks," he mumbled, face an endearing shade of pink as he shyly cleaned himself up. We'd made a little progress, though he'd been more than happy to use Grace as a buffer between us. Maybe one day we'd reach a point where he felt like he didn't need to do that, or maybe he wouldn't.

I was grateful for this, more grateful than I could express even if

I'd been able to say the words out loud. I'd never be lonely again, and that meant everything.

Grace tossed the washcloth aside, covering herself with the sheet to preserve her modesty and reaching for my hand to tug me down on the bed next to her. There was only a split second of hesitation on Bullet's face before he took the other side, pulling the sheet over him as well.

I could feel Grace practically vibrating with the need to talk about everything and Bullet huffed a quiet laugh, drumming a tune only he could hear on Grace's thigh.

"Let's not make it awkward, Amazing Grace. Everyone feel good?" Bullet asked.

"Yup," Grace replied happily while I nodded my head.

"Everyone comfortable?" he asked, eyes sparkling.

"Very much so," Grace assured him. I nodded again.

"Then we're good," Bullet said simply, shrugging. "Let's see where the Fates take us."

I nodded in agreement, closing my eyes for a moment and resting my head on Grace's. The Fates had been more generous than I deserved already. If this was as far as it ever went between the three of us, I would never complain.

We stayed in that position for a long while, too sated to move, Grace dozing lightly between us. Eventually the sound of the front door opening stirred me upright, but Grace's hand closed around my wrist, keeping me in place.

"It's Riot," she murmured sleepily.

The man in question loudly made his way through the living room, giving us plenty of warning that he was approaching before he opened the bedroom door.

"I bought you hydration, figured you'd all need it," he announced, tossing three bottles of water on the bed for us, mouth twisted up in wry amusement as he observed the three of us, still clearly naked beneath the sheet.

"Aw, you're not a regular soul bond, you're a *cool* soul bond," Bullet teased. Grace sucked in a quiet breath, and I was right there with her, hoping this would be the moment when the frostiness between the two of them thawed.

Unfortunately, it didn't look like Riot was there yet, since he ignored Bullet's words completely. "Well, as much as I'd love to sit down and get a play-by-play of how awkward your first threesome was, you all need to get dressed so we can go to Vasileios' place. Something big is going down with the agathos, and by some unfortunate stroke of fate, people are looking to *us* for leadership and guidance."

"What do you mean 'something big'?" Grace asked, taking a swig of the water before scrambling out of the bed and snatching up her discarded dress. Bullet and I moved slower, and it didn't escape my notice that he kept his eyes trained on the floor the entire time, cheeks pink.

Fucking adorable.

"Well, there's a sudden and terrifying influx of abnormally large scorpions in Athens. So there's that. Plus, the agathos who live here—and all agathos sent away on outreach trips—have been summoned back home by their original communities. We always knew the fact that the agathos were *organized* could be an issue, and it looks like it is. They're mobilizing."

Grace's expression lost of all its post-orgasm sweetness. "Then so are we."

GRACE

CHAPTER 27

We practically sprinted through the orange grove, my heart thundering in my chest. We'd always known that at some point, the agathos were going to take more drastic measures because *Gaia* was taking more drastic measures. They were following their goddess' lead, and that was more terrifying than anything.

We couldn't reason with their logic. Not without some divine backing of our own.

Vasileios' usually open, spacious living room with the dark floors and white furniture was *packed*, every daimon, agathos, and Kakodaimonistai in his community seemed to be here, many looking like they'd just woken up.

"There you are," Foster said, shoving his hand through his hair. Not for the first time, by the state of it. "My parents have been blowing up my phone for a couple of hours, telling me I need to come home. Saying that the agathos are going to war with the daimons once and for all. They said the natural disasters that have targeted daimon communities without regard for human life are proof that this is Anesidora's will. That our time is coming, a time of agathos dominance."

Despite the brave face I was trying to put on, I was hit by crushing wave of helplessness at Foster's words. Unlike every other time in my life where I'd been told that Anesidora had given her blessing for something, this time I believed it. She had a vendetta against me, against the daimons because they answered to Nyx and had supported me, maybe even against the *humans* now.

Frankly, I wasn't sure how *any* agathos could go along with this when we were hard-wired to protect humanity. Then again, the agathos I'd grown up with had always been good at picking and choosing who was deserving of help and protection based on their own set of standards.

"Grace, Grace's harem, come watch this," Vasileios called from the couch, one arm slung around Alesa. He yawned, tipping his head back and exposing the massive love bite on his neck as we wound our way through to the front of the room.

An international all-day news network was playing on the flat screen in English, stone-faced reporters spliced between footage of the most terrifying insects I'd ever seen.

Insects? Arachnids? I didn't want to look closely enough to count their legs.

"Those are not scorpions," Bullet said immediately, leaning into my side. "Not regular scorpions, anyway."

Wild gripped my shoulder, turning me to look at him and inhaling and exhaling slowly, encouraging me to breathe along with him as a combination of panic and bile climbed up my throat.

"They're the size of house cats," I gasped eventually, glancing at the screen out of the corner of my eye. Housecat-sized shiny black scorpions, scuttling through the empty streets of Athens as terrified residents holed up in buildings, panicked faces appearing in windows.

"They're not entering the buildings, see?" Foster said, pointing at the row of scorpions that shuffled past an open door.

"That building looks empty though," Riot pointed out. "Maybe they didn't go in there because there's no people inside to murder."

"They haven't gone inside any buildings," Alesa confirmed, tucking herself a little closer into Vasileios' side. "Not in the thirty minutes or so we've been watching. They're almost.... patrolling the streets?"

"Gaia sent a giant beast, Skorpios, to earth once," Bullet said absently. "Far bigger than these creatures I imagine, but scorpions are closely associated with Gaia."

"Where did they come from? Have they appeared anywhere else?" I asked Alesa, clinging a little to Wild as the world swayed for a moment. He wrapped a strong arm around my waist, holding me upright, while Riot moved in closer to my other side.

"They came out of the ground as far as anyone knows," Alesa responded, eyes glued to the television. "And yes, a few other places. They showed footage from Olympia and Delphi of the same thing."

Bullet and I looked at each other at the same time.

"The temples," I breathed. He nodded, mouth set in a grim line.

"On the plus side, we must have really rattled her. On the minus side, she absolutely knows what we're doing and is actively stopping us from taking our efforts to the next level," Bullet sighed, fishing his tarot cards out of his pocket to shuffle them absently.

"But what do we do now?" I asked, braving a look at the creepy scorpion-filled streets before looking away again. "We were planning on going to Olympia."

"I say we eat first. I can't think when I'm this hungry." Vasileios yawned. "I'll call the restaurant, see if they can bring pizzas."

Eat? How could anyone *eat* right now?

But everyone else seemed happy enough to go with that plan, and the moment Vasileios and Alesa stood to arrange food, I sunk into the spot they vacated on the couch, attempting to drag Wild down with me, but he seamlessly pulled Bullet in to take his place while he opted to stand over us like a bodyguard.

I had no idea how long we sat there, staring in silence at the screen, guilt churning relentlessly in my gut. The humans hiding in their houses and offices, staring out of the windows in terror as their city was taken over by these horrifying creatures, they had no idea what was causing this. But I knew. I'd known for a long time, hiding out here, living in comfort with my bonded.

Yes, I'd been carrying out multiple ceremonies and prayers each day with the others in the hopes of strengthening the Olympians, but was that actually helpful? Or was I just hiding behind the guise of doing something?

"I know you're spiraling right now," Bullet murmured quietly, speaking low enough that only I could hear him, "but remember that the agathos knew that all of this bullshit was caused by Gaia's rage and they not only didn't try to stop it, they used it as justification to attack daimons at will. They're probably not feeling even one tenth of the guilt you're feeling."

"The fact that *they* should feel worse doesn't make *me* feel better," I replied, watching a mother comforting a clearly terrified child through a third-story window as drone footage played on screen.

321

"What next, Gracie?" Riot asked, dropping to the floor and leaning back against my legs to watch the horror show. I reached for his hair absently, running my fingers through it.

Before I could respond to question how deadly a giant scorpion actually was and whether we could manage to get to Olympia anyway, the news anchors started saying something about breaking news, drawing the attention of everyone in the room.

"That's the Basilinna," Orion, one of the Greek agathos, said immediately. "My Basilinna, I guess. Technically. She didn't look... like that."

"She looks, um, unwell," I settled on, watching this woman walk up the center of the street as scorpions diverted around her ankles, giving her space as she approached the building where the camera crew were filming at street-level from.

"She looks like a fucking zombie," Riot deadpanned. He wasn't wrong. The woman's movements were jerky, her upper body contorted at a strange angle as she limped into the frame.

Strange zombie walk aside, this woman looked like she could be a goddess herself, with waist-length curly dark hair, half pulled back and secured with an elegant gold pin, and a sweeping navy dress that was entirely impractical for traipsing down the street with giant insects. Her age was hard to place though—she looked both old and not at the same time, her olive skin was taut but somehow withered. And her eyes... Agathos always had pale, opal-colored irises, but that was all this woman had. No pupils, no whites around the edges.

Orion shuddered, as he stood next to Wild. "She didn't used to look like that. Her eyes never looked like that."

Bullet made a sound of discontent next to me, pressing in a little closer to my side as the woman finished her slow and terrifying approach to the camera. The news anchors had fallen silent, the only sound was the incessant scuttling of the scorpions in the background. It was chilling.

"Humans," she rasped in a voice that was entirely *in*human. It had an echo to it, like it had been dredged up from a deep, ancient source.

"Gaia is speaking through her," Bullet said, loud enough for the rest of the room to hear. "That's why she looks like that. Mortal minds aren't equipped for that kind of thing, she's literally deteriorating from the inside out."

"You have enraged Gaia with your disrespect," the Basilinna continued. "She created this paradise for you, and you ruined it. She sent the agathos here to counter the evil daimons whispering poison in your ear, and you worship those daimons anyway."

"She's telling them," I whispered, clutching Bullet's thigh and Riot's hair. "She's exposing us."

"Gaia will make the world wonderful for you again, but the daimon scourge must be eradicated first, as must the agathos who have been tainted by their influence. Humans of Athens, stay in your homes. My scorpions will not harm you there, but if you leave, they shall *feast*."

I shuddered at the hissed declaration.

"Gaia invites Grace the agathos to come to Athens and end the misery she has caused. Come to me, Grace. Show the foolish gods and goddesses who seek to challenge me that you are unworthy of the prophecy they gave you. Sacrifice yourself to me, and no one else needs to suffer."

"Liar," Riot muttered.

"Come to me, Grace the agathos. Come to Athens. You think you are so brave, but you have never been tested. Come and show us what a coward you really are."

The Basilinna's head tilted back and up, a strange angle that exposed her entire throat, and a slow smirk spread across her face before she began to back away, the wave of scorpions parting for her as she went.

The screen cut back to the news anchors, sitting in stunned silence in their overly bright studio, and I could absolutely relate because I also had no idea how to respond to that.

Wild tapped on my shoulder to get my attention, holding up his hands to sign before seemingly not finding the words he wanted to say. Instead he just gave me a questioning look, head tilted to the side and eyes narrowed.

Was I going to go? There was no doubt in my mind that's what he was asking me. What everyone in this room was thinking.

"Grace," Vasileios called, strolling back into the center of the room while the Kakodaimonistai went to the front door to collect pizzas. "We do not negotiate with terrorists, yes? Tell us what it is you want to do."

I smoothed down the front of my sundress nervously as I stood to face the room, finding all eyes on me.

"I understand if you want me to go—"

"Let's just not even pretend that's an option," Riot cut in, standing behind me. "One, Grace is not 'sacrificing herself' to appease Gaia's temper, or whatever. Two, it wouldn't make a difference even if she did. Gaia has been flattening towns and taking the lives of all of our kinds—though especially daimons—and that's not the kind of behavior that just ends because she gets what she asks for. She'll demand more because she can."

"No one is suggesting sacrificing Grace," Vasileios said calmly, surveying the room with a cool look. "Or I certainly hope no one is suggesting that. Not about one of my friends, under my roof."

"No, no one wants that," Foster agreed firmly, crossing his arms over his chest. Estrella leaned against him, resting her head on his shoulder and looking around impassively.

"We are fighting, right?" Orion asked. "I don't know how—I have no idea how you fight against giant scorpions whose stingers can probably kill us. But Gaia would not have acted so rashly unless she was worried. We must have strengthened the Olympians."

"And I had hoped to strengthen them more by traveling to Olympia and giving an offering at the Temple of Zeus," I said quietly. "But that idea is looking less and less viable. While I'm not willing to go and sacrifice myself for Gaia's rage, I do think... Maybe I should go to Athens."

"*We* should go to Athens," Bullet corrected out loud at the same time Wild signed the words.

"*We* should go to Athens," I agreed, pushing my shoulders back and standing a little straighter. "Because I'm not a coward. Or maybe I was a coward, but I'm not going to be one anymore."

"Great," Vasileios announced with a loud clap that made me jump. "We are your willing soldiers, lead us into battle."

"Oh. Um, no thank you," I replied, though it sounded a bit like a question, and Vasileios laughed. "I don't know how to do that. And I can't ask you to come with me. It's too dangerous—"

"We're in this together," Foster interjected firmly. "We can be more help to you than just carrying out prayers and sacrifices from the safety of Leonidio, Grace. Use us."

Could I really ask them to come with me without a solid plan? Making a statement to rally support and strengthen the imprisoned gods had seemed like enough to go on in the heat of the moment this morning when I saw the wreckage of that plane floating off the coast, but now it seemed like nothing. Like a stupid, immature kid's idea of a plan.

There was no guarantee that it would work, and it didn't address the more immediate problem of an army of angry scorpions sent by Gaia herself.

"We want you to succeed," Estrella said in a quiet voice, holding Foster a little tighter. "We want change. We want the chance to ask the Fates to help us, to ease the restrictions on our lives."

"The scorpions—"

"They are just big bugs. We'll figure it out. I will get out all the knives I own," Vasileios said easily, flicking a hand dismissively. "Come, let us eat and pack. I will call Dimitrios, we can borrow his big tourist bus. The drive is three hours, plenty of time to plan."

"Absolutely," Riot mumbled. "A three-hour drive is plenty of time to plan how to take on a scorpion army sent by a deranged goddess. Why not?"

GRACE

CHAPTER 28

The sky was darkening as we approached Athens by bus. The daimons had started off the trip in an almost relaxed mood—well, not *my* daimons, but the others—but now everyone was quiet and nervous. The roads had been madness with people fleeing Athens, and the journey had taken much longer than three hours, but the closer we got to the city, the quieter and more eerie everything got.

"There's a barricade up ahead," Ezio, the daimon who was driving the bus, called out. "We're just outside the metropolitan area, no sign of scorpions yet."

"Who's manning the barricade?" Riot asked, arm draped over my shoulders as we sat together at the front of the comfortable air-conditioned bus. "Agathos or humans?"

"Humans, I think," Ezio replied, leaning over the giant steering wheel and squinting into the distance.

"Ah, then nothing to worry about," Vasileios drawled, his face buried between Alesa's breasts while he reached over to stroke Mathias over the top of his trousers. These Philotes daimons were really something else.

"Swap with me," Riot suddenly said to Wild, twisting to look behind him where Bullet sat with Wild. Bullet had his entire side pressed to the window, attempting to put some space between his and Wild's bodies, clearly feeling a little awkward after what we'd done earlier. Our timing really couldn't have been worse—Bullet needed some reassurance from me, and I'd noticed too late.

Wild didn't object to Riot's command, smoothly standing and moving into the aisle so he and Riot could swap places. I frowned, realizing a lot of the daimons on the bus behind us were moving around too.

"Hey, what's—"

Before the words were out of my mouth, Wild's lips were pressed against mine, one hand gripping my jaw, the other on my hip. I grabbed at his shirt to keep myself upright as he crowded my space in the best way, dipping me back until my head was resting against the window pane, his front pressed tightly against mine.

Everything about Wild was so big and commanding, he ate up the small space on the bench seat and I let him, parting my lips willingly as his tongue swept teasingly at my lower lip. I knew I had other things I was meant to be concentrating on, but he made it so easy to forget. To just live in the moment and let him lead. Let him make the hard decisions for me for a moment, just so my mind could have a little reprieve.

You're on a bus, I reminded myself vaguely. *Surrounded by other people.*

But when Wild's hand slid down from my hip to my thigh, giving it a quick squeeze before cupping the back of my knee and dragging my leg over his trunk-like muscular thighs, I didn't protest. *What were we doing again?*

"Done!" Vasileios announced, jogging up the stairs to the bus as Wild and I broke apart. *Done? What was done?* Vasileios grinned at my compromising position. "Count yourself lucky, Grace. Most of the other agathos were just pinned down in their seats. You got special treatment."

I shot Wild a withering look as my entire face flamed, and he helped me into an upright position with an absolutely unrepentant look on his face. Before I could tell him off, the other daimons who'd sneaked off at some point joined us on the bus and we began slowly rolling forwards, passing the now unmanned barricade.

I don't want to know, I don't want to know, I don't want to know, I chanted silently in my head, doing my best not to think of those humans and whatever they'd been encouraged to do. Logically, I knew that for almost as long as there had been humans, there had been daimons whispering wicked words in their ears, encouraging them to follow their worst instincts, and it wasn't my job to personally save all of them.

Logically, I knew that.

Wild draped an arm over my shoulders, pulling me into his side and dropping an apology kiss on my head even though he could sense I wasn't angry with him per se. His actions had come from a good place. Sort of.

"A little further to go, but at least there's no traffic," Vasileios joked, though the tension we were all feeling was palpable. "Welcome to Athens. Home of many ancient ruins and apparently, hundreds of oversized scorpions. Maybe thousands? Who knows."

I checked the knife strapped to the side of the jeans I'd borrowed from Estrella, my feet tightly encased in borrowed leather boots. All of us had dressed in the thickest clothes we could find and armed ourselves as best we could with knives, bats, and every household poison we could get our hands on.

Would any of it work against scorpions sent by Gaia herself?

Debatable.

But would Gaia have really gone to this much effort to guard the temples if they didn't pose a risk to her? I didn't think so. I had to believe that the Fates weren't done with me yet, that whatever nefarious plans Gaia had in mind, we'd find a way around them.

The bus was silent as we slowly rolled our way through the city, and I felt like a bug under a microscope as humans pressed their noses up to the windows of their homes, gesturing at us to turn back. Ezio was pulling obscene gestures at them all with a borderline gleeful smile on his face, so at least one of us was confident, I supposed.

"Usually, it would be maybe ten minutes from here with no traffic," Ezio said over his shoulder. "But I don't know. When the bugs come? Who knows."

Last chance to go back,' Wild signed, extricating himself for a moment to use his hands and then draping his arm back over me again.

"No turning back," I replied firmly. "We need to show strength. We need to take action now to slow down the trail of destruction."

Wild squeezed my shoulder in support, and I trained my attention outside, waiting for the first sign of the nightmares on legs currently haunting this city. Athens was nothing like what I imagined and so much more at the same time. I supposed after only seeing pictures of the Acropolis, I hadn't accounted for the fact that it was also a bustling modern metropolis where people lived and worked and went to school. Not that there was anyone outside, but there was evidence of modern life everywhere, and seeing it without humans around made it all a little haunting.

A little dystopian.

"This is creepy as fuck," Riot said, reappearing in the aisle next to us and opting to stand rather than take the empty seat next to Bullet.

Oh goddess, had he sent the humans at the barricade to their doom? Don't ask, don't ask...

"Agreed," Bullet murmured uneasily. "This feels a little post-apocalyptic."

"Fuck," Ezio cursed from the driver's seat. "We've got company."

"What kind of company?" I asked, grabbing Wild's leg and leaning towards the aisle to try see out the front window. I glimpsed some shiny SUVs in the distance that were definitely the first choice of agathos back in Auburn, but maybe they were just regular humans?

"The not-insect kind," Ezio muttered, pressing his foot to the gas. Riot stumbled back, falling into the seat next to Bullet.

"Technically, they shouldn't be able to hurt us while there are agathos on the bus," I mumbled, just loud enough for Wild to hear. He pressed his lips together, clearly unwilling to take any risks based on that information, which was fair since plenty of other things that weren't *meant* to be happening were.

"Okay, so let's floor it to the temple and hope for the best?" I suggested. "They want a confrontation, we're going to give them one. We just have to get to the temple grounds first."

"Got it!" Ezio yelled before anyone else could respond, pressing his foot to the gas. The bus lurched forward, the engine making a clear sound of protest as he took to the flat wide street as fast as possible. "I have never driven down this avenue with no cars on it before, this is fun."

"This is not fun at all," Bullet groaned from behind me. "Riot will for sure never speak to me again if I puke on him."

Riot grunted in agreement.

Ezio swerved ominously around some kind of giant roundabout with a sculpture in it, and the scorpions seemed to descend from everywhere at once.

Someone screamed—possibly me—and Ezio pushed the vehicle harder, not backing down as a swarm came towards us. Blessedly, they weren't as fast as I thought they'd be, but they weren't slow either.

"I'm going to run them over. Let's see how the tires hold up," Ezio called out. My stomach churned uncomfortably at the first *crunch* of exoskeleton under the bus' wheels. Immediately the vehicle slowed, the wheels churning through broken scorpion bodies, halting our progress.

"It's not far from here," Ezio gritted out. "We just need to go a little further. We're nearly there."

The SUVs stopped on another wide avenue ahead of us, the agathos climbing out of their vehicles and standing on the asphalt, not drawing the attention of the scorpions at all.

Shoot.

Shit.

We were sitting ducks in here. The bus wasn't going to make it to the temple, and we couldn't take on both the scorpions *and* the agathos.

The scorpion-proof agathos.

I stood, twisting to look at Foster and Orion, the two agathos closest to me, who'd clearly figured out the same thing.

"What are you thinking, Gracie?" Riot murmured, looking up at me with narrowed eyes.

"They're not attacking the agathos. Gaia didn't send them to attack her own," I pointed out uneasily, palms already sweating at what I was about to do.

"They're not attacking *those* agathos," Bullet replied, looking between me and the door. "Grace—"

"Let's go!" Foster yelled, the agathos already diving towards the driver's door. I half jumped, half stumbled out of Wild's reach as Orion hit the button next to Ezio to open the front doors, all of us tumbling out at once. The scorpions fanned out around us, carefully avoiding us as they continued to come at the bus over and over.

Foster launched himself at one approaching the still-closing bus doors, stabbing a knife through it with a crunch. It hadn't even tried to defend itself from him.

"Down here!" Orion shouted, grabbing my arm and dragging me towards a smaller side street, away from the agathos blockade. "Run. It'll take you out onto another wide avenue, follow it until you get to the ruins. We'll hold off the scorpions. Run!"

"This is not how I imagined exploring Athens," I muttered, forlornly remembering my perfectly organized Pinterest board of ancient ruins and gorgeous museums as I broke into a sprint, hoping that no one in the apartments above would start yelling and drawing attention to me. I was confident that if I could just get to the temple, I would be fine. Maybe I was just telling myself that to make me feel better.

My lungs burned as I ran, out of practice after so long, and I stumbled hard into a lamppost as the ground roiled underneath me.

We'd been protected at Vasileios' place, so close to one of the entrances to the underworld. We weren't protected here though. We weren't hidden.

Gaia knew exactly where I was.

It took longer than I'd hoped, despite me pushing myself as fast as my legs could carry me. The SUVs kept circling, agathos clearly choosing to follow me rather than the bus of daimons and humans, and I dived into small alleyways to catch my breath, flattening myself against apartment walls and shop fronts, waiting until they passed before I kept going.

I knew the others must have gotten off the bus, I could hear the shouts and sound of fighting spilling out into the streets, but I couldn't let myself turn back. Instead I forced as much love and apology through the bonds as I could before I kept going, panting a sigh of relief when I finally found the tree-lined enclosure that housed the ruins.

The Acropolis loomed overhead, the pale marble ruins standing in stark contrast to the bright sky. The history of where we were standing hit me like a freight train, despite the fact that I was supposed to be concentrating on where we were going. These ruins had seen so much—the Roman Empire at the peak of its strength, the Dark Ages, medieval peasants and the Ottoman Empire, world wars and Olympic games. That knowledge filled me with a sense of purpose.

I was part of a long history of change. Change was okay.

Those agathos driving around the city, attempting to block the temples, willing to fight or threaten anyone who got in their way, *they* were in the wrong. They were on the wrong side of change, even if they didn't realize it yet.

The ground shook violently beneath me, and I grabbed onto a tree, covering my face as the branch took a very *unnatural* swing at me. If the others hadn't led the agathos to my location, the incredibly targeted mini earthquake would have. The ground stopped moving enough for the agathos SUVs to assemble nearby, doors flying open as they made a sprint for Zeus' temple. I dodged whipping tree branches as best I could, stumbling back onto the street the moment the agathos crowd had cleared. Bloodied and bruised daimons, agathos and Kakodaimonistai alike stumbled towards me, but the scorpions weren't attacking them anymore.

They were streaming into the entryway to the temple as well, following their leaders towards the temple ruins to block our path.

"Wild!" I gasped, stumbling towards him the moment I saw him approach, dragging an exhausted looking Bullet along behind him. Riot jogged after them a moment later, all three stumbling into me at once.

"Don't you *ever* do that again," Riot snapped, pressing a hard kiss against my head. "You just took a decade off my fucking life, Gracie."

"The others are still catching up," Bullet rasped, bending over and bracing his hands on his knees. "As soon as the agathos realized you weren't there, they started directing the scorpions to different temple sites. What do you want to do, Grace? How do you want to do this?"

I could see Wild strategizing, looking through the restless trees and trying to figure out a way to get us across the wide expanse of sacred ground that housed the temple ruins while keeping us safe. He might manage it too. He'd come up with something and communicate it to me in ASL for me to relay to the others. It'd be something that kept me safe—Riot and Bullet too—but there wouldn't be any guarantees for anyone else.

I wasn't going to ask them to take risks that I wasn't willing to take.

Panic grabbed me by the throat at the idea of walking into a crowd of angry, *organized* agathos, but Wild grabbed my chin, guiding me to look at him before it could set in.

'*You are brave. You are strong. You are not alone,*' he signed in rapid succession. '*You are never alone.*'

"You know we'll always back you up, Gracie," Riot sighed, wiping his bloody blade on the thigh of his jeans, his irritation at me running off, already forgotten.

Was that the right thing to do? This was bigger than just me. The agathos, daimons and humans milling around, looking to me for direction, needed me to make the right decision. They were relying on me, and I didn't want to put their safety at risk.

"Tell me what to do," I whispered to Bullet. My fearless guide, my source of knowledge and insight. The bravest man I knew, who faced down impossible odds every day with a beaming smile on his face.

His smile was watery. "You know what to do, Amazing Grace. Everyone here knows what they signed up for. It's time to make some waves."

I nodded, my throat tight as I led my bonded out to where a few of our small group of misfits had already assembled. They were brave and adventurous, and they'd followed me here in the hopes of creating a better world. One that we fit into. I wasn't going to let them down.

There were humans in the buildings watching us through their windows, phones already held up, recording us. It was too late to go back now.

"No more hiding. We're going to approach as a group. Slow. Calm. Purposeful," I instructed, holding my head up high. The agathos among us nodded determinedly, faces set into grim masks, but it was the feral grins on most of the daimons that I found bolstered my confidence. They weren't afraid, so I wasn't going to be either. Their clothes were torn and filthy, but it looked like everyone had made it here, which was the most important thing.

"Once we get to the edge of the temple grounds, count to ten before you follow me," I continued.

"Gracie—" Riot said instantly, reaching for me. I grabbed his forearm and leaned up to kiss his cheek.

"Persephone told me make sure I had plenty of space," I replied with a weak laugh, patting my pocket. It made a rattling noise that made me feel vaguely ill. "Ten seconds, okay?"

There were twenty of us, but it felt like less than that as we filed out of our hiding spot, stepping through the gate where tickets were probably sold usually and standing on the edge of the flat expanse of grass. The remains of the temple loomed in the darkness, only a few crumbling columns on an enormous plinth. A few more broken pieces of marble column laid on the ground, and the roof had long since disappeared.

It wasn't the most majestic sight as far as temples went, but I could feel the energy from it. The power.

I gripped both Bullet and Riot's hands, Wild shadowing my steps and covering my back, and a stab of *something* hit me in the chest. A sense of something missing. Some*one* missing.

There was no time to reflect on it as the agathos shouted orders at us and each other in both Greek and English, scorpions scuttling between them, forming a barrier between our groups. A few agathos began chanting, much like they had when I'd been tied to the altar in the basement all those weeks ago. There were a lot more of them than there were of us, but we had a powerful weapon that they didn't, and it wasn't the pouch full of mystery magic Persephone had given me.

It was a *cause*. Resolve. We were fighting *for* something.

The agathos were courageous in the face of their fear of change, I supposed I could grant them that. But we had the courage of our convictions.

Bullet mumble-rapped *My Shot* from *Hamilton* under his breath and it brought a small smile to my face. He was like my own personal epic movie soundtrack to life.

"Still good to record this?" Riot asked, squeezing my hand.

"Let's do it. There were humans recording us on the way here anyway," I replied, nodding my head once.

My entire life, I'd been raised with Anesidora's command to *láthe biōsas*, to live hidden. Strangely, of all her compulsions, this was the easiest to shake off. Maybe because she'd exposed us first, or maybe because to hide and say nothing now felt like lying, and I couldn't lie.

"See you soon," I murmured, releasing Riot and Bullet and taking that first terrifying step forward on my own.

"Okay," Bullet agreed somberly as Wild's hand landed on Riot's shoulder, keeping him in place when he lurched forward to follow.

The ruins were illuminated by lights at their base, throwing them into stark contrast with the dusky night sky, and I focused on the majesty of that instead of the crowd in front of me, staring at me with such blazing hatred that I could feel it from forty feet away. My knees shook with every step, but I forced my chin up, daring them to make the first move.

I am strong. I am brave. I am not alone.

The agathos stiffened with tension as my group spilled out onto the dry grass that surrounded the temple behind me, a small but determined force to be reckoned with. We were warriors. Maybe not the conventional kind, but we were already fighting in a war bigger than the close-minded group in front of me knew about.

My heart dropped to my stomach as I loosened the leather pouch Persephone had given me, reaching into the bag without looking. Whatever was in there was smooth, yet *sharp*, immediately cutting my skin, though it wasn't deep enough to be more than an annoyance. A wave of nausea threatened to overtake me as I pulled out a handful of whatever it was, letting it fall loosely from my hand as I walked, just like the Queen of the Underworld had instructed.

Don't look, I told myself as each sharp seed-like thing landed with a quiet thud onto the earth, more little cuts piercing my skin each time I reached into the pouch.

I paused twenty feet away from the agathos, who had organized themselves in two military-style lines before the temple with two further rows of scorpions in front of them, stingers held high. Tilting my chin up stubbornly, I pulled out the sharp objects with more speed and threw them around me as they watched, blood running in rivulets down my fingers and dripping onto the earth.

They probably think you're crazy, I thought wryly as no one made any move to stop me. They probably thought I was doing some kind of ritual to La Nuit with ceremonial seeds or something.

I wasn't even sure what I was doing, other than putting my faith in Persephone and hoping she didn't entirely screw me over.

As soon as the pouch was empty, I folded it up and slid it into my pocket, growing increasingly nervous at the still silence around us. Shouldn't something be happening? Anything?

I'd take a field of flowers at this point.

But then the earth started to *move*. My heart stuttered in my chest—was this another one of Gaia's rage fits? Persephone had warned me this would anger her. But it didn't feel quite like Gaia's anger... The earth was moving, but as I looked down, the surface soil rippled—rippled, then *parted*. I screamed as a *hand* emerged, then multiple hands, shooting out of the ground like the most disturbing blooms in existence. Masculine hands in every shade that shoved the dirt away, revealing arms, and then *helmets*, shoulders, shining bronze...

"Grace!" Riot shouted, his voice drowned out by the sea of *men* that had just climbed out of the soil, dusting off their armor—bronze breastplates that covered the top of their red... skirts?—and assembling into what appeared to be a fighting formation either side of me, and at my back. They all wore bronze helmets that covered their foreheads and the sides of their faces, with dramatic red, feathery plumes running up the middle like a mohawk, and the bronze greaves that protected their shins seemed at odds with the leather sandals they were all wearing.

And their weapons. Their *weapons*. Each of them held an enormous circular bronze shield in one hand and a long spear in the other, with a *sword* strapped to them, the hilt barely visible behind their shield arm.

Oh my word. I'd just *grown* an army.

I looked with wide eyes at the man next to me—he stood at least a foot taller than Wild, with olive skin, dark hair, and a strong Roman nose—and he looked back at me, staring silently for a moment before placing his hand over his heart and inclining his head to me, bending slightly at the waist before returning his gaze straight ahead to the agathos I knew I *should* be paying attention to.

But the earth man thing that I'd just grown had *bowed* to me. Hand-over-heart *bowed*.

Did he even have a heart? Were they actual people?

Was I a mother now?

Not important. Well, it was a little important, but maybe not at that exact moment.

The haunted-looking Basilinna shrieked an order and the scorpions moved forward in a nightmarish wave, but my sudden army of men were there, using their long-handled spears to impale scorpions like it was *nothing*, flinging them off into the distance before doing it all over again. I shamelessly hid behind them as they worked, breathing a sigh of relief when Bullet, Wild and Riot reached my side.

"Make them stop!" the Basilinna shrieked, watching in horror as the scorpions' numbers dwindled away to none. Without even breaking a sweat, the men fell back into their lines both either side of me and behind me, the ones who'd been flanking me giving my bonded slightly disgruntled looks as they moved over to make room for them, with Wild and Bullet on one side and Riot on the other.

If I thought I was panicking about the sudden appearance of at least a hundred warriors, it was nothing to how panicked the agathos looked. They'd definitely lost their aggressive posture, shrinking back into the shadows of the temple they sought to block us from like it would protect them.

"Showtime," I breathed, taking a step forward. The entire line moved with me as one and I fought the urge to turn and look at the wave of *people* behind me.

"Oh, I think the show has already begun," Riot mumbled, standing as close to me as he could possibly get. "You just grew... humans?"

"*Spartoi*," Bullet volunteered from my other side, sounding awed. "Sown men. Men sown from the teeth of dragons."

"I honestly don't want to think too hard about that right now," I muttered, grabbing Bullet's hand.

We all fell silent as we approached the fidgeting agathos who looked like they were struggling with their fight-or-flight reflexes.

"Move," I demanded, straightening my shoulders and glaring at the possessed woman in front of me. I pitied the woman she'd once been, but this Gaia-controlled creature in front of me was dangerous, and I couldn't afford to have any pity for her.

"What have you done?" she hissed in that strange echoing voice. "Do you think you are a goddess, Grace Bellamy? Who are you to create a race of men?"

That was honestly a great question.

Had I known that was going to happen, I would have really given some thought as to whether the fact that I *could* meant that I *should*.

"The Spartoi were sent by the goddess, Persephone. You can't possibly believe I have that much power," I replied flatly. "Now, move. Who are you to block the entrance to Zeus' temple?"

"We are servants of Anesidora!" someone behind her yelled.

"Then go somewhere else and serve her," I said coolly, channeling my inner Persephone, remembering the way she'd commanded the space around her. I wasn't going to back down. I wasn't going to shrink in and make myself smaller and meeker and more palatable for *anyone*. "Leave."

"You can't harm us," the Basilinna said smugly. "You can't force your army to attack your fellow agathos, your instincts won't allow it."

"I didn't force them to attack the scorpions either. They're not my army, and I have no interest in commanding them. If they choose to attack you, that's their prerogative."

I wasn't actually sure I could stop myself from calling them off if they *did* attack, because agathos instincts were no small thing. But I'd spoken true—I didn't want to command them. I had no idea what to do with them now I'd accidentally brought them to life.

Could they even understand what we were saying? Their posture said they were ready to do battle, but their faces were completely impassive.

"We have come to pay our respects to Zeus, King of the Gods—"

"*Hubris*," the Basilinna hissed. She lunged forward, but between my bonded and the army, she quickly stumbled back again, limbs jerking the entire time. I didn't even think I needed their support at this exact moment— these grounds were sacred. I'd had a feeling that if I could just get here, we'd be safe, and it seemed I was right. "You are a fool, Grace the agathos."

"We have come to pay our respects to Zeus, King of the Gods, and you *will* move. Go worship your goddess of destruction somewhere else. I'm here to pray for *peace*."

The agathos shrieked, a pained noise, as the ruins of the temple behind them began to *glow*. It was faint, but the marble itself shone an almost iridescent gold, which probably would have been more terrifying if I hadn't just grown humans out of dragon teeth.

"It burns," one of the agathos screamed. "Basilinna! Anesidora! It's burning!"

Riot and Bullet both pulled me backwards reflexively, but the light wasn't burning any of us. It felt warm and faintly pleasant, if anything.

"Move away!" the Basilinna commanded, first in English then in Greek, encouraging the agathos to rush to the sides of the temple, away from the burning light. Despite their discomfort, they still manage to spare me looks filled with hatred, and it still hurt to be on the other end of it, but not as much as it used to.

I was learning that sometimes it was okay if people didn't like me. That some people were, in fact, awful, and I was better off with them not liking me.

The temple loomed over us, casting our now significantly larger group in soft light, but I didn't fear it. It felt welcoming, and the moment the agathos moved away, I took a step towards it, pulling Riot and Bullet with me. The rest of the group followed by default, and I sucked in a nervous breath as I climbed over the rope fence and stepped onto the ancient slabs of marble, moving towards the remaining fifteen columns, still standing strong and proud after this many years.

The sense of chaos that existed in the world around us seemed to disappear as we made our way towards the center of the structure, walking slowly and carefully lest the ruins picked *now* as the time to collapse. I didn't think they would though. I hadn't realized how much I could taste Gaia's thirst for vengeance in the air until we were engulfed in the warm glow of the temple, shielding us from it.

Bullet exhaled in relief, and while Wild's defensive stance didn't relax, Riot's did marginally. It was going to be hard to *leave* this place, this sense of security, knowing a vengeful goddess awaited us on the other side. The agathos, daimons and humans with us moved in closer, huddling into a tighter circle around me and warily watching the Spartoi as they did so. I didn't blame them—not only had the Spartoi sprung out of the ground fully armed, they also seemed to be saving their least intimidating facial expressions for me and me alone.

Definitely going to have to address that...later.

I exhaled heavily as I stood in the center of the temple, trying to come up with the right words to say. A traditional sacrifice would have been an *animal*, but I didn't have one of those on hand, nor did I have the stomach to sacrifice one. Besides, the prophecy had specifically said they were 'where no sweet smelling smoke or prayer can reach,' which was why we'd been bolstering their strength by celebrating them in other ways.

Like orgies for Dionysus.

"Your blood," that heavenly voice that sometimes appeared to give me guidance whispered. A teensy part of me was bitter that she'd only decided to pipe up now, after an entire day of me really needing some extra advice. *"Offer your blood and your service. Offer your devotion to a world of gods and mortals, a world of agathos, daimons and humans. To the ideal."*

To the ideal.

That was a future I was willing to sacrifice for.

CHAPTER 29

All of the hesitation Grace had been feeling—the doubts, the fear, the shock—had fallen away the moment we entered the temple. She'd quietly walked across the worn marble floor to the center of the temple as though she was in a trance, but I could feel through the bond that she wasn't. She was completely in control, no god or goddess had taken control of her body.

Grace was just at peace. Filled with purpose and confidence and light.

I'd never seen anything so glorious.

Bullet, Riot and I arranged ourselves in a circle around Grace, giving her a few feet of space. Riot's eyes darted to the spot between us and I wondered if he was thinking the same thing I was.

It felt unnatural to have a gap there. There was one of us missing, and we all knew it. The moment we were out of here, I was going to turn on the burner phone and follow up with Onyx. It wasn't like we were in hiding anymore, she'd probably seen us on one of the many livestreams that was currently broadcasting.

The group of agathos, daimons, and humans we came with filed in behind us, filling in the circle, while the Spartoi fell into unnaturally neat rank lines behind them, standing at attention with their eyes trained on Grace. I eyed them warily—not just because they were fully grown men that had sprung out of the ground like particularly terrifying weeds, but because they were looking to Grace for instruction.

If I thought for even a second that she wanted that responsibility, I'd stand aside and watch with pride as she took the reins. But Grace was no battalion leader and she had no aspiration of becoming one. We all had our parts to play—her and Bullet as messengers of the gods, and Riot as the unwavering support that kept her safe and steady in a sea of change. While I *felt* like I belonged with Grace, it wasn't until that moment that I really understood where my place was. What my *role* was.

Grace hummed softly to herself, a tune I didn't recognize, as she unstrapped the kitchen knife on her thigh we'd holstered there for scorpion-killing purposes. I narrowed my eyes, not particularly liking the look of where this was going, but not wanting to get in the way. Without any preamble, she ran the sharp blade across her palm on her already injured hand, slicing the skin open. Where there had been a trickle of blood from the dragon teeth, there was now a steady stream.

I bunched my fists at my side, fighting the urge to grab the knife out of her hand and wrap the wound, but Grace was already kneeling, setting the knife aside and holding her bleeding palm over the marble. Her wound dripped steadily onto the floor, staining it crimson.

"I offer my blood, my loyalty and my service to the ideal. To a world where agathos, daimons and humans live side-by-side, freely under the light of the sun or the moon. Where no mortal life is considered more valuable than another. I offer my blood, my loyalty and my service to a world of gods and mortals walking together again. To the liberation of those who have been imprisoned for too long, to those who were abandoned and forgotten finding their place once again."

She clenched her hand, stemming the blood flow and winced at the motion. For a moment, there was silence. That sense of peace and safety grew a little stronger, and I embraced it while knowing it wasn't something we could rely on. That Zeus' history of interacting with mortals was... fraught, to say the least.

There was a quiet thud, and I looked up at the same time as everyone else to find Alesa kneeling, already cutting her own palm with a pocket knife while Vasileios watched on with faint surprise. Alesa held her hand over the marble, mimicking Grace's actions and repeating the vow nearly word-for-word, much to Grace's surprise.

Alesa seemed to be the de facto leader of the Kakodaimonistai, so it made sense that the other humans immediately followed suit, finding clean blades they'd brought with them, ones that had been too short to risk using on the scorpions.

Both Riot and I looked to Bullet at the same time, and I caught a glimpse of amusement on his face before he turned to the Spartoi behind him, pointing at the guy's *sword* and then at his own palm.

If I could speak, I would have yelled at him. Instead, I was stuck saying nothing as the Spartoi withdrew his sword, the metal scraping ominously against the sheath, before holding it sideways so Bullet could roughly slide his palm over the blade.

Apparently, not getting beheaded by that one Spartoi was all the encouragement everyone else needed, as the other daimons and agathos who didn't have clean blades promptly did the same—though Riot looked extremely reluctant about it.

Grace watched him with a faint smile on her face, and I knew she wouldn't expect me to follow. Grace knew that my history with the gods was complicated, and that I didn't pray. I hadn't taken part in any of the offerings, not wanting to entangle myself in the world of the gods any further, knowing how capricious they could be.

But sticking my head in the sand wasn't going to work any longer. Besides, if we were going to engage with these gods, to free them from the prison Gaia had put them in, it was going to be on *our* terms. I couldn't avoid it any longer, and I didn't want to go through life, forever holding our breath in wait for Gaia to do something to hurt us—either because she was lashing out or because she'd lost control of her temper. Something had to give.

I pulled out the spare steak knife I'd taken from the cottage, kneeling down on the ground and letting my blood drip out.

I offer my blood, my service and my loyalty to the ideal, I thought, hoping that it was enough to feel the words if I couldn't say them. *I offer this freely in the hopes of building a world where daimons, agathos and humans are equal. Where gods and mortals exist in harmony.*

Grace caught my eye as I raised my head, her pride in me flowing freely down the bond, and a lump formed in my throat at seeing her look at *me* like that. I wasn't sure if I deserved her pride, but I'd work every day to be worthy of it.

The agathos who'd attempted to stop us were still hanging around at the very edges of the grounds, far enough away that the light from the temple couldn't reach them. I straightened, surveying the Spartoi and wondering if they'd be inclined to give us an armored guard to get the fuck out of here, while also wondering where we were going next. The tour bus we'd driven here in wasn't exactly cut out for a high-speed chase if it came down to that, especially now the tires were in shreds, and it was too distinctive if we needed to lose a tail.

But then the columns of the temple started to glow brighter, and suddenly our ability to get out of here unhindered didn't seem like a massive concern, since the agathos were sprinting as far away from this place as they could. Good. Let them see what they were up against. Grace wasn't just a rebellious agathos like they'd pinned her as for far too long. She was a messenger of the gods, and they were right to be scared.

The marble column closest to me emitted a whooshing sound, and I took a step back reflexively as a tunnel of light shot up from the floor, the movement repeating on all of the remaining sixteen columns like some sort of strange rave.

Bullet, Riot and I all moved quietly towards Grace, boxing her in as she stared up at the flashing columns in awe. There was a quiet groaning sort of sound, and I grabbed Grace's body, pulling her back against my chest as the cracked marble began to *knit itself* back together.

"We're all seeing this right?" Riot asked, sounding more than a little disturbed.

"It's *healing*," Grace said emphatically. Not completely—there were still only sixteen columns when the size of the floor indicated there had probably been at least six times that amount, and a restored ceiling didn't suddenly sprout overhead, but the weathered, damaged marble had healed itself, shining bright and new like the columns had been erected yesterday instead of two thousand years ago.

The light show ended and Grace shot us each a tremulous smile before focusing on Bullet. "Is there an area sacred to Gaia close by?"

Riot groaned out loud, and I silently did the same.

"Yeah, there's a little plot of land here at the temple complex that is sacred to Gaia, but are you sure about this, Amazing Grace?" he asked, sounding as unenthused as I felt at the idea of communicating with her again.

"I don't want a war with her," Grace replied firmly. "But I'm not backing down either, and she needs to know that."

"That's why the Fates picked you," Bullet shot back with a grin. "You're compassionate, but a little salty at the same time. It's a good combination. Follow me."

He led us to a rather unimpressive rocky piece of ground, and our strange circular formation seemed to form again automatically, the stoic soldiers Grace had summoned watching everything almost unblinking. Did they know what was happening? Could they understand any of this?

Foster handed Grace a small handful of seeds from the supply kit he was carrying, and time itself seemed to stop as Grace kneeled at the base of a small slope, digging into the dirt with her uninjured hand to make a place.

"I plant these crocus seeds in offering to Gaia. Anesidora, Sender of Gifts, Great Mother." Grace sighed heavily, taking her time to poke the seeds into the opening she'd made. I knew that whatever this was, it hadn't been planned. Grace was absolutely making this up as she went along.

"I'm just a mortal, and my life is over in the blink of an immortal's eye. I have no special gifts, no unusual talents, there is nothing particularly interesting about me, except that I asked for help from a goddess I didn't serve, and even then it was for my own selfish reasons. My own loneliness."

There was a pang in my chest at that, and I could see that same pain reflected in Bullet's face. We'd known about Grace before she knew about us, and for different reasons we'd stood aside while she suffered silently on her own.

"I didn't ask for this prophecy, not really, but I'm going to see it through because I believe in what it represents and I'll fight for a world where agathos and daimons are more than just good or bad influences for humans. Where we have choices too. Where humans *know* about the forces who pull the strings of their lives."

There was a murmuring of agreement from our small band of misfits—earth army not included—and I wondered if that enraged Gaia even more. It wasn't just Grace and her soul bonds now, she was slowly collecting up a band of like-minded people from all walks of life, and our numbers would only grow.

"I'm just a mortal, but perhaps the lack of time available to me isn't a bad thing. Perhaps it puts things in perspective. Mortals know how little we can afford to hold on to what grieves us, because life is short and our anger hurts ourselves more than anyone else." Grace smoothed the soil back over the seeds, kneeling in quiet contemplation for a moment before standing.

"You're not going to close the prayer?" Foster asked quietly, tilting his head to the side.

"We're not living hidden anymore," Grace said firmly, looking down at the fresh soil. It didn't burst into blooms the way it had at the community center, but a sinkhole didn't open and swallow us whole either, so perhaps this was progress.

Perhaps between the army and the temple, Grace had given an ancient primordial goddess a fright.

Grace leaned against my arm, her other hand finding Riot's. Despite the calm look on her face, I could feel how drained she was. We'd all been riding high on adrenaline that was rapidly leaving us.

"I think we're going to need another bus," she said wryly, giving the Spartoi a tentative smile. They didn't give any indication that they understood her, but there was a look of reverence and respect there that I recognized from the Keres daimons I'd coached and supported over the years. The ones who looked to me as a leader.

"And somewhere to stay," Riot added, frowning. "I don't like our chances of getting back to Vasileios' place after... well, all of that."

"I know of a place," Orion said, stepping forward with a solemn look on his face. "It's not too far from here and owned by my family, who I know have been called back to Larissa because I was called back too, so it should be empty."

"If it's not empty, it soon will be," Vasileios replied with a lazy smile. "We're not taking the dirt men back to my house, that's for sure."

Grace looked around the Spartoi like she was seeking out someone in particular, eyes lighting up when they landed on one. I fell into step next to her as she approached him, eyeing him warily. He straightened to attention the moment she got close. Unsettling.

"Hello," Grace said nervously, giving him an adorably awkward wave. "Do you speak English?"

His facial expression barely moved as he replied something in rapid Greek, his focus solely on Grace.

I looked around, tipping my chin at Vasileios then Orion, encouraging them over and scanning our group for Ezio and Galen who were also Greek.

"We can't help you, man," Vasileios laughed as he approached.

"It's Ancient Greek," Orion added apologetically. The Spartoi repeated himself, more insistently, forehead creased in consternation.

"Maybe if it was written down?" Vasileios shrugged. "It's been many years since I was forced to study it at school, but I could probably work out some of it."

"Do you think his brain will explode if we give him a pen and paper?" Riot muttered, his thoughts echoing my own. "The dude is wearing a leather skirt and speaking Ancient Greek. I'm not sure he's ready for ballpoint technology yet."

"Well they better figure it out before we get them on a bus," Foster pointed out. "The sooner they get comfortable with ballpoint technology, the sooner we can move onto internal combustion engines."

"I know a few words off by heart though I have no idea if I'm pronouncing them properly," Bullet said, stepping forward with a shrug. "I'm pretty sure they're going to follow Grace wherever she goes though. I saw your hand bleeding when you were scattering the teeth—I wouldn't be surprised if they were tied to you through blood magic somehow."

"*Xénos?*" Bullet said hesitantly to the soldier.

"What does that mean?" Grace asked immediately.

"I was aiming for 'friend,' but it's more like 'guest,'" Bullet admitted, giving her an apologetic look. "Like they're our guest and we're their host. I think."

Grace beamed at him, and I reached out to squeeze his shoulder, making him blush. He was so fucking smart, not just because of all the knowledge he'd been given by the gods but because he had constantly sought to learn more.

The man pointed at himself, jabbing his thumb into his breastplate firmly before gesturing at the other Spartoi still standing at attention. "Stratós. *Stratós.*"

"Army," Orion said flatly. "Some words don't change over the years, and that definitely means army."

The soldier pointed at Grace, saying something else that sounded similar.

"*Stratēgós,*" Bullet repeated, tilting his head to the side. "He's saying you're their General."

"Oh no. No, thank you," Grace replied immediately, looking at me with wide eyes. I felt my mouth quirk up at the alarmed expression on her face as she pointed at me. "He. Him. *Stratēgós*."

The Spartoi we were speaking to sized me up, not looking overly impressed with that news, and I got the distinct impression that if they *did* follow my orders, it would still require Grace's explicit blessing. He returned his attention to Grace, frowning at her like he was trying to work out what that made her, if not the General.

For dragon-teeth-dirt-people, they certainly seemed aware and intelligent.

"Grace," she said, pointing at herself.

"Grace," Bullet repeated, wrapping an arm around Grace. "*Prophêtis*."

"Prophetess?" Grace squeaked. "If anyone's the prophet, it's you," she added, giving Bullet a pointed look.

"You don't need to see the future to be a prophet. You've been charged with interpreting the will of the gods," Bullet replied easily. "Not just interpreting, but speaking for them. You're a prophetess, Amazing Grace."

I tapped her hand to get her attention because she looked about a minute away from passing out at that proclamation, despite all the prophetess-ing shit she'd done today.

'We need to go,' I signed. I was pretty confident the agathos were going to be too spooked to try anything today after all that they'd seen, but I wasn't taking any chances.

"Come on, daimons," Vasileios called. "Let's *borrow* some vehicles. We're going to go pay Orion's family property a visit."

Orion directed the convoy of "borrowed" buses to his family's home on the coast, just over thirty minutes from Athens. Vasileios had loudly assured the agathos present that the abandoned tourist buses had been legally acquired and would be returned in a timely manner, which was apparently good enough reassurance to at least get them on board.

The Spartoi had looked *terrified,* but Grace had made a show of reassuring them, speaking to them gently. She signed along as she spoke, whether it was a conscious effort to teach them to understand me, or just habit from signing to me, I wasn't sure. It would certainly be convenient if they could sign—even if I could speak, there wasn't a hope in hell of me learning Ancient Greek.

Riot let out a low whistle, standing in the center aisle of the bus and leaning forward to stare out the front window. "Orion, your folks live *here?*"

We were climbing up a long winding driveway that Orion had assured us would be fine to handle the buses because apparently, they had buses going up there all the time, though it was hard to see where we were going as it grew increasingly dark outside.

"They don't really *live* here," Orion replied with a grimace, his knuckles turning white from how hard he was gripping the steering wheel. "They hire it out as an agathos retreat for conferences and such."

Grace's nose wrinkled, a flash of discomfort floating down the bond at whatever memories that invoked. Probably some kind of indoctrination camp where they dressed the kids in matching khakis and made them recite a list of Gaia's greatest qualities.

"You're sure they won't be here?" Grace asked, leaning forward in her seat to speak to Orion and resting her uninjured hand on my thigh. I placed my hand over hers, linking our fingers together. I'd done my best to clean and wrap her cut hand when we got on the bus, but I intended to redo it when we were settled in just to be sure.

He nodded, eyes trained on the looming villa ahead. "My mother has been calling me nonstop, telling me to return to Larissa. I hadn't heard from her in years before this. But some of the agathos back there recognized me, so I'm guessing my family will hear all about what a traitor I am shortly."

"I'm sorry—" Grace began, but Orion shook his head, cutting her off.

"I don't regret any of the choices I've made, Grace. If my mother wanted me to take her calls, maybe she should have bothered keeping in touch with me," he said easily as he pulled the bus into park.

We piled out, the other two buses driven by Vasileios and Galen parking behind us. The Spartoi were trembling as they assembled on the circular driveway, sweat pouring off their faces. Grace quickly went down the rows, offering them smiles and platitudes in English, signing along the whole time.

"I'm not doing that," Riot told us flatly, watching her work. "There's a whole bunch of shit I never thought I'd do that I've done since meeting Grace, but I draw the line at comforting random ancient dudes who popped out of the soil."

"You have such a good bedside manner though," Bullet teased, ever the optimist that Riot would have softened towards him.

Riot grunted in acknowledgment, which was an improvement. "Did you see any of this?" he asked, staring straight ahead.

Bullet glanced sideways at him. "Sort of. There were a lot of visions of a crowd of blank faces dressed in ancient armor, and the Scorpio constellation. I assumed it was a metaphor. No one really predicts this sort of thing, you know?"

I tuned out to examine the house as he began dissecting visions and different cards he'd seen that may or may not have hinted at us adopting a hundred fully grown human beings from a whole different century.

A villa would probably be the best way to describe it, built from stone with a gently sloping terracotta ceiling. It didn't look big enough to house all of us from where I was standing, but I could hear the ocean and I guessed that the villa extended back further than I could see towards it.

"Ready to head in?" Orion asked me, jogging down the front steps to meet us. "I did a quick sweep and no one is here."

I nodded, glancing at Grace to make sure she had no objections. She slipped a hand through mine as we climbed the steps to the front door, pushing up on her tip toes to speak quietly in my ear. "Do we think the Spartoi eat normal food?"

Riot snorted, walking close enough behind to overhear. "They seem pretty much like regular humans to me—earth birth aside. Do they have bellybuttons, do you think? I hope this place has a stocked kitchen, Orion."

"We'll make it work," he replied, not sounding particularly confident as he opened enormous wooden doors that led us into a fairly grand room with cream stucco walls, high wooden ceilings with exposed beams and slate gray tiles on the floor. There was a decent-sized kitchen, a cozy living area with a brick fireplace and bookshelf with a few couches, and a dining area in the middle with a long table and benches that would probably seat twenty.

It was large as far as houses went, but there were about a hundred and twenty of us now. Grace's face fell, worry pulsing incessantly through the bond as she took in the accommodations.

"Don't worry, there's more outside," Orion assured us, moving around the dining table and throwing open the double doors and turning on the outside lights. Grace exhaled in relief as we walked out onto a stone patio with a second long dining table, sheltered by grapevines hanging overhead. Surrounding the patio on three sides were doors that seemed to lead to individual bedroom suites, and at the bottom of the stone stairs was an enormous pool. Beyond that seemed to be almost a sheer cliff drop to the ocean, glinting in the moonlight.

Let's hope Gaia doesn't treat us to a landslide while we're staying here.

"Each room has its own bathroom, and some have loft areas meant for sleeping kids," Orion explained. "Across the path is a converted barn with some bed rolls we could set out on the floor."

"The Spartoi might be more comfortable there," Riot pointed out. "They're in shock over the buses, and wheels were for sure a thing back in their day, right? What are they going to do when they see a television?"

"I don't even want to see a television," Grace murmured. "We might be on it."

"If we're not yet, we soon will be," Bullet agreed. "Which means we probably need to move quickly, whatever we do next. Not only will we have the agathos on our asses, but terrified humans to manage as well."

'The video?' I signed. Grace repeated the question aloud.

"Alesa and I were livestreaming, but our batteries are dead," Vasileios replied, flashing us his blank phone screen. "There were lots of people saying it's fake, of course, but we knew that would happen. Others saying this is the sign they've been waiting for, that they wanted to fight back after the disasters but they didn't know who the enemy was. You have momentum, Grace. Now might be a good time to make some kind of call to action."

Grace wrinkled her nose, and I could practically hear her rejecting the '*Prophêtis*' title in her head.

"Can I sleep on it?"

"Whenever you want," Vasileios agreed. "I have very many followers now." He looked almost smug about it.

"Yeah, let's focus on sleeping arrangements and food right now," Riot said, rubbing his temples. "I'm about at my limit for all of this shit for today."

I nodded in agreement. I just wanted a few minutes to regroup away from everyone.

"You guys take the master," Orion said quickly. "It's the only bedroom in the main living building, just up the stairs. It's got the best view of the ocean. The rest of us will figure out who's bunking with who. Grace and Wild, you, uh, might have to help us bring the Spartoi to the barn. I'm not sure they'll listen to us."

Right. Time to get our new army settled in their temporary barracks.

GRACE

CHAPTER 30

I woke up before my bonded, all squished together in the wood-paneled upstairs room we were occupying. The curtains were drawn shut over the enormous grid-like window that overlooked the entire property and the ocean view, but I knew it must be early. There was too much to do to sleep. Too many people depending on me. With some difficulty, I wriggled out from between Riot and Wild. Bullet was lying on Wild's other side, as still as a statue as he always was in sleep.

We'd raided the stores on the property for non-perishable food, and had all dined out on pasta cooked with canned tomatoes last night before going back to our individual rooms. The Spartoi had eaten in total silence, clearly alarmed by their surroundings, but they *did* eat regular food and seemed more than happy to sleep on the rollout mats in the nearby barn. In fact, it was the *most* comfortable I'd seen them so far.

I wasn't about to question Persephone's judgment, but the fact that she'd given me a whole *army* without any notice was a little bit terrifying. One that we could barely communicate with at that.

As quietly as I could, I freshened up in the attached bathroom and changed into shorts, a T-shirt and an oversized hoodie to keep me warm against the morning chill before tiptoeing down the stairs to the main living area. The Kakodaimonistai had grabbed the bags we'd packed from the wrecked bus, and we'd have to go through what we had at some point to make sure everyone had enough clothes and toiletries.

Would the Spartoi want to wear normal clothes? Maybe that would be too much change for them right off the bat.

Orion was already in the kitchen with two of the Kakodaimonistai—Leonie and Marek—preparing breakfast in hushed tones.

"Did we wake you, Grace?" Orion asked with a grimace. "This is the only proper kitchen on-site, though there's a huge barbeque outside."

"You didn't wake me," I assured him, rounding the kitchen island to see what they were making. "Let me help."

"You are the *Prophêtis*," Leonie said quickly. "You should relax. We're just making oats and opening canned fruit."

"Well, I can definitely help with that," I assured them, grabbing a can opener.

"The Spartoi are up," Orion mentioned. "I peeked my head in the barn. They're just... lounging about. Speaking Ancient Greek. No big deal."

My lips twitched in spite of myself. "No big deal. At least they're interacting with each other, right? Yesterday, they seemed so... robotic."

"They might have been easier to manage if they were more robotic and less human," Orion muttered, taking charge of the oats. That was true. I was incredibly grateful to the Spartoi, they'd protected us from the scorpions and had given Gaia a huge fright, but the responsibility of looking out for their wellbeing in a world they didn't seem to understand was daunting to say the least.

It didn't take the four of us as long to cook breakfast for a hundred and twenty as I assumed it would. Maybe if we got a system going and had a few more supplies, we could camp out here for the foreseeable future. Until... Until I decided what to do next, because apparently that was my job now.

Hello? Helpful voice that speaks to me sometimes, are you there? I could really use some advice.

Nothing. I guess that wasn't how it worked.

The guys came down the stairs and Wild immediately headed for the barn to fetch the Spartoi for breakfast, while Riot and Bullet helped set everything up on both the indoor and outdoor tables, though we had to eat in groups because we didn't have enough dishware or cutlery. I didn't know for sure, but it seemed like some of the awkwardness between Bullet and Riot had dissipated since yesterday. They still weren't back to their usual banter, but there was eye contact at least.

I picked at my food, encouraging the Spartoi to eat, which they did with great relish, and attempted to learn their names. The one I'd spoken to yesterday seemed to be their leader, and his name was Theras, though he seemed sort of baffled as to why I'd even want to know it. There was also Damatrios, Theodoros, Lycus, Philon, and Ariston, but after that they all began to blur together in my head.

I need to grab the burner phone from Wild and look up some Ancient Greek. I wanted to understand how much they knew about how they got here and why they were here.

If they even *wanted* to be here.

The words Riot had said to me not long after we met came back to me. *"You can't gift a person, Gracie. They have their own free will, goals, dreams that may be incompatible with yours."*

If the Spartoi didn't want to be here, I wasn't going to make them stay. I wasn't exactly sure where they would go or how, but we'd figure it out.

After breakfast, Wild instructed them to spar, gesturing dramatically to Theras to show him what he wanted them to do. Theras definitely appeared to be the Spartoi's defacto leader, but he nodded curtly and organized the others at Wild's direction.

'Routine,' Wild signed to me as the Spartoi spread out around the pool with their weapons, metal clanging against metal as they practiced.

"Routine is a good idea," I agreed quietly. We were probably lucky that this property was relatively low tech since it was used as a retreat, but even electric *lights* seemed to freak the Spartoi out. If Wild was able to create some kind of militaristic-style structure for them, maybe that was a good thing.

It didn't take long for the Keres daimons to be lured in by it too—Wild included. I shamelessly stared at the rippling muscles of his back the moment he ditched his shirt, forgetting for a moment that the Spartoi were practicing with actual *swords*.

As unsettling as I found it, they were the most comfortable they'd looked since they'd emerged from the earth yesterday, so I didn't say anything. If weapons brought them comfort, I guess I could learn to live with that?

I stacked up the last of the breakfast dishes and waved off Foster when he tried to take them off me, insisting on doing them myself. I needed a mindless, repetitive task to give myself space to think. We'd made a big splash yesterday, and today was the day to follow it up with *action*.

I needed to say something. To explain myself. To explain everything.

"Grace!" Orion called from the front of the house. "Can you and your bonded come out here, please?"

"One second!" I yelled back, drying my hands quickly and darting out the back to grab Riot, Bullet and Wild. There was something in Orion's voice that had me a little anxious, and the three of them picked it up through the bond, jogging after me as we returned to the front of the house without asking any questions.

Wild stepped in front of me before my hand could touch the front door handle, giving me a pointed look before letting himself out first. Riot snorted quietly, keeping a hand on my lower back as we followed.

"Grace," Orion said, standing on the front steps and facing down a group huddled nervously on the driveway. "These are some agathos I grew up with." He gestured at the five of them—two women and three men. "I don't know them well, they're younger than me. They claim they want to join us."

They definitely looked younger—closer to Mercy's age, if not actual high schoolers. One woman was holding hands with two of the men, so I guessed they were her bonded. The other two hung off to the side slightly, watching us apprehensively.

"Why do you want to join us?" I asked, genuinely curious. The agathos on our side so far were the ones who'd been rejected and sent away on outreach trips. They didn't have anything to lose by joining us—if anything, they had everything to gain.

"We've been uncomfortable with how things were going," the woman with the two bonded said, speaking slowly in heavily accented English. "They have been telling us to find you, that you are terrible, that you bonded with daimons. But I have my own bonded and I know you cannot... cannot *make* bonded. The soul bonds come from the heavens."

"We don't wish to hunt our own," her bonded added, looking at the ground as he spoke. "When we thought more, we realized we don't want to hunt daimons either. The violence was very bad. The earthquakes and disasters... So many have suffered."

I nodded in agreement when he chanced a tentative look up at us. The violence the agathos had carried out against the daimons had been horrifying, and it had made me more ashamed of my people than I had ever been in my life. "I want to believe everything you're saying without question, but my cousin is an agathos and she can lie. I'm a little wary of blind belief now."

The young man standing slightly off to the side gasped quietly, shifting awkwardly on his feet and immediately drawing all of our attention.

"You, kid," Riot said bluntly, pointing at him. "Can you lie?"

"His name is Alekos," Orion offered drily.

Alekos nodded. "Yes. My whole life. I thought it was only me."

"Guess they're some of the new model agathos," Bullet said cheerfully. "I say we let them in, see what they can do. They're grossly outnumbered if they decide to try anything stupid."

The entire group of them paled, stuttering assurances that they were genuinely here to help and they'd never betray us.

"Would you leave your phones with us?" I asked. "Just in case."

"Of course," the bonded woman said, stepping forward and pulling her phone out of her pocket. "My name is Xenia, by the way. These are my bonded, Nikolas and Phoenix."

The woman who hadn't said anything stepped forward, handing me her phone and wrapping her arms nervously around her waist. Orion said something to her in rapid Greek and she nodded quickly.

"Her name is Evanthia, she doesn't speak English," he told us. "She has no bonded either. I'm not quite sure where she'll want to stay—there are no single agathos women here. Maybe she can bunk up with some of the humans."

Right. Because she wouldn't be comfortable staying in a room with men. How quickly I'd forgotten what it was like to be a single agathos woman. "We'll figure something out," I agreed. "Let's head inside."

They only carried a rucksack each, and they all looked like they'd left in a hurry. I led them through the house, intending to figure out the sleeping arrangements first before making sure they were fed. The moment we got onto the patio, all those plans went out the window though.

Ovie, the Dolos daimon from Nigeria who I'd only met once at Vasileios' before he decided to come on this trip, emerged from the pool suddenly, swiping water off his face as he strode up the steps. Not that he appealed to me in any way—I only had eyes for my soul bonds—but I could appreciate the movie star quality looks as he crossed the stone floor and climbed up the stairs determinedly, shirtless and dripping water everywhere.

"What the fuck is going on?" Riot asked, sounding as baffled as I felt.

"Move," Ovie barked. I quickly took a step to the side so he didn't barge into me, and then he was on Evanthia, scooping her up against his wet body and fusing his lips to hers. She squeaked in surprise, arms hesitantly wrapping around his shoulders, relaxing into his embrace.

Bullet let out a low whistle. "Look at us, playing matchmaker."

"She has a daimon soul bond too?" Xenia asked, eyes wide as saucers as she clung tighter to her two agathos bonded.

"So does my cousin. The lying one," I replied absently. "It's like the Fates are weaving our threads closer together. At least that fixes the room situation," I added for Orion's benefit. Ovie was already carrying his new soul bond away, and she seemed remarkably chill about going with him. I hadn't handled meeting Riot that well at all.

"Maybe you have daimon soul bonds too?" Phoenix said to Xenia, glancing down at her before surveying the daimons lounging by the pool like he expected one of them to come and sweep his girl off her feet.

"It seems to be either or at this stage," Bullet replied. "All daimon soul bonds or all agathos soul bonds. I don't even know what a combination would look like," he added, grinning at me. "We might kill each other."

I shuddered at the thought. "No thanks, I think I'm fine with my harem of daimons."

"Just *fine* with it?" Bullet asked, gasping with mock outrage. "Clearly, we aren't doing a good enough job then. Get your ass back upstairs and we'll show you just how much better than *fine* we can do."

Now *that* was a tempting offer, but I had plans to make and Riot was glaring like he was annoyed that Bullet had included him in that 'we.'

"I'd like nothing more, but I need to figure out what I'm saying to everyone after we livestreamed yesterday's madness," I sighed. "And figure out if we have coffee in here somewhere."

"We're going to go on a grocery run," Alesa announced, approaching with Mathias, their arms linked together. "We're human and less likely to draw attention outside of the city. You just focus on what you need to do, *Prophêtis*. Let us handle the rest."

Those words were not nearly as comforting as she probably thought they were.

BULLET

CHAPTER 31

If there was one thing I'd learned while we'd been living like fugitives in Greece, it was that I wasn't cut out for normality. I shuffled my cards in my hands, fighting the urge to do a reading even though I wanted to more than anything. We were at a crossroads, a turning point, a key decision-making time in our lives, and all I had were a few fragmented dream visions to go on.

How was I supposed to live like this? How did anyone live without an on-call option to look into the future? This was torture.

No, I was definitely not cut out for a life of normality.

I closed my eyes for a moment, my hands on the cards, reaching for that strand of magic that connected me to the Fates, but a sharp pain knifed behind my eyes almost immediately, and I was forced to pull back. I opened my eyes, my vision always a little blurry in the aftermath, and shoved the cards away before I threw them into the pool in a rage. I'd been able to call on the Fates my entire *life,* and suddenly my brain wasn't able to handle it anymore. It was like losing a limb.

The stabbing pain eased off slowly, and I unscrewed the lid of my water bottle and downed most of it in one. These episodes often crept up on me even when I *didn't* try to use my gifts, and I was getting better at managing them. So long as I didn't push myself when the pain hit, I could avoid the nosebleeds and fainting, which were the most dramatic bits. Grace, Wild and Riot always knew when I was struggling, but the others didn't seem to, which was good. I wanted them to focus on the task at hand, on Grace, not on the Oneiroi in their midst who was teetering on death's door.

Grace was holed up in the upstairs bedroom, working out what she wanted to say to the world after yesterday. I didn't blame her for needing a minute to herself. Especially with the Spartoi staring at her like she was a goddess come to life, even if they'd reluctantly agreed to listen to Wild's directions.

I mean, anyone would have found those stares intimidating. Yesterday, I'd assumed they were temporary, golem-like beings. That Persephone had sent them up from the underworld to help Grace, and once their task was fulfilled, they'd disappear again.

Now, I wasn't so confident. They seemed very... human. They appeared to have human needs like food and water and sleep, they were afraid of things they didn't understand, and despite the language barriers, we'd made some progress in communicating with them. It made things more complicated by a long shot.

I made my way past the pool filled with lazing daimons—everyone was killing time while we waited for Grace—and took a seat in the shade next to Wild. I didn't even know why I did it, not really. Yeah, we'd had... whatever we'd had yesterday—a threesome? Did that count as a threesome?—but we'd basically been going at full tilt ever since, and had accidentally acquired an army, which had been a great excuse to not bring the maybe-threesome up.

Except that now we weren't growing humans or spontaneously repairing centuries-old temples, I couldn't stop thinking about it, and I wanted to know Wild's thoughts on it. And it was the hottest experience of my life, so there was that.

Basically, I had a lot of feelings, and it seemed like the mature thing to do would be to do something about those feelings.

I had no time to be bitter, and by that logic, I didn't have time to be a coward either.

Wild glanced at me, eyes flicking up from the burner phone he was currently turning on. His gaze ran slowly down my arm, ostensibly examining my tattoos, but it felt like he was undressing me with his fucking eyeballs.

Nope. This was a bad idea. Abort mission. Repress those stupid feelings before they make shit even more uncomfortable than it already is.

Riot already wasn't speaking to me, I couldn't afford to lose any more friends.

I went to stand, but Wild gently grabbed my forearm, holding me in place. His brow creased in frustration, and I cursed myself for not making more of an effort to learn ASL. He'd really come to rely on it these past few weeks with Grace. His hand lingered on my arm as the phone screen flickered to life, and he quickly opened the note-taking app and showed me the message he typed out.

'Stay.'

"Okay," I replied a little breathily. *No game whatsoever. So embarrassing.* "I'll stay."

Wild removed his hand, resting it between us on the seat, palm facing up, and raised an eyebrow at me. Tentatively, I placed my hand in his, linking our fingers together.

Okay. Okay, I guess we're holding hands now. Cool. This is fine.

'How are you feeling today?' Wild wrote, showing me the phone. He narrowed his eyes at me the moment I thought about deflecting, and I exhaled heavily. Wild saw way too much.

"Alright. It's an alright day." He raised an eyebrow at me. "Fine, I may have tried to dip into the Fates' magic just a little and got a headache for my troubles. I know, I know, stop looking at me like that."

Wild huffed, squeezing my hand and shooting me a disapproving look before resuming what he'd been doing on the phone.

"Are you contacting Onyx?" I asked since he wasn't making any attempt to hide the screen from me. He nodded, typing in a sequence of letters and numbers that I guessed was some kind of secret Wild-Onyx code. Very 007. "Grace was jealous of Onyx when she met her, you know."

So was I, but he didn't need to know that.

Wild reeled back like I'd slapped him, before quickly pulling up the notes app again.

'Onyx is my employee. That's all she's ever been to me.'

"And your friend," I pointed out. Wild vehemently shook his head. Goddess save me from idiot daimons who refused to accept they had friends. The phone rang, and Wild frowned at it as his thumb hovered over the green circle. It was pretty weird for Onyx to be calling a guy that she knew full well couldn't speak, but apparently his curiosity won out, as Wild eventually hit answer, putting the phone on speaker and holding it between the two of us.

"Oh, now you decide to contact me," Onyx snapped, sounding unusually agitated. *"Where the fuck have you been? Actually, don't worry. I know where you've been. I've seen the video footage of you doing whatever that*

shit was in Athens, frankly I don't want to know. I'm glad you can't speak, you can just listen to me—"

"I can talk," I interjected because Wild looked pissed. His grumpy face was next level, no wonder he had half of Milton terrified of him. "What's up, Onyx? Did something happen?"

"Did something happen?" she repeated with a laugh that bordered on hysteria. *"Aside from the freaky shit in Athens? Yes, something happened. I finally tracked Dare down and told him to sort his shit out and fly to Greece. That's what happened."*

"Okay. Well, that's good, isn't it?" I replied slowly. I'd been trying to get hold of Dare in the dreamscape to check on him, but it wasn't that surprising that I couldn't. Historically, he'd never been a big sleeper, and the time zones combined with daimon sleep schedules made things complicated. "We wanted him to come here. Did he not want to?"

"No, he didn't want to, but he's been a wreck since his mom died, he wasn't thinking straight about anything... Look, all I know is I told him to fly to Greece. Sent him the money for the ticket myself—well, from the Asphodel account—and he didn't make any commitments. But I've been trying to get hold of him since and I can't."

"So he's gone off-grid again. That seems to be his thing lately," I said, dread slowly unfurling in my gut. No, if something bad had happened, I would have seen it...

Wild swallowed thickly, gripping the phone tighter and looking over it at me, eyes wide.

'*Plane crash,*' he mouthed.

Fuck.

No, surely not. He couldn't have been on that flight. Surely, the Fates would have given me a heads up about *that*.

"It took me a bit to track down where he was staying—he'd been crashing at Rogue's for some reason and I guess everyone decided to just not mention that to me because they were worried I was going to push him too hard or something. Rogue said he'd gone and didn't know when he'd be back," Onyx continued quietly, all of her bluster seeming to leave her in a rush. *"I don't know if you saw, but a flight from New York crashed off the coast of Greece."*

"We saw," I rasped.

"I've tried to find out if he was on the flight or not, but I can't. I don't know what name would be on his passport, but I'm pretty sure he wasn't on the list of the..."

The list of the deceased.

"No." I shook my head, adamant. "No, there's no way. I've seen him, well not his face, but I'm pretty sure it's him. With Grace. I know she meets all four of her soul bonds."

"You just said you didn't see his face though," Onyx said forlornly, while Wild gave me a pointed look, clearly reminding me that my visions had been unreliable at best recently. *"Maybe I was wrong. Maybe we were all wrong and Dare was never Grace's fourth soul bond. Maybe you're seeing someone else, and Dare..."*

"No," I repeated, my voice steadier. "I haven't seen Dare's face in my visions of Grace, but I've seen enough snippets of Dare's future to know that this isn't the end for him. He's still alive, we just have to find him."

Though I didn't have the first clue how to go about that without consulting the cards and risking another episode. Shit, it'd be worth it.

I should have told Dare to come sooner. Maybe I'd been wrong to convince him to stay in New Jersey, knowing his mom was going to die. In the visions where he'd left before then, he'd struggled with his anger and it took him a long time to get closure, but was this really better?

Wild pulled up the notes, typing quickly before showing me the screen.

'If he encounters any agathos or daimons, he'll probably be able to find us.'

Okay, that was true. Those agathos defectors had found us without too much trouble, hopefully that meant Dare would be able to find us too. If he wasn't too badly injured that was.

"We'll look for him," I assured Onyx. "We're going to find him and bring him here. He's going to be fine, you'll see."

"Everything is chaos," Orion grumbled, pressing his phone to his shoulder to muffle the hold music coming through the earpiece. "Resources are stretched, things are a mess. I've been transferred six times and no one has any answers."

"There has to be something," I muttered, shuffling my cards frantically. Wild watched me like a hawk, and I had no doubt he would snatch them out of my hands the moment I closed my eyes and attempted a reading.

We'd cornered Orion in the room he was sharing with four other agathos men, demanding that he make some calls about the plane crash because we needed a native Greek speaker, but so far, no luck. And I could see Riot pacing next to the pool through the window of Orion's room, repeatedly messing with his hair and his lighter in agitation, and he didn't even *know* yet.

Obviously, I wanted Dare to be okay for his own sake, but also for my own selfish reasons. I missed my buddy, Riot, and he'd never speak to me again if anything bad had happened to Dare.

I didn't want to keep this news from Grace and Riot, but I was hoping we'd have a little more information to go give them first.

To soften the blow.

There was a tug through the bond from Grace and Wild blinked in confusion, glancing down at his sternum. It took everything in me not to laugh—I doubted this was a man used to being *summoned*. To be fair, I didn't think Grace actually *meant* to summon us either, she'd probably be really embarrassed if she realized she'd done it.

"Grace needs us," I told Orion.

'Can you keep making calls?' Wild wrote on his phone, quickly flashing it at Orion. *'I will track down contacts in Milton to verify he left town.'*

"Sure," Orion agreed easily, sitting down on the lower bunk bed and pulling a pen and notepad out of the nightstand. Wild nodded curtly, placing a hand on my back to guide me out of the room and back onto the patio, where all the cabin-style rooms opened onto.

He licked your cum off his finger, so I don't know why you're getting all fluttery about a hand on your back, I scolded myself silently, adamant he could hear my heart beating a little faster than usual in my chest. I was one second away from needing a fainting couch and smelling salts.

"There you are," Grace said, jogging down the stairs that led to the lower level where we were standing. Riot marched over from his pacing spot next to the pool, his expression softening a smidge when he saw Grace. Riot didn't like being around people all the time that weren't Grace and *maybe* her other bonded, and our increasingly large group was clearly stressing him out. "It's so pretty out here."

Grace looked out over the ocean to where the sun was sinking low in the horizon, and for a moment it was like *she* knew how ethereal she was too.

Maybe Grace didn't realize, or fully accept, how important she was, but she understood the importance of her task now just fine. The magnitude of what she had been asked to do, and how many people would be impacted by it—success or failure.

"Did you finish it?" Riot asked, nodding at the piece of paper in Grace's hand.

"I did. And I think I'd like to record it now, while the sun is setting. The transition from Gaia's day to Nyx's night."

"Good optics," I agreed. She was totally getting it now. I wished she didn't have to get it, that she didn't have to deal with all of this, but that wasn't what the Fates had planned for her.

Wild waved Vasileios and Alesa over, and they immediately dragged us to a spot against a stone wall surrounded by vines that they'd scouted out earlier, positioning Grace in front of it while getting their phones ready to record.

"I'm nervous," Grace admitted out loud, straightening the white linen blouse she was wearing and twisting the curls at the end of her hair with her fingers. "I feel like people will say... Like, who the hell do you think you are?" She laughed awkwardly, looking skyward and blinking rapidly. "And they're right. Who the hell do I think I am? I'm a nobody who was in the wrong place at the wrong time, and now the world is falling apart—literally—and it's somehow become my responsibility to fix it. No one on *earth* is qualified for this level of responsibility, especially not me."

Wild stepped into her space to catch her attention, signing something that had Grace nodding quietly in agreement. I didn't think it was something poetic and emotional, that didn't seem Wild's style. He was direct and to the point, and at that moment, Grace needed that to ground her.

"We stream live, yes?" Vasileios asked, glancing up at Grace over his phone.

"Yes," Grace agreed quickly as Wild stepped out of frame, joining me next to Alesa, with Riot on Vasileios' other side. "Ready when you are."

Grace looked down at the ground to steady herself as both Alesa and Vasileios started the live recording, and I felt a wave of calm wash through her via the bond as she looked up, the low golden light picking up the swirl of colors in her opal eyes.

"Hello. My name is Grace Bellamy, Grace the agathos, and I am a *Prophêtis* for the gods. Believe me, I know how insane that sounds, and I've tried to deny it many times, but I've seen too much and learned too much to deny it any longer." She exhaled heavily, a strained smile taking over her face. "I'm sure that for many of you, Gaia's message through one of her priestesses yesterday was the first time you'd heard the word 'agathos.' My kind have always lived hidden among humans, sent originally by Gaia to influence humans to do what is good and right and moral. Sent to counter what we were told were wicked influences from the daimons, who also live among you, whispering words of darkness and depravity in your ears."

Grace smiled wryly off-camera at the three of us. "They're children of Nyx, the Goddess of Night, and I was raised to think they're my enemy. But they're not. All of us are bound to serve in different ways, bound by restrictions placed upon us, and we want to be free. As free to live and to fall in love and make mistakes as any human is, not forever bound by instincts beyond our control."

Many of the others had gathered behind us, crowding into a tight semi-circle to hear Grace speak. They gravitated towards her—daimons, agathos, and humans alike. All of us had felt judged at one point or another for who or what we are, but Grace never made anyone feel that way.

"Over the last few months, I've been dealt a hand by the Fates that many will find impossible to believe, even my fellow agathos. I was raised to be the perfect agathos daughter, raised never to question anything, always trying to live in service of others until one day I made the choice to pray to a goddess who wasn't mine. In the time since, I've heard gods whispering in my ear, I've spoken to Gaia herself, I've visited the underworld and met the deities who reside there, and I've felt the power of Zeus in his own temple." She paused to let that all sink in. "I physically can't lie, but I don't blame you if you don't believe what I'm saying. It does sound unbelievable."

"Perhaps the most important thing about me is that I'm the reason all of these bad things are happening, the reason the earth is falling apart beneath our feet." Riot and I made noises of disagreements, and Grace spared us a reassuring glance before she continued. "When I prayed to Nyx—out of loneliness, out of frustration—I unintentionally volunteered myself for this prophecy I didn't know existed. It had to fall on someone's shoulders, and it happened to be mine. But even now, knowing what I know, I'd still do it all again."

"The prophecy is from the Fates themselves to liberate the Olympian gods—yes, *those* Olympian gods—from the Tartarus prison Gaia has held them in for centuries. And while I'm sorry for the pain and destruction this prophecy has caused, I'm not sorry that it exists. Liberating the Olympians, restoring them to power, means a more equal world for all of us. For the humans who have too much or too little, for the agathos who exist to serve those humans, and the daimons who exist to ruin them. For the deities themselves who have been at Gaia's mercy and Gaia's alone for too long. You've seen for yourself what happens when such an ancient and powerful being turns against us. It's easy to feel defenseless, but we're not."

Grace looked out into the distance again, collecting her thoughts, and I glimpsed a constant stream of comments appearing below the video feed on Alesa's phone. I looked away, not sure if I had the stomach to read them yet, not while Grace was still filming. If they were talking shit about her, I wasn't going to be able to keep my cool.

"The primordial gods—original, ancient deities like Gaia and Nyx and Erebus—they're eternal. They're forces we can't reckon with, not as mortals, not alone. But there are other gods, other gods who can provide checks and balances, and those gods, the Olympians, are sustained by *belief*. That's all I'm asking you to do. Please don't spill more blood when so much has been spilled already. If you want to help, if you saw the footage yesterday and it explains things you've been wondering about and you want to be a part of the change we're trying to bring... Just *believe*. Believe in the old gods, maybe pour a glass of wine in their honor, and perhaps one in honor of the many, *many* dead at the same time. The ones who never asked for the world to fall apart around them, who died not knowing *why* Mother Earth was raging against humanity. Believe that change is possible, but it's not inevitable. That a future worth having is worth fighting for."

Damn, Grace was *good* at this. Not that I ever thought she wouldn't be, but she was handling it with more calm and confidence than I'd expected.

Hopefully, she'd be able to maintain that calm and confidence after this was over and Wild and I told her about Dare.

"Decide what kind of future you want for this world. For your people. For *our* people. And if you want change like I want change, then *believe*."

CHAPTER 32

I zoned out for most of the ten-hour flight, watching movies and missing baby Quinn, gratefully downing the red wine the flight attendant gave me when I remembered that the last time I'd taken a flight had been with Mom. She'd convinced her rich Norwegian lover to spring for tickets for me as well on a trip to visit him, but that was where his generosity and her concern ended. I'd spent a broke few days in Oslo, traipsing around on foot because I couldn't afford the bus fare.

The plane shook with sudden turbulence, and the passenger across the aisle from me laughed nervously to himself, white-knuckling the arm rest until it steadied.

What were they all doing right now? They'd been hiding out in Greece for so long, charged with whatever mysterious mission they'd been charged with, and I knew nothing. Had they been busy doing mysterious god shit this whole time?

Had they been holed up in some resort overlooking the Aegean, fucking like rabbits and pretending the rest of the world didn't exist?

Don't think about that, *I reminded myself as the plane shuddered again. I hadn't touched anyone that way in months, which was hell on a Philotes daimon, and denial was the only way I was coping with the incessant itch under my skin.*

The seatbelt light came on with a quiet ding as the plane shook again. I was normally a pretty chill person, but even I was getting a little anxious at how much it was rocking and shuddering. There was a weird pressure coming from above, like a giant hand was forcing us out of the sky.

No, no. I was being ridiculous. Probably too much wine. Or not enough wine. Maybe more wine was the solution.

Except the flight attendants were all getting strapped into their seats, so I guessed no more wine for now.

There was a sudden jolt, people screamed, a sharp pain in my head.

Then nothing.

I woke up on a beach, people surrounding me, shouting things in a language I didn't understand. Everything hurt. Everything.

"Holy shit."

Bullet's horrified voice snapped me out of the nightmare I was reliving.

"What are you doing here?" I asked, blinking hard for a moment before sitting upright, all my aches and pains gone. The beach was clear of debris, of the injured and dying. It was just a beach, rocky and peaceful.

The power of an Oneiroi.

"Looking for you, obviously," he replied, reaching out a hand to pull me up. Despite everything, the anger I'd been holding on to for so long and the disappointment, the hurt, I clapped my palm into his and let him yank me to my feet. "Have you just not slept in weeks? I've been trying to find you, but you're never in the dreamscape."

"I was taking sleeping pills for a while. And when I wasn't, I was trying not to sleep," I admitted, surprised at how easily the words came out. Just because I wouldn't remember this tomorrow didn't mean Bullet wouldn't.

"I'm so sorry," he whispered, yanking his blonde hair harder than necessary. "I didn't see the crash. I knew you had trials ahead of you, but fuck. Fuck! Just tell me where you are. We'll come and get you the second I wake up."

"I don't really know," I admitted. "I woke up on this beach and this voice—I know it sounds crazy—she told me to get up, that I had to move, I had to run because the agathos were coming."

I gestured at the rocks behind me with a quiet seaside road that followed the coastline. "She told me to go up there and I did. I don't know how. I could barely move. Barely stand, let alone run, but she kept urging me to go. Giving me directions."

Bullet swallowed thickly, like my suffering was paining him too. "Where did you end up? Concentrate on the memory if you can, show it to me."

My lips twitched as I imagined us at the alleyway entrance to Jack's ground floor apartment, an absolute shit hole of a place that he spent his life doing drugs and playing video games in.

"What the fuck, man!" Jack screamed in a British accent that caught me by surprise, eyes wild and pupils blown wide as he stumbled back from the open front door. "Zombie! You're a fucking zombie! Look at your eyes!"

"I'm a daimon. As are you," I wheezed, bent double and slumped against the doorjamb. It'd be just my luck that the mysterious voice brought me to the doorstep of a daimon who didn't know what he was.

"I'm a daimon, you're a zombie. Look at you! You're all gray!" Jack attempted to rip his T-shirt off, but the fabric just stretched tight and held together. "Fine. Fine, I don't need my shirt off to fight you, zombie man. You and your gray skin. Fuck you."

I didn't like that mysterious voice, I decided, stumbling past Jack into his filthy apartment. Thankfully it was open plan, and I managed to fall against the kitchen counter and throw the tap on, shoving my hand underneath to show him that the "gray skin" he was panicking about was just sand and debris.

"See? I'm just a daimon who needs a shower and some first aid."

"Oh. Oh shit," he panted, leaning back against the wall, eyes still bugging out of his skull. "That's cool. Hey, you want a drink?"

"And that's how we became buddies," I told Bullet with a shrug. "There was some kind of giant scorpion infestation he said, and I had to stay. Not that I had anywhere else to go."

"Fuck. I need to find you. You must be in Athens, near the coast. So are we. I'm going to go to that beach and try trace your steps. Grace and Riot have been a wreck since they found out you might have been on that plane. I mean, we all have, but they basically haven't left the room. I'll find you Dare."

"I hope you do," I told him with a smile. "It's been really shitty on my own, you know? I hope you do find me."

"Are you awake, bruv?" Jack—my new daimon friend—announced, stomping into the spare room. He probably wasn't stomping, but everything hurt all the time now.

"No," I groaned, leaning back on the spare bed he'd assigned me that smelled faintly of cats. Not that I was complaining, I was lucky to be here. Lucky to be *alive*.

Now I got to alternate nightmares of my mother's dead body with nightmares of the plane I was on falling out of the fucking sky. Not just falling. They'd called it a "microburst" on the news. A column of sinking air, right above the plane. It was the most logical explanation, if you didn't believe in psychotic earth goddesses.

Gaia had been ripping the world apart, town by town, city by city, for weeks. It was always worse where daimons lived, and I couldn't help but think that plane would have gotten to Athens just fine if I hadn't been on it.

"It sounds like you're awake. I really thought I hallucinated the whole scorpion thing, but I'm sober as a judge right now and apparently I didn't. Isn't that mad?" Jack asked, shaking his head slowly, shoulder-length dark hair swaying with the motion. He was an English expat who'd moved here years ago and seemed to somehow make money playing video games, though I wasn't clear on the details.

I'd been staying at his place for a few days now—both to recover and for lack of a better idea. I'd lost all my shit in the crash, phone included, and I didn't know where to go from here. Plus, the world was falling apart around us, so there was that. The natural disasters had eased off slightly over the past couple of days, but the earth still seemed to *shudder* occasionally. It was ominous as fuck.

"Look at this," Jack said, holding out his phone.

"No." The light from the screen made the near constant headache I'd been battling worse. "I don't want to watch another trick shot video."

"Come on, just look," Jack whined, flopping down on the bed next to me with zero regard for my many, many injuries. He was tall and skinny—I'd yet to see him eat anything I'd consider proper food—so at least he didn't jostle the bed too much. "It's not trick shot video this time, I promise."

"What is it?"

"This daimon I sort of know, Vasileios, he's very popular. He's a Philotes, like you, and he's pretty much famous because he travels around the world and fucks everyone else's partners," Jack snorted. "He sent me this video with an agathos woman saying that all daimons need to see this, and I know it sounds like clickbait—"

I blinked, forcing my brain to focus on what he was saying. "An agathos woman? What's her name?"

"Hold on, I'll play it again," Jack said. "It's a livestream from two days ago. Here. Watch."

He held his phone up and Grace—*Grace*—filled the screen, eyes downcast for a moment before she looked up into the camera and directly into my soul. Grace.

My Grace.

I hung on to her every word, my chest cracking apart as she talked about the things she'd seen. She'd been to the *underworld*? How was that even possible?

"I need to go there," I breathed, grabbing Jack's arm. "Can you get me there? Can you ask the guy who sent it to you?"

"Uh, sure. I guess. I don't really know him that well, but we'll see what he says," Jack said, as though I wasn't staring at him with manic eyes, closing the video and tapping out a message before bringing up a different video from the day before. Grace walked alone towards a crowd of waiting agathos assembled outside temple ruins, scattering something on the ground as she walked.

"Holy fuck balls," Jack whispered as the earth at her feet shifted and rolled, hands sprouting out of the dirt like macabre blooms. Hands, followed by *helmets*, and weapons and fucking *men*. She'd grown *men*.

385

"Holy fuck balls indeed," I agreed faintly, those warriors with spears diving in to attack a wave of fucking *scorpions* the size of cats.

"I should check my messages more often," Jack said gravely. "The agathos are growing people now."

I didn't have a response for that. How had she done that? Was she safe around all those... hoplites? They looked like Greek hoplites—skirt armor and everything. Grace had grown an *army*.

"Are you sure you want to go there?" Jack asked as his phone dinged with an incoming message. "You can stay with me. It's been years since I hung out with someone in real life."

"I have to go there," I replied firmly, silencing the insecurities that reared the ugly heads, asking if Grace really needed me around when she had three bonded and a magic army. "She's the whole reason I came to Greece. I need to get to her. You can come with me. Stay with us."

"Chill, man, you're all injured and shit. Come on. I'll borrow my neighbor's car and drive you—the streets are still pretty empty. Let's go get your girl who grows people."

It wasn't an easy drive. The roads were damaged from the constantly shifting earth, and there were barricades and general chaos basically every step of the way. The people who were brave enough to leave their homes were fleeing to the countryside, hoping that would protect them from the disasters they didn't understand, giant scorpions that might emerge from the earth at any moment, and the terrifying zombie agathos who'd demanded Grace come to Athens.

They were panicking. Who knew how Grace's message was being received, really? It was one thing for the agathos and daimons to hear that, but a whole different ballgame for humans who hadn't known any of this shit existed.

"This is some place," Jack said, pulling up outside a brightly lit up villa just before midnight, and staring up at it with wide eyes.

"You coming in?"

"You first, mate. If you die, I'm leaving. If you don't die, maybe I'll come in."

I snorted, immediately wincing at the pain that radiated out from my face, and climbed out of the passenger side, forcing myself to move through my injuries with a renewed sense of purpose. My heart was beating faster—alarmingly fast, actually—but it didn't matter. Nothing mattered but getting inside and fulfilling a destiny that had always been mine, even when I didn't know it was a possibility.

There was no one around as I made my way to the front of the house. It was enormous—the kind of place they set reality TV shows in—and I couldn't imagine it being occupied by daimons, but when I pushed the front door open without knocking to find Bullet and Wild sitting next to each other on stools at the kitchen counter, it looked like they were completely at home there.

"Thank the gods for that," Bullet said with a grin, hopping off the stool and rounding the kitchen counter towards me. "Shit, you look terrible, but you're here. That's all that matters. You found us."

I'd been mad at him, but seeing the relief on his face made all of that rage I'd been holding on to disappear. Fuck knows, we'd all gone through the ringer lately. Bullet was doing his best. We all were.

I pulled him in for a one-armed hug, ruffling his longer-than-usual blonde hair. After everything, after all the bullshit and the suffering, I was finally *here*. My throat hurt with the sudden rush of emotion.

Also Philotes daimons needed touch and it had been a while. Bullet was patting my back gingerly, clearly concerned about my myriad of injuries, but it was still sort of filling my cuddle quota.

"I've been trying to find *you* all morning, but you beat me to it. Sorry I couldn't just demand answers," he said, releasing me and stepping back to catalog my wounds. "I'm trying to take it easy," he added, tapping the side of his head with his finger.

I caught Wild's eye, noticing the way he'd been watching Bullet carefully. Watching Bullet *possessively*.

"I'm here now. We can figure everything else out later," I told Bullet, tipping my chin in greeting to Wild before letting my gaze travel over the rest of the living area. I could hear voices through the double doors that seemed to lead outside, but it was the staircase at the back of the living area that caught my attention. My feet were moving before I'd even consciously decided what to do.

"Wait," Bullet called, laughing. "You're going to see something you might not want to see if you go up there right now. Or maybe you do want to see it, I don't know. You don't really look up for joining in, honestly, but they're going to be so glad to see you."

I didn't pay him any mind. Wild and Bullet were out here, Grace and Riot were not out here. Which meant they were in there, at the top of those stairs. And I wasn't about to wait any longer.

I'd waited, and waited, and fucking *waited*. I'd known Grace was mine for weeks, and I'd been on my own, dealing with my mom's death and the agathos bullshit while they'd all been playing happy families here without me, and I was so goddamn done waiting.

No more. Not even five more minutes. Or fifteen, however long Riot needed.

I opened the door and walked into the bedroom, finding Riot sitting on the bed with Grace's legs wrapped around his waist, their lips fused together, her dress in disarray. She broke away, twisting to look at me as the door clicked shut behind me.

Beautiful. So beautiful.

Grace was stunning, even though she looked tired and her eyes were kind of puffy like she'd been crying. Both her and Riot looked like they needed a good night's sleep. They were holding each other like they were desperate for each other, like one was the only thing anchoring the other to this world.

"Dare?!" Riot said in surprise. "Are you okay? You look... Fuck, man. I'm glad you're here but do you *knock?*" A startled laugh burst out of him as he adjusted Grace's dress to preserve her modesty.

"Mine," I said, staring at Grace. "You are mine."

"No," she breathed, staring at me with wide pale eyes, lips swollen from Riot's attention. *"You* are *mine."*

GLOSSARY

TYPES OF AGATHOS MENTIONED:

Arete = Virtue
Eusebia = Piety
Eutychia = Good Luck
Hygeia = Good Health
Sophia = Wisdom
Sophrosyne = Self-Control
Soteria = Safety

TYPES OF DAIMONS MENTIONED:

Apate = Deceit
Ate = Delusion
Dolos = Trickery
Geras = Old Age
Keres = Violent Death
Moros = Doom
Oizys = Misery
Oneiroi = Dreams
Philotes = Sex, Affection

THANK YOU

Here we are again! The end of another State of Grace book. This is a five-book series, so we've passed the halfway mark now. I hope you're still enjoying Grace's story, and her journey from the shy agathos who was always trying to follow the rules even when they didn't make sense to her, to the bold and brave character she's becoming. Grace is truly a joy to write, as is her harem! I'm so attached to this crew.

The next book in this series is Dare Not, and it is due for release on 20 December 2022. The fifth and final book in the series will be announced around that time. If you'd like to see more of Hades and Persephone, Dead of Spring will be out in August 2022.

I have a few thank you's I need to say—first and foremost to you, dear reader! At this point, you're three books into this series and I can't say how much I appreciate you coming along on this journey with me. I'm so grateful to each and every one of you.

To my amazing editor, Steph, from Rawls Reads—you are a magician, thank you for always pushing me to dig deeper into the story. Thank you also to Becky from Becky's Edits for doing a wonderful job on the proofreading.

And to the team of human beings who keep me from losing my mind throughout the writing process—Max, Lucy, TS, Rachel, Rory, Ashley to name a few—thank you for always being there for me and not blocking me while I whine incessantly about editing for weeks at a time.

Until next time!

For the latest news and teasers, join the Colette Rhodes Facebook Group or subscribe to my newsletter.

Colette x

ALSO BY COLETTE RHODES

STATE OF GRACE:

Run Riot

Silver Bullet

Wild Game

Dare Not

Saving Grace

SHADES OF SIN:

(MF monster romance)

Luxuria

Superbia

Gula

THREE BEARS DUET:

Gilded Mess

Golden Chaos

LITTLE RED DUET:

Scarlet Disaster

Seeing Red

Printed in Great Britain
by Amazon

47826565R00225